THE LEESHORE

A NOVEL BY
ROBERT REED THE

LEESHORE

Donald I. Fine, Inc.
New York

To Steve and Chellie

THE LEESHORE

I The sailer came out of the mist and the gently falling filth. Its wind fin was unfurled, the triangular slice of skin taut and dark and speckled with little patches of faint luminescence. Ahead was a floating island— an enormous plastic island—shaggy and rounded and seeping a gentle red light. The sailer tacked. As if hunting, it followed the curving shoreline, its head dipped, all of its eyes submerged. On the leeward side of the island, the wind fell away, and the water went smooth. The sailer drifted, furling its wind fin. Then it kicked with both of its tails and turned away from the shoreline, the steady noise of its labor muted by the wind overhead and the mist and filth all around.

At the edge of the smooth water, it quit kicking, resting now, acting like everything else in the sea.

It lay still on the water, much like something dead.

A pair of figures crawled out from one of the bright orange gills. They looked small against the sailer's broad back, wearing lifesuits and minimal packs and an assortment of lightweight equipment. Keeping low, they watched the island. Their voices were soft and cautious and not a little frightened by their circumstances. "At least the blood-oaks are doing well," said the girl, her tone caustic and cold. "Can you see anything?" she asked. "Jellico?"

"Nothing," her half-brother said.

She glanced at him. In the gloom, red-tinted and shadowy, all they could see was each other's dark faceplate. "Maybe we have the wrong island," she offered. "You think?"

"Maybe."

She pulled herself higher, trying for a better look.

Grabbing a long leg, he said, "Abby." He tugged on her once, then harder. "Abitibi."

She retreated. "It's got to be the one," she admitted.

The size and shape. Where it was drifting and the degree of rot. Neither of them had any real doubts.

Quietly, with a touch of heat, Abitibi said, "Damn."

Jellico laid still and quiet, thinking.

Abitibi asked, "What do we do now?" and then muttered, "Damn," again, the word delicate and slow. "Jellico?"

"What?"

"I . . . oh, never mind."

Because they came knowing the worst, they took what they saw too well. Between Abitibi and Jellico ran feelings of not grieving enough. Of not being properly devastated. Even if the Islanders hadn't been their family or their friends—not in any real sense—at least they had been the only other humans on Leeshore. Like them or not. And so now they felt guilt for having dry eyes, and guilt for their still being alive. As if the proper thing was to have been here and died. As if either of them should have preferred an ignoble end to what they had now.

"Stuhr," said Abitibi, a long, gloved finger making a gesture.

Jellico asked, "Where?" and then he saw the stuhr.

The island was an enormous sphere riding low in the water, its surface shaggy with a tangle of treelike things above the surf and kelp below. Most of the fungal trees were blood-oaks, small as yet, lacking the full crimson color of mature seed-bearers. Draped over the oaks, here and there, were ragged snatches of what seemed to be sheer plastic sheets. Stuhr, Jellico knew. Dead stuhr. Nothing else was left of the towering skyhook. The largest human thing for light-years around had collapsed into pieces nearly too small to be seen.

"I should swim in," he decided. "Have a look."

"Why bother?"

He thought a moment, then said, "There might be something we can use. Or maybe someone's left alive."

Abitibi said nothing.

"It would take two hours," he judged. "Maybe three."

"It's not worth the risk," she said. "They could still be nearby." They. The Alteretics. Their faceless, shadowy enemies.

Jellico wasn't listening. He was thinking about the Islanders and their precious skyhook. Decades ago, they came to Leeshore to build it all from scratch—a tower of hollow stuhr reaching into orbit; a fueling port ready to serve all comers—and, ever since, they had maintained the facilities and themselves with the same rigorous care, waiting for the day when a starship would come from Earth to relieve them. Saving them at long last. He could picture the Islanders now, and plainly— their thick, ageless faces and their careful plodding ways. He had never understood them. Not a bit. His mother had been one of them once, of course, but he had never known her to look or act like them. Not hardly. And now, what with them dead and the island ruined, Jellico was beginning to see the world through their narrowed eyes. Finally. He was understanding how it feels to have dangers all around you. To have hazards imagined and hazards real.

"Alteretics," he muttered to himself.

Abitibi heard the word but said nothing.

Mankind's greatest threat, the Islanders had called them. Alteretics were demons led by a god of their own making. Ruthless monsters without decency or honor or trust.

Jellico decided, "They're gone, I bet."

"I don't see any point in taking chances," she said. "The skyhook's down, and there's no repairing it. So far, the Alteretics don't know about us. I'd like to keep it that way.

"Abby," he whispered, aiming to soothe. "I really think one of us should go in and look things over."

"So go," she snapped, arguments and patience both spent.

He lay beside her, thinking, the thick steady wind pushing the island towards them. They began to see details—individual oaks and the milky white of a narrow shoreline. The island smelled like something gone sour, then bathed in a strange almost-sweet deodorant. Jellico put his head close to Abitibi's and said, "I'll open a channel. I'll put up my aerial. You can watch and hear me all the way."

She said nothing.

"If anything goes wrong, anything, just leave. All right?"

Her silence seemed to mock him.

He gave a voice command to his own helmet, beginning to broadcast now, and he put a hand to his throat and closed the speaker under his faceplate. If anything, his voice sounded closer. More intimate. He began backing away, saying to her, "Till later, Abby. All right? Hmm?"

"Sure." She made herself lie still, watching him. "Just go."

"With luck?" he asked, sounding boyish. "How about some?"

"Luck," she said, making a gesture.

He told her, "Thanks," and eased towards the water, every motion spare and secure. "Make it kick, Abby. When I say."

She used a code word, linking the controls in her helmet to the sailer's mind. The sailer woke from a fish-rich dream. Muscles rippled beneath them, shuddering and stretching. She looked down at Jellico, imagining the strong lean face behind the darkened glass. His helmet gave a nod. He was ready. So with another word Abitibi gave a command; and the sailer, thinking the command its own, beat the water with all of its might.

The island vanished behind a wall of red-tinted spray.

II   Jellico, braking with hands and toes, slid down the leathery flank and dolphined clear—his froth mingling with the sailer's and then subsiding, a golden phosphorescence softening and then gone.

The sea was black and cool. He could feel the water through his suit, floating belly-down, and the filtered air smelled of salts and must and cautious, quiet life-forms. He was wholly part of this world. Drifting, letting the island come to him, he tried and failed to envision any place besides this place. Once in awhile, without sound, he would say, "Alteretic," in a careful way. As if practicing. As if he could appreciate what the word meant simply by making it a part of him.

All the people he knew, but one, were dead now. He had to keep reminding himself—summoning the thought—his numbed will refusing to believe.

The skyhook had been the prize—an enormous straw of living stuhr that had been anchored to this island and that had reached up to a geosynchronous orbit, pumps and a power supply ready to lift water to hungry starships. The Alteretics had come to capture the skyhook, and the Islanders had tried to defend it. When it became clear they would be defeated, they scuttled it and were murdered for their trouble. And now the island was drifting free of its moorings—the skyhook gone, every building leveled and the ground grown thick with blood-oaks. He and Abitibi had been saved by chance. They were days away when the Alteretics dropped out of the sky in their shuttle. Like always, they had been doing research—studying an upwelling far to the south.

"Alteretics."

He imagined Earth and the other inhabited, half-mythic planets orbiting Sol. Most of them were ruined now because of the Alteretics. Because of their heresy. They had dared to build a god, and their god had dared to wage war against nonbelievers; and now, having lost their holy struggle, all were fleeing Mankind, riding stolen starships across the galaxy . . .

Words. All words. Drama without heart. Events without substance or shadow . . .

"Alteretics."

Fishy somethings began to approach, nibbling at Jellico with their tiny needling teeth. Ahead, red-lit and closing, was the kelp, papery strands held erect by vascular ribs. Their glow bathed the animals living among them—the ecological equivalents of fishes and crustaceans and such. The animals were red too, camouflaged, their ruddy faces peering up through Jellico's faceplate, their expressions uniformly calm and cold and slow.

Reaching, Jellico grabbed a likely strand of kelp, then pulled.

Against the light, he was visible, vulnerable, and so he kicked hard and lifted a hand, grasping the fleshy stalk of a small oak.

He wanted fear. More than weapons or wits, a palatable sense of dread could serve him here. He felt sluggish. He felt oddly calm. Something in all of this seemed contrived—contrived and foolish—and he began to think of himself as a boy caught up in the midst of a game, wrapped tight in a moment of silly pretend.

Climbing onto the shoreline, he crouched and looked about.

The fungal wood was low and tangled. The faceplate made it all seem bright—computers sewn into the glass itself augmented the natural light, electronically enhancing colors and edges. Thick as thighs were the stalks further inland. The only branches were clustered at the top, in tight tangled bunches. The tips of the branches were flattened and wide, resembling leaves, and the shapes of the pseudoleaves were what gave the oaks their name.

The stalks glowed weakly.

The leaves were the translucent heart of the light.

Jellico shuffled forwards. Away from the shoreline, the oaks grew taller, brighter, with room beneath for a person to stand and walk. The stalks were scattered in a regular pattern, as if planted by organizing hands. Here and there were winged things riding the thick, still air. The only sound was the steady, insectish hum they made while they moved.

Jellico knelt, taking off his pack and removing what he needed. With care he assembled sensors and a small gas-powered rifle. Then he said, "Deploy aerial," and his helmet sprouted a flexible glass wire. He said, "Broadcast visual," and everything he saw through the faceplate was broken down to code and squirted across the water to Abitibi, to her helmet and faceplate. Then, feeling set, he stood and shouldered the pack and walked carefully forward. "Alteretics," he said, as if to conjure them into view. "Beware," he told them without sound, without heart, all of this still some child's tired game.

The ground was buried under fallen waste. Corpses and excrement.

By measuring its depth, one could almost judge when people had last scrubbed the island clean.

Dark and moist, slick and worm-riddled, the waste acted like a greedy mud. Jellico's boots mired down, and he was forever twisting them to pull free. Buried throughout were the dead from kilometers above—winged things and small bladder plants, airgrass and remains too rotten to hold a name. The island itself was a hard milky plastic set down in layers, each layer pocked with neat round cavities. Sometimes, particularly when an island first surfaced, the animals living within the cavities were left alive. Like the corals building reefs in an Earthly sea, they had built the islands on the seafloor. Protected by hard clear lids, they seemed indifferent to the pressures without. But by using a knife, plus muscle, one could break the seals and watch the fragile bodies explode—a smelly goo, deeply orange, fizzing like some carbonated drink.

He moved sideways up the gradual slope. He was walking on his toes, holding the rifle tight in both hands and keeping quiet.

There was almost nothing to see. This must have been the windward side, he decided. Back before the scuttling. Then he came upon a storage shed, built low and blackened. He knew the shed. Sure enough, this was the start of the old leeward side—this island, like most, tended to spin while it drifted free in the sea.

Creeping close, Jellico saw the machinery that had been stored inside, protected by a pressurized atmosphere of pure nitrogen. The machinery was partly melted now, the bare metals all tarnish and rust. Sensors showed nothing worth a look. He whispered, "Booby traps," at the shed and stepped away, as if to tempt the dangers to come chase him.

There were more sheds. Like the first, they were built from milky blocks cut from the island's core. What hadn't melted and burned was honey to the oaks, their roots making a fine dark net visible inside the roofs and the walls.

In weeks, the oaks would seed and die, then give way to longer living, less adaptable fungi. Over months, the corruption, in new guises, would slip underground, seeking weakness and gnawing holes. Eventually, the island would crack and crumble—the succession process running on with every piece dislodged—and finally, the flotsam would be too small to balance even a baby oak, or feed a single strand of kelp.

"Succession," Jellico said with certainty. With a confidence. Here was a word he could use easily, and well. All those years that the plodding Islanders had protected this place, fending off the natural processes . . . and now, after just days, it was all for naught. "Succession." A thousand people couldn't stop the rot. Not now. Not this late.

He paused for a moment, kneeling and carefully listening.

The hum of insects had become a buzz. A vibration in the air. Up between the glowing trunks, flying with a slow and graceless form, was an enormous blind fly as white as the island. It was chasing some scent, most likely. He watched while it came over his head, then stood and walked after it, sniffing now, smelling something distinct. He spotted a mound ahead, flies covering it.

Some huge thing had died and fallen, apparently.

Under the feeding flies he saw a skull, half-cleaned and birdlike. The skull was longer than Jellico was tall, eye sockets as big as bowls and ample brains behind. "A boeing bird." The body and wings had already been reduced to flies and worms and soil. He thought of Abitibi growing sad while she watched the scene with him. The boeing birds lived overhead, up above the airweed pastures and the bladder plants. They hunted alone, their wings built for the hard, high, blue sky. When the skyhook was intact, its mirrored surface sometimes had attracted boeing birds that would see themselves and not recognize their own reflections. Some of the birds would come too close and hit the stuhr, breaking a wing or their necks. And the Islanders, angry for the inconvenience, would have to dispose of the corpses. Typically, they ran a line from a tugboat and dragged them into the sea. Neat and easy. And the fish would rise and pick the bones clean.

"The poor things," Mother would say. "They're smart enough, surely, but they've never seen mirrors. They simply don't understand." In her dreamier moments, she talked of building planes of some kind and climbing up to the boeing bird world. If the birds had a language, they could work to decipher its sense. Then they could educate the species. "Stay clear of the skyhook!" they would warn. "Beware!"

Naturally, the Islanders never gave permission. Supplies were too tight, they were told, and that was true. More important, though, there were enormous dangers involved. It wasn't easy or fun to fly in the airweed and up through the tightly packed bladder plants. Sometimes, secretly, he had wished his Mother's enthusiasms could have been leavened with a hint of reason. Just an honest hint.

"Maybe we could live up there," she would say, smiling. Nearly beaming. "Abby? Maybe we can coax a boeing into letting you ride . . . like you ride the sailers? What do you say?"

Maybe, he thought, but not now.

Not ever, most likely.

Turning, Jellico continued up the slope. The wind was a swelling moan, and dead stuhr laid in heaps and little hills just under the summit. It must have made quite a mess after the scuttling, he thought. Eighty thousand kilometers of wasted stuhr strewn across the ocean, the Islanders' ticket to a better world reduced to a tattered colorless film. With his hand, almost without effort, he ripped through a piece of stuhr. Tri-ply stuff, judging by its looks. The strongest stuff possible. Three layers of ultralight material had been made durable and strong by employing some exotic physics, plus a steady stream of energy. And now the remnants of the skyhook's base were little more than dust in his hands.

The first hints of wind began flowing over him.

The ground became clean, polished by years of endless wind, and every oak grew small and stout, shouldering the wind.

It was like stepping upwards into a flood, the thick air chilled and filled with blowing mist and grit. He thought of Abitibi. He pictured her watching and listening, experiencing everything he saw and heard and feeling tense and frustrated. Just like Abitibi would. For a moment, Jellico considered saying something reassuring. But then he realized that if anyone was near, trying to eavesdrop, they would surely catch his signal now. He was, after all, the tallest antenna in the world.

For a moment he turned, looking back the way he had come.

It was too dark to see Abby and their sailer. He told himself they were too far away, the island's shaggy wood lying between them and him.

He climbed to the summit, up where the skyhook had been rooted. The ground fell away into a soft-sided crater. At the bottom of the crater was the ruddy round mouth of a shaft lined with oaks. The shaft reached down towards the island's core. A fusion plant from the old starship *Kansas City* had been reassembled in the hollow core. It was what had fed the stuhr all these years—artificially strengthening the bonds between atoms—and Jellico remembered the Islanders caring for the plant. How they had patiently made the worn machinery last another year, then another.

Kneeling, he breathed and tried to rest.

A pair of miser birds came up out of the shaft. They were the color of another sky, a higher sky. They were legless and blue. And clamped in their shovel-shaped bills were chunks of metal—tarnished by the air and twisted by some nuclear fire.

"Be my guest."

If memory served, it was near noon. But there wasn't a hint of any yellow-orange sun. Save for a few phosphorescent scuds, all Jellico saw were the rising birds weakly lit against the inky sky. He thought of them

and what constitutes treasure—for them, a few precious pounds of trash
pried off machinery that was once, not too long ago, the basis of Jellico's
own tiny life.

III   She was aware of the steady mist, like some thin persistent oil,
clinging to her and to the sailer. A heavier rain of excrement and corpses
peppered them and the still water all around them. Sometimes Abitibi
would nervously toy with some of it—a solitary wing, say, or some deflated
plant bladder. Like Mother, she could never lie still for long. She had to
be busy—not just active, but involved too. Right now she was watching
the images displayed in one corner of her faceplate, watching what her
brother was transmitting. She studied the crater and the miser birds and
said to herself, "It's all ruined." Her quiet voice was more puzzled than
sad.

She could hear Jellico taking a breath. Then he stood and walked
around the summit, following the crater's crumbling lip.

"Be careful," she whispered. "Careful, Jel."

She watched him work his way down into the wood again, pressing
against the wind. The dormitories would be below him, then the docks,
and visible off to his left was a pathway cut in the hard white earth. He
was smart to keep clear of the pathway, she decided. Smart to stay on the
random, untraveled ground. Maybe he was right—no one was left to
bother them. Why should the Alteretics have lingered? But then there
was no sense in being brash, either—in testing their luck. So far as Abitibi
was concerned, they should never have come near this place. Not for
years. They didn't need salvage to live, and they didn't need Islanders.
And sure as hell, they didn't need to tempt Father Rot like this. He was
coming soon enough as it was.

"Careful, Jel."

Everything had seemed so fine in the south, down where they had been working. Mother had long ago taught them the skills and made them love her business, and Jel and Abitibi had been busy enough not to pay attention to the broadcasts coming from Skyhook Island. One day there was something about new messages from the direction of Earth. Conflicting messages, like they always were, instructing them to scuttle the skyhook and save themselves, and make certain too that they kept the skyhook secure. Then, days later, there was a garbled sentence—the atmosphere playing hell with the signal—the gist of it all being that some starship was moving into orbit. No warnings given. Then twelve hours later, give or take, Abitibi was shaken awake by the urgent voice of a male Islander. "—we knocked a hole in them. We surprised the bastards, I bet! They're sinking. Their shuttle's done!"

In the darkness, lying on the flat back of the sleeping sailer, Jellico had asked Abitibi, "Are you listening?" and squeezed her closest hand.

She had said, "Sush!" and quickly squeezed back.

"They're coming anyway," the Islander had reported next, the joy gone from his voice. "They're swimming and rafting in." It took them a long moment to recognize the voice and fix it to a person; never in their lives had they heard the man race his words so. "We're down to small arms now. Hiding. Waiting—"

The signal had vanished; now, thinking back, Abitibi wondered if there was more involved than ordinary interference.

Then the signal had surfaced again. "—the Alteretics keep promising charity," the Islander had announced. "We won't—"

Abitibi had asked the buzzing static, "What? You won't what?"

And that time it was Jellico who had said, "Sush." Only there was nothing left to hear anymore. Lying side by side, they had listened to the senseless noise, straining for anything; and suddenly every channel filled with an enormous roar. Thousands of miles of stuhr had failed. The giant skyhook collapsed at that instant, tearing to pieces and tumbling towards Leeshore. Useless. Wasted.

The Alteretics were to blame.

Them and their god.

All her life she had heard about them, learned what a scourge they were. Not that the Islanders who talked knew exactly what they were saying—Alteretics came years after they themselves had left Earth. But for decades now they had eavesdropped on the radio noise from home. As well as they could manage, they had followed the wars and guessed at the damage and the casualties; and not once, not ever, did they doubt which side they were on. Even when the Alteretics, back in the early going, had seemed terribly close to winning.

Abitibi glanced at the image on her faceplate. Jellico was managing the steepening slope. The island wasn't this big, she thought. Yet it all seemed so slow. She could feel her heart pressing at her throat and her breath trying to race, and she laid as still as she could, watching and listening, her hands clinging to the sailer's hard back.

On the windward side of the island, the debris was heavier. Bulkier. The fine stuff had been winnowed out, and the carcasses crunched and crumbled underfoot. Jellico was aiming for stealth. She could tell. Sometimes when he glanced down, picking his way, she saw worms in the carcasses, their blind heads ending in round mouths that chewed and chewed. She saw insects, palm-sized or bigger, with antennae like hairs and clear glistening carapaces of berry-red colors. Her brother was grunting. Was laboring. The fungal wood around him was bowing with the wind, the leafy tips brightening with every nod. Once he paused, turned and looked back the way he had come. All they could see were his empty tracks and bits of blowing crud. The aerial on his helmet was somewhere up in the oak. He turned again and walked faster. Then ahead, abruptly, the ground fell away. The hard white stuff had been cut and shaped with lasers. Years ago, the Islanders and Mother had sliced a wedge from the island itself, making an honest flat stretch on which they could build. The slope leading down was slick and smooth, Abitibi knew. Jellico carefully sat and gave his sensors a long look—infrared and sonics—then with his rifle at ready he slid down the slope, legs bent, picking up speed and softly squealing, "Weeee."

He hit the bottom, grunting. Then laughed.

Abitibi felt like scolding him.

Out on the flat ground was another storage shed gutted by fire, then a pair of empty missile tubes. Beyond, somewhere in the monotonous oak, were the dorms and galley—domes of bi-ply stuhr set in a ring—with the labs below, in tunnels, and the machine shop buried deeper still.

Jellico walked between the tubes, measuring his every step, his every gesture.

She remembered the Islanders building the missiles, adapting outdated designs from Earth. It had been just a few years ago, not long after Mother died of her cancers, and Abitibi recalled a dozen missiles and tubes in all, scattered and sometimes hidden. The guts of the warheads she and Jel had supplied at a cost—the explosives made from ripened bomb-stools— and afterwards the Islanders had felt like boasting, claiming no one could come close to them now without their blessing.

Abitibi tried to imagine the battle.

In her mind, she pictured the wedge-shaped Alteretic shuttle descending, bulling its way through the bladder plants and airweed and then coasting on the thick air below. The missiles came one after another. Or together. Somehow the shuttle evaded them, or destroyed them, the Islanders likely having fits. And then a lucky shot damaged the shuttle. When it set its nose into the sea, it began filling with water, doomed, and she wondered what kinds of people could get out of a sinking ship and come ashore and finish the attack—their chances of success tiny by then, their best hope a quick and humble surrender.

"Fanatics," she whispered. Fanatics would have tried for the skyhook anyway, she was sure. And then after the Islanders were dead and the great skyhook was ruined . . . then what? If their shuttle was kilometers deep and sinking still, how could they manage to get home?

Softly, to himself, Jellico said, "Damn."

Abitibi blinked and looked.

The big mirrored domes of stuhr were gone. The interiors were burnt and collapsed, melted frameworks and crumbling walls mocking the rooms that had been there. Everything was ruined with exacting detail. With ruthless determination. The place looked as if it had been doused in fuel, shin-deep, before a match was found and struck and tossed.

Here the oaks were few, small and whispery pink.

Overhead was a miser bird. It was hovering, apparently hunting, its bill to the wind and its wingbeats strong and slow.

"Any treasures?" Jellico asked.

The bird tilted backwards, squawked and lifted from view.

He looked down at his feet and edged forwards again. Carefully. The

ground around the ruins was all gloom and shadow. His faceplate had to
work to build images, and when he moved his head the images blurred
—too little light and too much confusion, the computers extrapolating a
landscape from the barest of glows.

Something somewhere was clicking.

A sharp, exacting sort of sound. From below.

Jellico paused, took a breath, then wheeled around. Formless pink
dissolved into a brutish armored face. Abitibi gasped, thinking *Alteretic,*
and Jel shouldered his rifle and aimed squarely at the chewing mouth.
Then he laughed. "Jesus," he said to himself, relieved, pulling his rifle
down; and the enormous blind crab, sensing vibrations, quit its chewing
—four pincers holding high some nameless grey meat. As if offering
Jellico a gift. A token.

"Look at you," Jellico said. "Damn you." For the second time, he
laughed.

This isn't some game, thought Abitibi. Act your age, Brother.

The crab, regaining its confidence, began eating again. Jellico moved
upwind, up into the galley. To himself, he muttered something about the
smell. A putrid stink. Lurching and tottering about in the wreckage were
dozens of big crabs. They're in the stores, Abitibi knew. Sipping the rich
offal of the recyke systems. She recognized two species, then another with
functional eyes, all of them wearing the same narrow high shells and thick,
jointed legs. Nothing else on Leeshore so easily and willingly tolerated
Earthly organics. The crests on their backs were like razors. The crests
were useful in warding off feeding birds and whatnot. A careless motion,
plus pressure, and the skin of a lifesuit could be slit open wide.

"Easy, Jel. Easy."

He walked around the crabs, climbing, the rubble loose and the going
slow and uncertain. Abitibi began to notice the weakening in her brother's
signal. The image was turning to fuzz. With a voice command, she told
her own computers to cut through the static. To extrapolate a clear, clean
image. But the fuzz worsened. She had to squint to see.

Jellico was in the dormitories now.

He stopped suddenly, staring at an indistinct something ahead.

"Do you see it?" he asked.

What?

"Abby?" he said without breath. "Do you?"

Reaching up at them, out from under a toppled wall, was the delicately curled, shiny-black burnt end of an arm.

"Abby?"

She started to talk, to tell him to please shut up; but then everything vanished into a sparkling pink snow, and all she heard was a high-pitched hissing.

The hissing and her own galloping breath.

IV   The diamond had red-tinted facets and was set on an ornate golden engagement ring. The ring had been dulled by the fires and oxygen, yet it still rode on a withered finger.

Jellico kneeled, sucking air through his teeth and staring.

All the fingers of the hand had melted together. He remembered the ring's wearer as a bright and kind woman named Sarah. She was sluggish like all the Islanders, but cheery. Mother hadn't liked Sarah much— Mother had had little good to say about any of them—but Sarah was always friendly towards Jellico, given the chance. Sometimes when he and Abby were on the island, resting and getting ready for another expedition, the three of them would sit inside her tiny dorm room and talk. Chat. The woman would tell stories about her husband—one of the main architects of the skyhook—referring to the photographs on the walls and mentioning in her practiced fashion how he had died just before the skyhook was finished, sadly, crushed beneath a piece of tumbling machinery. Then she would take another tact. "If you two ever tire of living out there," she would say, gesturing at the sea, "I'd sure like having you for neighbors. Next door to me." She was lonely, and Jellico had always had felt touched by her loneliness and her morbid widow's tales. And he had enjoyed having to be patient with her. More than Abby, he liked to smile and nod and make the weak promise:

"Some day."

Not that a closet-sized room, scrubbed and sweet-smelling, could ever be worth the boredom and the routine. The deadly sameness. And not that Abby and he could ever forget what Mother had taught them. What she had lived for herself, and then died to prove.

Jellico muttered, "Abby," one last time, standing and checking his signal and learning that the atmosphere now was choking it off. So he pulled in the long aerial and walked. Further along he found more bodies, all burnt and most partially buried.

He felt an odd sort of calmness. He moved in loops until he found a corpse lying exposed. The skin of the face had been pulled tight by the corrupting heat. The mouth was open and the teeth, in perfect rows, seemed to be threatening the world.

He knelt again, the ash crunching underneath him.

He took out a knife and began to delicately ease the blade in and out of the cooked flesh—pretending this was an ordinary specimen, not someone he had known, and almost hearing his mother, behind and to his left, asking, "Jel? Do you see the structures, Jel? Can you identify the functions?" She said, "Think of the selection pressures, love, and tell me what's important and what's not."

Deep in the chest was an object—a metallic bit of slenderness—and with his knife and free hand he cut and dug. Cut and dug.

"There."

He brought out the prize and laid it carefully on top of a boot. On top of his toes. It looked like a bullet. Except it was more machine than bullet. There were delicate structures and a small sophisticated nuclear battery. And clinging to the tip was a ragged flake. A piece of spent stuhr.

"Imagine," he said, unable to imagine half of it. The stuhr he knew had to be worked on an enormous scale, a starship's reactor for power. But Alteretic bullets wore jackets of stuhr. With a god as your mentor, he thought, you got incredible weapons. Standing, he slipped the bullet into a pocket and sheathed the knife—the workings of the sheath cleaning and sharpening the glass blade. Then he picked up his rifle and climbed out of the ruins, moving with slow deliberation past the feeding crabs. Again the ground sloped. The oaks and their glow increased.

He thought of Abby. He knew she would wait only so long before nerves and her nature drove her to search for him. He could imagine her listening to the empty static, seeing nothing, counting seconds and making plans. She was so very much like their mother—in both tone and temperament. High-strung, the Islanders had called her. "Spirited," Jellico liked to believe.

The pincered tracks of the crabs made the ground look chewed.

He breathed and walked faster.

At one point he complimented himself, telling himself how calm he was about everything. Considering. And then, as if hearing some dissenting voice, he glanced down at his hand and found it trembling.

Nothing around him was familiar.

The growing oaks shrouded the docks ahead. If they were still intact, that is. He felt halfway lost, landmarks scarce, nothing to follow but the crab trail.

This was how the Islanders must have seen this world, he decided. A confusing place of death and rot and grubby little lights. Being scared for days and days made him wonder how Islanders, scared for decades, had kept their heads fastened on. How they took the strain. Once more he thought about the poor dead woman with the ring—Sarah—and how Sarah had lived hunkered under a dome of stuhr, armed with cleansers and simple pleasures and memories and dreams.

He was almost careless, hurrying now.

If there were booby traps or trip wires, he reasoned, then the crabs would have set them off already.

He was going to miss Skyhook Island. It and its people had never been that important to him—emotionally, at least. And now suddenly, curiously, he felt as if he had loved this place and all of them all of the time.

He supposed Abby felt the same. In her fashion.

He sighed and glanced down the slope.

A smallish crab was climbing. Feeling belligerent, it stopped when Jellico approached and raised its pincered hands, looking brave and sure. Jellico was like a man in a dream; he watched himself pause and stare at the crab, thinking that he should step around the thing. Only he couldn't muster the energy. He felt numb to his bones. As if cold now, he shivered. And with the end of his barrel he reached and poked the hard eyeless face once. Then again.

"Come on, friend," he began. "Do me this favor—"

The crab exploded. Chunks of shell and orange meat blew upwards, and there came a loud *crack* ripping through the fungal trees. Jellico stumbled. For an instant, he believed himself dead, the crab some kind of walking bomb. And when he looked upwards at the red tops of the trees, he thought he was injured, and oh, was he stupid and would poor Abby have a handful now if he lived somehow.

He blinked and looked for the warning lights.

The inside of his helmet was dark. Unperturbed.

He sat up and saw the crab laying in a broken heap at his feet, one claw twitching, and beyond the crab stood a human figure armed with an odd twin-barreled gun and covered with curled plates of stuhr.

Jellico climbed to his feet.

The figure came closer and flipped his gun in the air, quick and easy, grabbing the barrels and swinging the butt into Jellico's helmet.

He slammed sideways into an oak, then crumbled.

A small strong hand rolled him onto his back. He started to breath in sips and gasps. A knee came down on his chest, torturing bruised ribs, and a voice said, "Hey! Fucker!" with a thick accent. "You hear me? Huh? You hear?"

Jellico moaned.

"Hey, asshole!" Floating above Jellico was a round face partly obscured by smoke-colored glass. The face was pitted. The pits were deep and ugly and made the man fearsome. Fearless. "Alteretic shit!" he shouted, stabbing at Jellico's face with one stout finger. "You shit!"

"No."

"What?"

"No!" Jellico screamed, hoping the sound would seep out and be heard. "I'm not!"

"Goddamn Alteretic shit!"

Jellico reached for his own throat, for the speaker controls, and the stranger struck him hard with both of his hands. The island began spinning. He felt himself flying. He slid fingers into the fallen filth, down into the round cavities of the ground; and he held tight, moaning softly, until the stranger quit hitting him long enough for everything to simmer down. To stand steady.

The stranger was tinkering with the speaker controls himself. Jellico could see the eyes narrowed to wicked slits and the hard thick mouth that was laughing. The voice, still accented and calmly certain, said, "I kill and eat Alteretic shit. Eat you whole!"

Jellico believed him.

Then the knee was gone. The hands had him and pulled, and he found himself standing, his body fighting for balance.

"You want die?"

"Sure," he whispered.

"Sure?" The stranger laughed and laughed. He said, "You sound scared, little God-boy."

God-boy?

"You want die?"

Please.

A clenched fist struck him in the sternum. He fell backwards into another oak and slid to the ground, fighting for air. "Look. Here!" He blinked and saw half a dozen figures behind Pitted Face. They looked the same. All of them carried the same twin-barreled guns, and their lifesuits were adorned with pieces of shaped stuhr—each powered by some nuclear battery, he guessed. All of them seemed tiny. They had tiny dark faces that were intent and calm, smiling without a hint of kindness. Without a trace of joy.

Jellico struggled to his feet again.

"I like you, little God-boy." Almost sweetly, Pitted Face asked, "You like me?"

Jellico watched him.

"You like me." He nodded and said, "I know." Gripping the stuhr over his own crotch, he rubbed himself. "What are you thinking, God-boy? Huh?"

Jellico's gun was on the ground between them, half-buried.

"What you want, Alteretic? Want godless cock?"

Jellico remembered his knife and grasped the hilt and pulled it out, waving the blade in the dirty red air.

Pitted Face brightened. He seemed genuinely pleased, turning his back to Jellico now and asking, "You want me first? Huh?" With all the strange faces watching, he squatted and presented his rear, hands on his knees, saying to Jellico, "Be first, little boy. Please."

Jellico flung the knife blindly, then turned and ran. Keeping low, trying to weave between the oaks, he expected the guns to open up. He imagined their roar, remembering the crab. He prayed to be killed outright, easy and clean as possible, hoping Abby would hear them firing and have the good sense to get away. And then, when he still hadn't heard anything, he turned and started uphill, running harder, believing that he was rid of them now and halfway safe.

Halfway home again.

V   The boat—*Little Fist*—was just offshore, shrugging off the wind. Its hull was pure stuhr, built low and broad. Its bridge and crew quarters, engine room and so on were enclosed in three bi-ply spheres set in a line over a deep keel. In ribs and patches and wiry lines, stuhr helped buttress the deck and everything on board. Large-caliber stuhr guns, freshly assembled, were smartly scattered about; and the crews manning them wore lifesuits partly made of the stuff—helmets and leggings and wide breastplates riding them without weight or weakness, throwing back the soft red light of the rotting island.

Mantis was standing on the bridge, watching liquid crystal screens and colored monitors. The bridge was compact and dark and smelled of the world—in spite of airlocks and filters and measured bursts of deodorizers. Mantis himself was a fair-sized man. There was French blood and American good intentions in his family's history, and if his face and color were Asian, still his build and bulk were nearly European—long arms and legs anchored on a trunk that a careless someone might have taken for fat, belly-rich and reflex-poor.

He was a contented man, mostly. It was his nature.

He loved to talk, and he was talking now, smiling, thanking Mr. Chosen for having given him command of the *Little Fist*.

Mr. Chosen was standing behind him—a small, blandly handsome man working to ignore the prattle. Up on the main screen was a view of the island, and he watched the island and the monitors that clattered and clicked, spouting data. Then after awhile he interrupted Mantis:

"What's our rabbit's status?"

The flow of words barely broke. The language was a stew of Asian tongues, plus the occasional Indian-English word. "The rabbit—the boy —seems to have smelled our intent, sir. He's now trying to lead Moon's people nowhere. And he's quit running." During the scuffle, on the sly, Moon had fixed a tiny sensor to the back of the boy's helmet. "Twice," said Mantis, "the boy has tripped small proximity mines without being aware. Alteretic models, I think. My guess is that the planet itself has somehow deactivated them. Some fungus or rust, maybe, has buggered up their workings."

"Where was he going?" asked Mr. Chosen. "Before."

"To the far side of the island." Mantis paused, cocking his head and listening to a hand-held pair of headphones. "He keeps muttering something about someone. Some girl, I think. Just who she is, I can't tell. And if she's the only one or not—" He shrugged in a large way.

Mr. Chosen said nothing, waiting while Mantis hit buttons. He was dressed in the same cut and color of jumpsuit that Mantis wore, the tropical green plainly out of place, and the emblems of their respective ranks were set on their shoulders.

"Moon's team has broken off from the boy now," said Mantis. "They've found a habitat of some sort. Destroyed." He was watching a small screen, toying with the images. "Sonics show tunnels. Underground chambers. A long-term settlement, I'll wager. Just the sort of things we expected."

"Are you sure?"

"The materials seem consistent with an old-style starship. United States class."

"The *Kansas City?*"

"I don't know what else."

"Fine," said Mr. Chosen. "Fine."

Mantis touched a control. The main screen enlarged its view of the island, focusing in on the lip of the flattened ground.

"Are those crabs?"

"Stony teardrops," said Mantis, inspired.

Mr. Chosen watched the crabs. The camera was mounted on a telescoping boom, and Mantis extended the boom as far as it would reach,
then focused on the broken dormitories themselves. After a minute, Mr.
Chosen became disgusted and said so. "Something less morbid, Mantis.
If you please."

"Sir."

The view widened and slipped to one side. Now they could see the boat
below them and the wind-stirred sea in the distance, colored like molten
tar, and a school of those sail-backed fish was hunting on the sea, letting
the wind carry them along.

"Are you still jamming?"

"No one is broadcasting anymore."

"And you're quite sure there are no Alteretics nearby?"

"As sure as I can be, sir." This atmosphere played hell with sensors.
Not to mention with communications and machinery and people too.
Mantis thought of the airborne jungle above, dense and self-supporting,
and all the refuse falling from the jungle. Earth was an airless, virtually
lifeless globe when set against Leeshore. Particularly now, thought Mantis. Particularly after the Wars.

"What's your range again?"

"Sir?"

"The sensors . . . how far can they see?"

"Give or take, a hundred kilometers. Depending." Assuming that the
Alteretics were navigating with sonics and radar, and assuming that they
couldn't jam or camouflage as well as *Little Fist*. It would help if they were
in the open, exposed—cluttered landscapes meant a natural jamming.
And of course it depended on what sorts of gear they had saved from their
shuttle, and too, what kind of boat or raft they were being forced to use.

Mr. Chosen was silent. Mantis, glancing over a shoulder, saw a contemplative expression, Chosen's eyes showing all the life and depth of a
rodent's eyes. "Just the same," said the bland man, "perhaps we should
pull Moon and his people off the island. We might be wise to finish this
with a tactical device. Don't you think?"

"In case they left us a surprise. Is that it, sir?"

"Their own tactical device, yes. Somewhere down in one of those
tunnels." He fidgeted nervously. "Maybe your sensors have missed it."

Mantis was quiet now, standing quite still. Thinking how very unlikely that was.

"Mantis?"

"I think nuclear weapons are premature," he said carefully, his words weighed. "I think we should wait a bit, sir. Let the landing party learn what they can."

"That boy, and whoever else—" Mr. Chosen straightened his back. "I don't trust them."

"Nor do I, and nor does Moon." Mantis showed a smile. "Moon's not going to fall for any trap."

Mr. Chosen nodded, apparently satisfied.

Then Mantis suggested, "We can pull Moon and a couple others. Drop them on the other side of the island and let them hunt faster." He was well aware of Mr. Chosen's fears. No one liked being partly blinded, much less having to hunt your mortal enemies at the same time. "Sir?"

"Fine," he said. "Let's do that."

"Sir." Mantis opened a channel to Moon, aiming the signal and keeping its strength to a minimum. No sense tempting eavesdroppers—

"Keep me abreast."

"I will, sir."

"And I'm glad you like your new post."

"Thank you again, sir."

Mr. Chosen left. Mantis took the boat in close to the shoreline and called Moon. At length, Moon and two soldiers appeared, climbed into an inflated raft and then pushed out against the wind. They boarded *Little Fist* up near the bow, and Mantis took them around the island, traveling in a slow generous loop. He was thinking to himself how Mr. Chosen hadn't had much of a choice in who would be piloting. With a tempered satisfaction, he thought how no one else on board had even half his ability. All things considered.

The sea had always been part of his life.

His father's father, for instance, had made a fair fortune by towing foam-metals from their splash sites to smelters in China and the Koreas. And his own father had commanded a hydrofoil during the early Wars, serving with distinction until his own capture and conscription, Alteretic-style, and then his subsequent death.

Mantis liked this boat already—a good sign, and rare. Already he was use to the heavy ride and the sluggish helm, and there were moments when he outguessed the computers and monitors, hands and eyes knowing best what was needed. The smartest speed. The safest, smoothest way. The boat and Mr. Chosen—they were alike.

The more Mantis thought of the two, the more their similarities showed. It's a question of handling them in the right way, he said to himself. A nudge here. A whisper there. And let their keels do the rest.

The island looked unchanged as they moved around it. Up on the main screen, it resembled the top of some furry red ball. Mantis increased the amplification and the magnification and held the camera on a single spot. He watched the mold forest growing, centuries of stored energies converted to stalks and seeds and light. He could see swarms of insects floating and flowing through the air. He saw things like birds, only huge and legless, descending down from the black, black sky. One of the stony teardrops, waddling like a crab, crossed the narrow shoreline and waded into the sea, and Mantis touched the controls and enlarged the image even more, tilting the camera to follow. He saw kelps bleeding light and small reddish fish hovering, and there were tiny colonies of nameless things growing snug against the white skin of the island. He saw detritus in the sea, drifting, and the largest bits and hunks showed fins and fronds and other traces of lazy passengers. The crab, or whatever, vanished somewhere in the kelp. The boat was pulling away from the spot. Mantis let the camera pan ahead, sweeping across the bow, and he saw Moon standing with soldiers and crewmen between the bow missile tubes and the superstructure, huddled out of the wind. A small searchlight was on and pointing at them; the faceplates had turned clear with the light. Everyone was watching Moon. They were staring at his hands. Mantis caught a glimpse of the scarred face, sternness and laughter mixed in equal proportions, and he panned downwards and watched the show. It's probably something he found on the island, thought Mantis. A trophy of some kind. And suddenly he was looking between the people, gazing down at Moon's tiny hands. In one hand laid a ring—a gold band and a diamond. In the other laid the burnt finger Moon had pulled the ring from, and while Mantis stood watching, curious, someone in the audience apparently made a joke. Because suddenly all of them were laughing. One of them—one of the young soldiers—took the finger and pretended it was one of his own. Then, giggling to tears, he used it as a false nose. And then, finally, as a more vulgar appendage.

"Moon's in his element," Mantis said aloud. That little man was the purest distillation of war, having survived trials that a poor fat fellow like himself couldn't imagine. Along the way, Moon had acquired treachery and cruelty and a reasoned brand of violence, and as much as Mantis loathed parts of him, he had to admire the whole. Just like he had to rely on him. There was not a better warrior left on the starship—on *The Righteous Fist*. He was smart in ways you couldn't guess, just looking at him.

Whenever Mantis was asleep and Moon came into his dreams, Mantis slept well—the warrior guarding decent souls like his own, even in their slumber.

Mantis raised the camera now, scanning ahead.

The island bent away, the sea calming, and out in the misty black a cone of light flickered off and on, off and on.

He enlarged the image, and the light grew yellowish, brighter and wider and held aloft by something enormous. Mantis saw smooth leathery wings and a stout body, eyes as big as platters carried beneath the massive head. Between the eyes was an organ sparking like a strobe lamp, throwing bursts of light down at the sea. A scavenger? he wondered. Probably. Using sonics, he probed into its flesh and featherweight bone. "Are you hiding any Alteretics, friend?" Mantis said aloud. It wasn't. So he turned the sonics back to automatic, and when the boat approached the scavenger, it turned and fled.

Softly, slowly, a monitor began to *beep*.

Mantis turned the camera and found a sail-backed fish kicking, making for the wind.

He thumbed a switch. "Mr. Chosen?"

Something, he realized, was hiding inside the fish. Tucked underneath a gill flap.

"Mr. Chosen?" he repeated.

"Yes, Mantis."

"A fish with a rider."

"That girl?"

"Perhaps."

Mr. Chosen was silent, likely marching through his options. Then he said, "As you see fit, Mantis."

"Thank you, sir." Mantis hit the throttle as much as he dared, not wanting to sweep people off the open deck. The hum of the engines rose, faint vibrations coming up through his toes. Then he punched on a pair of large searchlights, aiming the beams, and Moon came on the line and said, "It's what? The fish?"

"Right. I've got sonics on screen two."

They showed the bones of the fish and the girl. Mantis could tell she was female from her pelvis and the recyke system in her lifesuit. On the fish's skull, tiny and bright, was a nest of wires leading down into the brain. A primitive but effective apparatus, he thought. Someone here has been clever.

"Moon," said Mantis. "The boss wants her whole. You hear me?"

"Her," he said. "Right."

Mantis had them nearly on top of the fish. Moon was standing on the bow with a handheld stuhr gun, and with a quick and careless motion he pointed, putting a pair of bullets through the skull and neural meat.

The fish died, orange blood spurting in a fountain.

Moon went over the railing just as Mantis cut the throttle. He landed on his feet on top of the flopping sail. The girl climbed out from under the gill flap, aimed and fired a puny gun.

Moon staggered, the stuhr taking the brunt of the impact.

She aimed higher, trying for his faceplate, and Moon ducked and darted and got a hand on the barrel. They started to fight. Somehow the girl pulled the warrior down, and they rolled in the bright blood, kicking, and finally Moon kicked hardest and then stood and tossed away the gun, the sea taking it with a hushed splash.

Blood was skating down Moon's breastplate and down his leggings.

Mantis adjusted an outside microphone and heard Moon talking to the girl with his broken English. "You better than boy," he said. "You got fight."

She lay still, saying nothing. Mantis studied her snug lifesuit and fine figure and the way she laid. When she turned her eyes towards the searchlights, her faceplate went from black to clear, the face within sharp and lovely and the color of some rich and lustrous dark wood.

Moon was laughing. Prancing about on the dead fish. His soldiers came down on a spun glass rope ladder. The two of them lifted the girl out of the orange gore. "Is he dead?" she asked. "Dead?" said Moon. "Who?" "The boy. My brother. You killed him, didn't you?" "Sure," lied Moon. "Killed and ate him too." They carried her like a limp rag doll. She did nothing and said nothing, and Mantis, watching, felt a sudden ache. An empathy. They told her to climb the glass ladder and she tried, moving slowly. Mantis asked himself what she and her brother might mean—for the mission and for his own self both—and he caught sight of Moon standing on the corpse, staring up at her potentials. Beyond, far out on the water, the winged scavenger had returned. It was spitting light and waiting. Hovering. Spreading over the water now was the blood. To Mantis, it was a louder, prouder kind of color than the blood of men.

VI   "Who are you?"
"Who are *you?*"
"To you, I'm Mr. Chosen." The accent was thin and light and nearly charming; his English was more Indian than Anglo. The little man was watching her, his foreign face bland, his hands laid in a neat pile on the tabletop between them. It looked as though he had worked an hour to lay those hands just so.
"My brother—"
"Safe. I won't tell you again."
Abitibi was sitting without relaxing. She was wearing the jumpsuit she had had underneath her lifesuit—a functional piece of clothing much like Mr. Chosen's, lacking only the emblems of rank and a certain scrubbed smell. Taped to her ankles and wrists and sweating temples were wires made of some flexible glass. She stared at Mr. Chosen. More than any-

thing, she wished she could tie the wires around his neck and squeeze his face blue. Then do the same to the rest of her captors.

Again Mr. Chosen asked, "What is your name?" They were alone. The room was a galley, she supposed. There were sinks and slots where synthetic foods would appear on command. She sat looking at her surroundings, and Mr. Chosen spoke. The galley's tiny size and the silence made his voice seem larger than it was. "What shall I call you?"

She said nothing, staring.

"Very well." He lifted his hands and reached beneath the table, the motion slow and important. "Perhaps this will help," he said. Up came a stat-sealed folder. He withdrew a photograph frosted with soot and folded in a haphazardous way, like trash. Touching a corner made the photograph come alive. Carefully watching Abitibi, he laid it down between them.

She glanced at the image, holding her breath and carefully giving nothing away. Pulling on the wires, she felt what slack she had and how they were bunched and fastened to the floor.

He began to talk, telling how it was that a small spaceship came here some years ago and how its crew built a port. A place where starships like itself could come and be assured of water. She almost told Mr. Chosen that she knew the story, that this was wasting time. But then she realized what he really wanted—her reaction—something in his tone and his poise saying that he was very, very curious as to what she knew and was thinking now.

Water was the reaction mass of choice. Nuclear engines, he stated, could heat any substance and fling it out the rocket nozzles. But nothing was so cheap and easy to handle as water. Besides, its hydrogen was fuel for the fusion reactors. And of course seawater was full of the stuff of life.

She felt a prick in her wrists. A pain and then a numbness. She tugged once at the wires, straining, and then decided that there was no point in fighting anymore. A calmness swept over her.

Mr. Chosen went on, describing how the crew had assembled a skyhook and a power source by dismantling their own starship. At odd moments, from unexpected directions, he would use some technical term or describe some obscure technique employed years ago. Abitibi would react. She couldn't help herself. She would shake her head and say, "No," or say, "That's not the way they did it."

"Who?"

"The Islanders. They didn't do that."

"No?"

"That was the way they planned it. On Earth. But when they got here they discovered it wouldn't work for them." And she explained what she meant.

The Islanders had built the skyhook and waited. A larger, more advanced starship was to come to Leeshore in the near future. A portion of that second crew would remain, tending the skyhook, and the Islanders and Mother would go to some Earthly world. Some place where people could live in the open and have families and grow. This was how Mankind was to conquer space. Habitable worlds are scarce, and the distances between them are prohibitive. When all the factors were tallied—the rigors of deep space, the limits of fuel and the erosion of the tri-ply shields —a string of way stations was considered the best means to be had.

Mr. Chosen said, "Abitibi?"

"Yes?"

"Your name is Abitibi?"

"I'm Abitibi," she heard herself say. "Sure." Suddenly it seemed very important to tell the absolute truth.

"Very good. Now, if I ask you the name of this world, Abitibi, what's the first thing to occur to you?"

"Leeshore."

"Not this?" He read a complex set of letters and numbers off a data sheet.

"Not to me. No." She scratched her wrists and swore, "That's what the Islanders named it. Leeshore."

"And who, may I ask, are the Islanders?"

"The people who lived here." She pointed at the photograph from the folder. "That's Skyhook Island."

"Why do you suppose they named it Leeshore?"

"It's the dangerous shore. The shore a ship fears when at sea." She hadn't remembered knowing that. Odd as it seemed, the notion had come bubbling up out of her brain somehow. "The lee shore is where storms drive boats to their death," she said. "On Earth, that is."

"Not here?"

"There aren't any storms here," she said. "Never."

"No?" Mr. Chosen gave a strange smile. Something about him was terribly remote. He asked, "Is that how the Islanders, as you call them, looked at this world?"

"They hated it," she said. Rubbing her wrists, she felt an odd tingle. "They felt they had been washed up here and left for dead. Forgotten and sure to die here."

"Interesting," Mr. Chosen said, his face showing nothing. Not a hint of interest. Not boredom. Nothing. "You call this Leeshore too?"

She shrugged. "Sure."

"Do you hate this world?"

"No."

"Why not?"

"It's our world." What could be simpler? "We were born here and we know it better than anyone." She was thinking of Jel now, wondering when she would see him again.

Mr. Chosen said nothing for a moment, watching her eyes. Then he turned in his chair and said something, facing the ceiling, his words not words now but instead some frothy, birdy language.

Someone answered Mr. Chosen. He spoke the same nonsense, his voice falling from overhead.

Then he turned back to Abitibi, calm as ever, and admitted, "You're a problem for us." He paused, breathing through his nose. "We come here hunting our enemies. We land on this strange world and discover its inhabitants killed. Except, that is, for a young man and woman, people who don't exist in any record of ours, who claim to be siblings. Their common mother being who—?"

"Alice Carmichael." It felt strange to use Mother's name.

"Carmichael." He nodded briefly. "She's the mission's biologist, am I right?"

"She's dead."

"As of when?"

Abitibi told him the particulars, adding, "We're the biologists now." Except the mission was over now, the skyhook down and everyone else dead. She glanced at the photograph, at Skyhook Island and halfway listened to Mr. Chosen saying:

"The crux of this interview is proving who you are." He stared, the big dark eyes never blinking. "Proof. We need proof, I'm afraid. Or we'll have to start thinking the worst. The very worst."

She recognized the photograph. The Islanders and Mother had taken it years ago. They had mounted a camera on a balloon and hung the balloon out over the leeward side of the island, and the camera had made a high-density image of everything at once. She could see the rounded white landscape bathed in bright UV-rich lights. The docks were in the foreground—tugs and some smaller boats drifting where they had been tied. Above the docks, on the flattened ground, were the bright mirrored domes of the dormitories. And higher still, just visible, was the base of the skyhook itself.

"Would you like to look?"

She told him, "Yes," and reached as far as the wires allowed.

He nudged the photograph closer, always watching.

Slowly, clumsily, Abitibi began touching the margins. Hidden under the plastic veneer were pressure-sensitive switches. By handling them just so, she knew, she could enlarge any portion of the image. Mother had done this once with Abby watching, telling her jokingly, "This shows every human for light-years around." There was a certain spot on the island where everyone had stood together in three perfect rows. She remembered what she had seen—everyone wearing clear bubble helmets so that their faces would show, all the Islanders sporting smiles and holding onto each other's hands. Mother had stood on the end of the back row—tall and lithe and quite pretty, her pale fine face showing only traces of her age. In her hands and on her arms, sleeping, were two bundled babies. Twins. "This is me," she would say to Mr. Chosen, pointing at the sleeping girl. And if she was doubted still, she would magnify the namepatch on the baby's arm. "Abitibi Carmichael," she would read. "See?"

Mr. Chosen seemed to hear her mind. He asked, "What sort of person would bear children here? On Leeshore?" As if angry, he said, "At the very best, this is a marginal world for people. The Islanders could live here because they were few and picked and well-trained. But children require extra resources. They demand precious time. The care of the skyhook was the mission's central concern, and that would have suffered. Not to mention the sad suffering of the children themselves."

Abitibi glanced up from the photograph, her eyes tired of the blurring whiteness.

He went on. "The people here must have known about the Alteretics. About the Wars. There was a good deal of jamming being done, true, and a fair amount of false information spread to the colonies. But the Islanders must have realized long ago that no starships were coming. At least not according to the original plans." He paused, his breathing slow and light. Then he said, "They must have lived cautiously. Slowly. To insure their survival, I imagine they used heavy doses of antimetabolites and other elixirs. To fight aging. And of course, they nursed their scarce resources. Like metals and glass and everything else Leeshore couldn't provide."

Blinking, Abitibi said, "Miser birds."

"Pardon?"

"If you kill a miser bird at the right time, then cut open its colon, you find that its accumulated waste is full of metals. Half-pure metals." She told him, "It's part of their life cycle. Jel and I got the Islanders to sometimes pay for the miser birds we shot. If we'd wanted to, we could have put them butt-deep in shit and steel."

"I see. I hadn't known." Mr. Chosen piled his hands on the tabletop. He looked in charge and very pleased to be that way. "You did that?"

"We did a lot of things." She was sweating, and her jumpsuit worked to absorb the sweat. Her voice was louder now, and brittle. "We kept track of the islands floating upwind from Skyhook Island. We kept track of the ocean floor, guessing where new islands would surface. We did research, good general research, looking at the ocean and atmosphere and as much of the life as we had time for. We found some native foods that people can eat—not that Islanders ever got the stomach for fungus. And we learned how to survive out there, which is the best trick we ever managed—to survive out past lights and scrubbed ground and the stuhr." She rubbed her wrists absently, saying, "If you hadn't come along, Jel and I would have lived years and years on our own. We didn't need the Islanders. And we sure don't need you." She frowned and cursed at him, the words hot and honest, and she struck the tabletop once. Then again.

Softly, to himself, Mr. Chosen said, "Feral imp." He seemed a little startled, and he worked to hide the feeling. He asked, "What did the Islanders give you? For the miser birds and the rest?"

She shrugged. "What we couldn't make ourselves. Lifesuits and electronics and filters to cut and remix the air." She thought a moment before admitting, "We've got stockpiles. They're everywhere."

"You're a frugal team."

"Feral and frugal." She hit the table a third time, her fists aching afterwards. "Do you know why Mother had us?"

"No."

"She didn't agree with the Islanders. Or you. All of you think the best course is to sit and do a slow rot. Never try anything new, and never once take risks." She said, "When the Wars were over, the starships would come as promised. Or so they thought." Then she laughed bitterly and admitted, "They were right, weren't they? Starships came and look how happy they are now!"

"Your mother—?"

"She said Leeshore's a confusing place. Complicated. Full of demands. She said the things that lived best were adaptable. They were pliable and tough and smart." Abitibi pulled on the wires taped to her sweating temples, the tape not yielding. "You can't just stay in one place and take those drugs—the antimetabolites and whatever."

"She had children," Mr. Chosen prompted.

"Yes." Abitibi felt like jumping or running. She was quivering down through her legs and up her strong back. "She thought they should build artificial wombs and mass produce children. The Islanders and her should. Whatever the cost, the children would have been worth it. But the best she could do herself was to get pregnant. She had never taken many elixirs anyway—they slow down your brain and your living, not just your aging —but she went off them entirely when she got pregnant. It screws up the embryo development." She breathed, then said, "The Islanders were angry when they found out. They threatened to hold back the elixirs permanently if she didn't abort. Mother wouldn't though. She said, 'Go ahead. Save them for yourselves.' So they tried scaring her another way —by pretending they were going to throw her off the island. But Mother knew a bluff, and she knew the Islanders, and she reminded them that a trained biologist had certain skills that they would always need. They had no choice but to fold, and she had them in her pocket from then on."

"Who was your father?"

Abitibi paused, wondering if that memory would bubble out too. But finally she had to concede, "I don't know. She never told us."

"An Islander?"

"No, no." There was a sharp ringing in her ears now, and her vision was clouding. "Mother had access to the genetic stores. There were . . . I don't know . . . maybe some hundred thousand people stashed in the stores. As sperm and eggs. They'd been frozen and brought onboard the starship, so there'd be diversity in the new colony. For when they reached a new Earth." She couldn't get the Islanders out of her mind. Why not? "We still have part of the stores. They're hidden out there," and she made a sweeping gesture towards a random wall. "You never know—"

"You don't know any possible fathers?"

"I said no."

"Was there anyone she mentioned from Earth? Any individual she admired and who might be represented in these stores of yours?"

Abitibi tried to recall.

Mr. Chosen began drumming on the tabletop, plainly waiting for something.

There was something I was doing before, Abitibi realized. What was I doing? Something important, wasn't it?

"I wish we could believe you," Mr. Chosen said. "It would make our decisions a good deal simpler. The Alteretics, for all we know, might have left you and your brother as plants. As agents." He sighed without emotion, watching Abitibi. "It seems so convenient. We find you two, by chance, and you tell us a nice story, gaining admission to our ranks—"

She suddenly remembered. The photograph! She hunted and found it on the table, laying just where she had left it, and with the moistened tips of her fingers she began pressing on the margins, hunting for her baby self, magnifying the island's white slope and wondering how she could have forgotten something so simple.

Mr. Chosen was silent, waiting.

"There." She shouted, "There!" The Islanders were in three rows, sure enough. They were standing just below the skyhook—which made a symbolic sense—and through the mist and the unusually light fall of crud she saw the fat round faces smiling. Not as happily as she remembered them. But still—

Her captor stirred; she felt him through the table.

All at once Abitibi was frightened. It was as though she was suddenly a different person—someone coming apart at the seams. Her fingers were slow and stupid, working with the photograph. The liquid crystals formed and reformed, the image enlarging and sliding down to the end of the back row.

Drops of sweat splattered on the photograph's veneer.

Sweat, she thought, one hand reaching and finding tears. Big tears. She was crying now, almost sobbing. She was thinking about herself and the poor dead Islanders, and just then Mr. Chosen said, "If you and your brother *are* agents—" his voice sounding distant and hard, thundering like Doom itself.

"Here!" she snapped. "Look here!"

"What?"

"Mother and us! See?"

"And who?" He glanced up at her crying eyes. "Who do you see?"

She looked again, blinking and discovering Mother's empty arms. There was no baby, girl or not. "No!" She rose. "No!" She jumped at him, and the wires and binding tape began tearing loose. She felt her skin peeling away, the pain searing. Mr. Chosen's expression was one of startled fear with his eyes going round—

—and then Abitibi was down on the floor in a heap. Her limbs felt dead, and she felt dead inside, remembering nothing and feeling as if she had been down for hours now. Gradually she became aware of the ceiling voice again, and Mr. Chosen spoke with that voice, using the birdy language; and then there were boots everywhere—small boots with tiny feet inside—and Mr. Chosen was saying, "You seem to be whoever you think you are, Abitibi Carmichael." He told her, "My men will take you to your brother now, and then you'll sleep a good long sleep."

She was moved by the booted men. She felt them removing the tape and wires with some cool, stinging solvent. Then she was floating, drifting along a narrow hallway with bright light above. A doorway swung open with a hiss. She was sent down like cargo, on her back on the cold, hard floor. Someone was lying beside her, restrained somehow, and she realized it was Jel and that the booted men were lifting him now and carrying him away.

The door hissed shut again.

The room was dark and felt small, and she stared up into the darkness and muttered, "I am who I think I am. Imagine."

VII   With blandness comes consistency, and Mr. Chosen was nothing if he wasn't the living portrait of both.

He sat beside Moon—trusted Moon—while Mantis summarized their circumstances. It was half a day after his interviews with the boy and girl. They were an hour free of Skyhook Island now, heading upwind, retracing their course in hopes of finding some trail. Mantis wasn't sounding hopeful about their prospects. "If there are any Alteretics down here," he concluded, "then we've got a long, long hunt ahead. If this was Earth, it would take an hour to track them down. Given our resources. But in this place, with these conditions . . ." He shook his head. "I can't make guarantees."

Of course, the Alteretics were here, thought Mr. Chosen. It was just like Mantis to doubt the obvious. Everyone had seen their starship in orbit around Leeshore, and then the one shuttle embarking. Some time later, in a blink, the hair-fine tube of stuhr had collapsed into nothingness. Gone. And when no shuttle returned, the Alteretics had fled—rocketing out of the system, making for the comet belt and the dirty water it held.

"How close do we need to be?" asked Mr. Chosen. "Your latest estimate, please."

"To spot them?" Mantis blinked. "I think my hundred kilometer guess is solid, sir. Give or take."

Mantis. Always pretending to be the earnest subordinate—

"What about our satellites?" Mr. Chosen persisted. "Aren't they an asset?"

"Unfortunately, no." Three satellites were in high, geosynchronous orbits. Five more were skimming over the dense atmosphere. *The Righteous Fist* had placed them there to help with the hunting. "The trouble is they can't peer through the bladders as promised, sir."

"I see."

"There's too much between here and them."

In a stack before Mr. Chosen were more mutilated photographs—the same kind as the one he had shown the twins, minus the doctoring. Carefully, using both hands, he took the top photograph and touched a corner and watched the image emerge—a blue-black globe without features, without variations, resembling a polished ball of obsidian fringed with a skin of clear dry air.

Leeshore.

Mantis was discussing the atmosphere and remote sensing, grousing and using the technical jargon that always sounded so slippery and suspicious to Mr. Chosen. He ignored Mantis, picking through the stack, stopping with a photograph showing a landscape of feeble hills surrounded by shallow valleys—the apparent ground colored the same blue-black as the planet itself.

This was the airborne jungle, he knew. It wasn't ground at all, but, instead, a jumbled mass of enormous bladder plants fighting for sunlight. Enlarging a portion of the image, he brought out details. The skin of the bladder plants glistened with a self-made dew, and clinging to them were pastures of epiphytes and parasites as black as coal. In the clear blue air above danced legless birds—in flocks and winding rivers and sprawling nations. Mr. Chosen tried to imagine the scene in motion. He thought of the winds pushing everything westward; and he thought of the bladders lifting their own bulks, the air inside them heated by the sun and various physiological tricks.

The jungle was what made them blind.

Days ago, riding their own shuttle down to the sea, they had cut into the jungle with an unnerving crash. It was a startling moment. For an instant, secretly, Mr. Chosen had believed that the Alteretics were firing at them, hitting them with missiles.

Leeshore was a strange, strange world. It neither fascinated nor repelled Mr. Chosen; he was simply trying to recognize its strangeness and work at understanding what it meant to him, the mission's leader.

Or so he assured himself.

The planet was larger than Earth, more massive and yet not quite so dense. A greater proportion of its bulk was water and gas—thus the ocean that was many kilometers deep and the crushing, oxygen-rich atmosphere overhead.

The airborne jungle, according to the surviving records, was born as seaweeds on the ocean's surface. Mr. Chosen had read Alice Carmichael's research papers while on board *The Righteous Fist*—the stuff that had been sent home—and he recalled the heart of them. Ages ago, the seaweeds developed bladders to keep themselves floating in the sunlight. These bladders enlarged over time, strengthening, becoming more and more supportive. Selection pressures rewarded the seaweeds that used heated air to gain lift. Eventually, these seaweeds pulled themselves free of the water, drifting on the winds like living clouds. The bladder plants formed a cap on Leeshore. A kind of semisolid, self-repairing roof. And ever since it had been night on the surface of the sea.

Where on Earth the sea is the symbol of life, on Leeshore it was only a dumping ground for the dead and dying.

A zone of eternal rot, if you will.

A Styx without banks.

Even here, sitting deep inside the sealed boat, Mr. Chosen could smell the rotting going on. There weren't the simple Earthly stinks, either. No, these were alien chemistries breaking down. Odd unearthly proteins and fats and carbohydrates. Yet they bothered him just the same, his belly a little sickened and his meals always tasting tainted somehow. Even if the mission went well, he knew, he might have to endure another month or more of the stinking. And of course, there was the prospect that *The Righteous Fist* would not return for them—

Well, he couldn't think of that possibility.

He simply couldn't let the thought inside his head.

He looked up from the photographs now, glancing around the galley and settling on Mantis. Mantis had finally paused. Amazingly. He was holding a hot cup of broth in one hand, swilling the sweet brew through his teeth.

Mr. Chosen turned to Moon. He used the moment to ask, "If we *do* manage to find the Alteretics, what kind of resistance can we expect?" He wondered, How many are there? What kinds of weapons do they have? And how are they moving from place to place?

For an instant, nothing showed on Moon's face; it was as if no question had been asked him. Then he slowly blinked and reached and deftly grasped a certain photograph from the stack. "The Islanders had boats. Five, the boy says." He pointed. "Four were tugs. All robots. Muscle but no speed." He had focused the photograph—a more recent view of the docks, apparently—and now he passed it to Mr. Chosen. "This is the other boat." The image was of a whitish sailing ship, the masts short and stout and the hull low and broad. "The tugs were sunk off the docks. We've found pieces. But the boat's gone. Stolen by the God-boys, I think."

"Is it a good boat?"

"The boy says it is."

"When did you interview the boy?"

"Interview?" He smiled faintly. "I interviewed him on the island. After I caught him the second time." He blinked, the ugly round face calm. In control. "That boat has room for a dozen. Maybe more. I figure the God-boys got off their shuttle alive. Light guns, sure. Some explosives. And maybe a baby nuke or two." He sighed. "Whatever they slipped off their shuttle." Flattening his hand to show the shuttle, Moon made the hand tilt and sink over the edge of the galley's table.

"We're sure that's what happened?" He didn't wish to sound as skeptical as Mantis. Mr. Chosen simply feared surprises. "Maybe they assembled a boat like our own," he offered. "Maybe they're waiting somewhere. Ready to ambush us."

"No," said Moon.

"You're sure?"

Slowly, every sentence clipped in his fashion, Moon explained the physical evidence to date. There was the radio noise *The Fist* had heard, eavesdropping. There were the apparent traces of a shuttle beside the skyhook's old moorings—visual confirmation impossible due to the depth and the lack of time. Finally, there were the clues he himself had found on Skyhook Island. Spent bullets and ransackings and the assorted butcheries.

When he finished, Mr. Chosen thanked him and thought a moment, then said, "Both of you know our mission. We need at least one Alteretic alive." He looked from Moon to Mantis, then back. "Preferably their ranking officer, their priest, though a conscript would be worthwhile." An

Alteretic priest would constitute a coup, he knew. For a moment, he imagined himself on *The Righteous Fist* again. The Commander himself, a wizened old Afghan, would pin a medal of valor to his bare chest, the medal burrowing its sterile parts into the skin, whispering all the while, "You have done your duty. You have honored your comrades and your holy cause—"

"We'll need help finding them," said Mantis, breaking the spell.

"Help?" he asked.

"Guides."

"You mean the twins, don't you?"

Mantis said, "They know this world. They understand it better than we will ever manage to—"

"—or so they claim." He sighed. The image of the medal had faded. Sometimes, like now, Mr. Chosen wished for the imagination that other men seemed to possess. The visual imagery. He told his audience, "I am not quite convinced that these children are to be believed."

Mantis seemed ready for his doubt. "I assure you," he began. "When I served in Intelligence I learned to use the interrogation wires . . . better than almost anyone, I don't mind saying. Outside the Alteretics themselves, I'm one of the best."

"You think they're genuine."

"The twins? Absolutely."

He stared at Mantis for a moment, remembering how the fat man had let him run the interview. Except Mantis was actually in charge—the doctored photograph his idea, and he always manipulating the children with those wires—and Mr. Chosen had to wonder now if he had really mattered. If Mantis had needed him at all.

"All right," he said to Mantis. "Suppose we use them. How do you think we should go about this hunt? What kinds of strategies do you propose?"

Mantis spoke. Like always, his voice threatened to outrace his brain, the words flowing and flowing and Mr. Chosen wondering when, if ever, the effervescent man would breathe. There were a few photographs remaining. While Mantis tried to imagine where the Alteretics were lurking, Mr. Chosen sorted through the stack and found one photograph not made with an ordinary camera—but instead with sonics. For a moment he was puzzled by the landscape shown. Then he remembered. There was a second biotic zone on Leeshore, distinct and unique. A second region where life created itself from wild energies—order from disruption, structure out of formlessness.

He was looking at the ocean floor.

The sonic camera was beneath the skyhook, apparently. He could see the bright silver threads that were the mooring lines, each one sewn into the crust and made of tri-ply stuhr. The crust itself was covered with the rounded grey shapes of plastic reefs; the reefs thrived beside hot water vents and undersea geysers, feeding on bacteria that in turn thrived on the energy-rich compounds synthesized underground. Earth had its own similar communities. Organisms growing in high-pressure environments, free of the sun. The difference between Earth and Leeshore was one of magnitude—ten thousand-fold. Leeshore's crust was continually cracking and spreading, lava boiling up through the fissures to build new crust. Underneath Skyhook Island, Mr. Chosen recalled, the crust had been relatively new—thick and stable and covered with youthful reefs. Over thousands of years, the reefs could swell to virtual mountains, kilometers across and weighing billions of tons. Then the crust would crack and spread again, or sink away, and some of the reefs would break loose and rise. Like Skyhook Island had once risen. Rise and rot and eventually vanish away.

Such a strange world, thought Mr. Chosen.

He touched the photograph and felt himself shiver.

Mantis was concluding his lecture now. Pausing, he managed to breath before saying, "If we had some experience with this place—some edge on our opponents—I think our chances would improve."

"I see." Mr. Chosen turned off the last photograph, the liquid crystals collapsing into a bland grey. Then with both of his hands he straightened the stack, thinking, wondering not so much whether to use the children, but how. "What do you think, Moon?"

Moon shrugged.

I don't want them for myself, thought Mr. Chosen. His interviews were distasteful in memory. He might not like the stench of Leeshore, for instance, but the twins' odors were worse. Easily. And they sat as if they didn't understand chairs and spoke as if they weren't so sure about language either. It wasn't their words, it was their cadence. The way their eyes tracked when someone else was talking.

"Well," he said, "we certainly can't let them go."

Even if they couldn't find a use for them, they had to keep them. It was a standing order. Friendly natives had to be delivered to *The Fist*. It was the manpower shortage—talented, intelligent individuals were scarce.

"Do you think you could make them into soldiers?" Mr. Chosen asked Moon. "Good feral stock like them—" He cocked his head and waited.

Moon appeared not to hear the suggestion. Then, making a tiny sound, he shifted his weight and said, "The girl." He nodded once and said, "With wires, maybe."

"Not the boy?"

He shook his head, smiling. "Pees his pants." Placing a hand to his chest, he said, "No fire."

Mantis stirred. Mr. Chosen turned to him and wondered, "What did you learn? After all, you were handling the wires."

"Moon's likely right," he offered, his tone somehow guarded now. His voice quieter. "They are two very different people. At least so far as the wires could determine."

"Different?"

"Like Moon suggested, sir. The girl has a certain fire. She's full of it, and I don't think she's quite clear as to what it is." He took a breath, then said, "Jellico is different. I don't know . . . quieter. More likely to contemplate instead of act."

"He's a coward," said Moon.

Mr. Chosen leaned back in his chair.

Thinking, recalling the interviews, he saw part of what both men meant. When that business with the doctored photograph came up, the girl had tried to come across the galley table to do who knows what. The boy, on the other hand, had stared and stared, weeping quietly, Mr. Chosen assuring him that now he would have to die.

It was as though he had halfway believed what he was seeing.

Instead of lashing out like his sister, the boy had simply resigned all hope and given up.

Indeed, thought Mr. Chosen. A coward to his core.

He said, "Very well," and gestured. "You can have the girl, Moon. You and Mantis can work out the particulars with the wires. It's not my area, but I suppose you'll want to accent her alleged fires—"

Moon nodded once. It was as close as he came to saying, "Thank you, sir."

"And you," Mr. Chosen said, turning. "You can have the boy."

Mantis thanked him with smiles and grateful words.

Charitably, Mr. Chosen said, "He seems bright enough. If you use the wires, I imagine he'll cooperate. He can be that guide you want."

"Thank you, sir." Mantis glanced towards Moon for no reason, smiles fading. "I think he'll be helpful without prompting, however." He said, "Sir," in a large way.

"Whatever you wish." Mr. Chosen paused, then said, "I do remind both of you that no one else is responsible for their actions. Am I clear?"

"Yes, sir."

"And you Moon?"

Moon nodded, returning Mantis' gaze. Then smiling.

There was suddenly a slippery quality to what was happening. Mr. Chosen could not quite decide what either of his officers were thinking. He began to stand, telling them, "You're free to go, gentlemen."

Both of them stood too.

Then Mantis, using a quiet voice, inquired, "Have you seen Moon's new ornament, sir?"

"Ornament?" Mr. Chosen frowned, thinking of medals.

"On his hand, sir."

Moon was wearing a ring on his smallest finger.

"Am I right? Is that an honest diamond, friend?" Mantis asked, "Are you planning to make the girl an honorable offer?"

Moon said nothing.

"Or maybe you'll rely on the wires, huh? Since you've worked it so that she'll have to wear them for awhile, at least." He shook his head. "I hate to think of an innocent creature like that girl being subjected to treatment outside the realm of what is proper."

Moon showed nothing on his face.

"What are you saying?" asked Mr. Chosen.

Mantis wouldn't let his eyes drift from Moon. "It's just that he has acquired a reputation on *The Fist*. In the brothel, to be specific." He said, "She's to be your soldier. That is that."

Moon lifted the hand to his mouth and used the diamond to pick at his teeth. "You want her treated right. Right?"

"Exactly."

"Saint Mantis," said Moon, now laughing through his fingers.

"Just so we understand." He turned and said, "I have complete and final control of the wires. Correct, sir?"

"In view of your experience in Intelligence, yes—"

"And we're not like the animals we're hunting, are we? We don't just twist someone's will into whatever shape we wish."

"I wasn't aware of doubt," Mr. Chosen conceded.

"Then I'm satisfied. Thank you, *sir*," he said loudly. Then he settled into a final smile—the image of the amiable comrade—and he turned and left the galley, whistling softly in the hallway.

Moon watched him go. His face seemed harder now. One hand fell onto the tabletop, seemingly by accident, and then he made a small sound and swept the photographs off the table and across the polished floor.

"Moon," Mr. Chosen snapped, "that'll be enough of that."

"Sorry," Moon answered, his voice tight and dry.

Mr. Chosen watched him kneel and pull the photographs together, his hands squeezing them to life, the images appearing and changing, blurring, then freezing when Moon set them on the tabletop again. Then he watched Moon leave and stood staring at the empty room. He thought of the golden ring and the wires and what must have been on the two men's minds. He did not believe there would have been a problem; Moon knew the code of ethics as well as any officer. It must have been a contest over who had what power—that's what it must have been. To himself, softly, he said:

"We're not Alteretics, after all."

Though if the truth were said, he would have to admit that sometimes, particularly at times like now, he wished he could put wires on everyone always and always know them and always have them under his strict and steady control.

VIII "You're familiar with stuhr, aren't you?"

"Somewhat."

"You know the basic kinds? One ply. Bi-ply. Tri-ply. And how tough it can be to work with? How impurities of any kind, on any scale, will destroy its integrity?"

Jellico told him, "I guess," and sat in the darkness at the back of the bridge. "Sure." He was rubbing his sore wrists and temples. A few minutes ago he had been asleep—a hard dreamless sleep interrupted when this man had said his name and shaken him and then helped him pick himself off the floor. "I'm sorry. What was your name again?"

"Mantis."

"Mantis," he echoed. "I've never had to learn a name before."

"I understand," assured the man, nodding. "Many things should seem strange to you."

Jellico saw that Mantis was standing before a maze of controls. He had his back to Jellico, and Jellico stared at the matted black hair and tried to imagine what the head underneath could want from him.

"You'll be feeling tired a little longer." Jellico knew the voice; Mantis was the one who had spoken to Mr. Chosen from the ceiling. "Sometimes the tape irritates the skin." He turned and smiled, his face full of an easy charm. "I'm the one who handles the wire," he admitted. "I apologize for the discomfort."

Jellico quit his rubbing. He asked, "What do the wires do?"

"Simply said?" He turned forwards again. "They're rather like those electric probes you and your sister put inside fish heads—"

"Bridles," said Jellico. "And the fish are called sailers."

"Perfect." He nodded and glanced back over a shoulder. "Our wires are a less potent, nondestructive version of the same technology. They allow us a kind of mind control. A mechanical brand of hypnosis, if you will." He paused, then repeated, "Bridles. I like that word." Then he said, "We cut your bridle out of the sailer. We've got it back in our machine shop. I've seen it. I'm impressed, knowing how you built that from scratch."

Jellico said nothing, wondering where this was leading.

Mantis turned serious. Sober. He told Jellico, "The Alteretics use wires on their conscripted troops. Their wires, however, are a good deal like your bridle. Very powerful. Very sad."

Mantis sounded sad.

"But where was I?" he then asked. "What were we saying—?"

"Stuhr—?" Jellico offered.

"Why are we discussing stuhr? This is silly. We should talk about intelligence. And memory." He gave a short chuckle. "Do you understand the differences between the two?"

"Differences?"

"Intelligence. Memory. They're not quite the same, you know."

"I suppose—"

"But more to the point, what's the principle that hamstrings intelligence? Can you tell me that?"

"Paulson's Rule," he ventured. "Is that what you mean?"

"I don't know. Is that what I mean?" He reached and touched some control, the boat making some slow adjustment.

What's Paulson's Rule? Jellico thought. Increasing pools of data decrease the ease of interpretation—

"Memory is infinite, or nearly so." Mantis sounded buoyant suddenly. Jolly. "For centuries," he said, "we've been building computers that can soak up the damndest things. Like mental sponges. But when it comes to strict intelligence—" He shrugged. "It's got something to do with the business of thought. The numbers of cross-talking circuits. And so on." He paused for a moment, staring upwards at the gloomy picture on the main screen. Then he lightly touched his own head, as if in reverence, and said, "When your mother was riding the *Kansas City*, coming here, it was believed that the human mind was near the limits set by Paulson herself. Nature, by a string of lucky mutations, had already done as good a job as was possible—"

"You're telling me about Alteretics, aren't you?"

"Indeed." Mantis was smiling; somehow his expression showed through the back of his head. "It wasn't long after that that Paulson's Rule was revised. The trick was in the properties of stuhr itself. In the way it speeds the bonding forces between ordinary atoms." He said,

"Somewhere someone developed a new brand of stuhr. It wasn't constructed in two dimensions. It wasn't set down in layers like bi-ply stuhr, or tri-ply. It had structure not unlike the human brain, and its interconnections ran in every direction. In three dimensions. We call it i-ply stuhr, the 'i' implying—"

"Infinite?"

"Indeed." He turned, smiling. Practically beaming.

Jellico tried his sore legs now, slowly kicking the air. He felt his aching ribs and thought of Pitted Face whenever he looked at Mantis, at that dark round face; and he softly, almost timidly, said, "Is the Alteretic's god made of the i-ply stuff?"

"It is." Mantis returned to the controls, touching and adjusting. He took a long breath and then started talking again, the words running on and on with a life of their own. "The god was built inside one of the more secretive research institutes orbiting Earth back when. It was made by a group of crazies, or a team of misguided scientists. The truth depends on who you listen to . . . although I think it was a mix of crazies and misguideds." He said, "They were working inside a tri-ply stuhr shell, hyperclean and radiation-free. And they managed to build a chunk of i-ply about the size of this boat, if you believe the rumors. Or quite a bit smaller. Or quite a bit larger." He shrugged. "Who knows? What we're sure about is that they made a considerable amount of stuhr structured and programmed to act like a mind, and that stuhr would put that mind near the newly revised Paulson's limit. *Do* believe it if anyone tells you that he or she doesn't understand the implications. I've seen the figures. I've studied the issue. I don't understand." He said, "There's no knowing just how intelligent such a mind would be. You might as well be a worm in shit, your bitty brain working to figure out the thoughts inside a human cerebrum. As much good as that would do you."

The boy shifted in his seat.

Mantis said, "When they had the mind up and running, they began ladling in the knowledge. They plugged into the System's computer net —that vast, vast bank of memory that we'd been building for centuries. *Everything* was in the net. From art and science—the sum total of Mankind's achievements—to bank records and shopping lists and little girl diaries." He chanted, "The grand and the prosaic all thrown into one brain for the first time—" Mantis laughed without sound, facing Jellico again and pulling his hands through his tangled thick hair. "Then eventually, after properly digesting the information, the god spoke. Or so goes the story."

Jellico nodded.

"The god's first command was for a temple to be constructed of tri-ply stuhr. The temple enclosed the institute, and it resembled more a bunker than a place of worship, actually. And inside were a string of power sources that were thoroughly reliable." He explained, "Stuhr is stuhr, godly or not—"

"I know stuhr," Jellico said, thinking how the skyhook had crumbled when its influx of power was interrupted. "I do."

"I'm sure you do." Mantis paused, then went on. "The god's second command was to find converts for the Faith—to build a cadre of holy men and women and instill them with the proper love and respect for the newly born diety. Several thousand were converted of their own free will. No wires involved. The priesthood was filled with loyal and thoroughly trustworthy people—a few of them actually blessed enough to talk to the god, and to listen to it—and then the god decided to act, vowing this was the time and the priests were its instruments—"

"The Hardware War, right?"

"You've been reading ahead, friend. Naughty."

"The Islanders . . . they knew something about the fighting."

"Secondhand," Mantis reminded. Then he said, "The Alteretics' god was hungry to rule. And yes, it started the Hardware War. What better way to come to power, all things considered, than to remove the existing computers and their files and then impose the god in their place?"

Imagining the process, Jellico pictured fungi that kill fungi and then infiltrate the old root tracks.

"North America and Europe fell quickly," Mantis said. "The Alteretics managed to turn dusty old defense systems against their owners. Particle beams. Lasers. Some nukes to make EMP damage. Not a dirty struggle, but selective. With limited targets and goals."

"Okay."

"But the Asian Federation survived." He paused, then explained. "We had grown up since your mother left Earth, you see. The Federation not only occupied the whole of Asia, but also Australia and East Africa and the more temperate fringes of Antarctica. We were the dominant colonial power on Luna and Mars, not to mention the Belt. We were the seat of power for Mankind, you see. At last."

Does he want a reaction? Jellico wondered. Or is he boasting, plain and simple?

"We Asians survived the Hardware War, our portions of the computer net halfway intact. And afterwards, it was the Federation that fought and won the brunt of the Wars. On our own."

Jellico didn't know what to say. Thank you?

"The Alteretics were never abundant. Not even when you count their conscripted troops and their mercenaries. At the most they numbered in the few millions, and they never held an entire continent or colony. Because there were strict limits to their powers."

"Why?"

"Their god is a thing. An object." He made a pistol from his hand. "Better to have a god who is everywhere, unseen, than one with a home address." He shot the gun. Bang-bang! "We chased their god and chased it, and they built dozens of temples and tried to play sleight of hand with us. 'Where's our god now?' But we persisted, and here we are." He looked about. "We're chasing it still."

"What?" He shifted his weight. "It's here?"

Mantis put on a confused face. "Who knows?" He said, "The Alteretics, once they were losing the last War, stole half a dozen half-built starships—the giant starships that were to come to relieve the Islanders. Then the Alteretics finished them, installing a temple inside each of them, and they fled the System—each making for a different fueling station."

"Like Leeshore."

"Absolutely."

Jellico sat quietly for a moment, then asked, "Is it here?"

"There is no knowing." Mantis shook his head, shrugging. "If we can ever get close enough for long enough and then have some luck, we'll cripple their ship and get on board and find out for ourselves." He said, "One slim chance in six. That's what we're chasing."

Jellico stared at his own toes, thinking. He cared nothing for the chasing or the chances, and he wished none of this had happened to him and Abby. It wasn't their war, he believed. When Mantis spoke of Mankind, Jellico pictured some alien species he knew only from textbooks and the stories told by the Islanders and Mother. Mankind's perils and struggles and hopes were . . . what? Sad, of course. He felt for the dead and the maimed, but only on some abstract level . . . detached . . .

"What do you think?" asked Mantis. "Are you ready to help us? Hmm? We'll be needing a lot of help while we're down here."

"You'll be leaving when you're done?"

"When our ship returns for us, naturally." Mantis seemed to pause for too long a moment, catching himself before he said something else. Jellico wondered what it could be. Then Mantis declared, "You can be an enormous help for us. I mean that."

Jellico said nothing.

"So?" Mantis repeated. "What do you think?"

He didn't know what to think. He sat and argued with himself, looking past Mantis, looking up at the largest screen on the far wall. He watched waves on the water and the empty windswept bow of the boat, missile tubes and stuhr guns menacing the darkness. He saw fragments of old islands here and there—colorless hunks of plastic almost entirely submerged, the glowing kelp milking out the last vestiges of energy. Mantis was steering the boat around the fragments. He looked happy in his work. Even joyous.

Jellico had read a thousand books about Earth—about its nations and peoples, the passions and history that went into the creature called Mankind. Mother had made him and Abby study the place until they could name famous names and recognize important patches of land. But sitting here, listening to Mantis go on and on . . . it was a dizzying experience. Baffling. In his core of cores, Jellico thought Mantis an apparition first and a man last. He thought how in all of his life he had come face to face with only two other strangers—Pitted Face and that odd Mr. Chosen. And on the basis of those three he felt unsure of himself. What should he make of Earthlings? Of Mankind? He really, really hadn't a clue.

"It's a smooth ride," he heard himself say. "Your boat, I mean."

"Yes, it takes the waves well." Mantis nodded. Was pride showing? "The boat's guts pivot, you see. Inside the stuhr spheres. The boat's computers anticipate the waves and wind and keep us close to horizontal."

"Huh," he said.

"Not that we couldn't do better, starting from scratch now." He gave a little laugh and said, "*Little Fist* was designed between the stars. On our starship. Even at relativistic speeds, there was plenty of time to dabble. To construct computer models and then the prefab parts. The problem," he explained, "was that there were limits to our testing. We couldn't assemble *Little Fist*—there wasn't room. There were gaps in our knowledge about Leeshore—the winds, the lifeforms and so on. So there were a thousand little things we did wrong. The sorts of things you can't spot on models, no matter how good your software." He said, "The best test was when we actually landed in the sea and assembled *Little Fist*. There's nothing quite like doing to tell you what can get done."

Jellico asked about the starship. "Mother used to talk about the *Kansas City,*" he said. When he was little and forever dreamy, he would picture himself inside one of the gee-proof baths. *Kansas City*'s engines would ignite, and he would feel the acceleration in spite of the bath, crushing him. Then the engines would quit, and out he would emerge—the cosmic explorer—and Abby and Mother would be there, and the three of them would race across the universe together.

Jellico heard Mantis talking, describing the enormous vessel that had brought him here; but he didn't particularly listen. He sat without moving, trying to think, and suddenly he caught a glimpse of someone in the hallway. His head turned reflexively. Craning his neck, he looked out the door and saw . . . Abby! Abby was walking behind Pitted Face himself.

Hours ago, when Jellico first saw Abby, he hadn't recognized her.

Sitting back, he shut his eyes and pictured her tired face—lovely like Mother's, only young—and he realized that her temples sported the same round sore spots that he felt on his own temples. Abby had been asleep on the floor beside him. He vaguely remembered her now. Mantis had come only for him, and he had only mentioned him helping. Not Abby.

Jellico's thoughts returned to the present. "I'm sorry to interrupt," he said to Mantis, "but what do you want from me?"

"Of course." Mantis straightened his back and explained himself. "Simply said, I want your sense of the situation. Your knowledge. Your particular insights." He gave one of his patented shrugs, claiming,

"This isn't an interrogation. Not like with Mr. Chosen and the wires."

"You want *my* sense of the situation?" Jellico sighed. "Alteretics came and killed almost everyone I know. I saw what they did to them."

"The Alteretics ransacked the island afterwards," Mantis said. "You didn't go down into the tunnels, did you?"

"I would have been scared of booby traps."

"You would have been wise. Moon found them everywhere."

Moon? thought Jellico. Is that Pitted Face?

Mantis said, "Early on, I noticed that their traps were maimers. The kind to ruin a leg, say. Intended to slow your enemy without actually killing him or her."

"So?"

"Nothing." He seemed to think for an instant, then he said, "Actually, the traps were mostly useless. It seems the fungi on Leeshore like the taste of explosives." He shook his head, confessing, "We've had to make changes in how we store our munitions. We weren't aware of this problem," and he laughed. "The Alteretics, I imagine, are busy doing the same."

Jellico watched and listened.

"They ransacked your island, yes. Everything worth anything was taken or destroyed. We know they stole one sailboat—"

"The ugly one? Moon? He already asked me—"

"Yes," said Mantis. "It has a glass hull, right?"

"Poured over an aluminum frame, yes."

"Carbon cloth sails?"

"That's it."

"Is there an engine?"

"A small engine. Hooked to a glass prop." He said, "Everything runs on a set of nuclear batteries. Only they're old batteries. I don't think they've got much juice left in them."

"Go on." A board lit up to Mantis' left, a beeper sounding. "Tell me more. I'm listening."

"There's an airtight cabin below deck. Plus the engine compartment." He watched while Mantis studied different kinds of monitors, touching new controls now. Jellico said, "I wouldn't trust the seals or the airlock.

The Islanders, if they had a second chance, would have designed them
better to begin with."

"But it's a good boat basically. Am I right?"

"The best *I've* known," he answered sarcastically.

There was a small screen on the new board. Jellico caught sight of the
colorless jumpsuit his sister had been wearing, and Moon's unique face
and the tiny galley where he had been sitting, wired, answering the
questions while his nervous system went through a set of choreographed
stunts.

"Anything else?" asked Mantis.

"What do you want?"

"Maybe the two of us could decide what the Alteretics stole." He
glanced at Jellico and smiled brightly and said, "Help me. Tell me what
was on Skyhook Island."

He shut his eyes again, not wanting to see Abby now. In his mind he
walked through the burnt dormitories, then down into the cramped
tunnels. He named equipment, coming at last to the main computers—
ancient marvels ripped from *Kansas City*'s head.

Mantis asked what had been on file.

Jellico listed categories, worried for Abby and yet wanting to believe
Mantis too. That the wires did no real harm. That they were just an easy,
mechanical means of hypnosis.

Finally, without warning, Jellico said a word that tripped a switch inside
Mantis.

"Maps?" Mantis repeated. "What kinds of maps?"

"Of the various islands." It seemed an obvious answer. "So we could
keep track of them as they drifted. Abitibi and I helped find them. The
Islanders paid to know where they were." He said, "We fed their positions
and sizes and shapes into the computers, and the computers used the data
to guess where each was heading at a given moment. Which wasn't too
difficult. Leeshore's currents and winds don't vary much, if ever, and until
islands break apart, they're fairly easy to gauge."

Mantis nodded, turned and stared at Jellico. He seemed to be asking
questions with his eyes.

"If an island got too close to Skyhook Island, then the tugs went out and gave it a good, long shove." Jellico shifted. "What did they do to the computers?"

"The Alteretics? They drained them and destroyed them. They're experts at the stealing and destruction of knowledge."

"I guess."

"They almost certainly stole those maps."

"Maybe they don't know what they are."

Mother had always, always told her children to give no one anything for free. Jellico remembered the way she had dealt with the Islanders. He wondered if she would have been so open with Mantis, given these conditions; and he decided finally that it wouldn't have mattered. Not so long as Moon and Mantis had their own kind of bridle—

He said, "I have copies of the maps. So does Abitibi." He wanted to sound generous, giving Mantis a great prize. "They are yours."

"I know." Mantis nodded and confessed, "They were in the computers that are part of your helmets. We took the liberty of examining what you carried on board." Then he said, "Sorry, friend. It's our business to look over things."

Should I be angry? Jellico wondered. Or what?

He asked, "What good does it do you?"

"At the least, we have maps now. At the very most, we know better what the Alteretics know." The big Asian hit a button. A portion of a map was displayed on a screen to the right, up high. It showed a black field sprinkled with soft white blobs of lights, and Jellico wondered how long Mantis had been maneuvering him towards this very moment.

"Some of these islands are marked—"

"Stockpiles," said Jellico. "Or ongoing experiments. Or shelters." He said, "It depends on the symbols."

"The Islanders knew where to find you two? If they needed you?"

"No." He shifted in his chair again; he kept forgetting they were dead. "If they wanted us, they called us. We rarely told them where we were going or when we'd come back." He said, "Those marks were more for Abby and me. To help us remember where we left supplies and what not."

"I see. Sure."

Jellico sensed that this man had something in mind.

Mantis, seemingly toying with him, said, "The Alteretics are clever, friend. Terribly so." He wagged a finger at nothing in particular. "And they are trapped in somewhat the same bind that we are. They're on a very odd world, by Earthly standards. And they've got to survive somehow with the tools and skills on hand."

"So?"

"So I'm sure they know about you and your sister. We could have known about you two from the debris that wasn't burned or buried." He said, "They're in the same circumstances, and that means they're hungry for good guides. They'll take risks to find such people. Which is what they're doing right now, I'll wager. You and Abitibi are being hunted by them. Do you hear them sniffing at your heels?" He cocked his head and seemed to listen. To what? thought Jellico. Then he looked straight into Jellico's eyes, boring holes in his skull, promising, "If we handle this right, we'll get them easy and quick. Believe me."

Jellico didn't know what to believe.

Mantis returned to the controls. "Just a moment, please." He began talking to someone with that odd sing-song language. Mr. Chosen? Or Moon? He was standing now so the little screen showing the galley was blocked. Intentionally? Or not?

Jellico watched the map for a minute. He recognized Moon's voice on the intercom, ice in his spine suddenly and his heart racing. He looked over at the main screen again, watching the bow. In spite of the boat's balancing insides, he could feel every wave. Without moving, he set himself out into the wind and mist, the water breaking cool and strong over his body; and suddenly, unexpectedly, he spotted a lone sailer out ahead. It was running towards them, running with the wind, and it cut in front of the boat and skipped over the crest of a wave, lifting clear of the water for an instant.

Then it was gone as suddenly, and Jellico asked himself if he had seen a sailer, it had happened so fast.

"You're not going to let us go, are you?" Jellico asked. "Are you?"

"Pardon?"

"When we're done helping you, you won't—"

"How did you decide that?"

"I don't know. I smelled it."

"You've got a perceptive nose, friend." Mantis was beaming, the teeth

showing flat and white in the dimly lit bridge. "Talking to you, I've begun
to think you've got talents. Useful talents. And I bet you don't even know
they're there."

Jellico said nothing.

"I think we'll work together well. Here and always."

Jellico thought of the sailer in the wind, the sounds and stinks of
Leeshore all around—

"Trust me," said Mantis.

—and he stayed quiet.

"You're young. You'll adapt to whatever is coming."

That sailer had moved so fast, he was thinking.

So fast indeed!

IX   The island was long and jagged. It had sharp faces and deep
fractures, and someday it likely would come apart without warning, the
plastic of the dead reef taking only so much before it exploded along lines
of weakness.

That's how it is with people too, thought Abitibi.

She was standing on the rubbery, pebbled deck of the boat. She was
wearing her own lifesuit, tailored pieces of one-ply stuhr lashed onto foam
padding that were fastened to the lifesuit to make armor. Flanking her
were Moon's soldiers, all shorter than herself and armed, and Moon was
behind them, talking with that crazy blend of Asian dialects. She supposed he was telling his young lions what to do on shore—what to search
out, how to move and so on—and she recalled what Moon had told her
with his broken English:

"Keep low. Keep up. Keep near me."

Abitibi wondered why she had to go ashore. She had already told Moon
everything she knew and everything she could guess. He didn't need her
to find the cache of supplies that she and Jellico had hidden on the island;

and besides the cache, what had she to offer? The Alteretics themselves were mysteries to her. She couldn't know where they would set their traps or lay waiting in ambush. Maybe she could track them—assuming, of course, they left tracks—but then Moon could surely do a better job for himself. He must have hunted "God-boys" before. And besides, she thought, weren't the Alteretics gone? That tall fat one, Mantis, had guessed they had left days ago.

"Abby?"

She flinched at the sound in her headphones. Jel?

"Don't move," he told her, his voice gentle and dry. "Just look ahead. Like that, yeah. We'll talk a minute. Okay?"

"Where are you?"

"In the bridge." He said, "Mantis opened a channel for us."

Reaching slowly to her neck, Abitibi made certain that her suit's speaker was turned off. It was.

"How are you doing?" he asked for the hundredth time. "Abby? How do you feel?"

She remembered. Suddenly she remembered being mad at her brother. It wasn't a sensible anger she could admit to feeling—not to herself and certainly not to Jel—and maybe that's why it felt so intense. She blamed Jel for them getting caught. She couldn't help but think that if he hadn't gone for his walk on Skyhook Island, they wouldn't be trapped here now. Doing Christ knows what.

"Abby?"

"I'm fine," she said, her voice sad and tense.

"Where's your gun?"

"Are you kidding?"

He said, "Sure," and paused. "If you're not armed, no one will shoot at you."

"That's how it works?" she answered. "I'm glad."

Jellico seemed to be laughing. She supposed he was trying to cheer up her spirits, and she began feeling sorry for being so angry with him. It was a stupid, shallow kind of anger. And what made it worse, she realized, were the things beyond their control. Like Moon. Abitibi despised Moon and was terrified of him; and there was Jel, safe and comfortable, not having to cope like she had to cope. He was so damned lucky. Maybe I have a petty frame of mind, she told herself, but that's what I think. After the stress of these last days—their capture and the wires and now this— she felt fortunate to be able to think at all.

"Nothing bad will happen," Jellico promised. "Believe me."

"I do."

"And don't be brave," he cautioned. "Please."

"I won't. Don't worry."

She could imagine what he was thinking. Knowing Jel, he was probably feeling guilty for not joining her and guilty because he was secretly glad. Just like he was sorry for her being attached to the wires, Moon torment- ing her without clear reason; but glad too that all he had to do was sit over her afterwards, soothing the sore spots on her temples and trying to guess what was up.

It touched her in an odd way—his concern tempered with his own fears. She told him, "I'll be careful. I will."

"Do."

Moon had quit talking. "You'd better get off now."

"Bye," said Jel.

"Luck?"

"Luck."

"Till later."

The line squeaked and went dead.

The soldiers beside Abitibi were moving now, filing towards a gap in the boat's railing. The water surrounding the boat was flat and calm and glowing with a soft greyish light. An inflated raft laid on the water, waiting. One after another, the soldiers squatted and started climbing down a dangling rope ladder. The ladder swayed in a jerky fashion, the glass fibers creaking against the lip of the deck.

Abitibi stood back from the lip, watching, until Moon reached under the stuhr on her back and squeezed a kidney, saying, "Go."

Suddenly breathing was work. Abitibi moved without grace, the rungs of the ladder getting tangled around her boots. Once she simply had to stop to gasp. Facing the stuhr of the hull, she saw her own reflection— a silhouette with fuzzy margins. A silhouette bathed in the colored glow of the island.

Moon was coming. He prompted her, shouting, "Hurry, bitch." He tried kicking her hands.

She hurried. When she felt the raft she let go and stepped backwards, arms raised as if she was perched on a tightrope. The soldiers around her began to mimic Moon, saying, "Bitch," softly again and again. Laughing and smiling. Moon dropped the last meter and grasped her by an elbow, pulling her to a certain spot and pointing, saying:

"Sit."

She sat at her own speed.

Moon moved to the front, up to the pointed bow, and someone started the electric motor and eased the throttle open. The thick, thick air flowed over the raft. Everyone hunkered down as far as they could manage, heads to the wind. "Sit, bitch," the soldiers were chanting. One of them reached and began running a hand down Abitibi's thigh.

She still had her knife. Thinking what a terror all of this was, she pulled out the knife and put its point to the hand and applied pressure until the hand was withdrawn. Then she slipped the knife into its sheath again and looked up and forwards.

Moon's own hand was high and waving, feeding instructions to the back of the raft.

They slipped one way.

They skidded another.

Then the raft turned and ran straight for the shore.

This island was dressed in a larger, gaudier kind of rot. Most of the blood-oaks had died away, and the fungi growing up in its stead were taller and brighter, seeping a wealth of colors. The blood-kelps were gone too, and the new kelps reached a long, long ways out to sea. Abitibi had warned Moon which kelps to avoid and to always, always watch for hunks of the old islands that might be tangled with the kelp. Yet he surprised Abitibi now by doing just what she had wanted. Exactly. They came in over a streak of ruddy purple. Beet-kelp, Mother had named the stuff. Because it was heavier than most species, and less buoyant, when you saw it lying on top you were sure of room for propellers and keels.

The raft slowed. Against the force of the air, Moon stood and somehow kept his feet. The soldiers were quieter now. Less troublesome. Abitibi could feel the mood shift, every stuhr gun up and ready. Moon said a word or two. The driver cut the motor. The raft seemed to lift when its wake caught it from behind; and the shoreline loomed ahead, tangled and bursting with light.

"Move!" Moon cried.

Everyone was standing. As one, they leaped into the tangle feet-first, falling and thrashing, and suddenly there were dozens and dozens of small silver-white birds boiling up past them.

The soldiers crouched, ignoring the birds.

Abitibi moaned a little, startled, and Moon put a hand to her forearm and squeezed, holding her in place, waiting for the birds to vanish and for the woods to quiet again.

Knife-owls, she realized. A flock of knife-owls must have been lying in a ring, sleeping.

"Here," said Moon. "Come." He was looking at her face. He had let her arm go.

The shoreline had been washed clean in the past. Only a hardy few fungi tolerated the surf. The plastic earth was darker and slicker than the earth on Skyhook Island, and the cavities where the reef-builders had lived were of an entirely different shape. Half the size and four times as numerous.

"Now," said Moon. He rapped on her faceplate with the tip of a barrel. Her faceplate was clear, as was his. The wood was that bright.

The soldiers had evaporated. Abitibi looked and spotted one of them walking up the slope, every step measured and slow. Moon was ahead of her now. She could see herself in his armor, distorted by the stuhr's shapes. There was so much light she could recognize her own face. Her heart was pounding. She felt it inside her dry throat.

Walking now, she climbed after Moon.

The fungi came in every shape. Trunks were thick or thin, straight or curling. What passed for bark could be smooth as taut skin or lumpy and knotted. One enormous fungus resembled some ancient Earthly totem, its trunk sporting facelike features with lidless eyes and double sets of empty round mouths. Past the fungus the earth was covered with a meter or more of packed debris—shattered bones and bleached shit and airweed collapsing into dust. Overhead the canopy was like a roof. There were structures like enormous leaves—flat and broad and bleeding a hard, blue light underneath. Other fungi were topped with cups and basins and large bathtub-sized bowls held up to the sky. The falling crud was now being trapped by the fungi, and the mist was slowly collecting, forming tiny ponds. The fungi were feeding at both ends, the roots in the reef and the tops sipping on a sewerish brew.

Moon paused. He knelt. He held a projector he had carried on his belt, using it to throw a map of the island on the packed soil. "Where?"

Abitibi pointed. "We're here."

He nodded once, apparently agreeing.

Above them, hidden in a high valley, was a cache of supplies. She wondered, Why ask if you know? Hmm?

"Scared?" said Moon, his tone indifferent.

She looked at the way he was watching her face again, not answering.

"Scared," he said, satisfied. The map dissolved and he stood, setting the projector back in place and turning and striding away.

The slope steepened. The debris on the ground made hard walking. It was soft and fine-grained, worked and reworked by worms and insects, and it shifted easily and unexpectedly. Abitibi knew to use Moon's tracks to judge where to step and with what confidence, and she was pleased when she saw him struggling.

Here and there, in patches and alone, grew tiny fungi. Elsewhere the debris was drained of everything worth the trouble.

Nothing fresh and rich fell through the canopy anymore.

The woods were full of things like Earthly insects and strange, Earthly birds. Many were brightly colored, blending in with the general confusion. Some had eyes and some were all eyes, seemingly, and others did without entirely. Wings were the norm—transparent or feathered, stiff or not. Everything flew and with the same motion—not the graceful majesty of soaring boeing birds, but rather the lazy style of half-fish trying to half-swim.

Moon seemed to be slowing. Turning cautious now.

He knelt, and Abitibi automatically knelt too and waited, wondering what was happening.

There came a sound. She looked ahead of him and above. Wrestling its way free of the canopy was a giant grey-bat, its ratty face all mouth

and ears and nose. For an instant nothing changed. Then Moon lifted his
gun and aimed. Abitibi touched her speaker and said, "It's nothing, no,"
too loudly. Much too loudly. But Moon only looked back once and then
down, then stood and walked again, the gun relaxing.

She took a step and watched the grey-bat for herself.

It hung from both of its tails for a few moments, the tails like scaly
ropes. Then it spread its wings and beat them and let go of the limb.
Coasting downhill, it sang its cold precise songs and slipped between the
trunks. It came at Abitibi, straight on, and suddenly she had to kneel and
let it pass overhead with a faint rush.

It tilted, beat its short wide wings once and stretched its neck.

A beetlish thing was hanging in the air. She heard the sharp snap as
the grey-bat's mouth shut and the crunching snap as the carapace shattered.

Getting to her feet now, Abitibi turned and saw no one.

Where Moon had stopped, in the packed and lifeless debris, the word
"Quiet" had been written hastily with a finger.

She went on. Following the bootprints, she reached a point where the
ground leveled off and the high valley began; and Moon was standing
ahead, motionless, his stuhr gun up at his shoulder and his gaze fixed on
something she could not quite see.

The cache was fifty meters away, she guessed.

She came up behind him, thinking to make noise. She said his name
softly, without inflection, and he turned and gave a quick hard warning
stare.

Beyond him, one of the soldiers was walking oddly. Abitibi realized that
Moon had been watching the boy take huge steps, trying to put his weight
on certain spots. There was something faintly comical about the scene—
the boy holding his gun over his head, then leaping, a small package of
sensors carried in his other hand.

"What is it?" she whispered.

"Tracks," Moon explained.

She was beside him now. "Whose tracks?" she wondered.

He did not answer.

"They aren't ours," she offered. "We haven't been here in months."

There was a breeze under the canopy. All but a few centimeters of
debris had been swept away long ago.

"Where is it?" he asked, meaning the cache.

"There," she said. "Up and over there," and she gestured.

Soldiers began to emerge from the woods around them. They carried trophies—curious skulls picked clean or scuttling beetles with flashing lights on their bellies. One soldier had a tiny device—a remote sensor—its thick glass carapace cracked and its insides filled with beads of moisture.

"Yours?" asked Moon.

"It looks like ours." They had run some experiments near here. They had studied succession—the changes in fungi and animal life as the island matured and broke apart and died.

Moon said something to the soldier, and the soldier stepped forwards and gave her the sensor with a flourish. She saw his face. He was a boy too, she thought. Her age or younger.

Moon said, "The cache. Where?" and she turned and walked towards the spot, holding the useless sensor close.

All the soldiers fanned out and followed Abitibi. Moon stayed beside her, the butt of his gun wearing a hole in his shoulder. There were no tracks around the cache, she noted. Whoever had walked down the valley had passed the cache without suspecting. Apparently. "It's there," she said. "In that crevice."

There was a ceramic sphere—an old and durable fuel pod for an attitude rocket—and the sphere was covered with a thin layer of wind-smoothed debris. It was a meter across and barely showed, its hatch on top and still sealed. Jellico and she had rolled it up here and set it in the crevice for a reason. When the island broke apart it likely would come apart first at this point, and if their math was right, the cache would roll into the sea, safe and free, then drift alongside the assorted hunks and chunks—waiting to be found and placed somewhere new. Or used.

Moon waved, wanting her to open the hatch.

She undid the seals and pulled the hatch loose. Nitrogen gas made a little wind, escaping, and the lighter debris came up in a doughnut-shaped cloud.

There were no booby traps inside. Only supplies. There were synthetic foods and a pair of new helmets, filters and patches and a pair of lifesuits. Everything was wrapped in tough fluorocarbon plastics, packed with care and ready to use. The soldiers gathered, sensors working. Moon told her to step away now, and she pulled back and watched while they started removing the treasures. She was not surprised. During the galley sessions, Moon had made no secret of his interest in the caches. A moment ago, he had given her her own sensor, its value nil, and now without asking, they were going to claim the things she had struggled to collect and protect. And the stealing seemed wholly natural—she could not envision them doing anything else, given the chance.

"Jel?" she whispered. "What are we going to do?"

She turned and slowly walked away. It felt like an age since she had been by herself. She knew this place too, which helped put her at ease, and for an instant she thought of running. Not to escape, certainly. Not with Jel left behind, and not without a bridle and some distance first. But still, she thought, running and not having voices telling you when and where to turn and what to do or not do . . . the thought made her shiver. Finding a slight hole in the canopy above, she tossed the worthless sensor up at the sky—a defiant gesture. Then she rubbed her empty hands together and breathed.

There were weathered bootprints on the ground. A big man, apparently, had come down the valley with a single direction in mind. Like the soldier had done, she began to backtrack the man's course. To follow in reverse, her eyes down and watchful. Higher up the valley narrowed. The fungi turned squatter. The wind found a thousand ways through the canopy now, and the ground was bare and polished by the wind-driven filth.

The tracks, if they ever existed, were now wiped away.

We can't escape, she was thinking. She continued on in the same straight line.

If they gave us our chance, she realized, we couldn't take it. They have our maps. They know how to find our caches and shelters. If only Jel hadn't told them so much, maybe then . . . but she knew how ridiculous she must seem. With those damned wires of theirs, there weren't any secrets.

They'll take us away, she thought. In the end.

Mantis told Jel that on the first day.

Ahead, higher, the woods glowed with the same even color—a clear, cool brand of emerald green.

She was still thinking about those wires—another fine reason to be angry with Jellico. Except for that once, early on, he had not been stuck to them and subjected to the endless questions about Skyhook Island and the Islanders. He couldn't know how it felt to have your nervous system prodded and probed. How it was to have Moon and that fat man, Mantis, look into your soul and do whatever they wished to do . . . making you weep or scream, laugh like a maniac or just sit like a lump.

She reached the greenness now and began to slip between the trunks, the fungi packed close together. There was no way to walk straight on. She wondered if she was anywhere near the Alteretic's course. For an instant, she slowed and told herself to turn around, to go back to Moon and not get into deeper trouble. But then something caught her eye— an emerald patch that seemed wrong somehow—and she blinked and squinted and spotted a figure wearing stuhr, like a soldier, sitting on the barren ground like someone a little tired.

Slowly, aiming for quiet, she crept forwards.

The figure was a man. He had been shot through the forehead, the blast having shattered his faceplate. His stuhr helmet had failed where the stuhr bullet punctured it in the back, and it had collapsed into a tattered plastic shawl. The remnants of the face were snarling, the expression harsh and tireless. He was rotting. His own internal microbes were doing what alien chemistries couldn't manage, making him bloat. Kneeling, Abitibi reached beneath his breastplate, feeling the pressure against the fabric and wondering how long he had been dead.

He was Caucasian. Almost certainly an Alteretic, she realized; and she began examining him with that in mind. She tried to imagine the man up and walking under his own power, fighting like a fanatic for his own strange beliefs. This certainly wasn't the man who had made the tracks—he was much too small. But if the two men had been walking together—?

Abitibi paused and held her breath.

In most ways he was indistinguishable from Moon and his soldiers. Down to his equipment. Even down to his mortality, she thought in a hopeful way. But on his head, above the wound, was something else—a braid of tarnished metal wires that were sunk into the skull, into the brain. She remembered what little she knew. The conscripts, according to Jellico, were wired up permanently. They could have been anyone in their former lives, but after several weeks, they were loyal Alteretics. They loved their god and did whatever the priests and god said to do.

He had been a balding man. Reaching, she let her fingertips play over the dirty wires, feeling curious and something else too. Something growing and already intense. Some emotion she could not quite name.

Among the scant yellow hairs on the dead man's head, showing when she was close, was a round raised scar adorned with a crazy ornate tattoo. As if to embrace the head, Abitibi began to reach with both hands. Only her will melted away. So to have a closer look and still not touch him, she stood and bent and squinted at the tattoo—its pattern stained green by the light, something about its form implying religion somehow.

She stood up straight, her own head feeling light and her heart thumping crazily. The corpse was sitting against the trunk of a fungus. She squatted and did the same, putting her weight into another trunk; and she looked towards the corpse and said, "So. You're the enemy."

She thought about the Islanders who had been murdered, and now she wanted to cry. Jel had honestly grieved after the skyhook came down. She had resisted. On several occasions Jel had told her, "You miss them. You do. More than you know," and now suddenly tears were welling up in her eyes, and she blinked and glared at the killer, seeing her reflections in his armor . . . and his smaller reflections inside her reflections . . . both of them pulled apart and made tiny by the streams of bounding light . . .

She felt suddenly ill.

Ill and tired.

She knelt and slid her fingers into the holes in the ground, gripping, pitching her weight forwards and tugging now at the island. She was weeping. "You killed them!" she said. The Islanders. "You murdered them!" It was as if she had been suddenly shown the truth. For the first time she understood the Alteretics. At least in part. At least enough to conjure up the image of them as monsters—

"You!"

Touching the speaker on her throat, she turned it to its highest setting. Then she began to scream at the corpse, roaring, her voice making the woods shake and brighten ever so slightly.

"I'll kill all of you!" she screamed.
"All of you!
"Damn you!
"Damn!"

X   She told it, her voice level and calm . . . No, not calm. More drained than anything, in truth. The words were coming out grey and nearly lifeless, no traces of inflection or emotions or even interest. She sounded like one of the talking textbooks Mother had given them when they were five or six years old. Jellico was scarcely listening to her story; he couldn't quit thinking about what he had seen an hour ago. What he had seen her doing. Then Abitibi's voice broke, faltering for an instant, and she looked at him, and he wondered what he had wondered many times in these last minutes. Do I honestly, honestly know this person? His sister, yes, but he didn't recognize those eyes.

"I don't know," she was saying. "I lost control. I kept imagining the poor Islanders being butchered, and I got madder and madder. So I started screaming. As loud as I could."

"We heard you," Jellico said. "The instruments did, and Mantis piped the sound into the bridge."

She was on the floor, sitting against the far wall, her feet bare and her bare brown toes curled.

He said, "Go on."

He said, "Abby? What are you thinking about?"

"Remember Sarah? How we would eat in her room, listening to her talk about her poor dead husband?" She said, "We never let ourselves get too close to the Islanders. Remember? I mean, it wasn't just because they were different or because they wouldn't give us everything we wanted. I think there's more involved." She said, "We could have been friendlier. Only friendlier was too risky—"

"Risky?"

"Sure." She said, "We might have liked them. We were afraid to like them." She paused and then said, "Only we did. Secretly. All the time. At least I did."

Jellico had liked them too, and he understood what Abitibi was saying. At least in part. Sarah and the others had done nothing to deserve their fate. He still felt sad and angry. And yes, for years they had tried to avoid attachments with the Islanders. They didn't want to end up being like Sarah—alone with her ghosts. So they had made the work their lives, so far as was possible. He watched his sister's toes straighten and then curl again, and he said, "Go on. Tell me what happened."

He said, "What happened Abby? After you screamed."

"Moon found me." She lowered her eyes and told Jellico, "I expected him to hit me. Or threaten. Or something. Because I had wandered away. But all he did was pull me to my feet and make me walk up to the corpse again. I don't think he said a word to me." Again she faltered. "The other soldiers came and gathered in." A look swept across her face. "I do hate those sons-of-bitches now."

She meant the Alteretics.

For a moment she shuddered, then she found her pace again. She told how the soldiers had searched the area and examined the corpse in detail, recreating what must have happened. Again Jellico thought of a textbook, Abitibi's tone cool and direct and organized—sounding more like a much practiced lecture than a young woman's first slight taste of warfare.

"The two Alteretics had come up the island's other side. Three days ago, give or take." She said, "When they got to the green woods the taller one shot and killed his companion. He executed him. Moon says it happens every so often. He says the God-boys don't like their soldiers fouling up, and bullets to the brain are an answer." Pulling her knees to her face, she began blowing air between them. "Then the tall Alteretic went down to this side of the island. Moon says he's a priest. Their top officer. He says the Alteretic linked up with the rest of the landing party, judging by what the other soldiers have found so far, and then the Alteretics left the island and went on. Wherever."

Jellico looked away from his sister. Wondering who might be studying them now, he glanced around the little storeroom. This was where they had slept after that first interrogation, and now it was their own room—as much as anything was theirs on *Little Fist*—complete with foam mats that Mantis had given them, rolled up now and stacked in a corner, and a place where she would sit and a place where he would sit while they talked, nothing to do now but rest and wait for someone to need them.

Abitibi said, "I just had a thought."

"What, love?"

"Why didn't Mantis see the corpse before? Why didn't his precious sensors work?"

That sounded like the old Abitibi. Impatient. Critical. "Because soldiers wear equipment that blinds sensors to some degree," he explained. Mantis had explained the same thing to him. "Your armor, your stuhr, would normally seem bright to sonics or radar or whatever. Because it reflects almost everything. So built into the stuhr is a kind of camouflage. An electronic camouflage. Sophisticated and adaptable too."

"That explains the grey-bat." She described how a grey-bat had come straight towards her, taking a long look with its voice and ears and seeing nothing. "Could you see us on the island?"

"Not directly. Although Mantis had his ways." He thought and said, "When the soldiers used their sensors, Mantis saw them. And he heard the radio noise they made—not much, in case the Alteretics were nearby. And then you once threw something up over the canopy—"

Abitibi set her chin on a kneecap and said, "One of our dead sensors."

"That's what I guessed. Mantis said you were throwing glass at the sky." Just what is happening, Abby? Hmm? I look at you, and you seem so bloody foreign! "If there'd been a nuke on the island, then Mantis would have seen its fission trigger. He assured me. It has something to do with its density and the nuclear decay . . ."

She uncurled her bare toes, saying nothing.

"Did the soldiers find anything else?"

"Our cache." She shrugged. "Moon and the rest are bringing it now."

"Are they?"

"Something about the spoils of war." She shrugged again and spread the toes. One hand began to tug at the leg of her jumpsuit. "He said I'll make a good soldier."

"Is that what he said?"

" 'You want them dead?' he asked me. So I said, 'Sure.' And he told me that he would train me. He would help me be a soldier."

"When did this happen?"

"On the way back. On the raft." She sighed and thudded her head against the wall. "After I was done," she said. "Kicking—"

"Sure."

Over these last days, he realized, the two of them had seen each other more than during the last year. Face to face, at least. Riding sailers and sleeping on wild islands, lifesuits almost always on, meant there weren't many chances for this intimacy. Usually Abitibi was just a voice to him. A voice and a figure set in a series of postures. Maybe that's why I don't recognize her, he thought. Maybe it's a combination of little things, and what cues I have are distorted by the circumstances.

She said, "I'm tired."

"I bet."

She asked, "What are you looking at?"

"Nothing."

Fidgeting, she breathed through her nose and carefully stared at the bare floor and her toes, her mind plainly fixed on something. He knew that pose, only it wasn't her own. It was Mother who had had that same way of sitting and focusing, consumed by the problem at hand.

"What did you think? When you saw me?"

"I don't know." He shrugged. "Startled, I suppose."

"I was just so mad—"

"Sure. You told me."

"—mad like I've never been before. Not when Mother died, even. Not by half."

"I don't like the Alteretics either, Abby." He tried to reassure, saying, "We've been under stress. Particularly you. It's natural to surprise yourself. To have moments where you lose . . . perspective." He halfway believed himself, and whatever good his speech did for Abby, he felt better for having said it. "Why don't you tell me how it happened?" he suggested. "Start after the soldiers came and joined you."

"I'll try." Reaching behind her back with both hands, she pressed against the wall and pushed herself to standing. "The soldiers and Moon made a circle around the body. They were talking. In Asian. They were smiling and I guess joking, although it was a little like a ceremony too. Like something religious. And all of the sudden Moon pointed at a couple of boys." She paused, looming over Jellico, her arms crossed on her chest and her jumpsuit making a hushed hum as the fabric captured and condensed her body's sweat. "They couldn't be older than eighteen. Those boys. They got down on their knees, though, and pulled out knives and without looking twice between them, they cut off the head."

Her voice, if anything, had become more monotonic. She sounded as if she was reading data aloud at the end of a long, long day in the field.

"I wasn't surprised," she maintained. "When you look at their faces, you know the people behind them could do such things without blinking." She began walking the length of the storeroom—three lazy strides —telling Jellico, "And I was there, standing with them. This fury inside me. Nearly scalding me. Something saying to me that I was the same as all the other soldiers. That I had lost enormous things too and the Alteretics were to blame." One of her hands—long and elegant and as strong as Jellico's own—began to rub at a sweating temple, applying so much pressure that head and hand seemed to be waging a war of their own.

"They did what then?" he prompted. "Abby?"

There were shelves behind Jellico. They covered the wall and were filled with crates, all tied into place, and Abitibi grasped one of the tie-downs and then another and then assured herself and her brother, "The thing was a trophy to me. Not a piece of anyone." She said, "One of the boys stood, holding the thing by its hair, and he suddenly bolted past me and the rest of us. Running. And the soldiers started after him, laughing in that way they have. Like strange children, you know? And I found myself with them, running in front of them somehow." She let go of the tie-downs and turned, swearing, "I was not the first to kick it—"

"Abby."

"—but I enjoyed it the most. I did." With a breathless and flat voice she said, "The soldiers didn't keep up. I was booting the head down the slope and chasing it, and I lost it and found it again, and the soldiers caught up with me. We dribbled it to the sea, soccer-style. You saw me. Then I grabbed the hair and spun it and lobbed it out onto the water. The diamond-kelp buoyed it up, and the knife-owls tried a taste, and I stood and thought to myself that I have never felt so happy in all my life."

"Abby," Jellico said, aiming to sound warm and reassuring. "Do you know what's happening, Abby? I do."

"I'm insane."

"No," he said, "it's the wires, Abby. It's those interrogations." He said, "They've been tinkering with your mind."

"It's not them. It's me."

"No." He stood now, and she turned her back towards him, and he reached and gripped her tight shoulders, rubbing and feeling the heat bleeding out from her body. Islanders used to feel so cool and dry to the touch. With Abby, now the opposite was true; she felt as though her engines were turned up too high—as if some prometabolite elixir was coursing through her veins.

"I should have said something," he admitted.

"What about?"

"Mantis as much as confessed what they were doing with you and the wires. They want you to be their soldier, Abby. That's all any of this means."

"It doesn't explain . . . Wires can't do it all, Jel."

He paused and thought, then said, "We do much more to sailers, don't we? Using bridles?" He let go of her shoulders and stepped back, his mind replaying everything Mantis had said about wires in these last days. He had no doubts they were part of the explanation. What amazed him was that before, at least once, Mantis had implied that the Alteretics were considerably more willing and able to use their wire technology. At least on their conscripts. And yet, he couldn't imagine one person absorbing more change than his poor furious sister had undergone already.

Sailers are sailers, he thought. Smart fish, yes, but not people.

People are not machines.

Surely.

Abitibi was at one of the shelves now. Her lifesuit was balled up and stuffed into a gap between crates. She pulled out the suit, the stuhr clattering against stuhr with a dry light sound, and she began to tug at the fabric, testing it, carrying out a quick nervous check of the patches and the wear points.

Jellico felt hungry to understand everything. Moon and Mr. Chosen

were still little more than cartoon figures to him—incapable of casting
their own shadows. Mantis had been fleshed out some these last few days,
and Jellico sometimes found himself liking the man. But still . . . still he
felt a deep and biding urge to step away and watch them and everything
without passion, aiming for objectivity. He wanted the same deliberate
calmness that he employed whenever he had an odd new species of fish
or bird or glowing fungus.

He wondered if he himself was thinking these things.

He had, after all, been under the wires once himself. Not that that was
anywhere near what Abby had undergone—

She was examining the intricate workings of the lifesuit now. Jellico
watched, knowing she had her hands on the recyke systems, the suit
partway pulled inside out. He could smell the outside of the suit—soap
and strong deodorizers—and too the musty smell of Abby herself. "Who
made the armor," Jellico asked.

"One of the crewmen." She gave a wave. "Back in the machine shop.
What's his name? Cricket?"

"Is everything fine? With the suit, I mean."

"*You* don't hate them, do you?" she said.

"What?" he said. "Who?"

Her face darkened. "The Alteretics." She seemed ready to accuse him
of some crime.

"I hate them," he said, but the words came out too blunt-edged, even
for his own ears. So he added, "You aren't the only one thinking of Sarah
and the others. Believe me."

"See?" she said. "It's not just the wires. It's the same with you." She
nodded, seemingly satisfied.

But inside himself he remembered how he had felt when he had seen
Abby on the shoreline—when he had seen her throwing that severed head
into the water. He had been shaken to his core, horror-struck and furious.
He had wondered what sorts of people could do such things to his poor
sister, or anyone, and he had looked at Mantis. The round face was silent
for once, and yet Jellico imagined the familiar voice telling him, "You
were living in Eden, and Eden is gone, my friend. This is the real world
now! It's all grit and gristle from here on out."

The Alteretics were far, far worse. Worse than Moon, even.

Mantis had said it.

He wanted to believe Mantis. His intuitions told him that he and Abby were frightfully lucky to have been discovered by *Little Fist* first. Those same intuitions were what had helped keep them safe through the years in the wild, after all. Shouldn't he trust them? Unless it was the wires talking to him . . . thoughts programmed into his nature—

Stop!

Just stop! he told himself. Quit second-guessing yourself!

Again Abitibi was balling up her lifesuit, preparing to return it to its berth on the shelf. But then the door hissed and swung open, and Moon was standing in the hallway, hands on his hips, dressed in his own lifesuit and resembling a sea creature wearing a shell of mirrors.

He said, "Don't." He was looking at Abby. "Suit up," he told her. "Work time, now."

Jellico glanced her way, gladdened to see that she still disliked the man —even after discovering her hatred for the Alteretics. Her face was Abby's face now, something of the old anger showing.

"You too," said Moon. "Mantis wants you. On the bow."

"Why?" Jellico inquired.

Moon seemed not to hear. He simply stood and watched Abitibi with his frank dark eyes, not so much staring as he was studying. His hands were bare—his lifesuit equipped with stat-sealed gloves now riding his belt. On his left hand, on the littlest finger, was the gold engagement ring that Sarah had worn. Once or twice, after the interrogations, Abitibi would mention that Moon was wearing the ring. Then she would fall asleep, exhausted. Several times Jellico himself had seen soldiers or crewmen wearing bits of the Islanders' jewelry. And now, thinking of all this, he aimed to be objective. Dispassionate. He pretended Moon was some specimen dredged up out of the deep.

He thought of the wars Moon had emerged from, and the mores generated by those wars, and in that context the crime of stealing a dead woman's worthless ring was minor. Even forgettable. Certainly when set against the murder of whole planets and peoples.

Yet still—

Another voice, equally powerful and just as true, said to Jellico, "He is no different than the Alteretics."

Moon was a fanatic, surely.

He was plainly capable of anything and everything.

So what to do? he asked himself, dressing and then hunting for his helmet. Having confidence in intuition was one thing, he realized. But when a soul gives two answers in the same breath—

—*which do you take?*

XI The crew and soldiers were bringing up the latest treasure—that big ceramic ball that had held the cache—and then they pulled in the inflated raft and began to bleed out its nitrogen gas, readying both objects and everything else for storage below deck, everyone working together by the amazingly bright colored light of the island.

Mantis watched the show from time to time. He made certain that his own men were behaving themselves, Cricket doing the actual barking of orders so that Moon's people didn't feel alone. Who knew when Mr. Chosen would catch someone in a compromising situation? Chosen was that kind of officer. That kind of man. On *The Righteous Fist* they swore that when Mr. Chosen had no one else to watch, he spied on himself. Hoping to catch himself in some lax moment. Ready to come down hard on an improper gesture or an impure thought.

It made Mantis laugh, thinking of such things.

"Pardon?" said the boy. "Did I say something—?"

"No!" He turned and said, "It's nothing. I'm sorry." Staring at the darkened faceplate, he asked, "What were you just telling me, friend?"

Jellico was standing on the other side of the big bow stuhr gun. Fixed to the gun's base was a liquid crystal screen tied to the boat's computers, and projected on the screen was the precious map of Leeshore.

"From here," said the boy, "they *might* go here next." He laid a fingertip on a splotch of light. "What with the westerlies in their sails and assuming they wanted to be away from the equator and Skyhook Island, like you said—"

"Exactly." Mantis looked at the various splotches, gauging distances and transit times. "Can you guess where they are now?"

"When did they leave here?"

Mantis gave an estimate.

"I don't know. They might be here now." His fingertip implied a thousand square kilometers of dark, wind-tossed seas. "They might catch that island any time," he said.

"I see." The two of them agreed, it seemed. He thought of a joke about great minds working in parallel . . . but Jellico's mood didn't leave room for jokes, it seemed. Instead he simply asked, "Does that mark mean there's a cache to find?"

"Two caches."

"The same kinds of equipment?" He motioned at the helmets and food that were scattered on the deck.

"More." Jellico said, "The same and different too."

"Such as?"

The boy whispered a command to the helmet's computers, summoning a current listing. Mantis could see the display in the lower corner of the faceplate, the numbers and words reversed; and Jellico read aloud and made contemplative sounds, halfway muttering.

"What can they use?" asked Mantis.

"There are some tools." He described the tools. "And shelters." A pair of tentlike structures made from lifesuit materials. "Strictly for emergencies."

"What else?"

He said, "Bridles."

"For sailers?"

"Yes," he said. "Two of them."

Mantis wondered if there was any advantage in having bridles. For an instant, he entertained the image of a great school of the big fishes, each with an Alteretic straddling its back. But then maybe the Alteretics would miss the caches? So far they didn't show much evidence of having good sensors. Odds are they were lucky to get out of their shuttle with the portable stuff, and the rest was at the bottom now. Crushed. It and the shuttle too being slowly and steadily incorporated into the matrix of some new reef.

Motioning at the map, Mantis said, "All right. You're an Alteretic on this island—where would you sail next. Hmm?" He wondered, "What's your best next step, knowing what you know?"

The boy ran his hand over the map, then said, "Here."

"You're sure?"

"What else is there?" He was a touch defensive.

"Nothing," Mantis agreed. There weren't many candidates marked with the same cryptic symbols, and in this stretch of sea, there were very few islands of any kind. "How many caches?"

"One," said the boy. "And a biological station."

"Of course."

"Doing long-term experiments," he added.

"I see."

Mantis set his hands on top of his own helmet, linking his fingers and thinking. Mr. Chosen was the sort of officer who set his talented men against one another—like himself and Moon, each with his own team, and each team supposedly trying to be the best. Tricks like this were the kind that had made Chosen's career. He was the sort of officer who milked cleverness from others, particularly when the cleverness offered him an easy route to glory and recognition. That's what he wanted now from Mantis and Moon. Some clever plan. He was sitting below, in his room, watching them now and waiting. Mantis could feel his shallow gaze.

What we should do, he thought, is bypass this next island entirely. Forget trying to catch the Alteretics by their heels—particularly because behind them is where they will be looking. What would be smart was to skip ahead one island and wait on them, hidden and ready. Then when they came they could be fought on terms not of their own making. Beaten in ambush, quick and clean.

He looked at the boy again, imagining the face behind the faceplate. Mr. Chosen referred to him and his sister as being half-wild. "Feral," was the exact word. Mantis, however, believed the opposite was true. Growing up feral implies growing up without limits—no set culture; no honored traditions; and no clear morals. But Leeshore itself made limits mandatory. At least that's the way it felt to Mantis. The very alienness of the place—its hostility, its strangeness—served to press people together and make them depend more on one another. Love your neighbor or not, he or she meant more to you than any freedom. At least for the short-term.

On Leeshore, the most pliable morals would grow strict, given time. Attitudes would naturally calcify.

People would start moving in lockstep.

True, the twins were raised by an independent woman—their one parent and teacher and rigorous role model. But Mantis wondered if independence under those terms was independence at all. Someone like their mother, determined and self-assured and likely self-centered, most probably wasn't the sort of person to build truly fresh thinkers. Certainly not ones to rebel against her own norms. And the only counterweights to be found were the Islanders themselves—ageless, semifossilized souls maintaining a hunk of stuhr for people long dead and forgotten.

All their lives, thought Mantis, and the twins knew only two ways of being. Different in style, yet fundamentally the same in tone. Full of absolutes. Never yielding. Never forgiving, or so he imagined.

Was that too harsh? he wondered.

Maybe somewhat.

Maybe I'm confusing their world with my own, he thought.

Jellico and Abitibi seemed to be adapting—a good sign. The business with the wires still, after wars and wars of practice, was tricky. Even dangerous. The essential heart of the technique came when Mantis, or whoever, reached inside a mind and accented some of the existing tendencies. Like Abitibi's innate anger and short fuse. Indeed, Moon had been smart about her abilities. She was a natural fighter. Thinking back on what she had done today—playing that soldier's game, kicking the severed head down the hillside—Mantis felt sad and compassionate and yet at the same time glad too. Eventually, given the chance, she would have come to this stage on her own. He knew that as surely as he knew anything. But having it happen this way, what with her evolution being helped along, she stood a remarkably better chance of surviving.

Alteretics—they were the experts with wires.

Mantis, like every other Earthling, knew facts and stories and fables about what Alteretics could achieve.

Not that they were entirely miracle workers, either. True, their conscripted converts were fearless, yes, and fanatical—hungry to die for the Faith. To do their God's bidding. Or their priests'.

But the converts had no sense of self. No capacity to look after their own poor devoted butts.

They could be like sheep.

They were cannon fodder.

And sometimes some of them, too full of the Faith for too long, would suddenly lose their zeal. The wires would no longer do their duty—minds finally learning to ignore instructions from without—and some trusted priest would have to take the failed, unreliable Alteretic away from the others and finish him or her with a minimum of fuss.

That was what had happened to the Alteretic on the island. Mantis could almost be certain.

Almost.

A simple bit of housecleaning—that's what it must have been. And Moon's soldiers had extracted their own revenge, symbolic and thoroughly appropriate, slicing the head from its shoulders and so separating the infected mind from its unwilling meat.

Mantis sighed.

Jellico was waiting still, apparently watching the map and Mantis, his back to the island and his hands wrapped behind his back, his pose that of some altar boy halfway asleep on his feet.

"How are you feeling?" he asked the boy.

Jellico said, "Pardon?"

"Is your room comfortable?"

"Enough. I suppose." He gestured as if to say, "What right do I have to complain?"

"Are you sleeping at night?"

"Sometimes . . . I have trouble . . . "

"Stress," Mantis told him. "And a certain shock, I suppose."

The boy said nothing.

"A wire might help," Mantis said. "I use a wire to sleep."

"I've seen what wires do."

"It's just one wire. For sleep. I promise."

"No."

"You're sure?"

The boy was positive.

"I'm sorry," Mantis said. "We honestly didn't know your sister would find that body. We didn't know about the body ourselves." He paused, then said, "The sight of it triggered feelings that should have come out more slowly. Feelings good for her . . . that can help her eventually . . ."

"I'm sorry too," said Jellico.

Mantis stared at him for a moment, thinking what luck it was to have found him. Jellico was strong in several ways, not to mention smart and innocent—like Mantis himself, a soul born into a world split into two camps. Jellico had potentials. They weren't the easily tapped potentials of his sister, but by listening to his voice and following his reasonings, Mantis saw he had potentials nonetheless. Carefully, in stages, he would culture and condition Jellico's mind. Not with wires, but with words. With gentle compliments and sweet murmurs. That was the oldest means there was to subvert a will.

The boy might make a fine officer in Intelligence someday.

If things went as planned, thought Mantis, they would take their prisoners, and *The Fist* would snatch them off this sea. And maybe Jellico would hate *The Fist* at first, for the first year or two. But he would adapt, and someday he would fit in so well that he wouldn't recall belonging anywhere else. Mantis loved this business of recruiting new talent. New blood. And he had a feeling about this strange nonferal boy.

"If you or your sister need help, you can come to me."

Jellico said, "Okay," his voice wary. His manner watchful.

"Thanks for your help," Mantis offered. "I'm glad both of you are with us. I am."

He muttered something in return.

"Why don't you help the crew now." He spotted Cricket and said, "See him? Get to know him. Ask him what he wants you to do."

Jellico turned, and the light of the island made his faceplate turn clear. "Him?"

"Cricket." Then he said, "Later. We'll talk later."

Jellico walked away as though he expected to be shot from behind. He moved slowly. Mantis took a moment to watch the girl working, wondering if she and Jel were lovers and if Moon as yet stood a chance. Here, under these conditions, he knew Moon didn't dare anything too overt—

particularly since Mantis himself had served a warning at the first. "Don't use the wires to win her, friend!" He depended on Moon, sure, but Moon depended on him too. And so long as this was war and Alteretics were close, Moon didn't dare risk making Mantis too angry.

He turned and returned to the map, plotting their course and thinking to himself. Planning. Somewhere in the back of his own mind was *The Righteous Fist*—a glorious, self-serving name that made him laugh—and he wondered how its own hunt was progressing, how his fellow Intelligence officers were managing, and how the chances stood for a quick and easy victory out there among the watery comets.

Not that he could help them in the slightest.

And not that they could help him here.

Best think of matters you can affect, friend. He told himself: Don't waste energy and the lining of your gut on them.

He watched the map. Every so often, here and there, a splotch would change its position ever so slightly. The computers were showing the islands as they drifted and spun in the wind. This was not a map so much as it was a model—a dynamic estimate of reality—computations being applied to old data in an effort to rejuvenate them into some semblance of truth.

In months, there would be flaws in the model.

In a few years, Leeshore would be a very different place from this mathematical construct.

Mantis chuckled. To himself.

"Mantis," said a sudden voice. "Could you explain what you're doing? Please?"

"I'm sorry, sir. I was just weaving a plan."

"It must be a very good plan," said Mr. Chosen, "since you're standing there chuckling."

"Sir," he said, "it is a marvelous plan. I promise you. If we are lucky and smart we should win this little war of ours for good, and soon too."

"I see." There was a pause. Mantis looked at the crewmen and the soldiers, all the gear and treasure now stowed away and everyone busy with scraping the deck clean of the filth that had fallen in these last hours. On the deck, written in both Standard English and Standard Chinese, were the words:

Little Fist, plus the hand-in-hand insignia of the Federation.

"Sir?" Mantis prodded.

"Bring this plan of yours inside," said Mr. Chosen. "But I should warn you first. I too have a plan."

Mantis said, "Perhaps they're similar, sir."

"I wouldn't know."

"Well," he offered, "I can tell you mine and let you judge."

There was a pause, then Mr. Chosen relented. "Fine."

Of course he would steal the plan from his subordinate, claiming it as his own. Then, as if to prove to Mankind his worth as a tactician, Mr. Chosen would likely make little adjustments—enough so that nothing was changed, but his ego was fed.

Mantis cared nothing about the approaching theft.

To him, this was simply a means to make Mr. Chosen depend on him all the more.

He couldn't count the times in the past when other superiors had picked up Mantis' ideas as their own—all of them believing they had the right and the right too, to gain by what they stole. To further their careers, say. To acquire medals and cash rewards and more power.

And Mantis couldn't remember how many times the tactics had failed in the end. Ideas had a way of being marked by their owners. A Mantis scheme was recognizable despite what high-and-mighty officer was voicing it. It was his the moment he invented it . . .

. . . blessed with a life of its own . . .

XII   Mr. Chosen sat in his cabin, the door shut and sealed and the lights down low, an extra high-density filter humming behind him, suspended over his bed with shiny stuhr wires.

He was sitting at his desk, the small clean hands wrapped together in his lap and his gaze directed downwards at the glowing square screen. Mantis was on the bridge now. He was taking them away from the island.

Mr. Chosen watched Mantis from the steep angle the camera afforded, and he tried too to keep watch on the screens at the front of the bridge —the darkness spreading now, the mist and falling shit and cadavers apparently thickening, the seas striking the boat sideways with waves and foam and assorted debris.

They were moving towards the north now.

If all went well, the soldiers would soon be sitting on the next island, hiding and waiting, and the boat would be offshore somewhere—ready to rush in with a moment's notice. Mantis had sworn this was the safest plan. When Moon had heard it, he had agreed that there wasn't a better choice. "Just so long as we see the Alteretics first," Mr. Chosen muttered to himself. If not, and if the boat was separated from the soldiers on the island . . . well, he was frightened to think of those prospects. Without *Little Fist's* firepower, the soldiers could be picked to pieces. And then what?

Of course he had made the scheme his own.

After all, he was supposed to be the commander of this operation. It was entirely his own responsibility, and why should he not claim what he wished to claim? He was the officer most at risk, surely, and so shouldn't he acquire the benefits as they came?

Although this business about dividing his forces worried him . . .

Not to mention sitting day after lightless day without using active sensors. No sonics or radar. Essentially blinded. They would have to let the Alteretics approach and then hit them from some blind side of their own—hopefully gaining a few prisoners for their trouble.

Both his officers, each in his own fashion, had assured Mr. Chosen that nothing on Leeshore was entirely safe. There was no plan that could be honestly guaranteed. Now, sitting at his desk, he thought back to when he was given the assignment of leading this team and how then he had believed himself fortunate. Even blessed. The high echelons on *The Righteous Fist* had seen his talents, surely, and they were rewarding him with a rare opportunity. Or so he told himself—boasting to his fellow officers that he would bring back prisoners and parade them up and down *The Fist's* long hallways. Even through his first days on Leeshore he had believed that this was a coup. His poor unfortunate fellows were surely envious of him. And he had dreamed of himself parading before them, as a hero. Parading and then being decorated, his name entered into the Hall of Glory.

Only now, here and there, his convictions were faltering.

Ever so slightly . . . diminishing.

He hated this world. It baffled him and enraged him, and the simplest tasks always seemed next to impossible to accomplish.

Making an exasperated noise, he touched buttons on the desktop. The view on his screen jumped, leaving Mantis and the bridge and settling on a camera fixed to the stern. Mr. Chosen was looking backwards into the boat's phosphorescent wake—a bluish glow swept sideways by the wind, obscured and then lost. Thumbing another button, he opened an audio channel; the noises of water and wind filled his tiny cabin. The island they had walked today was now a faint far glimmer, colorless and low. Or was that some other island? He wasn't sure. He could remember a night on Earth, at sea, when he and his fellows had stood on the flight deck of an ancient People's Republic carrier, and when Mr. Chosen had seen a similar light he had remarked too quickly, "Isn't that Manila? Isn't it?" For a moment no one had spoken. A few throaty sounds had made him uneasy. Then someone had explained, "No. No, Manila's to the east. And distant. That's Hong Kong." The Alteretics had breached Hong Kong's defenses that day, setting a firestorm with half a dozen nukes.

He jumped to another camera now, looking starboard from high on the stuhr superstructure. The water all around glowed with its own faint light. By augmenting that light and enlarging portions of the image, he found eerie-colored splashes marking where organisms swam or drifted or flew through the spray. Everything seemed quite small. Spare. Mr. Chosen examined the largest organism, using taxonomic keys that he had compiled himself—partial, patchy keys wrung from ancient Earthly records and files left undestroyed on Skyhook Island, plus files milked from the twins' own helmets.

Whenever he named a finned or winged something, Mr. Chosen felt a small warm satisfaction. A name was a handle. A name was a kind of control. Yet, by and large, what he saw was handle-free; the sea seemed to be filled to the brim with creatures too minor to be known.

Now it was late evening, ship-time.

Mr. Chosen looked into the crew quarters. Half the bunks had opaque screens drawn, their occupants wired into sleep. One of the men was snoring, meaning there was some kind of malfunction. The wires were suppose to help people sleep, effortlessly and long. Snoring was a symptom of a partly collapsed throat, the normal flow of air choked off. Snoring was a mild but still important sleep disorder on par with bad dreams and insomnia.

Making a note, Mr. Chosen decided someone had to be told. Mantis, or perhaps Cricket.

Lack of rest, as much as stress, causes wear in war. He had read that somewhere. Probably back at The Academy.

Jumping from camera to camera, he made his rounds of *Little Fist*. The hallways were empty, silent and dimly lit. The machine shop was darkened, as were the armaments room and toilets, the shower and storerooms. In one storeroom he could hear the twins softly breathing. Switching to infrared, he found them lying apart. Chaste. The girl was on her belly, hands tucked under her face, pillow-fashion. The boy was against the shelves, on his side and curled into a fetal position.

At least they were a risk that had turned out well.

So far.

Moon was pleased enough that today, after the landing party returned, he had announced the girl would carry a stun gun next time. Provided he had a chance to run her through the basic training.

This was one success, he thought. Recruits. Recruits always looked good, particularly when they were young and strong and bright. Like these. Some Islanders would have been nice too—people born in a remote age that Mr. Chosen could only vaguely imagine—and he felt cheated for not having the chance to talk with such people. The Alteretics slaughtered them in seconds, probably hoping to keep them from scuttling the prize . . . and then failing . . .

He would have liked to have seen the expressions on their faces, the skyhook collapsing on top of them . . .

Watching the girl sleep for a moment, he wondered how she would look on his own arm, scrubbed and dressed formally for the awarding of his medals. He might be able to find a means to win Abitibi. Certainly he had the position now to claim her as his own—and for a moment he enjoyed the imagined compliments and envy of his fellows on board *The Fist.*

She was beautiful.

Moon would fume, or worse, but Lord was she ever beautiful.

"Wait," he muttered to himself. "Maybe later."

Pressing a button, he jumped to the galley. The screen filled with light, and he heard laughter and rapid-fire talk. Moon was standing beside the tiny galley table, dealing cards to a circle of soldiers and crewmen. The air hung thick with a grey narcotic smoke that seeped from a burner set on the floor. "Bets!" Moon called. Around the table they went, shouting their bets, and in the middle a pot grew into a sloppy stack—credit chips worth luxuries on *The Fist.* Like the brothel and alcohol and the tightly restricted supplies of drugs.

Mr. Chosen watched the game, hunching over the screen and squinting.

The cards were being thrown down like threats now. More bets, and the pot began to totter. To slide. Then suddenly, in a blink, Moon was declared winner. Reaching, he let a smile show, and with both hands he swept his loot into a bulging ammunition bag.

For an hour, Mr. Chosen watched them play.

He hadn't a clue as to what the cards meant, even after carefully listening to the bets and studying all the winning hands. Games like this were fundamentally senseless, he believed. Once or twice, as a raw recruit, he had been teased into trying his skill. And every time he was left broke and bruised. Spots on rectangular bits of paper or plastic—it seemed such an arbitrary business. He still wondered if he had been cheated somehow. Teamed up against by the others and made the fool.

Into the second hour, just short of midnight, one of the players said, "Enough," and left the game. He was a slight, pale crewman with a high sharp voice. "I have the helm," he explained, pocketing his credits and waving off the cards.

Moon grumbled. "Let Saint Mantis steer."

But the crewman, named Cricket, insisted on leaving.

"Saint Cricket," said one of Moon's soldiers, smiling, his tone light and mocking.

Cricket ignored him and the others.

He left the galley, and Mr. Chosen followed him to the bridge and watched the two men talk.

Mantis did not appear to have moved. He was still planted on his feet. "No, no," he told Cricket. "I'm fine. I'm fresh." He gestured, saying, "Go back to the game. Or bed. Wherever. I'll take this shift too." He sung something about loving to cross strange new seas, exploring.

Cricket, listening, glanced into the hallway and seemed unsure.

"Or stay. We can talk," Mantis said. "For a little while, friend? It's been an age."

They stood together, and Mantis set out on one of his famous rudderless monologues. Mr. Chosen considered returning to the galley and then decided to stay, leaning back in his chair and staring at the ceiling while the words washed over him—the subjects varied and confusing. And then finally exhausting.

Once, almost sheepishly, Cricket commented on the weather.

"It's always the same," he said with his distinctive voice. "Wind and near-rain and garbage falling and falling."

"The airborne jungle's to blame, friend." Mantis launched into telling him how the masses of bladder plants and airweed served to dampen the effects of sun and Leeshore's rotation—Mantis' voice gaining a certain vigor, his descriptions coalescing into a spinning blue-black world in Mr. Chosen's mind. "Clouds can't form in the usual sense. Not typhoons or squall lines, either. It helps that there's no moon overhead, meaning scant tides, and the axis isn't tipped. No seasons, see? Not to mention too that this sea traps heat and moderates everything still further." Mantis sighed. "We might see the wind drop as we go north. Otherwise, it's more and more of the same."

Cricket made an appreciative sound.

Then Mantis asked, "Don't you think there's a beauty in all of this?" He chuckled and said, "Don't shake that head at me. Think. If you and I were given the tools and the lumber, could we build a place so perfectly and thoroughly conceived? I doubt it. Imagine. Those huge bladders above us have to be lightweight, yet strong. They have to fight gravity and the winds, plus each other—and all the while trying to soak up as much sunlight as possible. For food and for the heat that gives them their lift."

He paused, breathing, and then said, "Millions of fully grown bladder plants. Trillions of youngsters. And yet by working against one another, they make a roof on this world."

"A roof," echoed Cricket.

"It's a matter of balance," said Mantis. "Of opposing forces cancelling out. It's purposeful intent—though I'm not going to drop God's name in on this. The true Almighty announces itself loudly enough on its own."

Some days, thought Mr. Chosen, Mantis was a staunch Catholic. Other days he was Buddhist. Then others—agnostic. For a long while, Mr. Chosen had believed it was a question of pretending faiths to impress others. To shine for superiors. But Mantis, he had come to realize, did not care for such simple sensible considerations. He was probably teasing his audiences, wearing different faiths for his own amusement.

Mantis was a little insane. Mr. Chosen had no doubts.

"Or miser birds!" the insane man cried. "Consider their role. If you are a bladder plant, big and strong and basking in the sunlight, you still have a problem. Where do you find your essential metals—the stuff a stalk of growing seaweed would find dissolved in seawater? Hmm?" Mantis said, "The miser birds are part of your answer, friend."

"Miser birds."

"Exactly," he said. "They pick and cut their way down through the gaps between the bladders, then find islands fresh off the seafloor or freshly broken apart. Because of the way the islands form, they can incorporate pieces of the seafloor. These pieces sometimes include nodules of metals—iron and magnesium, cobalt and whatever—and the misers hunt them out and ingest them whole, and their guts concentrate the metals to an amazing degree. Then back they go through the gaps, up through the jungle, and they shit on the bladders to start a bloom. To make the bladders beneath them grow fast and strong." He said, "You see, if the bladders grow, so do the epiphytes and parasites riding them. And *those* are the treasures the miser birds feed on."

"That's interesting," Cricket offered.

But Mantis wasn't finished. He began naming new examples—new marvels—to illustrate just how intricately drawn was Leeshore's web of life. Mr. Chosen shifted his weight, now resting on the desktop with his hands piled under his chin. He felt drowsy. He was thinking about Mantis and Cricket. The two of them had served together on Earth. On Special Forces. Then at widely scattered points throughout the System. In Intelligence. There were more members of their unit—all bearing those silly insect names—serving on *The Fist* now. Mr. Chosen remembered the files he had seen, and he found himself thinking about them in the hefty terms of an ecologist. Why had all those men remained together for so long? he wondered. They must make for a stable community, each one serving some distinct role. Filling some certain niche. For a time, Mr. Chosen had believed they were all lovers—not an unheard of circumstance from men at war—but he had seen no evidence that that was true. And some of them, like Cricket and Mantis, weren't even good friends in any sense of the word.

So what was the bond?

Why the loyalty?

Now, reconsidering the evidence, he thought he knew the answer. Some of the men in the unit had quirks in their personalities. Like Mantis, with his skeptical, confusing nature. By joining *The Fist*, they had left an Earth that had at last beaten its enemy in the field. There was not a single Alteretic unit remaining. But the high, high echelons were still concerned. A good many of them asked: "What if the Alteretics had planted agents among us? Unseen spies. They could just be biding their time until Mankind loosened its guard and forgot."

There had been talk of purges.

Not simple security checks, or diligent interrogations, but instead wide-ranging purges of a kind never seen in the past.

The wires would be used on unreliable or undocumented people. Or so went the rumors. If the investigators felt the slightest doubts, more traditional means would be employed—torture and execution and obliteration. And since any purge feeds on its own momentum, soon the semi-innocents would be swept away. Men and women like Mantis, always so slippery about their opinions and politics, would tend to vanish. *Poof!* Gone.

That was likely why Mantis and his ilk had joined *The Fist*.

Surely.

And Cricket—a quiet and competent officer—must have been motivated to do the same. Pressure from his fellow officers, perhaps. Or maybe just fear of incrimination through association with the rest of the wayward unit.

Mr. Chosen was slipping close to sleep now. He felt comfortable and competent. Suddenly he had a handle on Mantis, or at least a clearer perspective. He was no longer as intimidated by the man's wit or apparent intelligence, believing he too was scared in his heart of hearts. Just like Chosen was scared. And as for his slipperiness of belief . . . well, if there were failures in his nature, then that was fine too. A man like Mr. Chosen tends to build his career on the lapses of others. The thought of a purged and perfect world left him absolutely cold.

Still he could hear Mantis' voice reaching through his drowsiness. He was talking to Cricket about ecology still, and order in the natural world. "Think of *The Righteous Fist,*" he said. "Think of the troubles *we* have in balancing all of its environmental factors—and *The Fist* is a tiny world, at that."

Cricket found the space to admit, "I'm worried about *The Fist,* sir," his voice soft and fragile. "Where is it now, do you suppose? Is it fighting yet?"

Mantis made calming sounds. "I don't know how much fight either of those starships can find, friend. They're like two spent giants. They've had long, long runs, and they're low on fuel, and there's a lot of emptiness between comets. More than anything, they'll be conserving their energies. Shooting from a distance. Aiming for luck."

"I hope it's ours," said Cricket. "Luck."

"Speaking of which," said Mantis, "were you playing cards tonight? With the troops?"

"Some."

"Did you win?"

"And lost, too. Some of both."

"Just so you know whose team you're playing on," Mantis told him; and Mr. Chosen thought that was a strange statement to make. "Which reminds me, friend. What would you say if I found another partner for our team? Hmm?"

"Who? The boy?"

"A talented mind like his . . . it's a guess, but I bet it's so."

"Maybe."

Mr. Chosen realized Mantis was thinking of recruiting the boy for his own unit. For Intelligence. And he went to sleep with the world seeming right—all of the men on board striving for prizes, whether it was Mantis and Cricket trying to swell their own ranks, or Moon and the others having contests over sliding stacks of credit chips.

Then he was deep asleep, dreaming.

He saw a great range of mountains, at night, and heard giants somewhere grappling and snorting. Then the sun rose, and he found himself standing in a high pasture watching two great burly rams, foam in their mouths and blood in the foam; and the rams dipped their heads suddenly and charged, slamming horns to horns, and their skulls shattered, and their bodies slumped, and snow fell and buried them in a minute.

Mr. Chosen sat up again.

His neck ached, and he rubbed his neck and breathed deeply, feeling his heart pounding against his ribs. Blinking, he happened to glance at the screen. He thought he had been asleep for only a moment. Except Mantis now was standing alone, whispering softly to no one, and the clock built into the desk claimed it was nearly four in the morning.

Mr. Chosen stood and carefully straightened. Then by the light of the screen, he began undressing, pulling off the jumpsuit and folding it properly and using wetted thumbs to wipe clean the tiny emblems of rank. Nude now, he sat on his bed and began applying the wires to his throbbing temples, the adhesive cool and soothing. Four hours, he decided. He set the timer for four hours. Then, lying on his stiff back, he remembered that he had been dreaming just a minute ago, and he couldn't for his life recall what he had seen or done in the dream.

He began thinking back to Hong Kong again. He remembered how the ash had fallen on the deck of the Chinese carrier—black and cool, homogeneous and radioactive—and he remembered how he and his fellows had had to stay below while crewmen wearing all-stuhr suits plowed clean the flight deck. For weeks afterwards, the sunsets were doubly red. Everyone was required to take antimutagens and anticancer agents. One of the

Indian officers on board—a large and bitter man without any sense—
smiled and swore that the drugs would add weeks to everyone's life. So
why be so gloomy, troops?

Of course, all the Chinese blood had turned icy. There were stares and
a few muttered insults. Mr. Chosen remembered being secretly glad—the
man's stupidity had seemed to cancel out his own blunder about Manila
and the light on the sea. And then afterwards, the Indian had transferred
to another unit on another sea, rumors having it that he died eventually,
and badly, while in combat.

On the monitor, Mantis was singing now, softly, and Mr. Chosen
didn't feel like sleep. Not just yet. So he listened to the song, one hand
toying with the medals grown into his bare chest. When he squeezed a
medal just so, it would speak, explaining the circumstances by which it
had been won. The voices were tiny, unamplified and mostly senseless.
But he liked their buzzing, and he knew by heart what each was saying.
His favorites were those he had won for helping to capture Alteretics—
the greatest honor in the Hall of Glory. Moon and Mantis claimed there
were a dozen Alteretics on Leeshore. Give or take. Including a priest. So
for a little while, Mr. Chosen imagined the grand ceremonies they would
hold on *The First*—twelve medals given to himself for the conscripts and
the priest too—and he shut his eyes and saw himself in a hero's robes,
the tall and dark beautiful girl at his side, and he heard the crowd chanting
his name and applauding, the sound deafening, *The Fist* itself trembling
with the racket.

Eventually, almost reluctantly, Mr. Chosen roused himself from his
reverie.

Reaching, he tripped the SLEEP switch on the wall, and immediately
he felt himself falling, utterly relaxed and buried in darkness.

He was asleep for ages, it seemed.

When he woke, the timer was flashing OVERRIDE, and he blinked and
saw nine minutes had elapsed.

"Mr. Chosen?" Mantis was calling. "Sir?"

"I'm up." He sat up and pulled off the wires, then staggered towards
the desk. "What is it?"

"Look to starboard, if you would, sir."

"Starboard?"

"Yes, sir."

His fingers were clumsy, striking buttons. He warned, "This had better be important, mister."

"I'll let you be the judge, sir."

Upwind and towards the north, stretching as far as the cameras reached, was a colorless plain lit by quick and bright little fires and a soft uniform glow. The plain resembled an island. Mr. Chosen couldn't help but think of land. But when he enlarged the nearest fringe, he found no shore, only oblong shapes heaped against each other and bobbing in the waves.

"It's a fish kill," said Mantis. "I think it is."

Mr. Chosen sat and stared at the image.

"All part of Leeshore's recyke system," announced the crazy man. "I was just telling one of my men, in fact—"

"Shut up!" Mr. Chosen cried out.

"Sir—?"

"Please!" he wailed, feeling a strange sudden darkness inside himself. "Please! Just shut up!"

XIII   Standing in the open doorway, Jellico listened to his sister explaining the fish kill. Abitibi was surrounded by her audience—Mantis at the controls still, Moon and Mr. Chosen against the back wall. She was saying, "Anything will trigger one. A disease. Or a shift in deep currents. Or some sudden lack of dissolved oxygen." She was facing the doorway and glancing over one shoulder, eyeing the main screen while she spoke. "My guess is there's been an undersea eruption. As big as this kill looks. Not a disease," she said. "Too many species."

Mr. Chosen appeared tired and short-tempered. He was standing with his hands behind his back, his back arched, and his face outraged by everything. He addressed Abitibi, "What can you tell us about its extent?"

"I don't know." She glanced at Jellico, using her eyes to invite his help. "We've seen kills, what—? A couple hundred kilometers across, haven't we?"

"Several times," he offered. "Sure."

"Mantis," the bland little man snapped. "Where does this leave us? Assuming what they say is true."

"The way the kill is spread across our path," Mantis said, "we could either try swinging downwind or doubling back." His hands showed what he meant. "The trouble is that I'm sure there'll be no time, sir. We have to make that next island soon."

"Then we have to continue on course. Am I right?"

"Straight through." Mantis put on a mischievous face. "Kicking the fish out of our way, if need be."

Jellico looked past the dimly lit heads, gazing up at the screen and thinking to himself that this kill was indeed enormous. *Little Fist* was still pointed northwards. The bow was shoving against thousands of bloated corpses—colorless and bloodless and frequently huge. Their flesh was lit from within by the rot and from without by the scavengers feeding on them. Sometimes one of them would burst, letting off a stream of rancid gas; and every so often, the gas would catch fire in the hyperoxygenated air—a hot bright flare shooting skywards and then gone.

There were dozens of species of fish.

Maybe hundreds.

Abby's right, he thought. No disease was responsible. More likely, some wide-scale eruption injected sulfides into the deep water, robbing the fish of their precious oxygen.

Mantis and Moon were talking now. Planning. It was obvious the boat was being slowed by the masses of fish. Mantis, in Asian and with his hands, was explaining how he wanted the weight on board to be shifted. The bow should be lighter and ride higher, he seemed to say. Then *Little Fist* could skate over the bodies instead of acting like some dry-land plow.

Jellico had heard their language so often in these last days, he was beginning to smell the substance of everything said.

Turning, Mantis seemed to ask Mr. Chosen if he agreed.

Mr. Chosen nodded, his face now nervous and impatient.

Again Mantis and Moon talked. Moon sounded brutal and coarse, even in his own language, his eyes invisible in the gloom, and his face, if anything, more hideous than ever—the pits seemingly deeper, his head like some lump of porous synthetic cheese.

Jellico felt anxious whenever Moon was close.

The beating on Skyhook Island was part of it. And the ring Moon had stolen, too. But more and more it was Moon's relationship with Abby. It was the wires he had used and the way she talked about doing all she could to help them; and too, it was the way Moon would stare at her, like he was doing now, something about his expression predatory. Calculating and confident.

He felt jealous of Moon.

Without so much as a fight, Jellico wondered if he was to lose his sister.

"Jellico? Friend?"

He looked at Mantis.

"You have to suit up and join the rest. In the hold." He said, "We need your strong backs."

Jellico nodded, turned and stepped into the hallway.

Abitibi and Moon emerged after him, and then Mr. Chosen. The four of them walked in an uneven line. At one point, Mr. Chosen turned and stepped inside a ladder-lined tube. Moon paused, watching Mr. Chosen drop out of sight. Quietly, Abby asked where the man was going, and Moon said, "To hide away," his head shaking. Jellico remembered. He lived in his own cabin underneath the bridge, running the show from a distance. More and more Jellico thought of Islanders when he saw Mr. Chosen; and he felt an odd disappointment, and scorn and pity, all mixed in equal amounts.

Moon was walking again. He and Abby went into the storeroom together. Jellico hurried, thinking how illuminating it was to meet and decipher a stranger. Everyone at first had seemed essentially the same. The crew and soldiers and the officers. Simple and strange. But lately, the faces had turned unique, and the mannerisms became distinctions. It was like looking out over the fish kill and seeing only fish at first. Then gradually, in measured bits, the water is filled with hundreds of species.

He was beside Abby now. They were dressing. Their practiced hands knew the routine of slipping into their lifesuits, connecting recyke and waste disposal systems purely by touch. Moon was standing in the open doorway, waiting, watching only Abitibi. His breath came through his flat pitted nose, and his hands were clenched and resting on his hips. He would have to ask Mantis about Moon. Jellico couldn't decipher what was inside the soldier. Not by himself. He looked at Moon's eyes—flat and black and showing him nothing—and wondered if he really wanted to know.

Mantis' voice was blaring now, in Asian, coming across the intercom and sounding full of authority.

Jellico picked his sister's stuhr-coated helmet off the floor and handed it to her, smiling. She seemed distant now. Diverted. The face was Abby's own face, strong and intense, but the intensity was focused on things she couldn't seem to share with her brother. She turned away. He bent and grabbed his own helmet—scuffed and scratched by years of hard use—and he put it under his arm and followed the two out the door and away.

The stuhr spheres of the superstructure were connected with flexible tubes strung inside stuhr collars. The tubes were dark and bristling with handholds, and as the boat's insides tilted and twisted, anticipating the waves, the tubes stretched and relaxed with an odd, creaking noise.

A tired sound, thought Jellico. Sad and spent.

Moon led them through the middle sphere. Jellico caught glimpses of the empty crew quarters and the machine shop. He thought to himself what an awesome tool *Little Fist* could become, used for research. Someone could motor around Leeshore at will, with room and the power for several full-scale labs and a dozen scientists and the sensors needed to spot rarities and keep careful track of the grander picture.

They entered the second tube, then the rearmost sphere. They were surrounded now by empty space and sharp noise, and below them was the main fusion plant and the motors all wrapped snugly inside nameless pipes and insulating foams. This place wasn't anticipating any waves; Jellico very nearly stumbled with his first step. The staircase was built on the curved inner face of the sphere, various pipes and cable running alongside and up into the front of *Little Fist.* Jellico kept low like his sister. He clung to the railing with his free hand.

There was a platform at the bottom, sandwiched between the motors and an enormous airlock. Standing in a tight mass were soldiers and crewmen—everyone but Chosen and Mantis, he realized—all of them wearing lifesuits and armor and lightweight oxygen tanks. The roar from the motors was deafening. Jellico paused and slipped on his helmet, the seals working automatically. Then he was down among them, standing with his feet spread apart, and that officer from up on deck—Cricket?— was behind him, placing a tank on his back, cinching the straps tight for him and then plugging the hoses into his never-used intake valves.

Jellico suddenly felt heavy and clumsy. When the floor gave a lurch, the tank almost spilled him.

Cricket said, "Careful," and squeezed one of his arms.

Jellico turned and looked at Cricket.

"You'll need armor," he was saying. "Come sometime, and I'll make your armor." He was wearing a bright smile and shining eyes. He told Jellico, "You're a good man. Mantis says."

"He does?"

"A good smart young man." He nodded, something implied, and Jellico felt himself tugged in some new and confusing direction.

The airlock opened. As a unit, everyone marched into the chamber and then stood waiting. Jellico tried to stand beside Abby. The door closed behind them and sealed, and the place grew hushed for a moment, the motor sounds gone. Then a wind began playing over them with a mournful howl. Jellico became aware of the bitter, faintly oily flavor of canned oxygen. His lifesuit swelled a little as it stored several minutes of air. He found Abby's hand and squeezed once, and she reflexively did the same. Then the wind quit, and the outer door opened, and everyone marched down a long and sloping corrugated ramp, entering a tremendous and well-lit hall of mirrors.

The floor was metal—a soft grey metal covering the boat's bottom. It looked as though the bi-ply hull had been assembled, and then molten lead was poured into the hull as ballast. For balance. The appearance of the place was deceptive, all the mirrored stuhr making it seem huge and bright. It took Jellico a minute to find his bearings. Reflections dwarfed what was real. He saw himself in the hull to the right and the left, and in the spheres ahead and behind, and when he turned and the boat pitched, he felt uneasy in his stomach.

Moon was shouting instructions now.

Everyone was walking, ignoring everything but where they were going. Groups of three and four formed. Jellico kept his sister nearby. She and he and Moon were together, making for the bow. A triangular stack of squat black cylinders waited for them, four-high. Moon climbed on a cart and drove it close and locked the hard rubber wheels. Then he unfastened the tie-downs that restrained the cylinders, and he gave both of them short metal bars with flattened prying ends. He explained what he wanted. The three then set to work.

The cylinders had to be rolled into the cart.

Each made a banging crash as it tumbled.

The bottom four cylinders had to be lifted and set in place, then all of them had to be secured with more tie-downs. Moon unlocked the wheels afterwards and drove the cart towards the stern, slowly, letting the floor's pitching do most of the work.

There were crates and spare motors all around them, and gun parts and ammunition and exotic electronic wonders. The atmosphere was nitrogen, Jellico supposed—inert and pressurized and maybe tainted with broad-based fungicides. Everywhere he looked, he saw teams caught up in their labors. There was a certain discipline that infected the place. No one needed to be told what to do anymore, and everyone seemed to move with the same sense of shared purpose.

Jellico felt detached from things.

Inside himself a voice told him he belonged elsewhere.

Moon stopped beside a propeller shaft. He waited for them, then left them to it. Abitibi and Jellico lifted the cylinders one by one, together, building a new stack. Jellico sweated until his face was soaked and his eyes stung, his jumpsuit absorbing and cleansing the rest. He blinked and blinked, and then he happened to spy something painted on the end of one of the cylinders—an idealized atom, its nucleus a human skull.

"Well, how about that," he muttered.

Abitibi asked what he had seen.

"These are nuclear warheads," he announced.

"I saw missiles." She waved towards the bow. "Moon says they have more up on deck." She sounded like the proud warrior, telling him, "They can drop them on top of anything they can see. A hundred kilometers all around us."

"Sure. I remember." Mantis had described them, hadn't he? Something about having them but not wanting to use them, preferring to take their prey alive.

They finished the stack, blocking the cylinders so they wouldn't roll, then securing the entire stack—Jellico still trying to think of them as cylinders, not warheads, and so harmless. He went so far as to lean against the stack.

Abitibi asked, "What are you doing?"

"Resting," he said. "Why don't you take a break."

"We've got work, Jel. Now."

He stared at his sister for a long moment.

"Jel?" she implored. "Don't you want to catch the killers? Hmm?"

He said, "Maybe," and then thought that wasn't true. He meant to say, "Of course," only his pride and jealousy kept blocking his way.

She said, "Help me?"

He stood and he tried.

XIV   He was tucked into the front of the boat, sitting sprawled out on the sea-stained kits and field packs of his men, thinking now, thinking: What did you mean, a mission? Whose mission? He was enormous, hands twice the size of most hands and arms as thick as most legs and legs built up to the point where the fabric of his jumpsuit threatened to split, muscles straining the seams. He was a handsome man, too. Not in obvious ways, his features too coarse and his light-colored eyes too small; but the Alteretic women who grew up as priests beside him, never wired and so possessing their own pure and free wills, had

flocked to him over the years—because of his looks and the strength
and his enormous size. And too, because he was generally regarded as
being brilliant, much in the same fashion he was handsome. Not in
obvious ways. More on the sly. By surprise. His features and eyes hiding
a relentless, disciplined mind.

"Whose mission?" he repeated, aloud now. "Just what were you telling
me? Hmm?"

He was alone, thinking to himself. He could see the green-glowing trees
all around him still, the bare ground made of plastic, and the soldier—
a trusted man, or so he had believed, who had stood facing him, talking,
telling him that everything he had done or had failed to do was because
of very strict orders. No, he claimed, he wasn't able to divulge who had
given him the orders. No, it wasn't any of those priests, either. Or those
priests. Or those. No.

"Then who?" the towering priest had asked. "And don't say you can't
say. Don't."

"I can't."

"I order you."

"You shouldn't try," he had said, his voice edged with conviction. "I'm
not supposed to listen to you, Your Reverence. I'm sorry."

The priest had trusted him. Which, in the world of conscripts, meant
he had had complete faith in the conditioning process, the wires im-
planted into the brain just so. The Alteretic hierarchy of God above priest
above all else was in place in everything he thought and did. But it
couldn't be that the conscript had followed anyone's orders, or anything's.
Because he knew the God, and he had named all but the highest-ranking
priests before the conscript quit saying, "No. No. No," refusing to
confirm or deny. And he thought now that those high priests would surely
not have told this poor conscript to do everything in his power to ruin
the mission. Which is what the conscript had done. Without fail. He had
helped to make a crazy mess of everything.

"All right," the priest had said. "You can't tell me who gave you the
secret orders. All right. Can you tell me what they are? Hmm? Can you
explain just what you're suppose to be accomplishing?"

"I shouldn't."

"Is that so?"

"Again," he had said. "Orders."

The priest had reared himself higher, unconsciously trying to intimidate the conscript. "Do you know what I'm hearing? I'm hearing you telling me that you've lost your senses. That you don't understand who's in charge." He had said, "I am in charge. No one else. Down here there is no one else, is there? Hmm?"

The conscript had blinked, his expression hardening.

"Are you hearing me?"

"Absolutely, Your Reverence." It was the tone that the priest could recall now. Bullheadedness showing through and through. "I understand completely, Your Reverence. And you're wrong."

It wasn't just a case of trusting the conscript, the priest reminded himself. Conscripts are trusted to serve God as instructed, and serve the Faith. But the priest, for years and years, had recognized in him more than any simple-felt loyalty. He had been talented at one time. Bright and highly trained and enormously useful. Even vital.

The priest had been an important figure on board the starship.

A known and notable quantity.

It had been partly his responsibility to help tend for the vast i-ply god of stuhr they had smuggled on board—a shimmering, living chunk adorned with wires and power supplies and filling more space than did this sailboat, larger by half. Only the most reliable and skilled of the priests were normally allowed in the presence of the God.

But this particular conscript . . .

"Damn!" he said now. "Damn, what was I doing?"

There had been a problem, technical and obscure. The problem had surfaced while the starship was deaccelerating, the priests and conscripts safely tucked away inside the protective baths; and while it was never more than a minor problem—certainly not threatening the God itself— it was serious enough that every qualified hand was needed to help once the deacceleration was complete.

That conscript was full of skills.

He had proven himself on numerous occasions, with machinery at least as sophisticated and tempermental.

The priest thought back, replaying those frantic days while they approached Leeshore—straightening out the problem before it turned serious, at the same time planning to attack and capture the skyhook—and he grew cold thinking what an unreliable, possibly insane conscript could have managed in those seconds and minutes when no one was watching him with the God.

Then came the actual attack.

That conscript was also copilot to the shuttle, helping to take them down through those damned blue-black sacklike clouds, avoiding the missiles as the Islanders launched them, helping to aim their nose at a patch of still water just downwind from the island itself. The plan was to hit the Islanders hard and fast, giving them no time to scuttle anything. People like them, isolated and scared, might even be terrified into surrendering. That's what the priest went down there hoping. Scare them into giving up. Or knock them senseless before they could blink.

The last missile did the damage.

The priest remembered the jolt of the blast, and he was mad at himself now for not realizing what must have been obvious. That on a shuttle bolstered by stuhr, the chances of critical damage from a non-nuclear warhead were scant. Almost impossibly small. But a trusted conscript sitting in the cockpit, buttons all around, could have done anything. He might have leaked raw fuel out the rear to feed the explosion, say. Or intentionally flooded the stern, knowing there wouldn't be time to check the damage. The shuttle filling and sinking and gone, lost in less than a minute.

The plan had been to hit the still water and skate up onto the plastic island, the stuhr underbelly taking the abuse.

What happened instead was that the missile exploded, and the nose went down, the shuttle hitting short and too hard, salty spray coming up the aisles and everyone grabbing their packs and kits and guns, making for the escape hatches and the crushing darkness of Leeshore.

They still could have won, he thought.

If he had been on his toes.

If he had seen what was happening.

They had gone up on the island, soaked but still together as a unit, and the Islanders were holed up inside their dormitories, acting brave. They had shot down a shuttle, after all. They might just win this little war.

The priest had spoken to them, promising them safety. Security. And whatever else would sound and smell good.

At the same time, he sent his most trusted conscript—the copilot—around to the back of the dormitory with a couple others. Their orders were to force a stuhr hatch open using small shaped explosives. Time was essential, the priest had explained. Don't waste time. Don't give the prey an extra moment to think. Just blindside them, good and quick.

And in the end . . .

. . . what?

The skyhook was scuttled.

Scuttled and no one broke into the rear of the dormitory. No one killed the Islanders before they could switch their old starship fusion plant into OVERHEAT mode, melting it to slag and destroying the skyhook and setting the island to drifting and guaranteeing none of them would soon get off this wet hellhole.

It was later, in those next days, when the priest asked the other conscripts and learned that his trusted one was not to be trusted.

The ones who had gone around the dormitory with him admitted that he had worked slowly, and poorly, and made too much noise while trying to break inside.

Later, on the second island, he and that conscript had taken a walk. Alone.

He remembered the green trees glowing, and the ground, and the conscript talking endlessly about being on his mission. About doing what he was told to do. About following orders and the priest not being allowed to know what the orders said.

"It took me time," the priest had told him. "But I finally saw what was happening."

The conscript had said nothing to that.

"You didn't just botch up the attack. You got our shuttle shot down. Didn't you?"

The criminal's face had become more and more determined, the more his crimes were dredged up.

The priest had hit the conscript—just once—the enormous hand swatting the side of the head, the man's body tumbling and the resolve still there on his face. All those years as a priest, using wires and reading souls, and he had never once known a conscript to go bad this way. Not exactly. Never by hearing nonexistent orders from some fictional source. No, he thought, it had to be fright in combat—stresses built up past the point that conditioning could hold fright in check—and Leeshore was one of the stresses. Something knew, he realized. Something that might press a man's soul until it broke in curious new ways.

Sure.

The priest had gone to shore planning to deal with the problem, ready to use a discrete and quick bullet.

Straight into the traitor's skull.

But while they stood facing one another, talking, the priest had kept asking himself if someone had actually wanted the mission to fail. If the highest of the high priests had given the order to the most trustworthy conscript, knowing it would be carried out efficiently. Without questions.

But why?

The priest knew he himself was valuable. To the starship. To the work with the God. To everything.

So why doom him?

Why? And why lose the skyhook too?

He couldn't decide. There seemed no sense, no reason.

"What I need to do," he said, "is forget it. I did what was right. I did my duty." He was a cruel man once the need arose. He was willing to do a thousand things that would cause most people—even the most battle-tempered—to wince when they considered them. "I had no choice. I had none."

He had shot the conscript.

Once.

Suddenly.

He remembered how the faceplate and forehead had both shattered, the stuhr helmet collapsing away into a slight film. He could still watch the dead man as he was flung backwards against the green tree trunk, making it glow more brightly with the impact. Then the body fell slowly to the ground, looking like a man sitting down gently, something about it supremely relaxed. At ease. And the face glaring at the priest regardless. Even now.

He felt guilt. Not for the man killed, but for the mission. For the waste of having to kill the fighter, the talent, and the whisper-thin chance that he had made a mistake. If he wanted to survive down here—and he did, hating this place from the first, and hating the idea of death worse—then he would have to conserve his talents and resources better than he had in the past. Before now. He would have to be clever, imagining enemies all about. That's the only way he could win.

He was sitting in cramped quarters, looking about now, looking at the assorted prizes they had just found on the last island. An odd mix of equipment, familiar or not. Useful or not. In addition, he thought about the gear his own people had brought, and this glass sailboat, and what might be done with all of that.

Get clever, he told himself.

Your enemies think they're more clever, likely. So be more so still.

Starting now.

He was thinking about his people, looking towards the bow and the hanging black sailcloth that separated this part of the cabin from the rest. He could hear the men breathing, sleeping gently, wires keeping them under in spite of waves and the assorted groanings of the hull and rigging and the tired old seals. He could imagine the others up on deck, working hard, navigating to the limits of the maps available, aiming for another island that might or might not help him and them somehow.

He shifted his weight.

He was thinking how this crew, man after man, would do what he told them to do. Twice as hard, provided he said that God had informed him of the need.

He shifted again.

And thought.

And he stood, not yet knowing exactly what he was doing. More watching himself moving according to intuition, curious about why those big hands of his were reaching towards the packs and kits. He was hunting for something. For the dead conscript's stuff, sure. He found it finally, someone having placed it on the bottom of the pile, on the glass floor, a stained and water-tight bag and a heavy field pack made from the same materials. There was a glow, soft and faintly violet, coming from spots that were mold. He touched the mold and frowned, wondering what kinds of damage were being done to the contents. He hated Leeshore, particularly its rot, and if ever he had the chance, he surely would destroy it. Strap a rocket to a comet, aim and fire. That's how they half-destroyed the Earth, he thought to himself. Using asteroids and comets, impacting them on the surface. He would like to be in charge of this System someday, the Wars done. And won. He would blast this hellhole until it was baked sterile. Until it was made safe. And then he would start life over again, this time doing it right.

The kit was locked. He began working on the lock, small and metallic and tarnished badly. He said, "There," when it broke in his hands, and he opened the kit and carefully reached inside, holding his breath and not knowing why. There was a tension in his stance now. A wariness. The hard thick fingers probbed through folded jumpsuits and around spare ammunition, and then he was touching something else. He knew what he was touching. He felt a surface that was smooth and occasionally sharp and thoroughly solid—cool and warm at the same time, plus dry. Absolutely dry.

What he saw first were the big batteries.

Nuclear batteries.

Enough juice there to last a hundred years. Or more.

And then he said, "You," and cursed, his voice harsh and sudden and loud. Almost screaming.

"So you're the one!" he wailed.

"You!"

Nestled in his hands now, bright in the bad light and glittering where the stuhr-edged power chisels had been cutting, was a chunk of pure i-ply stuhr that seemed to weigh nothing and a ton all at once. The priest was sweating now, kneeling with the thing in his hands and cursing still. Staring at it and telling it:

"You think you've been clever, huh?"

Saying, "I bet you do."

Saying, "What if I rip off the batteries and watch you die? Hmm?"

A chunk of the god. That's what he was holding now, understanding now just what must have happened. Knowing the source of all the troubles.

The priest was raging.

Steaming.

But of course he couldn't let himself do anything to the god. Not when he knew what the precious god—the whole, complete god—meant to him and to his comrades everywhere. This double handful of i-ply stuhr, alone and by itself, containing more sheer mental power likely than all the people left living on all the worlds above this damned lightless sky.

XV   The trick was something he had managed in the field once or twice, no sleep possible and no one else able to do his job.

Mantis had been on the bridge for nearly a full day now, much of it spent steering manually. He was numb, he was so tired. Numb and slow, but still determined to see this challenge through. Mr. Chosen, wearing a dark and disgusted face, had informed him, "Officers should care for themselves, setting an example for their people." He was angry because Mantis had piloted through the night for no apparent reason, and angry because a mess of fish had decided to die in his path.

But that was Mr. Chosen. He didn't understand the fun you could have at the helm of a good boat, cutting your way across new seas; and he didn't recognize simple bad luck when it came to him and shook his hand, friend to friend.

"I apologize," Mantis had told him, chin dipped like a hunting sailer's. "I'm to blame. I'm the one who should suffer."

"And put us all at risk?" Mr. Chosen had trumpeted. "Mantis?"

"Honestly," he had answered, "I don't think Cricket or any of the others can handle this boat well enough, sir."

"You don't?"

"I don't."

"Is that so?"

"Yes." The little man had not looked well. Not at all. Mantis had turned to him and announced, "If you take me off the bridge, then someone will have to learn to cope with that." And he had gestured up at the screen. Up at the fish kill. And poor Mr. Chosen had made a tiny crinkling sound as his will collapsed. *He looks ill*, Mantis had thought to himself. *He looks like some half-crippled thing falling out of Leeshore's own sky.*

Doomed.

"Oh well," said Mantis, feeling cranky tired. "Just so long as he doesn't come apart entirely." And with that he stepped away from the helm for a moment, the autopilot on and the time ripe for the trick.

At the back of the bridge was a reclining chair. On the chair were the controls and the wire removed from his own bunk. Mantis pulled the chair up to the helm and plugged the wire into the sleep circuits recessed on the floor—benefits of modular construction, every room on board suitable to serve as any other in a pinch. It was a capacity shared with the human brain. Rugged redundancy. Extra neurons for hire. Half of him could be sleeping at a given instant, and if the balancing was done just so . . . the other half could manage alone!

He had done this before. The controls were his own—augmenting the impulses coming out of the floor.

Dolphins and whales, back before their unfortunate demise, had managed a very similar trick themselves. They couldn't sleep like fish sleep, motionless and passive. They had needed enough awareness to swim and blow and breathe. Thus they slept in pieces. In shifts.

It took Mantis time to adjust his controls. When he was satisfied, his head and body tingling with a vaguely familiar sensation, *Little Fist* was beginning to have troubles coping with all the dead fish. This was too much for the autopilot, what with the bow sticking up without grace or purpose and the stern buried in the sea behind them. "If we weren't so damned afraid of building thinking machines," Mantis said without sound. "Then *Little Fist* could reprogram itself for the situation, and all the poor tired human pilots could sleep according to their own designs."

It was the Wars that were to blame.

The Wars and the Alteretics.

It might be a thousand thousand years before people screwed up their courage to try artificial intelligences again. If then. And until then, Mankind would have to make do with a brain built on the African plains and fine-tuned by millenia of hunting and sowing and warring. Unless, of course, one counted the i-ply god itself—something that Mantis caught himself doing from time to time, stupidly, the years of practice not enough yet to teach him to keep his precious mouth closed and sealed tight.

Parts of Mantis were sleeping now.

He was aware only of the parts awake.

Sitting at *Little Fist's* controls, he made adjustments, dropping the power back a touch and then turning them more into the wind.

The wave-tossed sea was covered with floating corpses. The flesh was milked of its colors, the fins and tails tattered or gone. The enormous deep-sea eyes stared out in every direction with a kind of collective outrage, apparently searching for their killers. Those eyes played on Mantis' played out nerves—years hence, he supposed, he would remember their cold gazes without trying. Probably without warning. Flashback fashion.

"Is it the same for you?" he asked a scavenging bird. "I should hope not, friend." Likely this was Paradise in its mind.

He began toying with the image on the screen, boosting the brightness and pulling details out from the mayhem. He saw birds circling and birds hovering and birds laying on the water, faces buried inside putrid carcasses. The delicate wings and elongated bodies proved they had come from the high, thin air above—Mantis was developing a knack, matching form to function. Birds built for this realm, he had noticed, were stubby-winged and massive. They lived just above the waves, and they tended to approach the fish kill from its edges—like stealth bombers. But the birds around them now had dropped from the bladder and airweed realm, ICBM-style. If the bombers replaced them sometime, he reasoned, then *Little Fist* was getting close to an edge. To the end. "Just so long as the birds think like me," he said. "Perfectly." He laughed aloud, enjoying his own bluster.

More and more the bloating fish were exploding.

It was a static charge or some organic reaction that would ignite the gases. In spite of mist and the spray, the fires were searingly hot. The boat itself precipitated the worst of them—flashes of yellow dressed in thunder, the force of each blast making the floor shake ever so slightly.

Watching the fires, Mantis thought of Earthly scenes—oil shale fields burning and cities scorched to rubble—and he thought how the most unnerving sensation on Leeshore was not the alienness of Leeshore, but instead its familiarity. There you could be, staring out at something you had never dreamed of seeing; and suddenly, almost effortlessly, you saw a living bit of Home . . .

"Mantis," he warned himself. "Keep your mind on the Here and Now."

He was growing accustomed to halfway sleeping.

The sensation was buoyant and warm, soothing him from within.

Touching the controls of the helm again, he made small alterations in direction. Then he settled back into the chair and carefully did nothing. On the screen, a small scavenging bird was hunting, coasting in a lazy loop with its naked head dipped and watchful. Mantis blinked once. When he opened his eyes, he saw a dead fish rising off the crest of a wave, kicking hard. Then it took the bird by the head and pulled the thing, flopping and screeching, back down into the sea.

Mantis let out a gasp.

The bird was gone, and the fish suddenly was dead again—fins ragged and the color pale and the body flat on its side with a pair of creamy dead eyes upturned and watching for the next target.

Softly, Mantis said, "Imagine," and laughed. He thumbed a button and the empty storeroom appeared on a smaller screen. Where are you, my boy? He thought for an instant, then jumped to the galley. Sure enough, Jellico was sitting beside his sister and across from Moon. There were sandwiches and mugs of steaming broth, and on the tabletop between them was a hologram showing the island due north.

Moon was asking questions. Grilling them for details. Where would the Alteretics likely land, for instance. And what kinds of terrain would they find and have to fight in.

"Jellico," Mantis said. "Could you please come to the bridge?"

The boy looked at his sister. Abitibi was pointing at some feature, answering Moon. Then he looked at Moon and said, "I'll be back," and Abitibi nodded and replied:

"Fine."

He left the galley, his meal half-finished.

Switching to Asian, Mantis remarked, "Why were you using what is already mine, friend?"

"Fuck yourself," said Moon.

"Protocol," said Mantis. "It's what separates us from the slime—"

Moon kissed the ring on his finger—the gesture having evolved into an obscenity over these last days.

Mantis blanked the screen. He looked to the front again, studying the image and cursing softly. There were dead fish everywhere, and he couldn't decide which was the pretender. "You crafty bastard." By the time Jellico arrived, he had given up trying.

"What are you doing?" asked the boy. He was staring at the wire that was clinging to Mantis, his mouth left ajar.

Mantis explained briefly. Matter-of-factly. Then he said, "Come and sit here. With me."

Jellico brought a chair and sat, his back erect and his hands on the chair itself. He continued looking at the wire, but clearly his mind was elsewhere. He seemed small and lost and not a little disturbed.

"I just saw the damnedest fish," Mantis began, working to deflect his mood. He described the pretender to the best of his ability, asking, "Do you know what it was?" in the end. "Have you ever seen anything like it before?"

"Never," the boy confessed. "No."

"Really?"

The boy was disinterested. "No."

"Just hoping you would." Mantis shrugged. "I'm a curious beast."

Jellico shifted, then said, "It sounds like some kind of specialist."

"How do you mean?"

"It's rare," the boy said. "From what you told me, I'd guess that it occupies a narrow niche."

"Niche—?"

"Niche. What an organism does for its living." Jellico said, "That's the same as its ecological description. Its place in nature." He seemed more at ease when he talked about what he understood. "I can't say much. Abby and I have never worked on fish kills. What with the bodies and the fires—"

"They're hazardous."

"Fish kills? Very—"

"Say!" said Mantis. "I have a notion. If this fish has never been seen before, maybe the two of us should name it."

Jellico shrugged, suspicion showing.

"No, I mean it. Can you think of any names?"

He said he could not. Offhand.

"Well now . . . a sickly looking fish, but crafty." Mantis scratched his head, his style clownish. Overdone. "And it's watchful. Treacherous. No hint of its true nature shown, then it explodes into action."

Jellico was listening.

"We'll call it a moon-fish," joked Mantis. "We'll name it after our mutual acquaintance."

"Moon?" He seemed shocked at first. Startled. But then the joke must have soothed a sore spot because he smiled suddenly. Almost against his own will.

"Agreed?"

"Fine." He nodded.

"Then it's set." Mantis said, "From now until doomsday, that fish is a moon-fish. Always."

And Jellico began to laugh in spite of himself.

Slowly, in bits, Mantis steered the conversation elsewhere. Eventually he said, "Seriously, I am truly amazed by Leeshore's diversity." He gave a few examples of his own—facts and figures garnered from texts and his own observations. "I suppose Earth was once the same. Complicated. Diverse. But what with the population problems—too many people, if you can believe that—and then the Wars, there isn't a lot of nature left to balance—"

"Balance." Jellico seemed to taste the word. Pleasantly, aiming to be polite, he remarked, "Actually, that's a misnomer."

"Is it?"

"Balance implies a set of scales. A higher order. Some ultimate guiding state." With a strange conviction, he said, "Mother taught us early and often that everything is in a state of flux in nature. At least with complicated natural systems like Leeshore. None of that out there is in balance." He motioned towards the screen. "It's always in chaos of one kind or another. There's no controlling sensibility. None." He told Mantis, "Disorder just looks ordered, particularly when you're looking at it from a distance."

Mantis gave the controls a nudge. Faithfully and appropriately, *Little Fist* made its adjustments.

"Maybe this is a question of our different perspectives, too," Mantis offered. "You see, the Earth I know is a very simple place. A few people. A great deal of desert. No jungles or coral reefs anymore. Only wasteland, for the most part." He told Jellico, "On such a world there is one higher authority keeping everything plainly in balance."

"Mankind?"

"Exactly."

There was a pause. Then quietly, almost reverently, Jellico asked, "What's happened to Earth? Since you last saw it, I mean."

"There's no knowing for sure." He briefly related the troubles *The Fist* had had breaking through the Alteretics' jamming. Then he paused for an instant, concentrating on a lush green image. On something hopeful and yet possible too. "There was talk about a terraforming project. About making Earth into its old and honored self again. A goodly number of species did not technically go extinct, after all. Their cells were frozen in genetic banks—the same means by which your father and your sister's father were carried up here. In cold storage."

Jellico nodded, listening carefully.

"Imagine a whale," said Mantis. "You know whales, don't you? From your texts? Sure. Well, they were smart and aesthetically pleasing creatures. Somewhere someone must have kept a few viable cells—enough from which we could build a viable population. By cloning. So if someone had cleaned up the seas, you see, and then stocked it with plankton and fish—" He summoned an optimistic face, then burst into a smile.

"What about genetic maps?" Jellico asked.

"Maps?"

"Sometimes Abby and I tear apart a specimen's DNA. We map the genes and then record the data."

"Sure," he said. "A whale, or anything, might be synthetically produced. *If* the records survived the Wars, that is."

"But they did." Jellico shifted and breathed.

"How do you know?" Mantis was careful now, playing foolish. "Who told you that—?"

"You did." He wet his lips and said, "The Alteretics' god swallowed everything that was ever learned, right? So it certainly has all the gene records compiled up until then. Right? And so maybe if you ever capture the god, you could use what it knows." He said, "Couldn't you?" He paused, then asked, "If it's so smart and all—?"

"In theory," said Mantis. "Perhaps." Very little of him was sleeping now. He was quite alert, thinking quickly, judging what would be his best response.

"Well?" said Jellico.

"Let me give you a little warning. May I?"

The boy waited.

"You are very perceptive. A few clues and you're making all sorts of intuitive leaps. But at the same time you're surrounded by men who have come out of Hell, quite literally. All of us have lost dear friends and our families to the Alteretics. A high portion of us had no one left at home when we started starchasing. From birth we have been told how the Alteretics' god is evil and cruel and hungry to command Mankind. And all our lives we've seen evidence that that god is indeed at least as foul as promised. And likely more so.

"When you, an innocent, begin to speculate about using the god for this purpose or for that purpose, no matter how worthy your goals, you have absolutely no right to complain or be surprised when one of us offers to break your thumbs for free."

Jellico stared and said nothing.

Mantis thought of Mr. Chosen eavesdropping on them now. He reached and took the boy's elbow and gave a good hard squeeze. "You talk about chaos being natural. Well, maybe you're right. Maybe disorder is the natural norm, and there is no grand balance. No vast scheme of things. But never tell yourself that that means you should sit back and ignore the worst parts of the chaos either." He said, "Am I getting through to you, friend?"

The boy seemed distressed. He admitted, "Sometimes when I think about the Alteretics and the Wars—"

"Jellico."

"—something just doesn't make sense."

He gave the boy's elbow a jerk. He halfway expected Mr. Chosen to come across the intercom and ask both of them to please come downstairs to his room. But no one spoke, and Mantis, using a careful tone, said,

"Everything you need to know you already know. All the ingredients are there. Complete."

It was the sort of grey statement Chosen could never catch.

Jellico began to nod, comprehension and puzzlement mixed in equal parts on his face. Then suddenly his eyes and mouth changed, and his back at last relaxed, his shoulders dropping. "Okay," he said. "I'll remember."

Mantis said, "Do."

The boy began to stand. He seemed aware of the rules now, something faintly conspiratorial in his expression. Then he decided, "I should get back to Abby," and his face was concerned again. Distracted.

Mantis stood. He was several centimeters shorter than Jellico and not quite so heavy. Jellico had the youthful build that shows its muscles and hints at an easy, clumsy kind of strength.

"You want something," Mantis observed. "What?"

Jellico was staring at the wire clinging to his temple. "You look like a puppet," he said. Then, his voice deepening, he said, "Don't ever put Abitibi on the wires again. I mean that."

"You do?"

"I don't like what you did to her head."

"We did a good deal less than you think," Mantis began. "It's tough to accept. I know. But she is the same person she would have become without any wires. She just arrived a little faster. That's all."

"I don't know—"

He told Jellico how it was for her own good. He tried to blend his language, using enough of the technical talk so that the biologist part of the boy would absorb and retain what it needed.

"But why not me?" the boy asked. "Why only her?"

"She's the natural soldier, my boy. A born fighter." Mantis took hold of an arm and gave a soft squeeze. Then he admitted, "Moon chose her and yes, he's certainly after her, but the two of us understand him, and we'll work to keep her safe. All right?"

"And the Alteretics are worse than you?" Jellico blurted. He was ready to believe they were worse; Mantis needed no wires to know. His voice and face and stance all showed he was hungry to hate and fear them, just like his instincts told him to do. "They're worse with the wires? And with everything, right?"

"There is no comparison," Mantis assured him. "None."

"They slaughtered everyone else I know in the world . . . without flinching. And they would wire me up and use me. Right? If they caught me?" He squinted and seemed to make a decision while he stood beside Mantis. The same intuition that made him a good thinker now made him understand who was the enemy. The Alteretics were the enemy. Jellico bit at his own lower lip and nodded, his mind made up.

"In war," said Mantis, "people change. Or, rather, their hidden natures become apparent. And sometimes, yes, they seem rather like strangers for a time."

"It's the stresses."

"Sure. The terror and the death and all." Mantis told the boy, "In a month or a year you'll look back at this, Jellico, and ask yourself how you could ever, ever have been so young and pure."

"I guess."

"Don't go to the galley," said Mantis. "Go back to the storeroom. I'll have Cricket bring around a portable viewer and show you how to access the boat's records." He glanced at the control board, then back at Jellico. "Pipe into the history files. Go on." He said, "Learn all you can about the Alteretics. And if you have questions, ask. Cricket or myself would be happy to answer what we can."

"All right." Jellico turned. "Fine." And he left.

Mantis dropped into his chair again, wondering if he indeed resembled a puppet with these wires in tow. Relaxing now, the partial sleep came back over him like some clinging warm bath. He stared at the screen; the sea, it seemed, was more choked than ever with dead fish. He jumped to a camera on the stern and saw the chewed bodies being forced up and out by the big stuhr propellers. Fires bloomed and subsided in an instant. The air and sea were filled with scavengers, winged or not, eating with a tireless discipline—their bellies bloated to the point of bursting, the rancid meat held in throats and pouches when the guts could take no more.

Mantis replayed his conversation with the boy, in his head, wondering if he had said enough.

Or maybe too much.

Cricket had not looked pleased when Mantis suggested that they had a ripe candidate in their midst. If they had been completely alone at the time—out of everyone's earshot—Cricket likely would have debated him on the issue. Did they really need to recruit him? Why not wait until they were back on board *The Fist?* Why not play it safe? After all, this wasn't simply they recruiting a boy for Intelligence. They weren't an ordinary Intelligence unit, and who really knew this boy? Hmm?

Mantis was sorry Cricket couldn't argue.

He would like to have said to him, "I remember another young fellow, years and years ago, whom I recruited. Against the wishes of others. I had had an idea that he would make a good officer in Special Forces, and he did. And when we were upgraded into an Intelligence unit, he proved himself invaluable with the building and repairing of sophisticated equipment."

That would have cancelled the debate. Neat and simple.

Mantis didn't want to delay. The boy had talents and youth, and their unit certainly needed new manpower. On *The Fist,* cramped and efficient by necessity, new manpower was absorbed in quite literally a blink. In an instant.

So he was taking the initiative.

Educate Jellico, he had decided. Then make him one of us.

Mantis returned to the original camera, eyes ahead, and adjusted the course and speed again. Then he happened to catch a glimpse of something nearby, off to one side, and for an instant he believed it was an illusion of some kind.

Mantis made a sudden soft noise, part gasp and part laugh.

"What are you?" he asked. "And what, dear friend, are you doing?"

Running across the dead fish, moving parallel to *Little Fist,* was a crablike beast endowed with speed and incredible balance. It resembled one of the stony teardrops on Skyhook Island, except the body was smaller and the shell lighter and the legs were long enough to build a cage around a standing man.

"Goodness," said Mantis. "Who are you?"

He used sonics on the crab. There was a chance that the automatic sensors would miss the obvious among the clutter. He saw hearts beating and nameless organs pulsing with the hearts, but there was nothing worth showing concern. The crab was practically dancing on the corpses, racing the boat. Sometimes it would lift a pincer or two, acting like some ancient soldier brandishing a sword, and its four lidless black eyes would stare and stare.

"What are you after? Hmm?"

The crab was not quite fast enough. Gradually, *Little Fist* pulled away. Mantis found himself remembering when he was a boy, one of the hardy city birds—a pigeon or a starling—would see its own reflection in a stuhr bunker and attack. "Of course. Why not?" The crab could see itself in the hull. "You poor valiant fool, you." And now the boat was too far away, and the crab stopped and raised all four pincers high. "You certainly scared me away, friend."

He had to laugh.

Then he touched the controls once again, teasing *Little Fist* back to its proper course.

After a minute, the crab was out of view. The dead and bloated fish went on and on. The sudden fires worsened still more. Far away, in every direction, they were like cannons firing in the night—traces of some great and vital war being waged over treasures destined to be lost forever, and soon.

XVI   They were awake in the dark now, not sure of the time, and she thought how if only the floor would start to dip and rise a little now . . . then she could almost believe they were lying together far out at sea.

"I was just dreaming about the Islanders," she confessed. She was on her back on the foam mat with one arm thrown behind her head. By staying absolutely still and staring up at the invisible ceiling, thinking, she could recall the dream from its start to end.

"The Islanders?" prompted her brother.

"We were visiting. They were healthy. The island was fine. You know," said Abby. "Like before."

"What happened?"

She told him, feeling it all again. They had been inside the galley, she said. The island's big galley. The air had been warm and dry and stinking too sweetly. Too cleaned. The Islanders' senses had always been dulled by the antimetabolites; their world had to be overly perfumed if they were to have confidence in their worth as proper people and homemakers.

Abitibi described the galley and the Islanders, perceiving a thousand sensations for each one that she mentioned. She saw their round smiling faces with the smooth, clear skin. Naming names, she proved that she had seen all of them. Then she tasted the synthetic foods and drank a glass of lemoned water, sipping the water, everything too spicy and too tart so that lazy tongues could find the flavors. All the while the Islanders were talking—loudly and too slow. Not like old people's voices or children's either. Not like any voice you can pin to an age.

"They swore it was time for us to give up the expeditions," Abitibi remembered. "We had turned old, they said, and you told them we hadn't. Not yet. Except when I looked down, I saw I had Mother's hands." Wrinkled and delicate, stiff and slow.

"How did I seem?"

"Oh, you were still young." Except there had been something—an odd quality to the eyes, maybe, or in his posture. Old. It was as if there were different kinds of aging, now that she thought of it. His eyes had not seemed so young and clear as before. And his posture had been a little slumped, his back as broad as ever, but more burdened somehow. More tired.

"What did you tell them?"

"That they were right." She said, "I *was* old, Jel. Very old."

"And?"

"They said our room was ready. They took us to see our room."

Jellico stirred, then laid still.

"Remember the cave?"

"What? Where Mother died?"

"They had the room done up so we would feel at home. It was the cave again. Exactly."

Sometimes a dream could sound so trite when described. Like now, she thought. What had seemed so real when asleep turned plain and unremarkable. "It shook me," she said, struggling to convey her emotions. "Those worn old hands were mine."

Jellico said, "Dreams," his tone understanding and patient. Then, after a minute, he said, "The cave, huh?" and touched her lightly on the wrist.

The cave had once been some deep-sea animal's burrow. The animal had somehow carved out a home in the then-living reef; and later, when Mother found the cave high on a stable young island, nothing at all had remained of the previous tenant. "Ours now," she had proclaimed, and the three of them had added an airlock and filter systems and generator and lights. For five good years, on and off, they had lived in that fine cramped home. It was during the last year that Mother's cancers broke loose of all the petty medicines and small-scale treatments. And afterwards, according to her explicit wishes, Jel and Abby had left her wasted body on the bed and set a tiny fire.

The fire smoldered, creeping into the workings of the filters and airlocks.

Eventually the airlocks failed, imploding.

From a distance the two had watched the implosion, and they heard the roar of the inflowing oxygen; and there was a blast, scalding and quick, and a fine rain of ash. So in the end, in a fashion, Mother had cheated Father Rot.

Abitibi returned to the dream. "The Islanders left us to ourselves. To decide if we wanted to stay."

"Did we?"

"You did."

There was a pause. "What did you want?"

"To hunt Alteretics." Wasn't Jel able to guess? she wondered. Peering into the darkness, she waited, listening, wondering what he was thinking. "I know it sounds foolish," she finally confessed. "What with the Islanders alive still. But in the dream, that's what I was thinking—"

"Sure."

She shifted onto her side now. She asked herself if they were close to the island yet. Last night, late, they had finally pushed free of the fish kill and everyone had set to work leveling the boat again. She guessed the hour, thinking late. Then she asked Jellico if he could find a clock.

"Sure." A helmet bumped somewhere in the dark, then she saw the faint emerald glow of the faceplate's display. "It's early."

"We're keyed up." Abitibi stood and stepped by memory, finding the controls beside the doorway. The ceiling began to brighten, the yellow-white light the same color the Islanders had loved so—an approximation of Sol, minus UV wavelengths. Gently, never straining, she began to stretch. She put her nose to her knees and felt joints pop and hamstrings ease loose. Then she stood again and jumped, slapping both palms flat against the cool bright ceiling.

The dream was fading now.

She studied the storeroom and tried to recall the cave again, details jumbled inside her skull. She watched Jellico stand and stretch, and she shut her eyes, summoning back the blue-white plastic walls. What she so disliked about losing dreams was the way ordinary memories seemed so pale afterwards. She tried and failed to recall how large was their cave and how its walls felt to a bare hand, young or not. She could remember the layering of the reef, like rings in an Earthly tree—an enormous tree—but the exact dimensions were gone. At best, her mind held only a crude approximation of their former home.

"You're going in with Moon, aren't you."

"To the island?" She said, "Absolutely."

"For how long?"

"You'll have to ask the Alteretics, Jel."

Yesterday, slowly and without patience, Moon had gone over the plan. They would hide on the island and wait, shrouded by electronics. And *Little Fist* would hide at sea, using its own electronics to pretend to be a sailer. As long as the Alteretics had no visual contacts with either, Moon had sworn, their sensors would show only an empty island and a big lazy fish. Then their landing party would be hit with concussion grenades and stun guns, the aim being prisoners, and the Alteretic boat would be knocked useless—sails and glass no match for stuhr shooting stuhr.

Remembering the missiles and nuke warheads below deck, Abitibi had asked, "Why not kill them from a distance? All at once?"

"Prisoners," Moon had restated. "So we can ask questions. And get answers. Right?"

She had said nothing.

But he had watched her expression. Her eyes. "You want them dead," he had said. "But you can't kill God-boys. You can't."

"Why not?"

And Moon had explained. When a conscript is fully trained by the wires and ready, portions of his skull are opened up and neural tissue is deftly removed. The brain is a holographic organ. A piece of the whole contains the essence. A sampling of memories and the basic soul. What's taken is chemically deciphered and translated into something i-ply stuhr would understand. This then is given to the Alteretic god, the ceremony called the Joining.

"The Joining?" she had said.

"Yeah." The dead conscript, Moon had reminded, had had a scar on his head and a tattoo on his scar. He had never missed what was taken; the brain is full of redundant systems. Besides, neural tissue can regenerate itself. The newest medicines make it grow and heal.

"So the dead conscript is alive? Still?"

"Inside the fucking god, sure." Moon had said, "Maybe forever. Who knows?"

Abitibi didn't know.

"Maybe till tomorrow." Moon had slammed a fist down on the galley table, plates and mugs jumping. "Prisoners can tell us where the god's hiding, you see. Catch them, and we can catch and kill the god too."

She reached now, pulling her lifesuit off the shelf. She thought how clever the Alteretics seemed, putting pieces of themselves inside the stuhr god. Insuring a kind of immortality for themselves. She said, "I just want this done and over," and looked at her brother. "I'm just in it for the revenge."

Jellico said nothing.

She sat on her mat and crossed her long legs. Jellico watched while she worked, wearing that patient face that infuriated her whenever she was worn down. She knew there were things on his mind—a part of him was out wrestling with some issue, some nagging question. But still his eyes were focused on her hands while she checked the lifesuit's filters and patches, its food and water reserves, then next the batteries powering the stuhr armor and the electronics.

Abitibi felt guilty for not being more herself.

Yet more and more she realized that what she felt and wanted were as genuine emotions as anything she knew prior to today. Granted, the wires had made their marks. This new Abitibi differed from the old. But what had scared her about herself at the first—her fury and that business with the Alteretic's head—had grown comfortable and reliable, something on which she could lean when needed.

When she was done running checks, she looked at herself in the stuhr breastplate, saying, "Moon once went to Hell and sold something."

"What?" Jellico blinked, returning from somewhere. "What was that?"

"Yesterday, after you left, Moon told me that he went to Hell and sold his fear. He got his fear's weight in luck in the exchange."

"He did?"

"So he goes into battle lucky. Or so he claims. He told me soldiers with his kind of luck keep smart under fire."

"So?"

"So." Her black hair was starting to grow long, she noticed. The face everyone—the Islanders and Mother and Jel—had called beautiful looked so very tired now. "I don't know," she said. "I must be envious, that's all. I'd take luck over fear these days."

"I want you to be careful, Abby."

"I will."

"Keep near Moon. Do what he says."

"Always."

Jellico moved closer and took one of her bare feet, rubbing the cool toes. "Do you ever wonder what Mother would do if she was here?"

"Raise hell, I suppose."

"She was always so strong," he said.

"More so than us."

"What did she sell to be so strong, do you suppose?"

Abitibi was trying to imagine being smart under fire, and couldn't. So she thought of the poor Islanders and the dead Alteretic and suddenly, almost effortlessly, she turned angry again. Today, Moon had promised, he would teach her to use a stun gun. Jel had said something about watching history files, about learning what an Alteretic was. She already knew. She could have told him had she wanted. But instead she looked up and asked him, "What would you sell for strength, Brother?"

"I don't know." He dropped the foot and sat back and thought for a moment, finally deciding, "The trick, I think, is to borrow."

XVII   Their mother had built the biological station from one of the fuel pods they used for their caches. Working together, the twins had rolled it to the top of the island when the island was almost bare, it was so new. Inside was an assortment of communication gear and nuclear batteries, plus a complex and durable field computer. Growing around the station now was a mature wood of short and thick fungi. The fungi were healthy, but they had been healthier. A variety of parasites were beginning to root in their trunks. The parasites were the brightest things in the wood —their colors ranging from hot salmon to a dark and brooding violet— and the wood formed a canopy of several tiers that supported years of fallen waste.

The station was linked with hundreds and hundreds of sensors.

Abitibi and Jellico had planted them across the island, and whenever they returned they would move a few to more interesting and lucrative spots. The sensors kept tabs on dozens of variables at once. They recorded which species were where and what their circumstances were. They measured the wind and mist and the falling wastes, breaking the latter down into its nutritional value and approximate origins. Then they squirted the data back to the station, and the station categorized and collated the data, improving its own general picture of the island.

Old and heavy with rot, the island was beginning to break apart. Just weeks ago, a considerable portion of it had come free. Afterwards, the island had tilted several degrees—portions of the shoreline drowning while a good stretch of kelp was lifted into the air. Communities on the shoreline were changing now. Adapting. Tolerant fungi like the blood-oaks and kelps had established themselves early on. But succession was a quicker, more complex affair than on bare new islands. The reef was already riddled with root channels, its plastic partway digested, and the air and water were thick with seeds and spores released by the nearby fungi. Slower-growing species could beat the tolerant ones—chance and endless subtle factors, meaning nothing had dominion—and the station worked and worked at breaking down this biological stew, trying for a clear and consistent recipe.

A young frond of diamond-kelp, sparkling brightly, was sprouting out of the trunk of an old shagbark.

On the far side of the island, shagbark was rooting into a mound of dead diamond-kelp.

A long satin-skinned two-headed eel was laying eggs inside a drowned skybowl-tree.

A colony of nameless insects had nested in a stand of dried butter-kelp, and when the station recorded their presence, it assigned them a temporary name—letters and numbers chosen according to taxonomic guides. Since the twins last came to the island, some hundred new species had been found. A typical number. In the last thirty years, on various islands, the various stations had compiled a list nearly a thousand times as long.

Opera-owls were in the top of a big drowned needle-tree. They were heavily built birds scarcely different from their fishy ancestors—large round eyes without lids, wings buttressed with clumsy bone and hard white feathers that shrank to scales at the ends of their ropy tails. They were a breeding pair caring for their young. They had built a nest in the needle-tree with bits of shagbark and broken shells and their faces for cement. The nest was a bowl filled with seawater, warm and clear, and newly hatched young, their slender bodies soft and transparent, flopping about on soft gelatin wings.

By chance, there happened to be a sensor in the needle-tree.

Maneuvering inside its programs, the station focused as much as it could on the rearing of the opera-owls and the rotting of their home. The bowl was a couple of meters above the sea. With luck, the trunk would snap or crumble just when the owls were ready. The parents would watch their brood swim into the tangled kelp, knowing enough to hide and to feed when they could; and later, after a few weeks of swimming, the surviving owls would rise to the surface again and fly—hunting the dark open seas for a hundred years, or better.

The needle-tree was now on the island's leeward side.

Fixed high on its trunk, just beneath the bowl-shaped nest, was the small glass-covered sensor.

The sensor spotted a shape coming out of the mist now, running sideways to the wind. It was a large object, slow and making a hundred kinds of noise, churning up the water behind it.

For an instant, the station believed the object was alive. When nothing in the taxonomic keys matched what the sensor perceived—not even remotely—the station went so far as to invent an entirely new class of organism in order to suit it. Then it realized that no, no, there was a boat offshore.

Immediately, without remorse or embarrassment, the station cleared its circuits. The boat throttled down and nearly stopped. Suddenly, there were people on the deck, running—hunched figures calling to one another and gesturing. Bursts of concentrated sound began playing across the island, probing and then echoing back; and after a minute, the boat cut its motors entirely and drifted to a halt, its wake spreading and diminishing and then gone, the water flat.

The station continued with its duties.

It watched the boat and put nothing into memory. So far, the boat had done nothing it deemed important.

An inflatable raft was thrown overboard, unfolding and enlarging and finally lying flat on the windless black water. People climbed down to the raft, and the raft made straight for the shoreline. An opera-owl was roosting on its nest, and when it began to wail, the station took notice. The owl lifted, wings beating, and the station recorded the deep-throated call bulling its way through the thick and dirty air.

The raft came in over a stretch of diamond- and beet-kelp.

Moon, standing on the front of the raft, had to dip his head to miss the lowest needles. Then he deftly leaped to shore and waved on the others.

Both owls were overhead now, circling and wailing.

The station studied Moon and the others. They were people, obviously, and people were not defined as biotic elements on Leeshore. But they made bootprints and broke limbs, crushing fungi and worms, and organisms died, and others were given fresh opportunities when people walked. So the computer was full of calculations now—counts being revised and then weighed against the old, outdated forecasts.

There were voices. The station recognized neither the voices or the language. It was aware that the soldiers had spread into a line now and were moving inland, stepping slowly. They were carrying guns, but it wasn't aware of what guns could do. They had equipment on their belts, sensors in their free hands, and their lifesuits carried enough food for three lazy days.

"Radio noise," Moon muttered in English. "Too damned much!"

"We're doing long-term studies," Abitibi told him.

The station knew Abitibi's voice. With endless patience, it began to wait for one of the hundred prearranged commands.

"Loud," snarled Moon.

"It's the station."

"Too loud," he claimed. "If God-boys come, they'll hear and run."

The raft was lying on the shoreline. There were half-a-dozen kinds of fungi already rooting in its fabric. Both owls had settled onto the nest again. One of them spit seawater into their offsprings' faces. The other used a ropy tail to scrape clean the bottom of the nest, dumping spoiled food and feces into the placid surf. Then the first owl lifted again and began to hunt, its four big eyes gazing down at the bright tangled island and the drifting mirrored boat.

The soldiers were working their way to the summit.

No longer was the station on the summit. When the island shifted, it was tilted towards the windward side. A ceramic orb lay halfway buried in the dark grey debris, the second orb of a hidden cache nearby.

Abitibi and Moon approached. Moon was using instruments, probing. Abitibi asked, "Station? How are you functioning?"

"Well," it answered, launching into the particulars.

She said, "Station, stop please." She turned and looked at Moon. "The cache is . . . there," pointing now.

"Leave it," he responded. "Afterwards." He nodded once.

The station had its own eyes and ears. It studied Abitibi, waiting.

"What are you doing?" she said.

Moon was walking away from them.

"What is it?"

He was using the instruments.

She stood with her mouth ajar, and Moon stopped short of a stout and rounded fungus covered with scale-like bark. The fungus had very little glow of its own, blending into the debris on the ground. Full-bodied and dark, it was something like an Earthly mushroom—except for its mass, which was considerable, and its unique chemistry.

"A bomb," said Moon.

"Bomb-stool," Abitibi explained. "Young. Not ripened yet, luckily."

Moon knelt.

"When it ripens," said Abitibi, "its meat turns to unstable compounds. Explosives, actually. Then the shell hardens and the scales turn to tough, tough seeds. And the bush detonates, plowing up the ground and scattering the seeds."

Moon stood again. By the light of the woods, his face had the texture and resilience of plastic. He blinked. He breathed. Then he started back towards the station.

"They grow in old woods," said Abitibi. "Most fungi have allelopatric responses to them—producing toxins to keep bomb-stools from germinating. But here—" She turned and turned, her own face lit by the parasites dangling off the trunks and limbs. She moved quickly, without apparent weight, and breathed quick and shallow breaths.

Moon opened a radio channel, giving quick instructions.

Abitibi approached the bomb-stool, pulling out her knife, and with the sharpened point and all her strength, she managed to cut the shell and expose the soft pink meat inside.

"That's all," she said.

Moon asked what she was doing.

She said, "Booby traps spoil because fungi love eating explosives." Slipping the knife into its sheath again, she said, "The same fungi make their livings chewing on these bombs." Her voice was high and brittle. "Jellico and I have to come around every so often to check for them. It distorts the study, of course, when we kill them. But still." She said, "We can't let them grow at will, can we?"

Moon said, "Come."

She did not seem to hear him. She bent and rubbed a handful of soil into the bomb's open wound, making sure spores had their chance.

Moon walked to the station and leaned against its shell. Then he shoved the gun butt into the pulverized debris and let it lean too, and he said, "Over here," with a certain force.

Abitibi stood, rubbing both her hands clean.

He watched the way she walked towards him, betraying nothing with his expression. He said, "Sit," and gestured. He said, "Here," and stroked the smooth cool top of the station.

She sat so there was space between them, her posture prim and wary.

"I like girls," he offered, his gaze steady and his voice dry.

She said nothing.

"You like men?" he asked.

She said, "No."

"No?" Moon grinned. "Saving it for your brother, huh?"

She turned carefully, smoothly, and cut at him with her eyes.

Moon laid his middle finger over his index finger, making a womanly slit. Then he held the hand to his faceplate and stuck out his tongue, pretending to lick.

She watched him pretend.

"You make Jelly hard?" Moon asked.

She shook her head, her own face hard and impassive now. Resisting.

"Likes you on top?" He blinked. "I like top, too."

Abitibi tried to stand, and Moon grasped her forearm and gave a squeeze.

He said, "Virgin," and pointed between her legs, his eyes sly and knowing.

Softly, almost without noise, she said, "He's my brother—"

"Shit!" He shook his head. "Two people alone, wind and dark and all this all around . . . you want Jelly bad, I bet. Want him in you. Want his seed—"

"No," she said.

"No?"

"You don't know," she remarked, getting to her feet now and glaring at him. "You just don't—!"

"No?"

"We've had hormone treatments. Microsurgery. When we came of age, first thing, Mother made changes inside us. So we couldn't. So we wouldn't have to think about it. You see?" She breathed and said, "If you want me to want it, you're wasting your prick."

For an instant Moon was passive, studying Abitibi without hinting what he felt or believed. Then he smiled broadly, and a small laugh starting in his belly worked its way up and out until he was lying on his back on the top of the station, rolling, his face flushed and shiny with exertion and tears on his pitted cheeks.

Abitibi stood watching him.

Suddenly he sat upright. "Really? Snip-snip?" He made scissors with a hand and gestured towards her pelvis.

She said, "Yes," with great care.

"*Really?*"

"So?" she said. "What of it?"

He stood and smiled and said, "The only girl on Leeshore," and shook his head.

He said, "You poor stupid creature."

He gestured at the station. "Get this turned off too!"

"Quick as you can!"

He said, "Your crazy bitch of a mother," and strode off to hunt for a place to hide and wait.

XVIII   When they were approaching the island, Cricket made his armor. He showed Jellico how it fastened to his lifesuit and explained how the stuhr helped. "It won't stop a stuhr-frosted bullet," he warned, his voice distinctive and quite pleasant. "Not even a baby bullet. Not even a little." He wore a grin, but he sounded very serious. Very sober. "All the armor can do is deflect fragments—pieces of the deck, or bits of the man beside you. Bullets kick loose all sorts of things in battle."

Jellico said, "Okay."

"We'll have to put a skin on that helmet. Here."

"Let me," Jellico offered. "I'm tired of watching."

Cricket looked at his hands as if to measure their innate skill. Then he said, "Okay," and sighed. "We start here."

The machine shop was the largest room on board—excluding the enormous engine room and the nitrogen-filled hold. Yet it felt cramped to the point of suffocating, tools and workbenches and stores of materials set about with a combination of careful foresight and haphazard expediency.

Making stuhr proved simple and relatively quick.

Cricket showed Jellico how to size the helmet and apply a thin layer of high-density foam. "To absorb," he explained. "Impacts." He flattened his hand and described how the stuhr drummed before it broke, vibrating his hand in order to model his words.

Jellico listened.

The stuhr itself took minutes, and the process was almost entirely automated, a small machine gripping the battered helmet and another bending itself into the proper shape, new stuhr forced out through a long slot not wider than a single excited atom. A third machine planted the batteries and fastened down the edges with stat-seals.

Jellico lifted the helmet. "This is all?"

"Simple, huh?" Cricket said, "If you don't puncture the stuhr, it should last a year. If you recharge the batteries, forever."

"All right."

"Do you know how to recharge?"

"Show me."

Cricket, apparently glad for the audience, showed him twice.

"Fine," said Jellico. "Thanks."

They began walking down the cluttered aisles. The machinery was only vaguely familiar, Cricket pointing and explaining what he guessed would interest his charge. Jellico felt disoriented. The only object he could understand was the used bridle set on top of a table. Moon had cut it out of the dead sailer, and Cricket had given it a once-over study. Turning, Jellico told Cricket how he had been amazed by stuhr bullets—the Islanders had worked on skyhook and dormitory scales only—and how he had guessed that a god must have designed such an ultramodern wonder—

"No," said Cricket. "We thought it up ourselves."

"You're wizards."

"No." A look came into his face. "Well, maybe. A little," he said, smiling now. "Some." He was full of pride. This machine shop was his domain, and his alone. He stood before Jellico, beaming, and when Jellico thought to look at the man's hands, he saw that indeed they belonged to a machinist—calloused on the tips of fingers, strong and yet somehow gentle too.

Mantis came across the intercom then, telling everyone to be ready. Jellico already knew he had to dress and work alongside the crew, throwing the raft into the water and hurriedly saying good-bye to his sister.

"Luck?"

"Luck."

Abby looked tired. Jellico regretted refusing the wires now, standing in the open, out on the bow, and helplessly watching the raft pull away and beach itself on the drowned shoreline. He was sorry for all his little failures, named or not, and he blamed his sister for nothing. After a time, carefully, a pair of soldiers reappeared and deflated the raft; and one of them carried it inland while the other used an electric blower of some sort to cover the tracks near the shoreline. Then the members of the landing party took their positions, and *Little Fist* tested them by hunting for them with every sensor on board. The sensors did not detect their presence.

Jellico and the crewmen went inside again, two at a time, Cricket with him and each hosing the other down—hot water and harsh detergents, then a rinse with strong deodorizers.

Little Fist was underway once more.

Jellico waited in the storeroom. He pulled out the viewing screen and pretended to study the old records—news briefs and selected government reports showing the course of the Wars. It was the same as reading about Earth in textbooks. He felt detached. Only the graphic scenes of the dead and the maimed made a lasting impression, and then only because they built on existing impressions. He remembered the walk he had taken through Skyhook Island, and the dead Islanders, and the miser birds clinging to twisted bits of useless metal . . . and he felt an honest empathy for those who had suffered for the Alteretic crimes.

And yet.

Yesterday, suddenly, he had realized that the records might not be complete or completely accurate.

"Propaganda," he had muttered aloud.

"What?" Abby had asked. "What did you say?"

"Something is missing." A vague feeling had crystallized into a certain question; he knew the words but he feared using them aloud. "I just want something answered."

"What?"

He said, "Never mind."

"Are we fighting on the wrong side, Brother?"

"I know what side I'm on. Now."

"Whose?"

"Mine."

"And what does that mean?" She had turned angry, imagining that he was slighting her somehow. "Do you want me to stop helping Moon? Hmm?"

"That's not what I'm saying."

"What are you saying?"

"Forget it."

"I can't!"

"Try." He had said, "Please."

In all their lives and through all their shared troubles, Jellico realized, never had they been so close to fighting. And now, staring at the screen and thinking back, he recognized that Mantis had been telling the truth about one facet. The wires. This Abby wasn't a new Abby. Jellico had been nursing the hope because he hadn't wanted to know the truth. His sister was doing what she would have wanted to do eventually, forget the damned wires. And he knew this was fact because it was the same with him. From the start, he had helped Mantis, not to mention the mission, and he would keep helping both until whenever . . . however they wanted it done . . .

It's just this question, he thought.

Nagging at me.

Nagging . . .

His helmet was beside him, beneath the shelves. With its stuhr, it looked very new and rather strange. Unnerving. Stuhr never ages, he thought to himself. It's always the same, or it's dead. Unlike people, there's no middle ground. No weathering at the eyes, or shots of grey in the hair. Its shape changeless or worthless, and that is that . . .

Again he looked at the screen. Glass wires were clipped into a slot in the floor. *Little Fist's* computers were feeding in some dusty film made just after the Hardware War, the gist of it being that anyone might be an Alteretic agent. Thinking back, recalling the hours and hours of history he had watched, Jellico tried to pull it all together now into some firm verdict. What were the Wars about? Over all? Of all the people anywhere, he decided, I should be able to be objective. Detached and observant and clear-thinking.

Mantis had looked at him and sworn, "Everything you need to know, you know already."

He wasn't handling the clues properly. *Sure.* Jellico felt answers within reach, only a thousand years and a million more hours of watching film wouldn't give him any help. None. The right insight at the right time— that's what he was lacking. That and then not allowing conventions to keep him from accepting the truth.

Mother had been the expert at insight.

"The trick," she would claim, "is to steer between rock certainties." That was what Jellico was trying to do now. "You can always be sure, no matter what, that the fanatic is wrong." She had taught both of her children that fanatics were the intellectual equivalents of warning buoys. They were lashed to rock certainties in order to keep right-thinking people clear of dangerous waters.

What would Mother have said about these circumstances?

Turning his head, Jellico looked at the stuhr on his helmet and thought about the Alteretic god. For days he had speculated about its abilities and limitations, morals and goals. Now his skull was full of crazy, conflicting notions. If this were old times, Abitibi and he could talk the notions through, hunting workable answers. Not the absolute right answers, sure, but ones with sense and a certain potential.

Mother had taught them that trick.

"Brainstorming," she had called it—the image being light leaping from head to head and back again, gaining brightness and power with every passage.

Watching himself in the stuhr, he began drifting to sleep.

"Friend?"

His eyes opened.

"Friend? I've got a favor to ask of you?"

He looked at the ceiling. "What?"

"Dress, then go outside. Help Cricket, if you will."

Jellico sat up, his sense heightened by the quick sleep. "Where are we?" He tasted his mouth and smelled himself. "What are we doing now?"

"Drifting." Mantis explained how a stuhr gun had failed on the stern, and Cricket needed two more hands. "He asked for you. 'Give me our trustworthy guide,' he said."

Jellico stood, saying, "All right." He dressed, then walked to the airlock. Stepping up and in, he thought how everything was acquiring a kind of familiarity now. The hallways and airlock and the pitched deck, too. When the inner door sealed, the floor began to roll with the waves. The airlock itself shifted, aligning with the outer door and locking tight; and Jellico stood, hands grasping hot pipes, fighting for his balance while the air flowed over him and the sea bucked beneath.

The outer door finally parted.

He could see the water, empty and black, and the lightless thick sky. The wind curled around the door and slapped him backwards against a wall. He lowered his body. Instinctively, he pressed forwards, managing to reach the railing and never falling once.

There were soft green lights built into the deck, illuminating the scene. Jellico could make out the bow as it rose and fell, waves washing to either side. Mantis must have dropped a sea anchor overboard, he thought. "On a long, long stuhr line." That's how he keeps *Little Fist*'s nose to the wind, he realized. They were drifting slowly. They were keeping parallel to the massive island on their south.

"A sea anchor?" he said to himself, wondering.

"What if it is?" he whispered.

A dull dread almost made him retreat. To warn Mantis. Then he decided that nothing would happen, chances were, and almost certainly nothing soon. It was best to find Cricket and help him, because that in turn helped Abby. Abby came first. So he moved towards the stern, navigating by the tiny lights, holding tight to the railing with at least one gloved hand and thinking of his poor sister sitting on the island.

Once, then again, the cool seawater washed over his boots and made the deck icy slick. The second washing threw some large nameless fish against his feet, its face all eyes and a toothy mouth, its belly bright and swollen with a meal just eaten.

Inside the fish was a fish twice its own size. At least.

The skin was stretched until transparent. Jellico bent and peered inside, the larger fish still intact—folded into thirds and seeping a cold bright ruddy light of its own. Squinting, he could just see a third fish inside the second one's belly. It was tiny. It was colored the same as a big sapphire.

This was desert all around.

There were no fish kills, no islands, and the filth from above seemed scarce. Jellico glanced at the sea, nothing brighter than a burning match. Sometimes areas can stay deserts for weeks, he thought. It all depended on luck—a thousand different factors interplaying. Only the hardiest things lingered for long in these waters. They were the ones adapted to desert—able to make their meals when they came, or do without.

Carefully, using the side of his foot, he booted the struggling fish overboard. Then he walked on.

Cricket was kneeling, waiting, apparently staring inside the gun's workings and deciding what to do.

"I'm here."

"Here." He sounded like a knife-owl speaking human words. "Take this," he squeaked, handing Jellico a pair of components.

They could see the island as a faint, faint glow in the south. They worked together by the light of the gun's liquid crystal screen—a neutral ivory glow no one could have spotted past a hundred meters distance. Cricket was belted to the deck with glass ropes. Jellico did the same. Again and again, with care, Cricket handed him components from the gun's hard guts. Then he pulled tools from a pocket and began to work, every motion studied and slow.

Jellico watched him.

"He says I should learn to like you."

"Pardon?"

Cricket paused, a tool dipping. "He says you're smart and skeptical and could be of use someday."

"Who says that?"

"Mantis." The black faceplate was uptilted. The familiar voice said,

"Don't worry. There's only one audio channel back here, and I had to kill it to fix the gun."

"What do you want?"

"Nothing. What should I want?"

"Why are you looking at me?"

"Who says I am?"

Jellico stared at the faceplate. He told Cricket, "All right. No one can hear us." He said, "I bet you two planned this, huh? You and me having this little talk—"

"The gun *is* broken."

"Can you tell me some things?"

"It just happened to break. We're taking advantage of the opportunity." He was working again, the tools making soft sparks.

"Why aren't the Alteretics smarter?"

"Smarter than what?"

"You."

Cricket asked, "How do you know they aren't?"

"They have the same weapons. The same starships. The same armor on the same lifesuits." Jellico said, "With God as their mentor, shouldn't they have superweapons? Faster-than-light starships? Whatever?"

"Should they?"

"I think so."

"If you were to ask Mr. Chosen or Moon, they would tell you that guns and ships require factories and raw materials. New guns and new ships need revolutionary skills and facilities." Cricket said, "We fought the enemy hard, they would say, to keep them off-balance. The Alteretics never had a chance to gain a technological lead."

"If you say—"

"*They* would say."

"I say there's more to it." He told Cricket, "A god is born and its first act is to declare war. A few Alteretics and itself fighting worlds and worlds. And it loses. It doesn't win the quick, clean war it wanted, and in the end it's chased out of the System entirely—"

"Exactly."

"So why?" He wondered, "If I was so bright, I wouldn't pick a fight. Not if I couldn't win it quick and clean."

Cricket said nothing.

"I would act nice. I would do good things for all people, whether I myself was good or not." Jellico said the word, "Propaganda," with careful emphasis. "I would win the war with propaganda. I'd never fire a shot."

Cricket was working.

"I'd make Mankind depend on me. On my i-ply genius. I'd give them gifts—new technologies; new science; new insights—and I'd do everything I could to defuse any negative feelings towards me. From anyone."

"Only that didn't happen."

"Why?"

"Give me your guess."

"I bet I know what people would say. Moon and Chosen and the rest." He said, "The god is evil. Inherently evil. And no matter how intelligent it can be, it couldn't resist the temptation to destroy Earth and almost everything else. It surrounded itself with a few loyal subordinates, the Alteretics, and all it cares about is making mayhem and being safe."

"That's what they would say. You're right." Cricket looked up again. "Here. Give me that component. Please?" He began to reassemble the gun, his fingers working quickly. Then he said, "I'm about to turn on the power, meaning the audio channel—"

"You aren't going to tell me—?"

"What?" Cricket smiled. "What's really happening? Oh, no! No, I'm afraid we're all out of time. Sorry."

Stunned, Jellico simply watched and waited.

"There!" Cricket announced.

"Are you done?"

"I don't know. Try shooting it."

"The gun?"

Cricket stood against the restraining ropes and demonstrated. "Like this. Go on."

The barrels were long and lightweight and built from a tough glass substance laid over a series of thick coils. From what he had seen before, Jellico understood that firing involved two stages. The bullet, like in any gun, was first driven up the barrel by gas pressures; then the coils acted on the metal heart of the bullet, electromagnetic forces propelling it faster and faster.

Each barrel was a small mass accelerator.

Ages ago, on and around Earth, people had used such things to launch ores and heavy cargo into orbit. These guns were smaller versions of the same technologies. He could understand, imagining their power, why his armor was worthless if he was ever struck.

Jellico grasped the trigger and fired. The gun was empty. It made a quick dull clicking noise, soft and harmless.

After a minute, Cricket said, "Quit."

"It works?"

"Perfectly. And thanks."

Standing again, Cricket unfastened his ropes and walked the wet deck back to the airlock. Jellico followed. Helping one another, they began washing the detritus off their lifesuits while the air pressure dropped. In the middle of the domestic business, without warning, there was a sudden jolt and the floor tilted and they were lifted and slammed into a wall, the armor and padding absorbing the worst of the blow.

Jellico dimly recalled the sea anchor.

Outside, the boat was burrowing into a wave. The bottomless water came up over the bow and then washed over the first third of the super-structure, the hull tilting, the stern rearing into the air; and then the stuhr line broke or was killed, and *Little Fist* suddenly bobbed upwards and turned sideways, powerless, sliding along with the steady wind.

Jellico stood, trembling.

He and Cricket hurried, finishing their scrubbing and then climbing out of the airlock.

Mantis was standing in the bridge, blood over one eye, asking, "What was it? It grabbed the anchor, didn't it?" He said, "Like a marlin to a bait, wasn't it?" his voice racing while one hand absently mopped up the blood.

"Sure," said Jellico. "There are things that'll do that."

Mr. Chosen came into the bridge. He looked as though someone had picked him up by his ankles and shaken him vigorously. "Why didn't you warn us?" he shouted. More frightened than furious, he asserted, "If this kind of thing can happen, you have an obligation to warn us!"

Jellico explained his thinking. He was thoroughly honest. He learned that his years of watching Mother handling the Islanders had helped; his voice was level and slow and sober. Finally he gave Mantis several means by which he could avoid the trouble in the future, and he slowly looked at the watching faces, feeling in charge.

"Are we damaged?" Mr. Chosen said, "Mantis?" and turned away from Jellico. "What's our status?"

"Only cuts and bruises, sir." Mantis' own voice was cheerful. Sweet.

"*Only?*"

"An unfortunate lesson," the cheerful man conceded. "But a lesson learned, too."

Mr. Chosen asked Jellico, "What other secrets are you keeping?"

Jellico did not answer. He used his silence with great care.

"You *are* keeping secrets, aren't you?"

"You should have had me wired all the time. Like a machine. Then I would do anything and tell you anything." Jellico paused, his jaw set. "That's what you should have done."

Mr. Chosen frowned, tempted suddenly.

"But we're not those sorts of people," said Mantis softly. Sweetly.

"I'll help you," said Jellico. "I sure don't want the Alteretics down here. Not on my planet. And if it helps my sister, I'll do anything for you and the mission." One hand waved towards the island. "But remember. You need me. You need the both of us." He paused, then leaned forwards and laid his nose a bare centimeter from Mr. Chosen's nose. "I know of things in this ocean that could eat this boat whole."

Technically, that was a lie.

Mr. Chosen couldn't be certain, however. He was sweating, his forehead shining in the dim light, his black hair sopping wet and his knees shaking, structurally unsound.

"This is not finished," warned Mr. Chosen.

Jellico watched, waiting.

"Mantis!" said the frightened man. "Take control over your crew! If you can! Please!"

"*Sir!*"

And with that Mr. Chosen retreated, pushing past Cricket and hurrying down the hallway. Gone.

Jellico waited for a moment, thinking. Then he suddenly heard himself remark, "It's amazing. A god wages war against that sort of person. And somehow, somewhere, the god manages to lose."

"Indeed," said Mantis.

Jellico looked at the big Asian and saw him smiling, his round bloody face tough and watchful. Cricket looked much the same, particularly in the knowing eyes. And for another moment Jellico was thinking, everything suddenly turning clear now.

All the mysteries, in a motion, swept clean away.

XIX

Moon sat in the colored wood, on the bare plastic ground, entertaining himself by torturing a large beetlish thing. One by one he had pulled off its legs, and now he was chasing the head. Still, the beetle was struggling, an astounding strength left in its body. It squirmed and jerked, twisting, and it spread its wings against the pressure of Moon's tiring hand.

"No you don't," he whispered. "Quit."

He was using a knife to pry the head free—the razor edge of the clear glass blade making a grinding noise while it cut.

The wood was full of noise.

Always a part of Moon was listening to the wood, waiting for some sound not entirely native. A biped walking up the slope, say. Or a stuhr gun loading both its chambers. Already he felt adapted to this world—its rhythms and its crazy colors. He understood very little about the biology itself—the disciplines of taxonomy and ecology weren't worth the clutter they would bring to his mind, he believed. But by taking apart the beetle piece by careful piece, Moon taught himself to appreciate just how durable was the life around him.

They had been waiting for nearly two days now.

This was the fortieth beetle Moon had caught and dismembered.

With a dull *pop* the head came off. Only a greasy length of orangish nervous tissue still linked it to the body, and when Moon pulled, the tissue suddenly contracted, muscle-fashion. Neat and simple, the beetle's lumpy brain was pulled free of the head and drawn inside the struggling body, its hard-won memories presumably saved for some other time.

New legs and a head would grow, given the chance.

Moon knew because there were beetles on the swept ground around him, on their backs, all sprouting fresh appendages at an enormous rate.

An experiment occurred to Moon. He looked up and tossed his current beetle into the air, watching the wings open and beat. Headless and limbless, the beetle struck out in a random direction, flying vigorously, picking its way through the blowing trees by some invisible means. Then gone.

Two days now he had been waiting.

Two days of second-guessing Mantis' plan. Of fighting cramps and lifesuit sores. And of bolstering his enthusiasms with these methodical games. If the Alteretics didn't show in another day, he reasoned, he would wait another twelve hours. Then he would call Mr. Chosen, not Mantis, and cancel. His soldiers had their limits, as did he. Besides, if they were to catch the scourge, they couldn't afford passive schemes any longer. Leeshore was an enormous place, and dangerous, and Moon feared it somehow would claim the Alteretics before he had his chance.

His soldiers were scattered below and beside him, all sitting on swept patches of plastic ground. Apart, they were difficult to spot with eyes and impossible to find with all but the best sensors. The girl was closest to him, off on his right. Her long body reflected the straw-colored light of the overhanging rot, and she sat without moving. Maybe sleeping. He thought at least she wasn't fidgeting without reason anymore—those small, nervous motions she steadfastly blamed on her mother's precious genes.

"You're mine," he muttered. "More and more."

He remembered Mantis and that warning in the galley—that silly wind about honorable intentions and noble means, implying Abitibi wasn't a prize to be won with wires. Moon had become furious as a result. It wasn't so much that he had hated the fat man's tone, but more that Mantis had seen inside him and anticipated what he might do. He despised being understood. He prided himself on being mysterious, impassive and out-wardly complacent when need be—or savage and explosive if the situation merited such—and no one at no time had the right to guess his mind.

Moon believed Mantis to be a fool. Surely he was a man of enormous talents in limited realms, yes, but he was a cripple too—an intellect's soft pliant mind inside that pulpy failing body. Time and again during the Wars, Moon had discovered such people. He felt he understood their failings and could recognize their symptoms, subtle or not, and he could never make himself trust them for an instant. Not ever.

Mantis was an honorable man.

Infected by notions of truth and justice, he misled himself to thinking that the bones of the universe were built on such fancies.

Souls like Mantis couldn't appreciate the Alteretics.

Not really.

For all their intelligence, they believed the God-boys were merely a temporary and unstable mistake in the natural order—somehow wrong in the universe's eyes and doomed for that reason.

Moon knew better.

He was not a stupid man. Or uneducated. Or blind. Outside he might resemble a brute, but that was simply the result of hard, hard years of thorough schooling.

When Moon was a boy still, large for his age and handsome almost to the point of pretty, a herpes-style virus designed by the Alteretics and mutating pell-mell came racing through his home province, infecting both him and his two brothers. The sores, black and fearsome, blossomed on their faces and chests and clustered on their groins; and their parents—withered, prematurely aged souls—had stood and watched, immune for no apparent reason and mystified that they should be so cursed.

Both of Moon's brothers were older. The eldest was an honored student centimeters from a good position in a powerful government agency—destined to become the kind of son who could care for sickly parents, and for their extended family. So when an elixir appeared on the black market —a miracle medicine said to cure the disease completely—the parents joined with their siblings and cousins to raise the money; and then Father went to the capital one morning, flanked by some soldier cousins, and returned with a vial no larger than a thumb, the elixir within as black and fearsome as the sores themselves.

Foolishly, Father tried to hide the vial from Moon.

Theirs was a small home, the brothers side by side by side in the same room, and Father began administering the elixir while telling his youngest to look elsewhere, please. Think of Heaven, son, and please keep your eyes turned away.

As if Moon could help but know.

Or care.

The middle brother died after three weeks of unremarkable suffering —some soft cries, some clawing at the sores, and then a quiet coma and an odd smell extruded into the close damp air of their shared room. A pleasant smell, actually. Sweet, in its way. Sweet and memorable.

By the fourth week, the eldest brother was sitting upright and eating heartily, his sores drying out and falling away without leaving more than a whisper of scars. And Moon continued to linger somehow. To persist somehow. Now, thinking back, he couldn't remember his own suffering. Whatever private hells he had weathered, they were obscured by so much that was newer. What he remembered best were what his parents showed in their faces—the honest compassion for their youngest; then their stoic acceptance of his coming death; and finally a gradual horror when they realized that the germ would drain him but not kill him and then leave him wasted and spent.

Moon understood their guilt only a little.

They had chosen the correct son to save, he believed. Too many times Moon had seen fools split medicines two or three ways, or do nothing at all, rather than make the simple and obvious choices needed.

Those sorts of people deserved their guilt.

They had earned the privilege of misery.

But still, being "good" people, his parents had tortured themselves. Day by day, they watched the sores dry and peel away, the skin beneath left pocked and sickly. It was Moon's own immunological system that had won out in the end. The viruses retreated to where antibodies couldn't reach, entering the spine and the brain. Herpes viruses have always had an affinity for both, using them as havens; and in the process of burrowing and going dormant, they managed to kill and maim enormous numbers of cells.

The family managed a joyless and brittle celebration for Moon on his eleventh birthday. Now, thinking back, he only remembered people singing too softly, the songs ancient and rumored to be holy and healing—a mixture of Buddhist and Catholic drool.

That night, in his sleep, Moon had lost his hearing.

His legs quit moving the next day, and within a week his arms were dead at his sides.

Last to leave were his powers of speech and his control of his facial muscles; and then at least the disease was in remission, his body paralyzed and his mind injured and his parents beside themselves, wondering what to do with this useless hunk of a son.

It was the surviving brother, in the end, who had saved Moon. When he was healthy again and secure in the government post, he had Moon brought to the capital and given the best care. Autodocs built to serve generals and statesmen were set in bed with the wasted boy, cutting and probing, then injecting him with the newest elixirs. The last viruses were killed, and the surviving nerve cells were coaxed to divide and spread— slowly linking with one another and repairing the damage done.

Slowly Moon came alive.

Therapy was grueling and frustrating, yet instructive. It took years of isometrics, then wrestling and fencing, for Moon to build his strength and his characteristic quickness.

Only the speech centers and the muscles of his face refused to heal completely. Still, even decades later, Moon spoke no language as if it was his first language. To strangers he sounded like some low-born from a remote mountain village or a lost Belt colony. And his face was an impenetrable mask. Mostly. Its painful ugliness served to scare those same strangers—fear giving Moon a leverage from the start.

He had made that boy, Jellico, nearly die from fright.

It was his sister who showed spirit.

Who had the fight genes.

He sat watching Abitibi, thinking, remembering how in the galley before, Mantis had mentioned his reputation on *The Fist*. Moon's rumored loves and lusts in the brothel. The accepted word was that Moon adored inflicting pain, the stories ranging from simple beatings to knife-play, then worse. The fact of the matter was that he cultured those rumors of cruelty. Each of his women was sworn to secrecy, and he chose only the whores whom he could trust to play along. He enjoyed the sensation of a room becoming quiet when he entered, the spark of fear moving from person to person. Better than sex, he enjoyed the seduction and conquest of a new girl—young and fresh and trusting in rumors—the girl believing always that Moon is about to be savage and then discovering slowly, in pieces, that there is no one who is ever so gentle as him.

He thought of Abitibi and that incredible, unexpected business. That crap about being left without any sex drives whatsoever. If he was the Moon people expected, then that wouldn't matter at all. Indeed, the lack of feelings might be an added enhancement. A novel feature. But the truth was that he wanted her only so far as she could enjoy his wanting, with the help of wires or not, and he hoped she would be surprised by the lightness of his touch and the grace of his motions—passion making her accept a cock more scarred even than his face.

Perhaps some cure for the girl was possible.

There were two autodocs on *Little Fist,* plus medical facilities on board *The Righteous Fist* itself. Certainly someone somewhere could find some way to reattach what was severed, or perhaps circumvent the trouble altogether, bestowing lust upon a woman too beautiful and spirited to stay cold and dead.

"Or maybe she lies," he muttered to himself. Maybe all of this was a fiction invented to protect herself from his advances.

Only he didn't believe that was likely.

Not very.

From the first, he thought, he had noticed a remote quality. A kind of chill masked by her beauty. Wires hadn't hinted at the truth. He laughed, thinking how a knowing eye still was the best judge of human character. The eye and the well-timed threat, too. To Moon, wires were merely modern tools to give speed and ease to affairs as old as Mankind. Like so much else involving the Wars, all that was labeled fresh and new was merely improved a little and then repackaged.

The essentials of the universe had not changed.

Still, in spite of gods promised and in spite of gods made, there was nothing decent or sweet or kind or charitable anywhere.

Altruisms were fictions.

Peace came only to the lazy and the idiotic.

Mantis, the poor brilliant fool, could never appreciate the brutal truth. Settling back against the stout trunk of a tree now, relaxing, Moon thought of the fat man and happened to look at one of the first beetles he had caught. Its new legs were kicking and reaching. A new vitality was emerging from the maimed body.

"You understand," he said softly.

"We are two of a kind."

And with that he tossed the beetle overhead and listened to the *buzz* as it hurried away.

XX   Moon had explained the Alteretics over the course of several days, focusing on what they did in battle and afterwards—the wiring of prisoners, the bridling of wills and then the opening of the skulls and the holy Joining—and she must have been listening, because now, sitting and waiting, she could play back the whole of his monologue without consciously trying, the broken voice strong and steady and oddly familiar.

If all went to plan, she knew, the Islanders' sailboat would drift out of the wind, and the Alteretics would split in two, a portion of them coming to shore and then climbing up towards them, unaware, using their portable sensors and so signaling their presence.

"Which seems stupid," she had said. "If they were quiet like us, wouldn't they be more secretive?"

And Moon had growled that things weren't so simple. An Alteretic on patrol, unable to track his own brethren, might turn and fire at the first shuffling sound beside himself. He wouldn't know if the sound was friendly—not in the confusion of a jungle—and so of course he'd never let the circumstance arise. He and all of his brethren were using sensors whenever and wherever they had the chance—as much to make their own noise as to hunt for others.

"They sound like cowards," Abitibi had said.

"No," Moon had sworn. "Not and never. No."

She had wondered aloud what they would look like. Particularly that priest. What was he like? How would she know him when she had him in her sights?

"Big," he had promised. "Probably a round-eye." Caucasian. "Priests usually are round-eyes." Judging by the tracks left on the earlier island, Moon went so far as giving a height and weight and a weightlifter's build to the priest. Over two meters tall, he made an imposing figure. Even inside Abitibi's head.

"You want him as a prisoner, right?"

"Sure."

"What will you do with him then?"

"Nothing." He had shrugged. "Mantis may try things. With the wires. But we'll save him. For *The Fist,*" and he had smiled, his eyes dark and wise.

"He's the one who ordered the Islanders killed—"

"Stupid people. They deserved it."

"—and everything destroyed."

"That's it. Get red-faced mad."

"Can you hurt him with wires?" she had asked.

"Grind his soul to sand. We can."

"I hope we get him alive." She had brazenly pointed at the stun gun on her hip. "I hope I'm the one."

And Moon had nodded, staring at her face and body like always and seeming satisfied with what he saw.

Now Abitibi shifted. Gently. She found herself thinking about the two starships dueling far out in space, imagining the cold emptiness and the scattered far stars. While she thought of stars, suddenly, she recalled what *sand* meant in strict geological terms. Pulverized stone. And then a poem or two came to mind—rhythmic snatches of tortured English that Mother had made Jel and her read when they were little. Too little to resist, it seemed.

Sand and stars were both used as symbols in literature.

She remembered how they could represent the infinite. The timeless. Or some such grand scheme.

Blinking, she consciously took a deep breath and brought herself back to where she was sitting. Alone. For nearly three days, she had tolerated this one place—in spite of soreness and boredom and plain fear. The anger that had buoyed her up for so long was gone now. Exhausted, no doubt, and resting for when she would need it again. Most of the food she had brought was eaten, the cold soups and synthetic honey finished yesterday. Her drinking water tasted salty, the filters not scrubbing her urine and sweat as thoroughly as she liked. And the disposal chute was filled with dried and compressed shit. Moon had warned her not to void in the chute—the smells were distinct, particularly on an alien world. If the wind was wrong, and if an Alteretic had something called a blood-hound sensor, he could find her in minutes. So she sat very still and ignored the pressure, trying to act the part of the good soldier.

"How much longer?" she muttered.

There was no knowing.

For the millionth time, Abitibi studied the wood all around, waiting for an Alteretic to emerge suddenly, unexpectedly, with his stuhr gun raised and his eyes narrowed and watching.

More than anything, she wanted to talk with Jellico now.

Desperately.

"Isn't it unnerving?" she would say to him. "Humans build the greatest mind possible in all the universe, then give it the sum total of their knowledge. And it turns on Mankind. It shows its gratitude by butchering billions . . . and why? Huh? Can you tell me why, Brother?"

"Abby," said the imaginary Jellico, "why are you so certain about that word?"

"What word?"

"God."

She paused and thought.

"Think of what we know," he said with authority, sitting on the ground before her, his hands playing intricate games in his lap. "This alleged god we're fighting . . . it has no body. No limbs and no grasping hands. It spent the Wars inside various stuhr fortresses—its temples—as much hiding as anything. And since then it's been running. Fleeing for its life. Which all in all is not the most becoming behavior for a god . . . do you think?"

She could hear his voice plainly. It was like old-times, the two of them hunting answers with their wits.

"And while we're talking about fear," he went on, "what about the stuhr this god is made from? Remember stuhr's nature. An instant without power and the stuff is ruined. Completely and forever. It *seems* indestructible, sure, but really it's a very mortal substance. In some ways more mortal than our own flesh and guts. Without the capacity to heal itself. Or, for that matter, without the capacity to care for itself either."

"Sure," she muttered to herself. "I see."

"Are you getting my point? The term 'god' is a misnomer. A bit of hopeful nonsense applied to it by its builders." He shook his imaginary head and told her, "It's smart, true. We can't guess how smart. But when you consider its circumstances—chained to its power source and forever in peril—then you begin to realize how little brains and brightness can mean in this world." He asked, "Do you see what I'm preaching, Abby?"

"Sure."

"You do?"

"I understand part, at least."

Only she couldn't fill the gaps. She knew what Jel had meant about something somewhere missing, the answers hovering partway between intuition and articulation.

She should have asked more questions.

If not to Moon, then to Mantis or even Mr. Chosen.

Mother wouldn't have hesitated, she realized. Not if it would have helped generate solutions.

Mother never understood the meaning of the word *hesitate*. Not with anything or anyone.

Suddenly Abitibi's mind shifted gears. She remembered what Moon had said about Jel and Mother. She should be feeling sexual urges for her brother, he had claimed, and what Mother had done was less than kind and considerate. She had certainly never hesitated when it came time for turning off their glands. "There are just some things that can't be risked," she had proclaimed. "I'm doing this for your own good, and for everyone's." Remembering back, Abitibi couldn't bring to mind an instant when they had argued with Mother. Because you never dared to argue with Mother. Nor could she recall Jel or herself ever doubting the wisdom of the act. Not even in passing.

Maybe they had assumed it could be undone later . . .

. . . something which was technically likely, she understood. Though difficult.

And surely they had been too young to appreciate what they were losing. Even now, the breath of maturity on them, lust seemed like some faint far concept best delineated in the appendixes of ancient texts.

Certainly not in terms of herself and here.

When she thought of sex, she envisioned opera-owls circling a newly made nest—the courtship dance elegant and chaste, sperm and eggs released into the air as fragrant clouds; and the clouds would fall on the clean seawater and unite, then grow furiously, eating what their parents brought and what fell into the nest by accident, and sometimes each other, too.

The image wasn't so inhuman as it might seem.

Not to Abitibi.

Once or twice in the last year—after hard, hard stretches of field research—she and Jel had honestly planned ways to have their children. They would use the biological stocks left from the *Kansas City*, plus Mother's old ideas. On Skyhood Island, they would build artificial wombs of some kind and produce infants opera-owl fashion. En masse. That way they could insure a few surviving long enough to become toddlers, and afterwards their work, and Mother's, would be continued uninterrupted —a genuine living colony begun on Leeshore at last.

So much for idle dreaming.

They would have needed the Islanders for that kind of future—their time and resources and their collective experience.

All that was ruined now.

Entirely.

Maybe it was best, being caught by *Little Fist*. She didn't dare tell Jellico how she felt, but sometimes it was good to think that they had no choices. No hard decisions to be made. Like with Mother, they could let someone else lead them to wherever . . . Moon having promised that she would become a true soldier inside a year, ship-time. *The Fist* would need all the manpower it could find for itself. In his mind, there was no questions where she would end up. Regardless of what she or her brother wanted.

Sitting in the yellowy glow of the fungi, she stared down the slope at nothing in particular. Abitibi's mind was blank now. She did not blink or breath deeply or move in the slightest. For three days, she had watched the fungi and every bird and bug that came drifting through the woods —besides when she slept—and some small part of her pretended this was a professional adventure. An exercise in nonstandard field observations. By watching the shreds of wind that pushed through the canopy, she had decided that the island had made half a revolution since they had landed. Her helmet's internal compass proved as much. And by listening to the stubborn groans of the trunks around her, she could estimate how much filth laid on their broad, strong limbs—a meter's worth, at least, with an assortment of finer branches and brightly glowing sexual organs lifting up over the highest tier and bowing in the wind.

Abitibi blinked.

Suddenly a part of her said to look down, and she did, the eyes seeing a bright blue light on her faceplate, the light turning off and on, off and on, and she remembered Cricket had installed that light and explained it would flash when her antidetection devices were activated.

Someone was scanning.

She looked up, hearing a sudden noise. There was a buzzing and a hard *splat*, and she wheeled and saw a heavy-bodied beetle clinging to a trunk with pale soft legs half their natural size. New legs, apparently. With a fresh head sprouting from a dark, glossy thorax. And she told herself, there must be a nest nearby, because it looked like one of the colonial plastic-eating beetles she and Jel had found—

There was a motion in the woods.

She turned and focused in time to see Moon let go of another beetle. He was pushing it like he would push a paper glider. It buzzed and flew and passed just over her head, its belly stripped of its legs and its head a glassy blister on an orangish scab.

Moon gestured at Abitibi.

He shouted with his arms and all of his body.

She stood slowly and carefully, her knees complaining about the sudden weight. Somehow she couldn't believe in Alteretics now—even with the blue light and Moon's animation. All this was some mistake. Maybe the boat and Jel were simply coming close again, tired of the senseless waiting, and soon all of them would be on board again, showered and well fed.

Moon wanted her moving. Now.

She stepped off the plastic ground she had swept clean three days ago.

The island had turned and the leeward shore was to the far side now. Paralleling Moon, she started up the slope, hanging back enough so he could stay between her and them. Like she wanted. She could just make out the stuhr of his helmet and parts of his gun and the instruments he held in his other hand. The soldiers were doing the same things, she supposed—moving along and watching the Alteretics by watching their sonics and radar and such. What Moon had called a passive sensor mode. On Leeshore, she thought, almost nothing stalked its prey in a human sense. Not crabs or fish or even the boeing birds. She imagined ancient Earthly jungles and tiny people toting long bone-tipped spears, and she tried to take her own sudden fears and focus them into a dream spear. A fearsome weapon to grant her a sense of purpose. A calm, strong feeling to clear her head—

Moon had paused.

Suddenly.

Now he was turning back in her direction, the listening instruments pointing overhead for some reason. He was standing very close to the summit. Nearby, partway buried in shit and bones, were both the cache and the dormant station. She could just make out Moon's face, lit up by a salmon glow, and she wondered if she was right to think he was puzzled by something—eyes narrowed and his jaw set and something in his stance saying that not everything was right.

The canopy groaned, weight on wood.

In the distance, softly, an opera-owl hooted a warning.

The canopy groaned again.

Abitibi looked upwards. A dead limb suddenly broke and fell, tumbling to her feet, and then a single boot came down into the clear bright air, and then a leg, the boot probing blindly for some perch. For some other limb on which to trust its weight.

"Alteretic," she whispered.

At once, automatically, she had the stun gun out and aimed. There was a dull *thud* and a sack filled with metal shavings was coughed from the short, wide-throated barrel. The sack was spinning. It hit the heel of the boot. There was a harsh quick crackling sound, then a yelp, and the Alteretic fell through the canopy kicking, his leg numbed by the impact and a dose of nerve-scrambling electricity.

He crashed to the ground beside Abitibi.

She aimed again, suddenly furious and fearless. She could see the poor Islanders lying dead in the ashes. As if she had been there, she knew this man had done the butchering. His faceplate was clear. She could see his face. He was a dark man, nearly black, and of medium height and build. He had eyes full of a strange cool fire that seemed perfect on a fanatic, and above one eye was a distinctive, bright-colored tattoo.

He had dropped his gun when he fell. He was reaching for it now, snatching it up, flinging himself backwards to take weight off the useless leg.

She fired.

The second sack struck his faceplate, cracking the glass, and the helmet's interior was lit blue by the electrical discharge.

And still he was conscious.

Abitibi was looking down the barrels of his gun. She threw herself backwards and something roared at her feet. Stuhr bullets pushed up through the canopy, just past her nose, and she landed on her butt and bounced and thought now she would be shot too. Only she wasn't. She looked and saw the Alteretic was torn apart. Up and to her left Moon was running towards her, waving at her with his gun, and she thought with remarkable calmness, I am glad to see you.

There was another noise from above. A *click* and *pop* followed by an oblong metallic object bouncing from limb to limb, falling with a thud out past the dead Alteretic and then making absolutely no sound at all.

Abitibi stood and ran.

She was down the hill, thinking only of speed, when the grenade detonated, and the shock wave flowed down the slope after her and picked her off her feet and deftly tossed her between trunks and falling limbs. She could not remember the force of the blast when she woke, lying face-down with the woods all around leaning but not quite breaking yet and the rolling thunder fading away into the sharp rattling noise of stuhr guns sweeping and firing at random.

Some fungus creaked, wood splitting.

Abitibi got to her feet again, turned and looked up the slope. The blast had set a hundred small fires—dead wood and the ground itself now burning, smoke coming off the fires and hanging like a thick black paste in the air. She saw the dead Alteretic; he had been thrown a long, long distance. He looked broken. His legs had crazy angles. He looked tiny, lying dead on the burning ground.

Something cracked and shattered.

Abitibi stood and stepped backwards. A fungus came tumbling out of the smoke, pulling down its neighbors—their colors brightening for an instant, startled to die, and then diminishing and vanishing under the flow of the semiliquid filth coming off the branches and bowls.

She turned again, hurrying downhill.

Bullets were cutting through the trunks and limbs above, hitting with a soft wet *plop* and emerging out from the far side spinning, chewing the woods to bright bits. She was running. The air was thick with filth shifting down through the canopy. Abitibi paused, guessed a direction, then ran faster, taking her air in gulps. Out of nowhere came a soldier. She hit him and fell over him, hearing him curse in a half-wail, in Asian. Then the ground came up and drove the wind from her lungs, and she gasped and felt her senses reeling.

The soldier got to his feet. He rolled her onto her back, still cursing, and he swatted at her faceplate as if dispensing punishment. In the gloom she could barely see the dark round face. She watched his anger fall away. Then he stood—a child-sized man, one of the ones who had cut off the dead Alteretic's head—and he began to hunt for his gun. Leaving her alone, thankfully. She tried sitting upright, breathing in tender bites. The soldier seemed to say, "There you are," because he paused before bending to pick up the gun by its nearest barrel. A big stuhr bullet passed through the reaching arm. It shattered his armor and his bone so that his hand fell limp towards the ground. For a stunned instant, he looked as though he would try grabbing the gun again, with his good arm, blood snaking down his stuhr leggings. Amazed, Abitibi watched. She was startled by the blood's bright, bright redness—how it bloomed in the hyperoxygenated air.

A figure stepped into view—an enormous man twice the size of the child-soldier.

Abitibi tried standing, reaching for her empty holster—where was that stun gun *now?*—and the man turned and slugged the soldier's bad arm and turned and slammed his flattened palm into her faceplate.

She went unconscious.

Later, coming awake, she had the distinct sensation of being lifted. One arm and her head were dangling in the air somehow. She opened sore eyes and blinked. Below was the island—tangled and bright and maddeningly complex—and then she was past the island and over the sea, feeling the wind and tasting blood in her mouth and trying to roll into the air and fall, something grabbing her now and applying pressure to the kidneys.

For an instant, in her confusion, she believed that some Islanders must have survived somehow, rescuing her and maybe Jellico too. She was glad to think of them as alive, and she promised herself to make them friends and family now, to make up for times before, and then she thought that wasn't it at all. She was forgetting something.

Breathing made her skull ache.

Abitibi tried sitting up. A hand larger than some dinner plates took her by the helmet and pulled her away from the edge of the platform. She was on a hard platform, on her back. Above, round and huge, were an assortment of tents and sails that had been sewn and glued together, making a balloon, and she saw the balloon's open throat and an assortment of tanks and a bright sudden flame that roared.

Then she thought: *I'm a prisoner.*

The revelation came at her swiftly, like an ambush, and she accepted it before she could feel surprised. "I'm an Alteretic prisoner," she whispered to no one, lying still and sore, shutting her eyes and taking her breaths now like medicine. Slowly, and in measured amounts.

She would never again see her brother.

They would make her a conscript, she knew. She would lose her soul to the wires and die one of them. It was inevitable.

And then her head went clear. She was worried for Jellico, wondering how he would cope. Badly, she thought, but he would adapt. It was a strange thing to think, but true. The trauma surely wouldn't kill him, she realized. He would grieve a time and then heal. And she wondered what would have happened if Mother hadn't cut their urges early on—if they had grown up into romantic lovers and not just siblings. Maybe they would have been too closely tied now. They might be inseparable. Symbiotic partners, in effect.

"That's why you did it," she muttered, thinking of Mother and crying now.

Gifts inside cruelties; cruelties inside gifts.

Abitibi felt very old suddenly, and painfully wise; and she shut her eyes for a little while and failed to wish herself to death.

XXI
Mantis was in the bridge, standing and talking, assuring both Mr. Chosen in his room and Jellico just behind him that things were falling into place with a machined precision.

The Alteretic boat had been visible just a minute ago, briefly, lit by the island as it swept to its south. They had seen it with the camera mounted on the boom high on the superstructure, the boom extended upwards to push the horizon backwards. Mantis was still hearing the boat's feeble radar and sonics. "All they've got is portable gear," he commented. "They're halfway blind. Just like we guessed." Any moment they would slide onto the still water and split into two groups. Mantis would start a gradual, mostly silent approach. Then when Moon was ready to strike, he would make a noise—a quick radio squawk—and Mantis would sweep in, and Cricket would take the crew up on deck, using the big stuhr guns to cut the sailboat apart.

"You watch," he had promised the boy. "The crew are like surgeons. They'll slice down the masts, but never puncture the hull. We'll go in afterwards and pick up the pieces, neat and easy."

Jellico had blinked and nodded, wanting to believe him.

"Neat and easy," Mantis had repeated.

"I'll watch," he had promised.

"Do."

Jellico was watching now. Mantis could feel the eyes while he worked, glad for the appreciative audience, and then he heard the boy ask, "What's that?" softly, more curious than worried by whatever he saw.

Mantis asked, "Where?"

"On the main screen," he said, stepping closer. "Not the island, no. Above."

Over the island's rounded summit was a spherical, faintly vegetable shape that had sprouted sometime in the last minute. Mantis stared for an instant, curious too, and then he heard monitors coming alive as new data arrived. Infrared was on to something—

"It looks like a bladder plant," said Mantis. "I'm guessing, but isn't it a dying bladder plant?"

"No."

"Why not?"

"It looks wrong."

Suddenly someone high on the island was using sonics and radar.

Mantis said, "Shit," in Asian.

There came more sounds, quick and sharp, and when a computer decided guns were firing, an alarm was sounded. Automatically, in a flurry of motion, Mantis took *Little Fist* out of its passive mode—electronic fingers now reaching, playing over the mayhem.

Mr. Chosen came across the intercom. "Mantis?" he squeaked.

"I'm checking, sir." *Calm yourself. Be in control.*

"Where's that boat—"

"I'm certainly looking, sir."

It was southwest of the island now, in the wind, the sails full of the air, its whitish hull softly reflecting the colored glows. They were running, Mantis realized. The boy, in English, wondered about the boat. Mantis pointed. He wondered to himself how the Alteretics had built a balloon. On infrared, to him, the thing sure looked like a dying bladder. Who would have guessed? What were they burning for heat? he asked himself. Maybe hydrogen gas. Sure. They had those nuclear batteries on board. They could have electrolyzed the seawater and bagged the hydrogen in spare tanks, and they had plenty of fabrics to make the bag with—

Another alarm sounded.

"Okay," Mantis said calmly, sucking air through his nose. "Mr. Chosen? We have to make decisions, sir."

"What sort?"

"There's a baby nuke in the water. It's lying just south of the island. On some kind of raft—"

"You're certain?"

"Absolutely," he said. "Its shape and mass . . . well, it's tough to hide a nuke. And it's going to make a bang soon—"

"And?"

"I want to break radio silence. With your permission."

There was a pause that was too long, even for Chosen. Then he gave a grudging, "Granted."

He had already begun signaling Moon. There had been an explosion, small and chemical, and now there was steady gunfire—plus more scrambled signals between the sailboat and balloon, Alteretic codes. From the running sailboat came new bursts of radar and sonics—stronger, focused bursts—presumably squinting at the stuhr hull as they realized it wasn't a sleeping sailer after all. Mantis began the transmissions and the sensors. He buried his line to Moon inside a hundred false signals thrown in every direction. It would take the Alteretics minutes just to learn what was real—

"Talk," said Moon.

"We got fooled, friend. We underguessed them."

"Balloon?"

"Exactly."

"Fuck," said Moon.

"Do you have prisoners?"

No answer.

"You've got a nuke drifting offshore," he explained. "Move north. Fast. The island itself should buffer you."

The boy called out, "Abby?" his English out of place. "Is she there?"

Mantis told Moon, "Their balloon just lifted. I guess you've got till it's safe in the distance." He paused, then asked, "Who would have guessed, friend?"

"Is my sister all right?" Jellico was standing at the controls now, his voice tight and urgent. "Ask him! Ask Moon!" He turned to the screen and shouted, "Where is she?"

In Asian, calmly, Mantis asked, "Are there casualties, Moon?"

"Three." He sounded more frustrated than sad. He was running, tearing through the rot and grunting. "The girl. The two boy-soldiers. Lost them somewhere."

Mantis looked at the board, thinking, watching the displays for clues as to what was happening.

"What did he say?" asked Jellico.

"Your sister?" He gave an absent wave. "He didn't. Relax. Go over there, please." He pointed towards the back of the bridge, then said in Asian, "Mr. Chosen."

"This is what I feared would happen—!"

"Sir," said Mantis. *Calm.*

"Someone was too clever by half!"

"I'm going in after Moon, sir. Now."

"And let the Alteretics go free? Is that it?" He sounded small and feeble on the intercom. "Whatever happens happens with him. What we need is to hit that sailboat—"

"Sir—"

"—and that gas bag too."

The line to Moon was still open. Mantis had left it open, saving himself time. He wondered how it must sound, your commanding officer not thinking twice—not thinking once!—before he abandoned you and your soldiers to Fate.

Mantis knew how Mantis would react, set in the same bind.

Betrayed like this.

And there were practical concerns. Without Moon, he couldn't beat the Alteretics. Not with them alert. Not and get prisoners, too. Besides, it was ridiculously cold and calloused to leave the soldiers behind. For the simple sake of morale. Mantis knew the fire would go out of his crew if they thought those were the terms of this fight . . .

. . . Alteretics accepted this shit. But he knew his crew, and they weren't any pack of fanatics.

"I can't guarantee a live Alteretic, sir. If we chase them now."

There was a silence at the other end.

He wants it all finished now, Mantis decided. He is actually considering the most cowardly act possible . . . if only just to be done with this sordid business for good.

"Sir?" *Stay calm.*

"Yes?"

"Would you like Moon's input, sir?" Mantis smiled inwardly. "He's been listening to our conversation. Front to back."

Mr. Chosen was absolutely, unremittingly quiet.

"We've found our Alteretics. From here out, we can shadow them, wait and choose our moment." Mantis said, "Sir?" He played his own waiting game—*patience!*—and said, "Sir?"

"The island," the voice allowed, almost inaudible. "Get Moon."

He hit the throttle at once. There wasn't any time left, he felt, and he second-guessed himself. He wondered if the island would buffer Moon and the rest . . . whoever was left. Both the sailboat and balloon were gone from view. The round bulk of the island seemed too tiny still. Too remote. The boy was standing behind him. He felt the boy's presence and turned and saw the young face drained of its blood. Again, the voice stumbling, he repeated his concern for his sister.

"Wait and see," Mantis advised, failing to soothe. "Be patient, friend. Please."

The boy understood. That's what Mantis was thinking now. After the leviathan had snatched their anchor—after the comedy of Mr. Chosen's hysteria—some tangible switch labeled INTUITION had been flipped inside Jellico's head. Suddenly his expression had changed, and his bearing, and he had asked, "They've got wires everywhere, don't they?" Talking about the Alteretics. Appreciating what they were and what they were doing. "It's not just the conscripts they've got wired, is it? What we're talking about here—"

"Is their god," Mantis had answered. "Yes."

"They've got it wired too?"

"Absolutely." He had sworn, "They're trying to enslave it. There is no better word to describe what they're doing."

"Trying to?"

"Exactly."

"They haven't managed it yet?"

"Apparently not." Mantis had reminded him how wiring was not foolproof with people. Think of the dead conscript. Conscripts go bad or go scared all of the time. "And this is a god. Complex. Vast. *A god!*" He had promised, "We need to talk. Later." Only there hadn't been an opportunity as yet. "We'll explain everything. Promise." As soon as they could . . .

Now the island filled the screen.

Mantis blinked, and there was a flash of blue-white light behind the island, the screen automatically dimming, and the light flowed partway around the island and swallowed the woods and then broke apart and faded almost before Mantis registered the explosion in his mind. Suddenly, there were strange fires burning everywhere—the fungi dried and ignited by the blast, and maybe the plastic burning too. Tremors passed through the floor. There was a ripping roar in the sky. *Little Fist's* electronics coughed and sputtered and came back to life; and Mantis called to Moon, hacking at the static walls, asking, "Did you get clear, friend?" and halfway expecting no answer.

"Get the fuck here!" said Moon.

"Your status?"

"Same."

Mr. Chosen has to be in a stir, thought Mantis. I was stupid for letting Moon listen, and he was a fool for saying what he did. "Half a minute and we're with you, Moon. Hold on!"

"What are we doing?" asked the boy suddenly.

Mantis said, "What?" over a shoulder.

"You can't go in—"

"Watch me."

"No!" he said. "Abby knows. She should have them swimming out to us. Now."

"Why?"

"Old islands come apart," he reminded Mantis. "They're weakened to begin with, and a blow like that—"

"Dear Lord," he shot back, remembering now and furious with himself. Immediately he began scanning, boosting the sonics' power and reaching into the plastic of the old reef. The sweat on his forehead felt cold. It ran into his eyes, burning, while he watched the monitors; and when he was absolutely certain, he signaled Moon again and said, "Have you been hearing us? The island's coming to pieces. Swim at us! Moon?"

There was static.

"Moon?!"

A *pop.* "What?"

He repeated himself. "Your ground's unstable. The force of the blast is shaking it apart!"

"Are you telling him?" asked Jellico. "Abby knows. Let Abby explain."

"Moon?"

"In the water!" Mantis could hear the sea and Moon's breathing, water sloshing with his exertions. "Swimming!"

"Good!" said Mantis. "Go!"

It seemed faintly preposterous—in spite of what the sonics swore, the island looked bruised but solid enough. Not liable to break apart or flip over at any instant, surely. He cursed under his breath. He hadn't been thinking. Now he tried not to make that a habit, studying the monitors and extrapolating the fissures into the future, deciding how the island would break and guessing the aftermath.

"Mantis?" said a hard, faraway voice.

He ignored the voice.

"Mantis?" Mr. Chosen repeated. "I know you are listening. And I know now what you wanted all along."

"Sir?"

"It took me a time to see. I'm not so clever as you, of course—"

Mantis said nothing, listening, concentrating not so much on words as he did on the noise wrapped snugly around the words. He heard Mr. Chosen's tone—self-assured and self-important once again—and he could imagine him sitting in that tiny cabin, clinging to his desk, sweat sliding off his face and down onto the square viewing screen, pooling.

"You wanted me to fail, didn't you?" Mr. Chosen said, "You arranged this entire catastrophe for your own sick amusement. Didn't you?"

"Not at all, sir—!"

"Don't lie." He waited, then said, "I won't forget what you've done. To me and to this mission."

The stupid, petty man was sure this was planned. All planned. Mantis could scarcely believe it. What a *fool!*

"Are you listening?"

"Sir," said Mantis. "Please pardon me."

He hit the intercom, paging Cricket, halfway asking himself what kind of troubles Chosen could bring on him later. Formal charges? He doubted as much. According to records, after all, the attack plan had been his own. Which made Mantis want to laugh—

"Here!" said Cricket.

"Take two others. Climb into the airlock and pressurize," Mantis told him. "When we stop, get out on deck and pull the soldiers out of the drink. All right? Then get everyone inside fast. No showers today. All right?"

Cricket said, "I'm in the airlock now."

"Good man!"

Jellico came closer. "What is happening?"

Without turning, Mantis laid a finger on his lips and blew. *Shush!* Then he saw a string of dots up on the screen, bobbing in the waves. Throttling down, Mantis aimed the boat to swing in front of them, counting now and counting all five—three missing, shit!—and using the moment to think ahead two minutes. An age! The audio channels were picking up the grinding roar of the island itself—a deep, mournful sound from near the core, plastic ripping and slipping along lines of weakness. He called Cricket and said, "Now," and then killed the motors. He watched the soldiers reaching for the lines thrown overboard. They came out of the water too slowly, winched up and over the edge; and at a crawl, it seemed, four of them managed to squeeze into the airlock and the other four line up and waited, resembling particularly desperate office workers vying for the elevator.

The island was still smoldering. The rising streamers of smoke and hot gas dissolved into the endless mist. Birds were circling and calling out. They seemed fully aware of what was happening, their faces downtilted and watchful, their eyes huge and full of an anticipation.

The airlock began opening again.

Mantis touched the throttle, buying distance as fast as he dared.

On the deck, Moon was shoving the soldiers and crewmen into the empty airlock. Behind him, the island was screaming, splitting into two pieces now; and for an instant he turned and watched, his stance and his face telling the island to come and try him. He was ready! Then he deftly leaped backwards, squeezing into the tiny chamber a split instant before the outer stuhr door closed and stat-sealed itself.

Mantis pushed the engines into the red and held both of his hands on the throttle, and the halves of the island fell apart and began to feel themselves out, twisting and rolling in the water. The burnt remnants of the woods were drowned. Great pastures of kelp were pulled up into the sky. Waves lifted, chasing *Little Fist;* and when there was no beating them any longer, Mantis turned and went straight at them, then angled, sliding up their faces one after another, the floor bucking back and forth as it tried holding them level.

In a minute, the sea was only rough, churning and combed by the wind.

In from the hallway came the sounds of exhausted men and the strange rich stinks of Leeshore; bombs of deodorizers automatically began spraying their scents, swamping the stinks.

The islands were side by side, kelp up and a few brave birds descending to feed. The kelp was very bright as it began to dry and die. It looked matted and oily, crabs and flopping fish showing in places.

"Where's Abby?" Jellico was asking. "I didn't see Abby."

Mantis turned and was very careful when he said, "I'm not sure where she is now, friend."

The boy said nothing and did nothing whatsoever.

Mantis said, "I'm sorry."

The boy just stood.

"I'm analyzing the telemetry now. She may be a prisoner." Then he said, "I'm sorry," once again. "I am."

"Yeah." Jellico's face was pale and empty. He was staring at the floor, at nothing, his mouth left open because he hadn't the sense to pull it shut.

Best to be quiet, Mantis decided, turning away and returning to the controls now. He tried to get a bearing on the Alteretics. He felt very sad for the boy and his sister, and everyone. *Little Fist* passed close to one of the islands, following the sailboat, and Mantis watched the birds while they hunted for the treasures exposed.

They're just like birds anywhere, he thought to himself. Looking at them, you'd swear they always know just what they're doing.

XXII   Moon came into the galley last, fresh from the showers
and the autodocs; and Mr. Chosen glanced at him and then looked away,
feeling an obligation to feel shame. And refusing! Then Moon sat at the
opposite end of the table and stared. Mr. Chosen felt his eyes. He tried
to wonder what Moon was thinking and got scared for trying. He told
himself that no one else was in charge and that his officers, being officers,
should understand the pressures he felt and the prospects he had to
willfully consider as a part of his duty. His burden. Surely Moon, he
thought, wouldn't allow himself a grudge. And with that, at last, Moon
turned and looked towards Mantis instead. Purely by chance.

"A bright, bright God-boy," he said, no hint of anger. "Who would
have guessed?"

"Indeed," said Mantis. "Who?"

Mr. Chosen lifted his head, the motion an effort. He said, "Gentlemen," once, his own voice cracking. Then he repeated himself, aiming
for clarity and feigning confidence. "Gentlemen." Eyes rose to meet his
own. He said, "Please." He said, "Status?"

"Sir?"

"Mantis." He nodded. "Go on."

Mantis smiled, his expression a little less joyful than Mr. Chosen
remembered. "Our damage was minimal. *Little Fist* is still fully functional. Contamination was mild and has already dissipated." He paused,
glancing across the table at the boy. "We're on the sailboat's path. We've
got a clear view. The balloon splashed down some time ago, and the boat
picked up whoever was on board." He was still watching the boy. "They're
running towards the northwest. My guess is they know they're being
followed."

"Can they see us?" Mr. Chosen asked.

"I think not." He sighed. "Cricket's jamming their sensors now, plus
weaving the occasional false echo. It's clear now that they're using only
weak portable sensors."

"And their prisoners?"

"I've enlarged and enhanced our best images of the balloon." Mantis reached across the table and grasped one of the boy's hands, squeezing. "Both the soldiers and Abitibi are theirs. It's all a very, very bad piece of luck."

Jellico sat without moving, his eyes warm and wet and his expression . . . what? Hurting, yes, but something else too. Something new.

"We'll get her back," promised Mantis. "Don't worry."

The boy nodded once and pulled his hand free.

"Sad luck," said Mantis.

Luck indeed! Mr. Chosen sat upright in his chair, hands on the smooth cool tabletop with the fingers spread, and he felt the blood pounding in his head and wished for the privilege of rubbing at the soreness. Mantis seems to be forgetting my warnings, he thought. I don't for an instant believe this was luck, sad or bad or anything. He planned this to happen. He gave me that scheme of his, knowing I would bow to his experience and his vast intellect, and he sat back and waited for everything to unravel. *Why?* With Mantis, who knows? Perhaps he is secretly the same as all of us. Hungry for advancement. Willing to do anything. Even ruining a senior officer's career, making his own value rise by default.

"Yes," he said. "Well." Even to himself, his voice sounded frazzled. He said, "Gentlemen," a third time, then asked, "What are we to do?"

Moon shifted in his chair, saying nothing.

Mantis blinked and seemed to focus his gaze on the middle of the table, on nothing, perhaps knowing Mr. Chosen's thought and daring not to venture a new plan.

The boy made a sound.

Mr. Chosen, welcoming the distraction, turned and asked, "What was that?"

Jellico breathed and looked at him, saying, "You can't kill her," and the tip of his tongue darted once. "I don't care what you do to me . . . I'm not helping if it'll endanger her one centimeter more than it has to. I just won't."

"You won't. I see." Mr. Chosen laced his hands together, then said, "Help us come up with a suitable plan. If you can, and if it works, then naturally you'll get your sister again."

"A plan," the boy echoed, nodding and beginning to think.

Moon said something to Mantis.

Mr. Chosen started to look at Moon, then caught himself. He instead forced himself to remain calm, turning to Mantis now, and he said to the plotting man, "What about the priest?"

"Sir?"

"What do we know about him?"

"Yes, sir." Mantis smiled and said to everyone, "Cricket and I brought our Intelligence files for just such a case. The priest may be a certain high-ranking Alteretic. Or someone else entirely. But the candidate we know matches his physical description, plus he has a reputation for both tactical skills and a gambler's sensibilities."

"I see."

"Whoever he is, he is good." A certain conviction showed in Mantis' tone. "That knowledge in and of itself is important to us. And to the mission too."

"I don't see—"

"It's a question of allocations, sir." He grew more energetic, saying, "There are only so many Alteretics as skilled and daring as our priest. In part, this stems from the high attrition rates they've suffered over the years. The quality, front-line priests are more likely to be lost since traditionally they're assigned the most dangerous missions. Also, and maybe more importantly, the priesthood is first and foremost an organization of birth and the Faith. Priests arise from a limited pool of children—the Alteretics' young. Limited pools mean limited diversity, and that decreases the chances of truly gifted leaders being found—"

"I still don't understand—"

"I'm not saying that Alteretics throw competency out the airlock. It may sound that way, but I'm not." He paused, then said, "Ask our friend," and motioned towards the boy. "Jellico knows, being a biologist. Whenever you start with a small population, you're shackled. It's true in genetics, and it's true everywhere else too. If all your children need to grow up into good Alteretic soldiers, then only a few will excel. A precious few."

"You're saying the priests aren't good soldiers?"

"Not at all. Indeed," Mantis said, "almost all of them are quite competent. Well trained and disciplined." He gave Jellico a twinkling look. "With a god as their teacher, why not?"

Mr. Chosen shrugged. "But you're telling me that this priest we're chasing . . . he's one of those isolated remarkables. Am I right?"

"Absolutely, sir."

For a moment Mr. Chosen wondered what Mantis wanted—what was the scheme this time—and then he decided that since he wasn't trusting any of what Mantis told him, without exception, he could trust his own self enough to sit and listen.

"Okay," he relented. "I will accept, for the argument's sake, the brunt of what you're telling me. For now. But what can this possible mean for us and for our mission?" *Which you care little for, obviously!* "I want to know."

Mantis nodded and smiled too brightly. Beaming. "I served in Special Forces, then Intelligence, and Cricket with me much of that time. At all sorts of places, on Earth and through the System." He said, "We know how the Alteretics operate. How they utilize their talents and hide their weak points. They'll inject their finest leaders into the most critical of situations, not wanting to waste them on the routine or trivial." He breathed and swore, "They sent a top man on what amounts to a suicide run. We know this now. And from that point, we can surmise a good deal more."

"Can we?"

"We know where their god is living."

"Do we?" Mr. Chosen began to comprehend. At least a little. "Aren't you extrapolating with very little data—?"

"Sir," he said. "Think of it in these terms. The Alteretics had so many starships but only one god, and they put their god on board one ship, in secret, and fled the System. But of course, they had to pick and choose which of them were going on board which starship. And I assume they didn't do such a thing on a lottery basis, but instead on merit." He paused, then said, "They certainly shuttled their best onto the starship with the god. It stands to reason. And since that's the case and since this fellow in the sailboat is proving himself to be a fine, treacherous opponent—"

"Perhaps." Mr. Chosen allowed there was a possibility. Just that. "Although we're a long, long ways from hard information."

"Nonetheless." Mantis stabbed the air with a finger.

Mr. Chosen began to understand something else too. Mantis was trying to manipulate him again. Not to trick him this time, but to salve his wounds. To nurse his pride. What I have to do, he thought, is reassert my role as commander. For once and for always. So he sat and tried to remember some means . . . something he had seen officers do in the past, in his circumstances, or something he had learned in the Academy . . . anything at all . . .

"We are fortunate," Mantis maintained.

"Are we?"

"It all could have gone much worse."

"Nonetheless." This was Mr. Chosen's turn to stab the air. He was surprised by his own decisiveness. "I think it's time for a reappraisal."

Mantis blinked, waiting.

"No longer are you commanding this vessel."

"May I ask why?"

"I have not been satisfied with your performance to date." He reminded everyone, "This is all I need say."

"Then," asked Mantis, "who commands?"

"I will. Myself."

"I see." Mantis glanced at Moon, neither man showing his feelings. "Shall I continue to be its pilot, sir?"

"Of course. I don't pretend to understand that job." Immediately he began to regret his move. Now he would have to stay on the bridge at all hours, watching every small thing. But his hand had been forced. Mantis was to blame—"Now you and the boy leave. Check on Cricket, if you will. I have to have a word with Moon."

Both of them rose. Mantis, he noticed, was walking as if on shards of razored glass.

"Would you come sit here, please? Moon?"

The others were gone. Mr. Chosen heard them in the hallway, the boy talking now, lowly, his words ending in a question mark.

"Moon?"

Moon rose and approached slowly.

Mr. Chosen heard Mantis answering the boy, both of their voices now diminishing. Now gone. Swallowing, he felt his dry throat ache. He took a shallow breath and said to Moon, "Sit." He said, "We have some items that need discussing."

Moon sat beside him, saying nothing.

"About the plan." Mr. Chosen swallowed once more, the ache greater. "I want you to know that I was not entirely responsible for that plan. I had a good deal of input . . . a good deal . . . from Mantis."

"I know."

"You know?"

Moon nodded.

"He told you?"

"No."

"Then how—?"

"You're not smart enough." Moon blinked slowly, then in a careful certain way said, "Sir."

Mr. Chosen coughed into a clenched hand, the hand trembling. "Fine," he said. "I want you to realize something else," he said. "When I told Mantis to leave you and your men on that island, I was trying to do what was best for the mission."

Moon said nothing.

"Not for you. Not for me. But for the mission."

There was a strange, sickly-sweet smell coming from Moon. He sat, watching Mr. Chosen and saying absolutely nothing.

"It was a bad decision," Mr. Chosen confessed.

Moon smelled rather like Leeshore. Like death.

"I am under pressure," Mr. Chosen said. "I am not used to this kind of circumstance. It is taking me some time to adjust." He was sweating, and both of his hands were trembling. He told Moon, "I hope you don't hold a grudge for what I did."

Moon blinked, slowly, and said, "No."

"You don't?"

"Should I?"

"Oh, no!" He was glad for a moment, then more puzzled than glad. "I just guessed you might be . . . that you'd think—"

"You were scared."

"Which I was—"

"And stupid."

"Perhaps—"

"Leaving us for dead and no good reason at all, besides stupidity and piss in your pants."

Mr. Chosen said, "That's rather harsh. Don't you think?"

Moon laughed. Reaching, he grasped both of Chosen's hands and squeezed, grinding bones and making bolts of pain run up his arms. "Don't ever, ever pull my command out from under me. Not like you did to Mantis."

Mr. Chosen squeaked, "I won't."

Moon let go of the hands and said, "When I get the girl back, she's mine. Okay?" He lifted his own hand and kissed the bright golden ring. "Okay?"

"Moon," he said.

"Any way I want her. Okay?"

"Just don't tell me . . . what you want from her . . ."

"You can't imagine." He said, "What I'll do."

Mr. Chosen sat and painted terrible wicked scenes inside his head, and he oddly saw himself, not Moon, in the midst of them; and when he looked again, he discovered himself alone in the galley, Moon gone, *Little Fist* quiet and still around him—an elaborate series of shells running hard across this bankless Styx.

XXIII   She was sleeping, sitting upright with her perfectly formed head thrown back against the moldering fabric of a random pack; and he was standing over her and checking on his work—the braid of wires rooted in the freshly opened skull, each wire clean and new, the free ends linked into a control box shaped like and no larger than a full-grown peach. "Damn," he said, "wouldn't I love a peach now." He wiped his mouth with the back of his free hand, the dark hairs tickling. "Know where any grow, lady? Hmm?" She was breathing smoothly, softly, and the eyes under the shut lids were moving this way and that. "What are you dreaming? Hmm?" He said, "I know what you're dreaming. I know."

He turned and crossed the narrow cabin, thinking, listening to the sounds of the boat and the faint high thumpings of boots on the deck, all the crew up top and working—manning the guns or milking a touch more speed from the sails or repairing one of the innumerable problems that had developed over these last days. The girl was a blessing, he was thinking. A gift. When he discovered her in the midst of the firefight, almost at once, a burden went off of him and made him feel light. Made him breath easy again. Now he had his guide, he knew. In less than a day, using wires, he would make her helpful. Then in a few weeks, give or take . . . a conscript, full and clear.

"Whatever else," he said aloud, "you're bringing me luck. You are."

Perched up towards the bow, up on a stack of spare equipment, was a lone helmet with its faceplate directed towards the stern, lights showing inside the faceplate, all of its systems up and running. A couple days ago, working alone, he had managed to splice the i-ply endings of nerves into the helmet's guts. The chunk of the god was inside the helmet, hidden from the crew. Not certain how to explain the god's presence, the priest had voted for secrecy. For the easy way. Besides, he realized, if a conscript was ever caught and if the enemy ever got him to talk honestly, he wouldn't know to tell them the truth. That there was a chunk of the living god at large. That it was somewhere down here on Leeshore.

"See?" he said, his voice frustrated. Coarse. "I'm looking out after your better interests."

The helmet made no sound nor showed any change.

"I was just thinking how I'm protecting you."

Nothing.

"Do you hear me?"

Nothing.

"Can you communicate, hmm? Did I get the splicing right?"

And nothing.

The helmet was Islander-made. They had found it inside a cache. Its computers had come with existing files—not the maps, which by their nature were temporary; but keys to the flora and fauna, all the research done by the twins and their mother, and too, an assortment of records that this girl and her brother had considered worth keeping. Photographs. Recorded conversations. A textbook begun but never finished, written on the fine art of Leeshore survival. All in all, a good if not solid image of life in this hellhole.

As had been the practice for years, the priest made all of what he knew available to the god.

Not that the god ever offered anything in return.

Not willingly, at least.

But the reasoning was that someday, in the fullness of time, the god would become loyal and sensible and then invaluable too—taking the legions of data and drawing a course to Paradise for the priest and all priests and their conscripts too.

For all Mankind.

Once or twice, without warning, the priest had checked on the helmet. Had the files been accessed? He thought not, but then there might be ways of covering tracks. Of not showing what you know or what you could do.

"Sneaky bastard."

Is that a judicious tone? he asked himself.

"What? Did I do the splicing wrong?" There was no knowing, he told himself. He wasn't even sure that this size chunk could operate as an entity. A self. The literature on i-ply still and all was sketchy. A lot of ideas and not much practical experimentation. Though, thinking it all through, he had to admit that the whole god would not likely have made a mistake about itself. Not after all the trouble it had gone to.

"You recognize me," said the priest. "Go on. Talk to me."

The god had talked to the conscript—the trusted man he had had to shoot himself. He knew that now. The conscript had been working in the central chamber where they kept the god, wires shrouding most of its stuhr surface; and probably while the conscript was clambering about alone, unattended, the god had seen its chance. "I have a mission for you," it must have said. "I am God, and do as I say."

A holy mission.

"Tell no one," it must have said. The priest imagined a voice appropriately self-assured. Probably midway between a boom and a whisper.

And naturally, the conscript did as told—chiseling off a certain segment of the i-ply, then attaching a string of nuke batteries, then smuggling the chunk down to Leeshore in his kit and ruining the assault and then finally being cornered by his own priest, the next closest thing there was to God in his life, and still he had refused to admit what was happening. Speaking nonsense about a mission.

The priest felt no remorse for shooting the conscript.

What he resented, frustrated like he was, was that he had not tortured the conscript before the execution. There would have been satisfaction in torture. A justice. He resented the misplaced compassion that had moved him to shoot quickly. To try to end things there.

He wondered what else the god had told the man.

"Kill the priest at such-and-such a time," he imagined.

Or: "Throw me into the sea when I say."

He had to admire the i-ply's scheme. It had found someone to cut free a part of itself—enough to hold a consciousness, presumably, and yet not so much that it would be missed at once—and then it convinced the same ally to take it down to an unmapped, ill-settled globe of wild seas. To give it a strange kind of freedom.

Then what? The god must have had some plan. Some purpose. Or maybe it had felt willing to take the chance, improvising as things happened. For freedom's sake.

"So you wanted to be free?"

Nothing.

"Leeshore's the perfect place. With the bladder clouds, no one up there could see you. Even if they knew where to look."

Nothing.

It won't talk, he believed. Not now. I bet not even if it had to, he decided. I bet if I threatened to unplug you, to kill you, you'd let me. Just so I couldn't win. I bet you would.

All his life, in one way or another, the priest had worked to conquer the god's will. And as with the dead conscript, he felt no remorse for his actions. He was pragmatic and disciplined, without a shred of doubt in his bones. Maybe he would never see the end of this struggle, true. And maybe it wouldn't end well . . . though he never allowed himself a chance to think of defeat. Whatever happened, he felt confident with the logics of his actions. And his inactions. Even in the worst times, like lately, all he needed to do was shut his eyes and think of Paradise coming . . .

"*Sush!*" said a sudden voice.

He turned. The sleeping girl had said, "*Sush!*"

Along the other cabin wall, set up in similar poses, were the two sleeping soldiers captured on the island. One had a bandaged stump in place of an arm, a single wire taped to his temple. The other had a permanent braid installed sloppily, and the control box attached was larger and more powerful, not to mention cruder, than the girl's.

"You're so smart," said the priest, standing with his back to the helmet. "What do you think I should do with them? Hmm?"

Nothing.

"I know what I'll do with the wounded one."

Nothing.

"For my crew, as a prize for their sufferings—"

Nothing, but he wheeled this time. Fast. He came around and for an instant—a fraction of a heartbeat—he believed he saw something displayed on the faceplate. *What?* Only it was gone then. If it ever existed. And the sleeping girl, dreaming, said:

"Sush!"

She said, "I don't believe you. You're not real. *Sush!*"

XXIV   The fusion plants, underneath the insulation and the assorted controls and fuel feeds, were built almost exclusively of stuhr. Absently, without any interest, Jellico recalled how in Mother's time it was stuhr that made the skyhooks possible and stuhr that made fusion cheap and reliable. Bi-ply and tri-ply could withstand nuclear bombardments; in a very real sense, stuhr in a fusion plant was truly self-propagating, feeding on the energies produced and giving off the abundant excesses—like flowers in the old Earth texts, eating sunlight to live and to give away the sweet nectars.

He was standing on the platform at the bottom of the engine room, and Cricket was beside him. Both of them were holding an assortment of tools vaguely like those that the Islanders had used to clean and service the *Kansas City*'s fusion heart. Cricket was saying, "Remember. This is not actually a secret, what you know. At least it's not a simple secret that could kill you."

"Really?"

"Only there could be trouble. Questions." He said, "If Moon caught us. Or Mr. Chosen—"

"Or I could turn you in to them."

Cricket gave a start. He believed Jellico, which was what Jellico had intended—a little jolt to keep him honest and to keep him appreciative. For a moment, there was something disapproving about Cricket's stance and his smooth mild face. Then he suddenly smiled, deciding to play that nothing had happened. "You've got your questions." It was the years in Intelligence and the experience with interrogations, Jellico supposed, that made him and Mantis so much alike. That gave them that easy charm. "Pretend to work—here, like this—and ask me your questions." He raised a tool and made Jellico do the same. "Well?"

They weren't talking so much as screaming softly, the dull roaring of the running motors blurring every word into the next.

"So," Jellico wondered, "how did you find out?"

"About the god?"

"Being wired, yeah." The tool was cleaning the surfaces which weren't stuhr, a static charge wiping clear dust and grime. "It's something almost no one knows, right?"

"No one."

"But it's not a secret, right?"

"Not like most." Cricket nodded and said, "The Federation doesn't work night and day to protect the knowledge. They don't have to, you see. Most people, hearing the stuhr god is wired, think they've heard a lie. A knot of strange propaganda. All their lives they've been told the god is evil and the god is the enemy, and so when they're instructed otherwise they simply don't listen. They bristle and growl, yes, but it's too strange a thought for their minds to accept."

"Wait," said Jellico. "Stop. Start at the beginning, why don't you? Tell it all."

Cricket said, "Sure," and began.

He had met Mantis years ago, by chance, and Mantis was the one who had recruited Cricket into the unit. He explained how tight manpower supplies had been on Earth—and how units, particularly high-quality units, had to devise means to replenish their ranks themselves. If they wanted to be assured of the best people. And Mantis had been serving as a kind of scout for talent. He had approached Cricket with an offer. "Enlist now," he had said, "and we'll take you as is. We'll make you one of us."

"Like he wants me to do," said Jellico. "Make me one of you."

"Exactly." Cricket was nodding, pushing the tool across the dirty faces of the machinery. "If you think manpower is scarce on Earth, think of us on board a starship. You don't let candidates slip free. Never."

"I see."

Then the unit was in Special Forces. Cricket described how he had dropped his real name to take *Cricket,* much as Mantis had once been someone else too. Taking a new name was a popular trick . . . partly because you were becoming a warrior and deserved a warrior's name. But also because the Alteretics hated Special Forces, and if they learned the family names, they sometimes hunted down and killed your brothers and cousins and whoever. So to everyone and always, always, he was Cricket. He could scarcely remember any other identity.

Special Forces were highly trained and accustomed to taking high, high casualties. The high and mighty ones—generals and such—injected them into situations that had gone sour, expecting them to do miracles where appropriate and not complain. Cricket told some horror stories. He described a firefight in which half of them were killed or wounded. After that, for the simple sake of self-preservation, the unit had decided to change professions. That and extinction seemed to be their choices.

Intelligence looked like a good "breeze duty," but to change from Special Forces to Intelligence required conviction and brains. The unit managed the trick without official permission. They taught themselves the assorted tricks of their trade—like Mantis learning interrogation with the wires—and between fights, on their own, they applied what they had learned, studying the Alteretics' circumstances and possible goals, and then making predictions. Eventually, the predictions began to outperform those from established Intelligence units. And generals, being pragmatic if not always competent, began to rely on them. They began holding the unit back from the fighting, wanting to save them for their brains. Wanting Mantis and Cricket and the rest to tell them what the Alteretics were thinking and what they were about to do.

"So we had saved ourselves," Cricket explained, shifting his tool. "Here," he said. "Scrape here. We can't just pretend to be working, can we?"

Jellico went through the motions.

Cricket described, in brief, how they had worked as Intelligence people. They had enjoyed their own bunkers and a certain freedom of motion. They had asked whatever questions they wished and were usually answered promptly, lies from their comrades kept to a minimum and a lot of souls owing them favors for favors rendered. They had commanders. Everyone has commanders, he said. But mostly they ran their own shows. The unit had a reputation for having "bi-ply balls" because the colonels and generals squeezed and squeezed and never made them flinch.

Cricket told about the conscripts they interrogated. Not the priests; priests were to be pushed up to higher echelons. Always. "But we got a conscript or two sometimes," he said, describing how Mantis would use wires and deception to make them talk. To make them believe Mantis himself was an Alteretic priest, say. To wear them down and break them. Not by turning them against Alteretics, but instead by using their fanatical nature against themselves. "Accuse them of doing poor work for the Faith," Cricket said, "and they'll defend themselves by naming names and places." He said, "They are absolute fanatics. Once fooled, they're fools. Do you see what I mean?"

Jellico felt his arms tiring. He thought of the last twenty-four hours— how he would think of Abby, forgetting she was gone, and how he would start to turn to speak with her, remembering suddenly and feeling guilt for having forgotten and feeling the same dull aching loss once again, as if for the first time.

Cricket was talking while he worked, his voice blending in with the roaring machinery. He described how the Intelligence unit had once operated in the Belt, orbiting a little nickel-iron asteroid that had been mined between two Wars. When the current War began—when both sides had had enough rest to refurbish stores and manpower—the Alteretics had snatched the asteroid. Then for several years, they had used the mass launchers and ores, flinging ingots at Earth or wherever. The Intelligence unit was attached to the soldiers who were trying to recapture the asteroid. It was boring duty, Cricket told Jellico. There was nothing to do. The fighting was so dirty and so close that every prisoner snatched had a habit of dying accidentally in the hundred or so kilometers between the asteroid and them.

Jellico nodded.

"Do you know anything about pride?" asked Cricket. "Can you imagine how a group of people, smart and sensible, will do the most foolish, even dangerous things? Just on the strength of pride?"

"What did you do?"

"We were bored. We deserved prisoners, we felt, and so we went in ourselves. Out of pride. For one day, we were a Special Forces unit once again."

Jellico waited, nodding.

"We caught a priest," Cricket said; and he went on to describe their prisoner—a youngish woman—and how they had kept her presence a secret, locking her up tight inside their private bunker while they tried to identify her with their files. "She was a prize," he declared. "A big, big prize." Maybe twice in the past, if that, had an Alteretic of her rank and status been captured alive. She was the sort of dream prisoner on which careers and easy living could be based. Provided the credit went where the credit was due. "Meaning we couldn't just bump her upstairs," Cricket explained. "We'd lose her if we did that. One of those high-and-mighties would claim her as his own."

Jellico said, "Okay."

Cricket said, "We interrogated her. Ourselves." He told Jellico what he already understood—that priests were not wired in the brains like their conscripts, and that they were born into their positions and not recruited—and he told new nuggets too. For instance, how the priests were taught from birth to resist interrogations. To defend against the wires. And how there was a certain amount of physical conditioning done too. The brain insulated to probes of all kinds. The knowledge within kept hidden away from all prying eyes.

It was work, Cricket admitted. Mantis and a couple others—their best interrogators—began working at the priest's seams, trying to tear her to pieces and learn what they might. Meanwhile, the battle below, on the little asteroid, wore itself down and was done. Engineers moved in to restart the mine, and terraformers came to build habitats, the recyke systems primed with the corpses from both sides. Alteretics or not. And the unit was moved to another front, put in charge of different duties, under different commanders; and still no one outside of them knew there was a potential windfall locked inside of a cell within their tri-ply bunker.

"Mantis broke her," said Cricket. "If you ask him, I think he'd claim her as his greatest moment. His finest conquest. Whatever."

Jellico listened.

"Imagine," said Cricket. "All those years of hunting and killing the Alteretics, and being killed by them, and for the first time, we were able to hear firsthand how it was to be a true, true member of the Faithful. Not just some conscript with plugged in sensibilities. But someone who had actually seen the god several times in her life and who could name names and give descriptions and list lists and summon up details that might prove critical in the future. To the Wars and to Mankind." And of course, they had been glad, he said. She was a great coup. They had taken an enormous risk in hiding her presence, and if they hadn't come up with a breakthrough themselves . . . well, they likely would have suffered. Particularly if they had ruined her with their trying. If the information inside that precious head was tainted in any way, or lost.

The top Alteretics live like some extended family—intermarrying and utterly reliant on each other, trusting each other as totally as they mistrusted those outside the family. The captured priest had seen every facet of Alteretic life. She knew the layouts of the various bunker-temples and their defense systems, and not only had she seen the Alteretic god, she had heard it speak and could describe its power supplies and even told how it communicated with its few permanent attendants—a complex tangle of wires laid over its surface, interfacing with the enormous mind below.

"Of course," said Cricket, "we didn't realize just what the wires meant. Maybe we had suspicions, but none of us said a word."

"No?"

"Until afterwards. After we thought we were done." He said, "That was when Mantis began asking questions. I remember him and the rest of us in the galley, and him swearing that she was hiding something still.

Some bigger something. A secret he could almost smell, they were standing so close to it."

"I can imagine Mantis talking," said Jellico. "I can hear him."

Cricket described the next stage, and Jellico saw everything with his
mind's eye. "Tell us about your god," Mantis had said. "But this time,
tell us everything you know. Tell us what it thinks and says. Don't cover
up anything anymore. No secrets." He had prompted her, saying, "Please,
friend. Be honest. What do you know? Hmm?" Ask Mantis, said Cricket,
and he would tell you no one on this side of Right had ever handled the
wires as well as he managed on that day.

And she told.

She went back to the starting point, back on the other side of the Wars,
and told how a group of people—her ancestors—had given birth to a god.
From i-ply. Building a living, tangible god that would give them guidance.
That would show them the way to Paradise.

"They weren't crazies," said Cricket. "They were smart enough to
manage what they started, and smart enough to guess at the conse-
quences. Some of them were scared or at least cautious. They wanted to
know what if the god turned out evil. If they couldn't control it somehow.
What then? And so they took the simple wire technologies then known
—the stuff you and your sister use, bridling sailers—and they improved
them, and they stuck the wires into the stuhr god. In case. And then they
fed in everything that was known. Like you've heard. They got the thing
up and living."

Jellico was listening.

"Some of it still has to be guessed," said Cricket. "Maybe some of the
first Alteretics were trying to do good for Mankind. But some of them
were greedy. Power-hungry. From Day One, some of them plotted to gain
control of the god and the Faith, and the wires were a convenient means.
We *know* a handful of them set themselves in charge of the wires, and
that's the group that eventually became the high priests of the Alteretic
movement."

Jellico imagined how it could happen. It was like promising to stand
beside a safety valve on some enormously powerful machine . . . and then
you use the valve to control the machine, and everything else too. "Sly,"
he muttered. "I can picture them."

Cricket was talking about what the captured priest had said. He reminded Jellico that wires were not perfect, even with people. Conscripts went bad. At least from the Alteretic perspective. The human mind was too sophisticated a machine to win over simply. And so of course the god was tougher. For decades, Cricket swore, the Alteretics had been trying to gain control—adding to the wires, trying new schemes, and generally improving the technology. They wanted a god that they could trust. A god that would give them its fruits and turn the Wars around in a day. Easily. Neat and quick—

"They're sure the god's alive?" asked Jellico. "And thinking?"

"The priest told us about . . . what?" Cricket shrugged, apparently hunting words. "Plans. Theories. A stew of wonders." He said, "Every now and then, due to the wires influence or maybe its own desires, the god gives gifts—"

"Gifts?"

"Of a kind." He said, "For instance, she told us about a starship that only exists on paper. The Alteretics think it might prove faster than the speed of light. But they can't decipher its power source or the materials from which it is built. Or even its scale."

Jellico nodded.

"The god claims to know ways to make stuhr out of any substance. Damn purity and all the other limits we have today." He said, "It has built an elaborate mathematics showing people how to travel between universes, if only people could understand the theory. And it knows how to terraform cheaply and mine whole stars for metals and power, and it has drawn up a set of plans for enclosing the Milky Way galaxy and making it eternal—powering everything with a string of small white holes—"

"And you believe all this?" asked Jellico, not sure of himself. "I mean, maybe it's just fooling people."

"True," Cricket admitted. "Who can say? What I want to explain is what the Alteretics believe. I want you to see why they've gone to so much trouble for so many years, holding the god tight and trying to make it behave."

If it is true, he thought, then what?

Unlimited travel.

Unlimited power.

A partnership between a few individuals and an i-ply genius . . . leading where? he asked himself.

His mind choked on the scale . . . galaxies being rebuilt to order and natural laws being deftly stood on their heads . . .

For an instant, he was caught up in the dreaming, imagining himself in a universe fashioned into any form chosen . . .

. . . then he blinked and felt the old guilt reemerge . . .

Abby . . .

. . . she was needing him. Everything else would have to wait, even dreaming. She needed him and he swore to himself that he never, never would rest until this was done . . .

XXV   For years he had known all of it, naturally—the capture of the priest, the endless interrogations, and then the sudden revelations that had come only as a partial surprise—but this was the first time Cricket had actually told anyone the story. The process surprised him by pleasing him. Events long passed were suddenly rearing up and casting shadows, not only becoming real again but turning sensible and reasonable and right.

This whole business about the god being wired . . .

. . . it had been a strange thing to learn, yet no, not unexpected. All his life he had grown up hearing that the stuhr god was the enemy; and yet there he was, barely a man then, and he heard the truth and immediately thought: "Of course. I always knew we couldn't be kicking the shit out of a god."

Funny, he thought. I had to wait years to get this chance, and my audience is some half-wild boy who couldn't keep his mind off his poor lost sister. Who seems to be barely listening now, at his best, wearing a face full of . . . what? Pain? Concentration? What?

Cricket was telling the rest now. He explained that the secret had gotten out somehow—that their unit had captured and interrogated a priest—and a contact with a contact called them on a secure channel, telling them that a top-echelon person was traveling from Earth to see them. To have a good long chat, as she put it. And Cricket described their panic. Telling it, he remembered how some of them had suggested losing the priest and wiping clean the files and sweeping out the interrogation room, building up a cover story too plausible to disbelieve.

Another unit might have tried that trick.

Most units, he confessed, would have done the obvious.

Only Mantis and several others had argued that they weren't the sort. There were codes in fighting and codes in living, and you didn't flush an important prisoner to save your precious butts. So instead, they took the opposite route. They hid nothing. They were prepared to be forthright. They even secured copies of their files in an assortment of locations, here and there throughout the System. As insurance. For safety's sake.

Cricket remembered the Federation man, telling Jellico the heart of it. He had such rank that he had no true rank. No title. Not even a name that was mentioned. Only power and his own swift ship and a guard of a dozen or two Special Forces thugs. Immediately, without hesitation, the Federation man had told them what he knew—everything, in other words. Then he had demanded to see the prisoner, transcripts of the interrogations and a brief summary of what had been learned. Mantis supplied the summary and a light attempt at charm, saying, "Friend," once too often, the Federation man actually lifting his gaze and snarling at Mantis, snarling from deep in his throat and warning all of them:

"I am not patient. Don't test me."

Cricket paused. He looked at the boy, the boy squinting at nothing and nodding. He decided that he had talked too much and described too much and should probably now push to the end. Mantis was the one to ramble. Get this business done, he thought.

The Federation man had said, "So. Now you know a secret. We're not fighting the stuhr god. We're fighting its makers, and it's fighting its makers too, and if we're not allies exactly we're certainly not the enemies most people imagine either."

The boy said, "It's obvious, once you see—"

"To you. Yes." Cricket breathed and explained how it was different for the rest of Mankind. For generations, with conviction and desperate energy, people had hated the god. They had had hundreds of explanations as to why the god wasn't more powerful and more successful—"Mantis must have told a few"—and too, there were the billions dead and maimed, each one helping to insure that emotions reigned. People couldn't, even if they wanted, purge the thought of the i-ply god as their enemy.

The Federation man had chewed on them for several hours. Cricket remembered how he had spoken—his voice level and chilled, the words clipped and practiced—and then suddenly, without warning, he had glared at their sweating faces and announced, "All right. So you're warned. I don't ever want you to pull this shit again. Am I clear? You made a mistake. You were a cocky unit and thought yourselves invulnerable, and now you know better. Priests go upstairs. To me. Priests are not your responsibility, and I never want you touching one again."

They had nodded. As one.

"All right." He had said, "All right. I want you to clean up your files here. No traces of the priest. And I want you to erase any other evidence that you might have stuck somewhere. I'll warn you, what you know is so big and so strange that no one will listen. So don't think of using what you know. Is that understood? Don't tempt me." He had said, "With a minute's work, I can cause you a wicked amount of suffering—"

The boy interrupted, asking, "How?"

"He didn't have to explain," said Cricket. "We knew. Because then he looked at each of us and said our names. Not our warrior names, but the family-given names. Do you see—?"

"He'd tell the Alteretics—?"

"In an instant. And they'd manage his retribution for him. Free of all charges."

Jellico asked, "Did you ever see another priest?"

"No, no." Cricket said that not long afterwards the final War wound down, and the Alteretics, in desperation, snatched the starships and fled with their god. A call went out for volunteers. As a unit, Cricket and the rest had embarked. There were many reasons. He wouldn't go into them now, he promised. Politics were part of it, and the fear of getting swept up in purges too.

"So why did you want me to know?" asked Jellico. "About the god."

"Mantis guessed that you'd decipher the puzzle on your own." He nodded, admitting, "Mantis has a way of knowing what people can do. He does. And I don't know . . . maybe he thought it would be better for you, learning it down here. He didn't want you asking the wrong questions on *The Fist.*"

The boy stood, the work finished. He was dropping the tool to his side and thinking, his face hard and his eyes intent on something imagined.

"What are you thinking?"

"Mantis wants me in your unit."

"We don't get quality like you. Not often enough."

He blinked and said, "I won't join."

Cricket said, "No?"

"No." His voice was hard and certain. "I'm staying on Leeshore. With Abby."

"Are you?"

He nodded, something in his face scared too. Vulnerable.

"I wish you luck," said Cricket. "But we will chase you and catch you eventually. We've got your maps, and we've got the speed."

Jellico sighed and said, "I'll tell what I know."

"Pardon?"

"I'll go to Mr. Chosen. I'll explain what the god is—"

"What? You're planning to make trouble? Hmm?" Cricket was amazed, the conversation taking this turn. "You're threatening us?"

The boy seemed very young. Timid now, and unsure.

"You believe Mr. Chosen would do what? Hmm? If he knew our secret, what would happen?"

He said nothing.

"Nothing." Cricket told him, "Mr. Chosen is the sort of man, living a thousand years ago, who would believe the Earth is the center of the universe. No evidence would sway him. Public opinion would be everything. He simply lacks the imagination—"

"Or Moon."

"Moon?" He was ready. "Moon is no fool. He may already suspect." Cricket said, "What's your plan? Hmm? Are you going to spread discontent? Is that it? Do you think you can start a rebellion on *The Fist* because you, a strange half-wild boy, claims an equally strange story is true?"

Jellico said, "Do you want the risk?" and he summoned up a moment of courage. "I'll do it."

"Don't threaten," Cricket warned. "I'm sorry. We can't, in all good conscience, let you remain here. You're doing no one any good. Not even to yourselves." Then he said, "Least of all to yourselves."

The boy said nothing.

"Come on. We're done," Cricket announced in a large way. He set down his own equipment and said, "Thanks for your help," with a careful voice.

Jellico made no sound.

Working together, they gathered up the tools and left, each thinking his own thoughts. They climbed out of the engine room and into the next stuhr sphere, and Jellico, deflated, said something about needing time to think. Alone.

"All you need," Cricket promised. "We want what's best for the both of you." He meant that and made it sound earnest. "Go on."

Jellico continued forwards. Cricket turned and took the tools into the machine shop, then stopped and stood and tried mightily to remember what he had wanted to do now.

The stuhr-fabricating gear. That's right.

It had been acting up. He changed tools and approached the bench while thinking about stuhr in general. In his mind's eye he saw the bright mirrored hull of the starship—layers upon layers of tri-ply to protect the crew from dust and particle bombardments—and the enormous empty fuel tanks and the enormous trailing engines; and he thought about how *The Fist* was home now, how he took his identity and purpose from people on board the ship and how he understood what Jellico must be feeling, sitting alone in that storeroom with his tiny life unraveled . . . his poor sister captured and her prospects, at best, dim . . .

He set to work, shifting gears, thinking about the god now. *The Fist* was chasing the stuhr god. Mantis said the chances were good. Their orders were strict. The enemy starship was to be crippled, not destroyed, and then captured. The god had to be captured intact, alive, so that they could be sure just what they had found. So there were no mistakes.

Then they would wait.

For orders.

For someone back on Earth to decide what to do with the i-ply stuhr that had caused all the suffering and waste.

Cricket did not know how others felt, but he himself lived for his simple tools and the splendid things they could build and care for. He knew a workman's love for machines, and he knew too a responsibility that came along with the building. A deep, profound responsibility which said that he must maintain what he built at whatever the costs . . .

. . . and they would wait for orders.

For years, perhaps.

And in the end, maybe, they would be told to destroy the god.

Or maybe set it free.

Or maybe the i-ply would simply get a new set of masters.

He stood over the bench, thinking. He considered starships faster than dreams and dreams larger than universes, and he wondered what he would say, given a say. Kill the god. Or set it free. Or what?

What?

He didn't have the wisdom to decide, and that was the most he knew. He was too tiny and stupid. Everyone was.

"And we always will be too."

XXVI Before her eyes came open, sleep falling away, Abitibi felt the hull behind and below her and heard the whimpering sounds of men and the steady rush of waves. She could smell that the seals of the cabin were failing, the stinks of Leeshore thick in the air. She wasn't the least surprised when she actually looked forward and saw a giant kneeling before her—a long chiseled face with lips pressed tightly together and the eyes close and colorless and unblinking.

Reflexively, Abitibi tried to move.

The Alteretic was holding a tiny sophisticated control in one hand, and by scarcely moving a finger, he caused her muscles to turn to putty and her bones to hum, a bitter bright whine in her ears.

"Who are you?" she asked, the words catching in her throat. "What are you doing to me?"

The Alteretic said nothing; he simply stared, blinking once, and then reached above her head. She felt a tug. She tried turning her head and couldn't, her neck rigid, and when she breathed now, she smelled his breath and the perspiration leaking from his lifesuit. She saw herself in his big stuhr breastplate. He wasn't wearing a helmet, but two were nearby. She saw him fiddling with a braid of glass wires rooted in her head, her head shaved smooth and clean. There was a round control box on the other end of the braid. He had it in one hand, the big fingers fiddling. She said, "Am I finished?"

He said, "What?"

"Am I one of you?" She asked, "Am I?"

"Everyone everywhere's an Alteretic." The giant had a clear, smooth voice lacking any hint as to age or emotion. "The wires and patience are all it takes, and then they realize their nature."

She said nothing.

He sat back down on the floor, smiling absently. "Abby," he said, waiting for her eyes. He said, "Did you dream while you were sleeping?"

She couldn't recall.

"You did. And later you talked. You told me about yourself and your brother and the wicked men with their boat and guns and their wish to catch prisoners. To catch me." Again he smiled. She was looking at the size of him, then his face. She noticed there was a glassy wire attached to his right temple, and she thought of the soldiers she had seen on *Little Fist*, sleeping. She started to ask about the wire, and he anticipated the question. He said, "I never have to rest all at once. I'm awake and under at the same time," and he smiled a third time. Only it wasn't a smile, she realized. He was merely pretending the expression. And she looked at his face, concentrating on his eyes, and saw something that made her wince. A coldness of some kind. Moon had had the coldness, but not so much. Not nearly. "I'm your priest," he said. "Abby? What does priest mean to you? Hmm?"

She had been dreaming. She could almost remember—

"Abby?"

Again, only more slowly this time, Abitibi moved. She reached with one hand and felt the wires, touching and cautiously testing. Her skin was itching. She leaned against the cool sweating glass of the hull and rubbed her head gingerly against the glass, soothing her scalp. The wires were nothing like the wires she had worn on *Little Fist*. She felt how they burrowed through her bone and into the brain itself. Tugging once, she felt pain. She let her hand fall away.

"I don't want this," she said.

"Don't you?"

"No."

"No?"

She looked at her reflections in the armor, and again heard whimpering from men nearby. In pleasure or pain . . . she wasn't sure.

"What else did I tell you?"

He blinked, saying nothing.

She looked past him, towards the bow. She saw the equipment stacked high and noticed one of her own helmets set out and operating. Why? "What do you want from me?" she squeaked.

"You do *sound* like an Alteretic." He nodded, smiling once more. "We Alteretics are always asking how we can serve our fellows." He waited for a long moment, then explained, "You were telling me about these things." He motioned. "What are they called? Bridles? And they work on what fishes? Sailers, you called them?"

"Sailers. Yes." Abitibi recognized the contents from two caches, and also scattered gear and supplies from Skyhook Island. One package was labeled *Medical Supplies*—antimetabolites, she guessed, judging by its looks. To the other side was the bulk of the cabin, hidden, some screen or sheet hanging . . . no, sailcloth. Carbon cloth, black and lustrous, hung in two sections overlapped slightly to form a simple doorway.

The whimpering sounds were coming from beyond the carbon cloth.

Over the wind sounds and water was the unmistakable soft moaning of someone suffering.

"Sailers," he repeated.

"What are you going to do with me?"

"What should I do?" he asked. "You killed one of my precious few."

"Not me," she said.

"No?"

"I didn't." Taking a deep breath, she smelled . . . what? There was a familiar odor. Fishy. It had been in the air all this time, and she could almost identify the source—

"I'm not interested in punishing, Abby. You killed him or you didn't. It doesn't matter." He said, "What I want is for you to repent and be mine," and he shrugged, the gesture charitable. Forgiving.

She was smelling sailers. They were sailers.

"Where are we?" she asked.

"Here." The Alteretic had a small projecting instrument in one hand now. He threw a familiar map on the hull beside Abitibi's head, and then he carefully pointed.

She had been sleeping . . . what? A couple days? she guessed. Judging distances and sailing times, she felt glad that they had gotten far away. But *Little Fist* had to be shadowing them somehow. North of the priest's finger, she noticed, was a cluster of dots on the blackness of the sea—one of the random aggregates of islands that happened every so often. Accidental archipelagoes, Mother had called them. Their whiteness penetrated into the glass of the hull, sparkles showing where there were imperfections in the aluminum frame.

"Sailers," he said a third time.

"We're in a school, aren't we?" she said. "You can smell them."

"My men up on deck, as of now, have counted hundreds of them." He moved the control box in his other hand, causing fire inside Abitibi's skull. Not a painful fire, but cleansing. Scouring. She felt fear and distrust fall away. She was aware that her breathing had slowed, and the beating of her heart too; and she stared at the priest's lean ascetic face and waited and waited, him finally asking, "Do you remember? When we were talking about the sailers?"

"Before?" She thought and said, "Maybe."

"I've got us moving like they move. They're affording us a measure of protection. A camouflage." He waited, then said, "Tell me what you can about sailers."

She thought of all the ways she could answer, her mouth open and no sound coming.

"I've been through your records. Your research. You never quite say how they decide where to go." He asked, "Are they like Earthly fish, each responding to pressure waves and to dim-witted neighbors? Or like higher organisms, with leaders and many followers and discipline and purpose?"

"In schooling species, usually, the school is led by a large bull." Listening to herself, she sounded calm. Matter-of-fact. "The bull's near the leading edge. Watching for food and what not."

"Can you identify the leader?"

She thought, then said, "Most of the time." She blinked and thought how very much she loved the man's voice—its tone and timbre—and she remembered when she had hated him, wanting him and all the Alteretics dead, only now when she thought of her reasons why . . . what? The same reasons still held, plus some powerful new ones. Only they mattered for nothing any longer, and she felt as though she had been reborn. All she wanted was to be told where she could best help this man, or any Alteretic, and she breathed and looked at the priest and said as much to him.

"Fine," he said. "Very good."

"What do you want with the bull?"

"To catch him," he explained.

"And?"

"Use a bridle, too." He had more questions. He wanted to know specific commands that a bridle recognized, and also the strength and endurance of a sailer. Abitibi talked, the matter-of-fact voice holding steady. Would a sailer do such-and-such? he wondered. If properly told, she decided. Then suddenly, the conversation finished, and he stood up as straight as the close ceiling allowed. He said, "Wait."

"I will."

And he was gone.

Abitibi was ready to wait until she starved. Or so it felt. Touching the glassy wires, she imagined the currents laced through her brain. The priest was very much holding onto her soul, and she could not think of a man whom she would trust more with whole worlds and Mankind. She felt a pride for being allowed so close to him and pride for having the chance to help him and his cause; and a part of her consciousness said that no matter what happened in the future, Abitibi was never forgetting the joy she felt now, selflessly serving a cause.

She waited, and waited, and still waited.

Up high was that one helmet, its systems running. She sat staring at the black faceplate, wondering if she should turn it off and save the batteries and save it wear . . . and the priest returned, saying, "What are you looking at?"

She told.

"What? Did it do anything?"

"No."

"It didn't make a noise, did it?"

She said, "No."

He stared at the helmet for a moment, his expression complex and shifting. Then he said, "All right. Come," and he kneeled and grasped a bridle, the control box and map projector both in his other hand. "With me. Come on."

She rose, joining him.

They moved towards the stern, between the hanging sails. When they were in the larger part of the cabin, she saw conscripts sitting on both sides, all suited up, guns and helmets close and large glass knives in every other hand. Lying on the floor between them, tiny and nude, was the young soldier who had been shot on the island. She remembered him being shot. She looked at him and at them and thought: *This reminds me of what? What does this look like?* The soldier was covered with wounds; the knife blades were self-heating, apparently, cauterizing as they cut. The wounds were interlocking like the boundary lines of countries, and she thought: *I know. This looks like people at a galley table.* It did. The conscripts were waiting to eat.

Abitibi felt numb in her knees.

The priest said, "Sit up there. They've saved you a place," and he set down the bridle and manipulated the control box. "Go on."

The numbness subsided. She walked around the soldier and squatted and sat on the cool bare glass of the floor. She pulled out her knife without thinking about what she was doing. The soldier was watching only her, his head adorned with wires glued and taped in place. His wounded arm, she noticed, had been cut away and the stump bandaged. There was sweat on the soldier's face. Pain made him weep. She thought: *Of course he's dampening the pain,* meaning the priest. She had no doubts as to the correctness of what everyone was doing. She loved the priest and the Faith, and the scene was full of an intense beauty unlike any she had ever known.

"You get the head," said the priest. "The head is an honor."

She remembered the earlier island and the conscript whose head she had kicked. *But he was dead,* she thought. *Dead and past pain.*

"All right," said the priest. "Now."

The conscripts began cutting at the living flesh, the hot blades sizzling and the meat curling and cooking. The poor soldier flinched and went rigid, his eyes turning glassy. Abitibi did nothing but watch him. She realized that he felt everything, that the wires only deadened his voice and kept him from passing out. He managed a quick whimper. He couldn't move. She was sweating now, like him, and her sweat dripped into his eyes now and again. She made herself move backwards, the knife in her hand still and her arm resisting, and she glanced at the conscripts and saw a uniform joy. This was a feast to them. A great occasion.

Past them, kneeling again, the priest was working. He had removed a new helmet—one of Abby's—from its fluorocarbon wrappings, and now he was detaching its bridle controls. Beside him, sleeping, was another soldier from *Little Fist.* Another prisoner. The priest had the soldier's helmet in his lap now. He was starting to add the controls to that helmet, and all at once Abitibi understood his plans.

Deep inside her head, out of reach of the wires, was a voice.

Kill the fucker! said the voice.

Grab a gun and kill them all!

Now, it said. *Do it!*

Only she couldn't force herself to try. The wires kept her eyes off the guns and drew strength from her folded legs. Instead she had to watch the soldier's face—slick with sweat and the pain—and she heard the cooking sounds and the savage eating sounds, the conscripts laughing among themselves with smooth hard voices—compassion something forgotten in another lifetime, it seemed.

She remembered the crabs she had watched as a little girl, and the full-grown boeing bird they were eating. The bird had struck the skyhook and tumbled. Its wing was shattered, but it was still alive somehow, barely, and the crabs were eating, and Mother shouted, "Enough," and shot the boeing bird twice in its big elegant skull.

Abitibi said, "Enough," in a whisper.

She drove the knife downwards into the soldier's throat, killing him in an instant.

Then the conscripts were yelling, pointing with the hot knives and screaming for the priest; and the priest stood and said, "So. So this is how it is," and he told her, "Come here. Now. Help me tell this man what he needs to know."

She got to her feet and returned his gaze.

He saw something in her eyes. He said, "Get over here," and grasped her wrist, twisting hard. "He's got to get right next to the boat. Tell him how, Abby." He wrestled the knife from her hand and said, "Tell him," his face strange.

Scared and relieved at the same instant.

XXVII

Mantis remembered like yesterday, perfectly, how he had heard of his poor father's death. A friend of the family's had sent them word along with a picture. The picture had showed a body sitting upright against a snowbank on some unnamed battlefield, the body stripped nude and the familiar head adorned with colored tattoos and the braided wires, not to mention a single bullet hole just above the open eyes. Father had been a conscript for more than two years. According to physical evidence, he had been executed by a priest who had been dissatisfied with his work and fervor. In the end, in spite of wires and his training, he had rebelled against his Alteretic masters; and now the terror was done. The family could sleep nights and know one of their own wasn't serving the stuhr cause somewhere . . . each of them taking a strength from the fact that the Alteretics had had to kill him themselves . . .

Only he wasn't dead, the young Mantis had thought. Looking at the grisly picture, he had touched the tattoos knowingly. Pieces of Father's brain had been removed. There had been a ceremony—a holy Joining with the i-ply stuhr—and Mantis had imagined a real part of his father living on inside the stuhr god. Safe and intact and very much real.

It had been a comforting image, he recalled.

Then years later, interrogating the priest, Mantis had thought of his father again. If ever he helped capture the god, he owed it to his family and himself to make contact. To try to learn what remained of the man. The god would tell him. In his daydreams, Mantis and the god chatted. Friend to friend. And the god would say, "I know your father. What they gave me I fleshed out into a whole person, and I made him happy. I did. I built a world inside myself where he and all the conscripts could live for all time."

"A heaven?" Mantis would ask.

"Indeed." He imagined the god with a soft sweet voice, neither male nor female. "An authentic heaven."

Of course, there was no knowing. Not about the god's capacities or its desires, or even about the prospects of holding conversations with it. A worm can't talk to a man, Mantis reminded himself. The gulf between them was enormous. Too big to be bridged, surely . . .

. . . though he loved daydreaming. He did. Sometimes he imagined himself asking, "How do you build a faster-than-light starship, Lord? Hmm? Can you teach me?"

And the god does. Happily.

"You're the first person I've liked," says the god. "You're a damned fine entity, Mantis. You are!"

Mantis began to laugh softly. To himself.

Mr. Chosen, sitting behind him on the bridge, said, "What is it? What's funny?"

"Nothing, sir. I was thinking . . . nothing." And he blinked and was back on the bridge himself, standing, watching the monitors and the ship and the sea all around. Somewhere to the north and west was the Alteretics' boat. He could make out the great school of sailers, and within a few hundred meters, give or take, he could pinpoint the sailboat itself. Mr. Chosen wanted them followed. The man seemed scared senseless that they would slip away somehow, and so from time to time, he ordered that Mantis should close in even more. "Are you sure they're there?" He asked, "Can they be using that school to escape? Hmm?" It was exhausting work, this cat-and-mouse business. Mantis felt the tiredness whenever he moved—in his muscles and in his bones. And to his credit, Mr. Chosen noticed what was ailing Mantis. "Are you sure you're up to this, Mantis? Hmm?" He asked, "Should Cricket come up and give you a break?"

"Probably so," he said. "Yes, sir. Please."

Mr. Chosen called Cricket, explaining. Cricket arrived with a small meal—galley sandwiches and steaming broth—and Mantis sat and ate and drank, feeling better already. Then he confessed, "I should sleep," and Mr. Chosen told him that he could. Here. He said:

"We can't have you off the bridge."

Cricket was doing a fine job. Mantis watched while he worked, finding the wire and applying it to his temple with the cool odorless glue. Then he glanced over the monitors once more, checking, and sat back in his chair and relaxed. "If anything happens—" he began.

"I will," said Cricket.

"We will," Mr. Chosen assured, his own voice tired.

Mantis touched a button. The darkness flowed around him, and the chair softened underneath his butt, and he heard his own breathing—a moist dark length of air drawn in and warmed and then let out again.

He was dreaming.

Standing in his dream, he was beside Cricket. The bridge behind them was enormous, maybe endless, and he couldn't turn to look, but he felt the presence of many others. Up on the wall were images of the outside, bright and blue now. He was looking up at the smooth face of the Pacific.

"A whale," said Cricket. "Look!"

Indeed. A huge whale was ahead and towards port, finning lazily in the sunshine.

"What do you suppose it's thinking?" asked Cricket.

"I don't know," Mantis heard himself say. "Maybe it's dreaming about rich meals to come. Do you suppose?" He sounded knowing and wise, his voice filling the bridge behind them.

Nothing changed for a long while.

Then a mirrored wall suddenly appeared on the Pacific, perpendicular to the water and endless; and the whale struck the wall and its own mystified reflection, then spun and swam away.

Their own boat kept running towards the wall.

Cricket wondered, "What is it?"

"I imagine," said Mantis, "it's the end of God's mind," and they were approaching the wall and approaching, seeing themselves now. Mantis began to lean forwards, squinting. He wanted to see who was behind him on the bridge. But then there was a sound, and he was awake, blinking and sitting up straight in his chair.

"Sir?"

"Yes?" He pulled a hand across his face. "What's wrong, Cricket?"

"It's the school of fish." Cricket was watching monitors, his face more puzzled than concerned. "They've turned."

"Where?"

"Around." He said, "They seem to be coming towards us."

Mantis stood, pulling off the dead wire. At once he was making guesses, trying to read the priest's mind. "How about the Alteretics?"

"Pulling ahead. They kept going."

Mr. Chosen said, "I don't like this," with his tired voice. He was sitting in his own chair, hands in his lap. "What do you make of it, Mantis?"

"I don't know." The priest could have guessed their general position. Sure. But could he have influenced the sailers in some way? Jellico would know. For the sake of time, he assumed the priest could and with a reason. With some motive in mind. Best give up on the cat-and-mouse stuff, he decided. Use all his sensors. He took over for Cricket, telling him, "Go get the boy," and he punched up the sonics and radar, one monitor immediately sounding an alarm.

A thousand sailers, or more, were bearing down on *Little Fist.*

"What is it?" asked Mr. Chosen. "Mantis?"

"A fission trigger." A nuke was riding on one of the sailers. He hit the general alarm. Explaining, he touched the throttle and slowed *Little Fist.* Up on the main screen, straight to the north, was a solid mass emerging from out of the mist—the sea pricked with triangular sails and flat slick bodies.

Jellico came running into the bridge. Cricket followed, and then Moon.

"How's the crew?"

Cricket said, "Dressed and ready."

"Weapons?"

"Operative." He was standing over the weapons board, making checks.

"Keep close," Mantis said. "I may need your hands, friend."

The sailers were closing on them. Mantis thought, aiming for cool deliberation. It was too late to maneuver around the school, and judging by the yield of their first nuke, the island-buster, whoever was coming had to be pretty damned close to do anything against bi-ply stuhr. "Besides," he thought. "If this priest is so smart, maybe this is the ploy. The diversion. Maybe the priest is trying to herd us towards the true, unexpected attack."

Jellico was standing nearby. Moon was in the doorway, Mr. Chosen still sitting beside the door with his hands tied in knots.

Mantis explained the circumstances, keeping with English so the boy could understand.

"Some rider?" asked Moon.

"On the fish?" He gave a tentative, "Yes."

"Is it Abby?" asked Jellico.

Mantis enlarged and enhanced the image. There was too much distance and too much crud, he realized, and he said so. Sensors were having fits for the same reasons. There was a nuke, yes. It seemed to be lashed to a big sailer. But, he said, if the Alteretics had bridled a sailer and sent the school back on its tracks . . .

"Can they do that, Jellico?"

He said they might. He said the fish had bosses.

. . . so maybe all they would need is a simple automated system of controls. Not a living person. Not so long as they didn't want to do anything fancy, that is.

Mr. Chosen said, "What should we do?" with a soft voice. "Moon? Mantis?"

Moon said, "Hit them."

"Who?" asked Mr. Chosen.

"The fish. Now."

And Mantis nodded. There wasn't any choice left for them.

Up on deck, on the bow, were two missiles in their tubes with nukes on their tips. Not baby nukes, these. Mantis armed one and instructed it when to detonate. "I'm going for an air-blast," he told everyone. "Three hundred meters over the school's leading edge."

Mr. Chosen said, "Shoot." He breathed and said, "Now."

A button was flashing red. The missile was absolutely ready.

"They wouldn't use Abby," said the boy.

Mantis used a thumb on the button.

"They wouldn't want to waste her, would they?" He sounded confident. "They need her. Right?"

The missile was off, out of the tube with an electromagnetic burst, then igniting, flames showing already against the high far black sky. Mantis was watching monitors and the screen. He could still see the tiny fission trigger but not its position. Not well enough. He saw the sailers pushing on towards them, the wind sweeping sideways across their broad backs and their wind fins erect and pulled taut. The blast came suddenly. For an instant, looking at the monitors again, Mantis thought something was wrong, and he wondered what his instincts were telling him. But then the glare blew over them, and the sea was on fire, it seemed, and the sensors began shutting down to save themselves from the EMP blast—electrons outracing the heavier, slower nuclei and scorching any circuits too slow or too close to protect themselves.

The noise shook *Little Fist*, but the stuhr dampened the sound to where everything seemed abnormally quiet.

Mantis heard Moon breathing beside him. He and Cricket were with him, all of them watching the monitors.

The screen went blank as the cameras shut down. They were in the dark now. Besides buttons and dials and the light pouring in from the hallway, there was nothing to see. He began working on the sensors, checking for lasting damage.

Moon said, "All dead."

Mantis had to agree.

Mr. Chosen wondered, "How long will we be blinded?" standing now, stepping into the light from the hallway.

"A little while," said Mantis. "Not long, sir." It was unnerving. He had to admit as much.

Jellico sat down in a chair against the back wall, the motion tired and anxious at the same time.

Moon moved back and sat too.

Cricket was working with Mantis, checking systems. He said, "The stern gun's down again," sounding frustrated. He and that gun had been feuding since they came to Leeshore. "It's inoperative."

Mr. Chosen asked, "Can you fix it from here?"

"I'll have to go outside," Cricket said. "It should be done now."

"Is that wise?"

"We might need it," Mantis said. "We destroyed the nuke, yes, but we don't know what else is planned. We should be ready."

He could see Mr. Chosen against the doorway's light.

"Cricket?" Mantis sensed that his orders wouldn't be cancelled under him now. He felt that nerves and exhaustion had removed some of Chosen's bite. "Suit up. Take someone." The boy? he thought. "Take a crewman. Someone who knows guns. I'll throttle down when you're set."

"Sir." He turned and left.

The cameras were coming back on, and also the rest of the sensors. The main screen filled with a diffuse light, faintly pinkish, and then the sea was where the sea belonged, with the coal-colored sky above. On Earth, that blast would have reached kilometers into the air. On Leeshore, the endless humidity and choking atmosphere had dampened the nuclear fire, minimizing damage.

Nothing visible remained of the sailers.

Mantis killed the motors and told Cricket to get outside. He watched the bubbling sea cool and looked out across the water. Nothing showed. There were corpses of fish and birds around the blast zone, and also things that tumbled from above. He saw a full-grown bladder plant, as black as new velvet, quiver and flatten when it struck the sea. Punctured, perhaps. He watched birds race at the bladder and pick at it with their bills, flapping and tearing loose lengths of what seemed to be fabric. Hot air blew out of the holes, and the bladder deflated further, vanishing against the waves and the struggling birds.

The nuke had been clean, relatively.

Nonetheless, Mantis was impressed by Leeshore's tolerance. The blast and rads had done less than he would have guessed. He wouldn't take *Little Fist* into those waters. Not for a time, at least. Not even dressed in stuhr like they were, if only for fear that their sensors would take a further beating.

Cricket and the crewman were at the gun now, bent and laboring.

Mantis was still a little blind. In places. That's probably what the Alteretics had wanted to accomplish, he supposed. To even out both sides

for a little while. Scanning ahead, he found the sailboat again. Nothing
was changed. He made no attempt to camouflage *Little Fist.* He guessed
that the sight of them might dishearten the priest.

Cricket had the gun's guts out on the deck.

"Hurry," Mantis told him, the radio channel thick with static.

Moon was talking to the boy. Laughing. "I'm looking at you, and I
don't know you. You're changed."

"Am I?"

"Yeah," said Moon. "Ever since your sister got stolen—"

"Fuck off!"

"Yeah." Moon laughed harder. "That's what I mean."

It was ten minutes after the blast.

Then twenty minutes.

Finally, Cricket was standing, as though he were finished. He and the
crewman began walking towards the airlock. With ten meters to go, no
more, the monitors began to flash. Suddenly alarms came on, and Mantis
said, "What is this—?"

On a side screen, up from the water, came a dying sailer. It was a
smaller species. He knew which species. Mantis could make out the
rigging ropes on its body and the sitting form of a soldier who was knotted
into the ropes. On the man's back was a tank of oxygen. Beside him was
the small dark shell of a nuke. In an instant, Mantis realized what was
happening. The rider must have made the sailer dive the instant the
missile was launched. It dived and the rider—Moon's soldier?—kept it
swimming against its own nature, pushing deep enough to escape the
worst of the airborne blast, then striking out towards its loud and confident enemy.

The sailer was kicking, coming closer.

Mantis said, "Cricket," knowing it was too late and knowing what he
had to do now. Only he couldn't summon the will—

Moon was standing. He was beside Mantis in an instant, his face tight
and his nearest hand reaching towards the throttle, pushing it into the
red, the floor tilting as the motors kicked alive and then leveling, Mantis
shouting. He said, "Cricket!" and he heard Cricket's voice through the
static. He and the crewman, neat and simple, rolled the length of the deck

and grasped the railing, holding tight for an instant and crying out before their hands slipped free, and they were gone.

Moon was sounding a collision alarm.

"Strap in!" he shouted to everyone, pulling Mantis away from the front and making him sit. Making him cinch tight the belts.

The blast came an instant later.

The bridge and all of *Little Fist* went black. Outside the atmosphere burned, sweeping across the deck and cutting off guns and sensors and the missile tubes, polishing the bi-ply stuhr clean and then causing it to drum ever so slightly, the atomic bonds stressed and finally holding, the dull drumming quitting and leaving everything so still and terribly dark that Mantis wondered if he had indeed died—asking himself if this was any god's mind and if he was some phantom, some sketch made whole, existing in the midst of it all.

Then he heard Moon. Close.

Moon growled and began moving.

The control boards found the energy to come awake, monitors blinking and flashing, telling everyone there was nothing left on the other ends of their lines. Nothing with which to see.

Little Fist was bobbing in the furious sea. Mantis knew. He could feel the sea, the floor aiming for level and not quite managing the trick. Moon was standing. Jellico was standing. Mr. Chosen was between them, sitting, his dry dead voice asking:

"What is the damage?"

"We're shit," said Moon.

"Accent the positive," Mantis said. "We're breathing." Except poor Cricket wasn't breathing, he thought. Never again.

"Can we catch them?" the boy asked.

"I'm not going to be blamed for this failure," Mr. Chosen said. "I am not."

"We can't let them escape!" said Jellico.

Mantis looked at the boy. Moon was right, he thought. The boy had acquired an intensity since the last island—

"This was entirely your failure," said Mr. Chosen. "Moon!"

Moon said, "What?"

"You will sign an affidavit. Mantis will be officially blamed—"

"What are you saying?" The boy couldn't understand. They were talking in Asian. "Tell me." He said, "How are we going to catch the bastards?"

Everyone was silent.

Poor Cricket, Mantis thought. He probably thought it was me pushing the throttle open—

"Get moving!" Jellico seemed to tower over everyone in the gloom. To Mantis, with his voice and hands, he said, "Now! Go!" He seemed full of a fire. "What do we have to do? Tell me what I should do!"

Mantis couldn't say. He was numb, crying for Cricket, thinking of how he had died and that he had truly died. No pieces of him had been saved. No better mind than Mantis' own would ever remember him now.

XXVIII

He was standing on the bare stuhr of the deck, thinking, knowing the situation and telling himself that there was some answer to all the tangled problems. He could almost taste it in his dry mouth. Save his sister and make certain that the Alteretics were dead or gone, then escape somehow and avoid recapture. Somehow. Jellico wasn't sure of the means yet, but he knew his responsibilities. Abby was in mortal danger. Nothing else seemed important any longer. Not to him.

The deck of *Little Fist* had been blown away. The stuhr remaining had been sandwiched between the deck and the hold's ceiling. On Jellico's feet, covering the boot soles, were flat static generators keeping him securely in place. He had to contend with the wind and the boat's motion, not to mention the slipperiness of the bi-ply itself. He was near the bow, facing the superstructure with his back to the wind. *Little Fist* had been wiped clean by the nuke. More than ever, it resembled a construction of mirrors. Moon had strung spotlights—small, portable models—on the high points. He himself was wearing static generators on his hands and feet both, clinging to where cameras and sensors had ridden on a telescoping boom. There was no trace of the boom itself. Where the glass wiring had bunched and been strung through an access hole in the superstructure, the radiation and fire had entered. Not all the damage was on the outside. The delicate electronics within had taken their share of the beating. Moon was shouting instructions, in Asian, to the crew. Jellico hadn't a clue as to what he was saying, much less the reasons backing up the words; but he watched them working and appreciated the organization, smooth and practiced, and understood without being told that he helped best by not helping at all.

Mantis had said, "We'll need a week, maybe more, to shape up."

That sounded like an age to Jellico.

"With a crew of this size, plus the damage, we'll be lucky to get back ninety percent of our capacities."

Jellico walked the deck, thinking, remembering how he had told Mantis, "You'll lose track of them, won't you? After a week, they could be almost anywhere."

"We'll string up a minimum of equipment," he had answered. "A couple stuhr guns. Cameras. Some sensors. And the motors are in good shape. We can manage maybe two-thirds speed." Then he had reached and touched Jellico's arm, saying, "Friend," one too many times. "You have to remember. We want what you want. The trouble is we're not so strong anymore. If we go in now, half-blind, we'll be asking to be killed outright."

They all wanted to take this slow.

Slow, at least as far as Jellico was concerned.

At first, wrongly, he had decided they were scared or somehow defeated —that their spirits had been vaporized with *Little Fist*'s skin. But then he had realized they were doing only what their training and experiences had taught them to do—when wounded, act wounded. When you are crippled, limp.

"If Abby was here," he whispered, "then fine. Perfect."

But the priest was inside her head instead, using the wires. Time was critical now. At the most, with luck, he had a week to save her.

The crewman and soldiers were bringing up the new equipment. The stuhr hatches now slid on the bare stuhr deck, and in the airlocks laid guns and sensitive instruments and kilometers of new clean wires. The reflections were a crazy stew of distorted people and objects. It dizzied Jellico and made him glad for the gripping soles he was wearing. Stepping slowly, he made certain one boot was secure before moving the other. He was making for the little airlock, ready to step back inside.

Mantis and Mr. Chosen had sent him out to check on the repairs. They were looking at bare screens in the bridge, still steering by feel and by guesswork. One still angry with the other, and the other still grieving for his dead friend.

Facing the sea one last time, Jellico stood beside the airlock. The explosions, oddly, had started a short-lived bloom. Stalks of dead airweed and young bladder plants were falling, and also shreds of mature bladders; the water was glowing with the first soft traces of rot, and fins broke the surface as countless fish hunted treasure.

It was dark around the airlock, spotlights and deck lights gone.

When Jellico stared at the sky, letting his faceplate adapt to the blackness, the blackness acquired a weak, yet distinct orangish light—Leeshore's sun hanging directly overhead.

He opened the airlock—the controls burnt away and replaced with a simple emergency system. He stepped inside and closed the outer hatch and waited, scrubbing himself and watching the soap and water drain off his lifesuit. There were thin brown streams of crap in the suds. Airweed fell and stuck in the drains. The water began rising, the drains clogged, and Jellico knelt and pulled the weed loose, a sucking noise and a tiny, fierce vortex signaling that he was done.

The inner hatch opened.

Jellico removed his helmet and walked to the bridge, the normal motion suddenly novel.

Mantis had one camera working, but something was wrong. The image had peculiar colors and blurred edges, the calibrations off. He turned and said, "Friend," and smiled weakly. "How are they doing outside?"

As well as they could, Jellico told.

Mr. Chosen was sitting against the back wall, his face empty and tired. "Are they keeping watch?" he asked.

"Moon has someone scanning with handheld instruments." Jellico said, "As well as they can, yes."

Mr. Chosen shifted in his seat. "How much longer until we're underway?" he asked Mantis.

"Another half-day. At best."

Jellico was standing between them, thinking.

"You seem preoccupied, friend."

"I'm thinking." Jellico felt transparent, his moods too easily read. "I'm working on something."

"On what?" asked Mantis.

"A plan."

"Indeed?"

Mr. Chosen coughed, then said, "To me. If you have a plan, talk to me." He explained, "The fat man has used up his opportunities already."

Mantis seemed to stiffen for a moment, then relax.

"Suppose I invent a good plan," said Jellico. "What happens?"

Mr. Chosen asked what he meant.

"This is your war. Not mine. My sister and I have lives here. Not on some starship—"

"You want your freedom." Mr. Chosen shifted again.

"And supplies. And your promise to leave us alone."

"If your plan works."

Jellico said, "Yes."

And Mr. Chosen said, "All right. Fine," too quickly. "You have my promise. Absolutely."

A lie, thought Jellico. He could smell it. But he told himself that this was something; at least they would listen to him. And he certainly wouldn't trust them any further than was necessary. This whole business was not unlike dealing with the Islanders.

"I need to go," he said. "Work out the particulars."

Mr. Chosen said, "Yes."

Mantis said, "Good luck," without his usual joy.

Walking down the hallway, Jellico imagined how he would respond if he lost Abby. He pictured himself grieving. It would be a thousand times worse than how Mantis felt now, surely. The pain might kill him, the purpose gone from his life.

The storeroom seemed smaller than before. The blast had caused a shelf to collapse, the crates broken open on the floor. He hadn't begun to clean up the mess. There were nameless tools and instruments, plus nuclear batteries. Everything had been packed into beads of a glass foam, clear and virtually weightless, and the foam was ankle-deep on the floor,

showing where Jellico had walked when he had come for his lifesuit.
He began undressing, the process made slow and careful by the mess.

An idea came to him suddenly. He found himself staring at the floor,
imagining Abitibi, asking her, "Do you think it would work? It seems too
damned easy."

In his head, softly, she said, "Maybe it will."

"I don't know about the math of it," he admitted. "It's not something
you could model easily. Not with what little we know."

"So take a chance," she said. "Be brave."

"Bravery," he said to himself.

"Jel," she reminded, "I'm waiting for you."

"That's right. You are."

"So what is there to doubt? Hmm?"

It was truly simple, he thought. He couldn't believe that no one else
had seen it first.

He worked quickly, kneeling, pulling off the lifesuit and filling a box
with the glass beads. Then he returned to the bridge and said, "We can
catch them tomorrow."

"Who?" said Mr. Chosen. "What do you mean?"

"You've got a bridle in the machine shop. I'll help you catch a big sailer,
and some of us can ride it until we reach the sailboat—"

"How?" asked Mantis. "How can you locate them under these conditions?" He motioned toward the darkness.

Jellico said nothing.

Mr. Chosen interrupted. "Leave him alone. Let him say."

Jellico breathed deeply, then he turned the box and dumped all the
beads onto the floor. With his bare feet, he herded them into a round
mat. He asked, "Is there someway you can launch your missiles? And I
mean soon." He said, "They don't have to be accurate. Only powerful—"

"We can't risk sinking the sailboat," said Mantis. "You aren't thinking
that, are you?"

"I'm not. No." The corners of his mouth turned up in a smile. "I want
you to shoot upwind. Up at the sky." He kneeled and looked at the foam.
"I want you to aim for the airborne jungle."

Mr. Chosen shifted.

Mantis made a knowing sound.

Jellico took in air until his ribs ached, then he braced himself and blew hard, scattering beads across the bridge and leaving the floor exposed. "Do you know what I'm saying?" he asked. "Do you see my plan?"

Mantis said, "I believe I do."

"And?"

"Clever," he said. "It's simple but clever." Something of the old Mantis reemerged. He seemed to halfway wink and smile. "You're a marvel, friend."

Jellico turned and looked at Mr. Chosen.

"But will it work?" Mr. Chosen asked. "Mantis?"

"I should think so, sir."

Mr. Chosen dragged his tongue across his lower lip. "If this scheme works," he said, "both you and your sister can go free."

Another time and Jellico would have said, "You're lying. I know you're lying."

But this time, carefully, he said, "It'll work. Believe me," and he nodded and tried mightily to look like a trusting boy.

XXIX

What amazed Abby was the time she had for herself, even though she had no will of her own.

She could sit with the other conscripts, rarely moving, listening to the ways they spoke with each other and understanding more and more of what they said. Or she could walk up on deck with the priest as her escort, hearing the wind up in the sails and in the rigging. She had watched the conscripts wrestling the baby nuke out of the little cargo hold, then securing it to the docile and waiting sailer. The priest and she had stood more than once on the deck, him handling her with that hand control, asking her endless questions about the sailboat and Leeshore, *Little Fist* and their pursuers. Abitibi had answered every question, volunteering nothing. The priest had promised that pleasure would come with honesty, and mostly that was true. Most of the time she felt happy, and when she was honest she was full of a strange, strange kind of joy.

A priest was a holy man.

In small, half-formed ways she understood what a priest meant to an Alteretic. He was a man or woman who could have spoken to God and heard God's great wisdoms. He was wise and strong and should be trusted in every function, small or not, in her own tiny life. The priest she knew had been brief about the Faith—he admitted as much, telling Abitibi that a true conversion requires time and effort he could not now afford. Plus the holy Joining. He did not apologize for the sketchy nature of her conversion, but she accepted his words as an apology and felt patient to wait for more relaxed times. For the days and years when this priest could make her a complete Alteretic, step by blessed step.

She had helped instruct the soldier, teaching him to ride a sailer.

The priest had devised the attack; and Abitibi, willingly, had worked to translate his plans into something the soldier could manage.

Then later, standing on the stern, Abitibi had seen a bright scalding flash to the south. Then a second, smaller flash. And the priest had asked, "What do you think?" He said, "Your friends are now dead. And so is your brother."

She had felt nothing, yet she was fully aware of feeling nothing. She was learning about the Alteretic wires, particularly how they made a person feel when bad news came suddenly. You felt flat and empty. Not sad. The wires dampened the soul whenever the soul threatened to emerge. They hid true feelings so very well that you were alert to the hollowness within yourself.

Later, his voice stubborn and calm, the priest had admitted, "I was wrong, it seems. They're still alive. Injured, no doubt, but breathing."

That's when the hollowness was filled in a little. Abitibi could again feel the soft hidden corners of her soul, and she clung to the feeling for as long as possible. A trace was left even now. She was below deck, on the floor, sitting with her legs crossed and watching the other conscripts. The conscripts were talking. "God," they were saying, "is great. God knows our misery, and God knows our salvation. He does. There is some final place He has intended for us. A paradise. And whether we make it to Paradise or not, *we* will make it to Paradise." They said,

"The Joining puts us with God, now and forever. We're living in the living stuhr. Always."

They were a strange group in Abitibi's eyes.

Every race. Every color. Every shape. She recognized them from the old textbooks, and where they were not pure they were blended—Africans and Asians, Europeans and Latins. She knew at a glance that each was a full conscript. It wasn't just the tattooed scars or the braided wires; it was also the intensity in the eyes and the way they effortlessly, endlessly, spoke of God.

She was one of them now.

At least partly.

Sometimes she went so far as to talk with them, saying, "I want to see Paradise. I do."

"You will," they chanted.

"I hope."

"Fight well and you will."

And then she would wonder about her brother. A part of her earnestly wished him luck, while most of her honestly wanted him dead. Jellico was the enemy now. He was a Nonbeliever. All the Nonbelievers would someday be vanquished, the conscripts said. Killed or conscripted. Maybe Jellico could be conscripted somehow. She thought there was at least a chance, now that the last nuke had been used. Sometimes she allowed herself to wish for him to be with her now. Both of them wired and speaking endlessly about God and the joyful times coming.

Sometimes, off and on, the conscripts would talk about battles.

They were graphic. They loved best the images of cruelty, particularly when Nonbelievers suffered and died. Each of them would remember his favorite kill, painstakingly describing the corpse and the way they cut up the corpse, cooking pieces and slowly eating them. A part of Abitibi remembered Moon telling her that he had eaten Jellico. It had been a joke; she couldn't imagine Moon doing any such thing. Not willingly. But now she understood the source of the joke. In hard times, Alteretics easily turned to cannibalism. Probably every Nonbeliever feared he or she would end up as someone's feast. And thinking that, Abitibi laughed softly. To herself. On Leeshore, everything in some way ended up as something's feast.

One of the Islanders—a pale little man with a sleep face—happened to resemble a certain conscript.

Or at least he had.

She could remember the Islander. Without trying, she saw his features and heard his voice clearly, thinking that the wires must be helping to access her memories. She was remembering too much for it to be natural. Maybe the wires had to expose memories in order to destroy old allegiances, building better things in their place. And then she remembered Mother, hearing the familiar voice. "Don't succumb, Abby! Don't let them get you without fighting!"

"I can't fight, Mother."

"You can!"

"Look at me. I can't."

If Jellico appeared now, coming through the airlock, Abitibi would try to kill him. She knew she would want him dead. But when she imagined the moment, suddenly, flatness and the emptiness came into her. Somewhere down deep, hidden, her true self and soul was biding its time.

She was tired now.

Tired and frightfully hungry.

They had given her some of the soldier-meat, but the act of setting it on her tongue was enough to make her vomit. And the priest had said, "Let her go. When she's starving, she'll eat. Wait."

He had sounded like someone who knew from experience.

The conscripts still talked about God and the war, their enthusiasm endless. While she listened, never moving, the priest himself came out from the front of the boat. He was thinking. He walked past everyone, occupied with his own concerns—his strong face the kind of face that gains energy and purpose when troubled. Abitibi did not doubt for an instant that solutions by the plenty would come when he needed them.

Little Fist was still on the hunt.

From what the priest had said to the others, Abitibi guessed it had dropped behind them for a time, licking its wounds. But now it was moving again—more slowly—and its sensors were working, minus their old punch and subtlety. Eventually, the Nonbelievers would have them in their sights again. Unless fortunes changed, that is.

The priest paused and gazed down at Abitibi. "Put on your helmet," he said. "We're going topside." He took his own helmet and set the seals, and she rose and joined him in the cramped airlock.

Leeshore's atmosphere flooded downwards, the odors suddenly familiar and almost pleasant. She didn't like the stinks from unwashed people. She preferred the sea smells that crept in through her filters, memories coming whenever she inhaled.

The hatch overhead hissed and slid open.

He climbed and she followed, effort making her vision narrow and her heart welling up in her chest.

She breathed, staggered and then caught herself.

He said, "Follow me," and she clung to the glass mast beside the airlock. "What? Is your head swimming?" She walked, feeling the wind and looking in every direction. A string of distant glows circled the sailboat. The sailboat's name was *Four Winds*. Abitibi had forgotten that unmemorable fact. It was a silly name, Leeshore owning only one wind. But islands it had in abundance. They surrounded *Four Winds*, seeping a cold and colored stew of lights.

The priest was waiting on the stern.

She joined him, and he talked, his questions clean and trimmed so that there was no mistaking what he wanted. And she stood motionless, thinking about what he needed to know and what his questions sometimes missed. A truly converted Alteretic would have interrupted him, saying, "Lord, there's something you should know. Please." Only Abitibi wasn't so converted. She could take everything he said literally. She answered and felt happiness, and yet he wasn't learning enough.

The priest wanted weapons. Or an ambush. Or both. He was going to miss the nukes, he confessed. Fighting a bi-ply hull with anything less was impossible. Or so it seemed.

Finally, in disgust, he paused.

She sensed there was something else on his mind. Some other burden, secret and crushing.

There came a rumbling from somewhere to the north. The priest heard the noise and listened, muttering something about thunder or exploding gas. Abitibi knew it was a bomb-stool. She made herself turn away, watching the conscripts who were handling the sails and helm. She thought of bomb-stools blasting islands free of woods and the tired debris; and suddenly the priest said, "Abitibi," with an odd tone. "Abby?" He was staring at her faceplate. "I have a special assignment for you and only you. Listen to me."

She did.

Toward the bow, hidden inside a helmet, was a lump of i-ply stuhr. He described it. He said, "If I am ever killed, you must find it and pull the batteries off of it. All right?" He gave her the technical particulars. "And don't listen to it. Don't! Never do what it says."

She thought of the i-ply god.

"Do you hear me? Abby?"

"Kill it," she repeated.

"And don't tell any other conscripts. Never."

"I won't."

"I know you won't."

She thought it couldn't be the god. It was too small, and why would the priest want it dead?

"I should kill it myself," he muttered. "This minute."

She asked, "Why don't you?"

"Because." He seemed to shudder. "I've got too much at stake. It's my emotions talking, but they won't let me." He said, "I've helped kill worlds so we can keep that thing alive, and I'm sure as hell not going to unplug it now. Not when we're so close to escaping."

"What thing?" she asked.

"Never mind."

In the distance, towards the west, another bomb-stool ignited.

The priest tilted his head, listening, and when the thunder was gone, he turned and said, "We'll go inside now."

She said, "Fine."

"Remember," he said. "Whatever happens, remember."

And she promised to never forget. Ever.

XXX The sailer was big and young and just about ideal. Jellico called up to Moon, screaming, telling him they'd find none better. So Moon gestured once, waving them ahead. Faster. The raft was running with the wind, its motor screaming. The sailer, apparently oblivious to the raft, dipped its head once and then again, hunting.

The easy way to catch sailers was on the leeward side of the islands. While they're sleeping, thought Jellico. While their wind fins and defenses are down.

He was sitting behind Moon, keeping low, the raft hitting stride now that the air spilled back over them, the wind apparently reversed. In his mind, step by step, he went through the procedure. Bridling a sailer was never entirely easy. A hundred things might go wrong, particularly when the sailer was alert and in its natural element. Out in the wind. Tension made Jellico sweat, his muscles twitching and trembling. For too many days he had been inactive. He felt like a stranger to his own body. He shut his eyes and saw the sailer, making himself breathe slowly and grow calm. There was much, much more to consider than bridling. But for now, somehow, he had to force those issues from his mind.

"Jelly?" Moon called. "Ready?"

His eyes opened. The sailer looked enormous and vigorous, kicking now, aware of the raft at last.

"Jelly?"

He screamed, "Ready!" and felt his body stiffen, muscles aching. "Like I told you. Get close, and fast!"

Moon waved once, the motion decisive and self-assured.

The raft responded, cutting sideways, and then the bulk of the sailer was suddenly beside them, dark and shiny with spray. Jellico stood and made a clumsy leap, hands stretching overhead. His aim was a lucky perfect. He landed high enough to get a solid grip, the sailer's flesh yielding without being soft, slick but not to the point of slippery.

He heard the raft roar away.

Blowing hard, he found the strength to muscle his way clear up onto the broad flat back. Then there was a new noise, closer and frightening.

He felt the sailer's position change abruptly, and suddenly the wind fin came to sweep him away. *Damn!* He was too far back. He had jumped too soon. The fin was fringed with long flexible bones, and it was the bones that were trying to get rid of the rider, that blindly slammed against his body, his hands already tired and starting to slip.

Jellico concentrated for an instant.

The sailer had turned up into the wind, drifting now, the great fin like some enormous paper fan used to beat a fly senseless.

Jellico moved. He scrambled further up the back, closer to the stalk of the fin. One blow smacked the breath out of him, but he persisted and reached the stalk and held tight, gasping. The fin dropped and rose and then dropped again—but the angle and momentum were lost. He hardly felt the glancing blows.

Mimicking a fly, Jellico began creeping forwards.

The sailer, like all sailers, tried diving and pulling its rider under the water and off. Jellico was ready. Spreading his hands and feet, he gripped the muscled back and applied steady pressure—the motion automatic and practiced—and the sailer rose up out of the waves and shuddered. Then it dove again.

Most sailers would wash themselves a dozen times. Give or take.

This big solitary bull persisted into thirty, Jellico creeping forwards whenever he saw his chance.

On his own back, in his personal field pack, was his equipment. The bridle was easiest to reach, but he didn't dare try. He didn't want to risk being thrown, some fin or tail having its chance to break the pest. So he hunkered down and waited.

The key spot was visible now. Almost beckoning. Jellico saw it on top of the sailer's skull, some rounded patch of a bright yellowish fungus lying on the flesh between him and it.

The patch was like a marker.

Jellico took it as a lucky sign.

The sailer dove a fortieth time. Then a fiftieth. Then Jellico forgot to count, reminding himself to tell Abby what sorts of hell he had gone through for her sake—picturing the two of them alone and laughing, riding sailers and having a fine time.

Finally the sailer tired of fighting.

Jellico felt the body relax, muscles loosening; and so he reached into the pack and found the bridle waiting, grasping its smooth glassy head and aiming at the one small place where no sailer skull has bone, using all his strength for the stab.

The sailer made a noise. It was part whimper, part raging curse, and its body stiffened as if Death itself had come.

The pointed end of the bridle had pushed into the brain.

Immediately, Jellico shouted instructions to the helmet's computers. A fine net of wires were deployed while the bridle came alive, its own sonic functions seeking out special regions and making certain each was properly and permanently taken over.

A grisly operation. He had no love of it and never had.

Eventually, following the automatic programs, the bridle made the sailer relax and fall away into a sudden sleep.

Jellico began checking all the systems.

"Done?" asked a familiar voice.

He ignored Moon and took a certain pleasure from the act.

"Jelly?"

"Yes, Ugly?"

"I am," he said. "How is our fish?"

"Perfect." Jellico felt mauled, but the sailer was ready. "He'll take a little nap. Now's the time to load."

From somewhere came the raft. Or, thought Jellico, maybe he hadn't heard its motor. Distracted as he was. Turning, he happened to watch Moon make the same leap he had just managed. He took some small satisfaction when the ugly man lost his footing and fell, his own enormous pack nearly pulling him into the water. But then, thinking of Abby, Jellico jumped up and took hold of the small strong hand, hauling Moon to safety.

Here, riding sailers, Jellico was in his native environment.

It surprised him how much of a difference it meant to him. Before, on *Little Fist* and even on the raft, he was nobody. Not even a soldier. But here all the boundaries blurred. On a fresh and healthy sailer, Jellico in control of the bridle—the helm—the relationships had shifted without effort or a word between any of the participants.

Maybe I'm making too much out of it, he told himself. Maybe it's because I'm more confident here. Even cocky.

But the old Moon, he thought, wouldn't have grasped his hand.

Not willingly.

And the old Moon wouldn't have asked, "Where?" and waited to be told what to do next.

The two soldiers were climbing on board. They moved with a slow certain caution, not knowing what to expect from the giant fish. They kept their knees bent and their field packs low. The packs looked like burdens, swollen with equipment. Behind their darkened faceplates, Jellico guessed, their faces were likely tight and pensive and watchful.

The raft's driver gave a shout, saying whatever it is that Asians say before battle. To Jellico, it sounded like, "Luck!" Then the raft accelerated and turned and pushed into the wind. *Little Fist* was a considerable distance away. All that showed were the spotlights burning, the glare white and sharp, the boat resembling some tiny island rotting at an enormous pace.

Little Fist was drifting again, thought Jellico. Its depleted crew was assembling the assorted missiles and warheads, Mantis likely plotting their trajectories and impact points. The goal was to kick the biggest hole possible in the bladder plants, letting in daylight. "Terraforming," Mantis had said. "Maybe someday we'll come back here. We'll make Leeshore into a habitable world. A garden. What would you think about that, friend?"

"I like it as it is."

"Because you know nothing else." He had shaken his head, frowning. "Sometimes I wonder . . . you are so quick, so bright, and yet you never seem to recognize that there's more than this," he said, gesturing. "You've got ample potential. I know. And surely you could change. Adapt to *The Fist*, and someday you might love it."

"We're staying."

"Yes, well—"

"I wish you luck. I do. But that's all." He had said, "Mr. Chosen promised me—"

"That he did. You're right."

Mr. Chosen had lied, and then Mantis too. Neither man had any intention of letting them go free. Not when there were shortages of manpower. Particularly after the casualties they had taken down here.

Mantis had shaken a finger, warning, "Things might not turn out so well as you hope. I'm sorry, but it's true."

Jellico had said nothing.

"Neither of you alone could live down here. Could you?"

"We'll see."

"Come with us. All right?" The charm was brittle, exhaustion and Cricket's death weighing Mantis down. "Friend," he had said.

Jellico had kept silent, thinking: *No, I'm not.*

"What are you thinking, friend?"

"Maybe you're right." He was imagining being locked up in a glorified can—*The Fist*—with Mantis beside him for the rest of his life, smiling, calling him, "Friend."

"I *am* right," he had assured.

"Perhaps."

"Think it through."

"I will."

And they had shaken hands, Jellico remembering the moment now and feeling the sturdy warm grip again. He blinked. He glanced across the dark back of the sleeping sailer. Moon and the soldiers were waiting, packs off and legs spread, standing near the bridle and the gills.

"Jelly," said Moon. "Where?"

Jellico pointed. Two men and their gear would fit in a gill, and he quickly showed the soldiers how to climb inside and stow their packs. Then he was back on top, alone. Moon was making their nest, he presumed, moving to the end of the longest bone in the wind fin and working —attaching a camera and sensors no larger than one clenched hand.

Out on the water, in schools and alone, were more sailers.

The bloom had become locally famous. Birds were hunting and sailers were hunting, and the sea swirled where big fish tore at bladder plants and crippled animals.

Working, Jellico watched the scene and thought about what Cricket had said. About the stuhr god. About its brilliance and its plans for the future—reassembling worlds and the Milky Way, for instance. He tried once again to imagine the intellect behind the plans, and how it must feel to be shackled and wired up by its apish builders. He had better luck imagining why people would build such an entity—scientific curiosity, of course, and also the promise of power—and why billions would die over such a possession. He understood the basic natures of these people around him; they were the same as the dead Islanders, and Mother, and himself, too. Good or evil, he thought, people seemed eager to find causes. To chase dreams. It was in their blood, he believed. And only the lucky few ever actually could pick and choose their devotions.

If anyone ever really did.

"Jelly," snapped Moon. "Come on. Now."

Jellico looked at Moon, then woke the sailer with a word. He told it to toss its head from side to side, and it did so. Moon slipped and fell, sliding towards the open water; and Jellico said, "Quit," and the sailer went rigid, Moon standing and shaking himself dry.

"Jelly's ready," Jellico announced.

He felt entirely in charge.

Gods and grand causes were receding now. In his own heart of hearts, he had come to do nothing but save his sister's soul.

That, he thought, was an ample mission.

All that one mortal man could ever need, surely.

XXXI   He woke with the sea in his ears and stars overhead, and in that instant between waking and honest recognition, when the mind gropes for *place,* Moon imagined he was on a beach somewhere on Earth, packed sand below and a tropical breeze blowing.

Then the beach gave a shudder, a fishless stomach complaining with a stomach's wail. And he remembered. Sitting upright, he breathed and collected himself in the time most people use to lick their lips. The sailer, he saw, was still lying out of the wind. Islands were on either side, and

he looked at their colored woods and decided that they had lost a touch
of their brilliance. Again he stared at the sky, at the stars, and found the
line where the airborne jungle remained intact. The stars themselves were
a sickly lot, scattered and partly obscured by the thick and filthy air
between them and him. Moon hoped to see a satellite passing overhead.
Mantis had promised to use them when he had them in position—
spotting the sailboat, then forwarding the information with subtle codes
that eavesdroppers should miss.

Little Fist was to the south, hunting in a loud fashion.

The core of the idea was to drive the sailboat northwards through the
archipelago. Let the big stuhr boat be seen. Chase in a sloppy way. Make
the sorts of mistakes that a wounded hunter would make. Then the priest
would think of escape or of some final firefight. It didn't matter which.
The trick was to fill the priest's head with guesswork. With schemes of
his own. And when the sun was on the sea, visibility stretching to the
horizon, the priest would have to do the human thing and relax. Just a
little. For the first time in ages his eyes would have worth. And maybe
he would trust the eyes a bit more than he would normally dare.

Moon stood and stretched, studying the islands again.

They were duller now. The colors seemed washed out and forgettable.
It must be the sun, he thought. It's coming soon, scattered photons
already filtering down through the mist and the surviving bladders.

He laid his hands together, palms flush, and pressed until his arms and
chest burned and ached. Then he released and relaxed, breathing himself
clean. The clock displayed on his faceplate claimed he had overslept by
five minutes. This was sloppy for Moon. He prided himself on never
needing alarms, some internal clock of his own prodding him awake when
he wanted. Shaking his arms, he looked across the sailer and found the
two soldiers sleeping. On each he used a firm boot. Once. They knew
better than to try ignoring him, and in a moment they were standing,
blinking but mostly alert, waiting for their first orders.

"Check your equipment," Moon said. "Twice," he said. "Then once
more. Go!"

There were nods. Feigned enthusiasms. Moon turned and walked towards the head and the lazily beating gills, drinking body-warmed honey
and washing his mouth clean with lemoned water. Jellico was inside the

right gill. For whatever reason, he preferred sleeping in that stinking hole. Yesterday, he and Moon had shared what was little more than a shelf—a structure made from a cartilage-like material—set centimeters above the water and the orange gill hairs. Jellico had steered the damned fish with the bridle and navigated with the sensors and camera high on the wind fin. Normally, in more typical times, the boy would have used a radio to link up with the bridle and such. "But won't the Alteretics hear the signal?"

They might eavesdrop, yes. Moon had admitted as much.

"So we'll string wires," Jellico had said. "I can rig a system. I'll plug it directly into our helmets . . . so you and the soldiers can keep tabs on what we're doing."

"Fine. Do that."

The boy was thinking—that much Moon had to admit.

He wouldn't let himself trust him. Not for long, at least. But he was working as hard as anyone when it came to making this mission a success. A good think to shove at your soldiers when they acted lazy. "You're going to let that kid, that *outsider*, show you up? Hmm?"

Moon bent and slid into the gill, the motion smooth. Practiced. The boy was where he had left him, sprawled out on the shelf. Moon could see by the steady light of fungal parasites—patches of fine, fine hair resembling miniature forests when you pressed your faceplate against them, their fauna complete with half a dozen kinds of bloodless bugs grazing on the fungi and nothing else.

Jellico had insisted that the sailer was not an organism so much as it was a community onto itself.

He had told Moon that this great fish would likely live for several centuries, wandering and feeding. On the surface of this sea, what with the stable environment, there were strong selection pressures to prolong lifespans. The benthic regions of Earthly seas had the same tendencies. And since Leeshore's lifeforms were so tremendously durable—

—but Moon knew that lesson.

The boy felt Moon coming and stirred.

"Did you sleep?" Moon thought to ask.

"I doubt it."

"Nerves," he said.

"I'm sure."

The cartilage dimpled under their combined weights. Moon was kneeling, looking squarely into the black, black faceplate. "Come upstairs," he said. "Once in a life you should see sunrise."

The boy was slow to move. Not stubborn, but definitely ill-at-ease.

"Come."

"I will."

"Dawn," he prompted.

"I don't know what that means."

Moon turned and climbed up into the open air. Changes were coming swiftly now, the empty eastern sky filling with a cherry-colored glow. The stars dimmed and vanished and the sunlight brightened while it spread across a broad front, bulling its way through the heavy air. Turning a circle, Moon examined the flanking islands. Currents and the wind had driven them together, their plastic deforming and sticking below the surface, transforming them into a single two-lobbed island. Under the pressure of light, their features were dissolving into a soft grey fuzz that resembled mold and rot and ruin. If anything glowed, it did so dimly. If anything had color, it kept its color a secret.

Jellico was standing beside Moon, watching.

The soldiers were busy cleaning gun parts, fending off the corrosion, and one of them and then the next lifted his head and paused, hands frozen in midmotion.

The sunlight swept overhead and broke against the jungle in the west, the bladder plants pushed by the raw high winds to form a straight blue-black wall stained with a faint red. Moon could just make out the lowest of the grown bladders—like spherical bricks set flush to one another. All were whole and intact, everything damaged having died and fallen to the east. The mist was not as thick as he would have guessed. The heat of the nukes may have cooked the air dry. And without any jungle overhead, nothing fell. No shit. No feathers. No random, picked-over corpses.

The island blocking the wind was south of east now, and their sailer was drifting northwards into open water. Directly south, high and slowly circling, was an albatross-shaped something almost too distant to be seen.

"What is that?" asked Moon, pointing.

Jellico said, "A boeing bird."

Without reference points, Moon could only guess its altitude and size. He wished for its eyes and its position now, scanning islands and the open water at will. He thought about the Alteretics, imagining them coming up on deck now and staring at the waterscape, mouths ajar, their priest taking in the scene and asking himself what it would mean for him. Moon respected that priest. The business with the balloon had shown him something, and the nuke-bearing sailer had convinced him to never underestimate this one. Mantis had been right. The Alteretics had sent their best. This wasn't one of their average wire-your-troops-and-charge fools. He had skills and a way of daring you, and Moon didn't simply respect him, he felt admiration. In other circumstances, in an earlier war, they would have been equals working for the common cause—

"There," said Jellico. "Isn't that it?"

Up from the sea came the dull red top of the sun. It was flanked by the island on one side and a few scattered clumps of bladders on the other. The wind was steady now. The sun looked flattened and slow and sticky, rising up from the horizon without effort or hurry. Days were long on Leeshore. Moon remembered that fact—either from the briefings or from the boy's chatter. He felt the wind and sunshine on his faceplate, and the faceplate began to darken, shading his eyes. Jellico muttered something about Skyhook Island. Moon asked him, "What was that?"

"From a distance, when it was all lit up, the island looked like that. Like the sun."

"Did it?"

"Yeah," he said. Then he turned and said, "It is pretty, I suppose," and he started to walk toward the gill. "I'm going to wake the sailer. I'm slipping us back behind the island. Out of this wind." He sounded like the officer in charge, and knowing better, Moon let him trumpet and strut.

It did no harm, he thought.

As soon as this was done, assuming it ended well, he would bully Jellico back into submission. One way or another. Because if he didn't he'd have to fight for the girl. For Abitibi's hand. Assuming that part of this ended well too.

Again he began to turn in circles, watching the sea become a brassy color while the islands grew small and plain under the light of day. The wind, if anything, was stronger than yesterday. One gust threatened to tip him over on his butt. Everywhere he looked, the water and the plastic ground, everything seemed utterly lifeless. It was as though the planet itself was holding its breath, making no move and waiting for the outcome.

XXXII In those moments between the needs of *Little Fist* and his links with the satellites, Mantis thought how he could have done things differently—run the ambush, chased the sailboat and so on—and he felt sick to himself and told himself that at least he wasn't a god. A god's failure amounted to something in the long run. That was what separated gods from Men.

"A question of magnitude," he said aloud.

"What is that?"

"Nothing, sir. Never mind."

Up on the main screen was a strange sunlit vista: midmorning on Leeshore's watery face. To its right was the same scene on a smaller screen, the view from two hundred kilometers overhead. One of *The Fist's* satellites was broadcasting images, peering through a hole in the world's roof. By touching controls, Mantis picked and enlarged key portions. The Alteretics were obvious—the sailboat a bright white slipper running with the wind, five crewman showing. If this had been Earth, Mantis thought, he could pull out a host of details. Their faces. Their guns. How many bullets and how many grenades. But Leeshore had too much atmosphere, and the sun shone on the endless spray. A layer of haze was forming, gaining depth and whiteness without actually obscuring. A computer model had predicted the haze. By early afternoon, it would burn away.

"Any change?"

"No, sir."

"Is it stable?"

"Our clear skies?" he said. "More than we guessed."

They had water-launched the missiles, one after another, and then the east was lit up with a cutting white light. Bladder plants had dissolved over thousands of square kilometers; heat and pressure had pushed at the wounded jungle, the hole turning enormous. Models hadn't predicted the hole. The limits of computers, thought Mantis. And their ignorance. He wondered what else hadn't been predicted. The long days and the steady sun beating down on the water, warming the surface . . . what about clouds forming? And storms?

"Does Moon know their position?"

"I'm about to update now, sir." He glanced over a shoulder, Mr. Chosen sitting in his usual spot. Straight-backed and hands in his lap. "It all seems to be going as expected."

"I've heard *that* before."

Mantis said nothing, knowing better. Instead he fluttered the radar, making it sound like a faulty unit. The sailboat's position was inside the flutter, plus speed and direction. Maybe Moon didn't need to know, he told himself. Hopefully he had the boat in sight already. He could actually be making his final approach. Counting quickly, Mantis saw half a dozen sailers hunting those waters. Or pretending. Maybe they'd get lucky, and a satellite would catch the attack. Whatever happened, win or not, it was up to Moon and his crew. They were out of it.

"So," said Mr. Chosen. "Just where are they going?"

"I'll see," and he squirted a command to the satellite, making its cameras tilt. Looking westward, the next images showed a number of varied-sized hills sticking up out of the blue-white sea. Islands. An enormous cluster of islands had run together and stuck, probably acting like pontoons on a fat boat. Or like bladder plants shoulder to shoulder. The Alteretics were making for those islands. He told Mr. Chosen the bare facts. No embellishments. Then he enlarged the view, bringing out the kelp-choked channels between the islands and thinking to himself what a wonderous and disgusting place that would make for an ambush.

Which was probably what the priest had in mind.

Make us come in after him and his. Have it out in the jungle, like old times. Like in the first Wars. Firefights up close, stuhr boats and fancy gear not meaning shit—

"I've been thinking."

"Sir?"

"About this mission."

Mantis said nothing.

"Whatever the outcome, I think we can salvage something." He breathed softly, deeply, and held the breath for a moment. " 'Accenting the positive.' You said that once or twice, didn't you?" He told Mantis, "What we need to do is accent the positive. Everyone."

"Whatever happens."

"Exactly."

Mantis thought: It comes to this. He steals my ambush plan and the plan goes sour. So he takes command of the boat, in punishment, and we're assaulted and injured while he is in command. And so now he's scared about this attack too. He wants to cover his soft butt. In case. What he's offering me is a deal. When *The Fist* comes, he says, we're all to be the best of friends. We'll talk only about how well we worked together, and how we tried our best to do what needed doing.

"Mantis?"

"I'm always willing to help, sir. You know that."

"And if I've ever been short-tempered—"

"It's forgotten," he said. "I understand."

"Thank you." Mr. Chosen sounded supremely relieved. Mantis turned, catching him as he stroked his medals through his jumpsuit—his expression vaguely happy; his face never so bland.

Mantis thought for a moment, then said, "I am right about the priest. I'm sure."

"That he's important. You've told us—"

"And that he signals where the stuhr god is sitting now. Up in that starship we're chasing." He paused, counting the seconds, then went on. "When we capture that god—and we will, believe me—you and I are going to be among the most famous men who ever lived. They'll talk of us for ten million years, sir. We'll be legends!"

Mr. Chosen sat thinking, saying nothing.

Mantis let him dwell on the images.

Finally he muttered, "The Hall of Glory."

"Just what I mean."

"Enough," said Mr. Chosen, stern-voiced and secure. "Quit this talk. You should concentrate on the business at hand."

"Sir." Mantis snuck a look. The flat dark eyes and the pulpy bland face were serene. There was no other word to describe them.

Quietly, slowly, Mantis yawned.

Looking upwards at the main screen, he considered wiring up and doing a partial sleep. Only as tired as he was, and with as much as he had to do, he was better off doing without. Or so he judged. This wasn't just a jaunt across the quiet Pacific. He was hunting. What he needed was a strong cup of broth laced with pep pills . . . and to that end, he called Cricket's replacement—a virtual boy—and made his request known.

He yawned again.

He blinked and stared up at the sea.

On the bright blowing water was a tiny island. It was a fragment of a fragment, apparently. It took Mantis several seconds to recognize the blood-oaks growing on its crest. In the strong light, the oaks resembled those he had seen on Skyhook Island, complete to the false leaves. Only the fungus looked boiled now. It was a lifeless grey passing into a faint pink-white at the points where the false leaves sprouted from the stalks, and he stared and decided that the oaks looked disgusted as well as boiled. They seemed disgusted at all the sunshine falling on them, robbing them of their splendor; or maybe they just didn't like to resemble what they were in fact: glorified toadstools, no more and no less.

Mantis was feeling tired of Leeshore.

What had been novel and intriguing was wearing through. Growing old. Making his nerves tingle, overloaded as they were.

He missed Earth now, and *The Fist*, and Cricket too. He wondered what would have happened had he made Cricket stay inside. *Forget your damned gun!* Or if he had hit the throttle at once, running from the sailer but not so fast. Not like Moon had hit the throttle and run. Buying distance but not sweeping the two men off the deck in the process. Giving them the chance to climb inside and be safe . . .

In came the crewman with the steaming broth. Mantis thanked him and sipped the contents of the cup, feeling his insides tingle. He glanced once more at Mr. Chosen. He said, "Sir, would you like a cup?"

"No," he answered. "Thank you, no."

"You're sure?"

He paused, then said, "All right. Fine."

"Another," Mantis commanded.

"Just broth," Mr. Chosen added.

Said the crewman, "Very well," and he turned and left them.

Again, yawning, Mantis gazed up at the main screen. The seawater had no color whatsoever. It shone brightly, resembling some crazy new kind of stuhr. Liquified somehow. Lifeless through and through.

Mantis felt better now. A little.

The depression was slowly seeping out from his bones.

When he was like this—and only when he was this bad—he used a certain cure of his own invention. He told himself that all this was unreal, that he and the planets and the stars were nothing more or less than dreams conjured up inside a stuhr god's mind. That what he was, was living because and for that god, wherever it was.

Maybe there was no universe as he knew it.

Maybe stuhr had been born in the remote past, and the stuhr had grown and won out over the protoplasmic life-forms; and now all that remained was stuhr and stuhr and stuhr, painting worlds inside itself to suit its own private needs.

Maybe Mantis was the hero in some daydream.

Sometimes he told himself so.

He muttered, "I wouldn't mind," and Mr. Chosen, hearing him, asked: "What? What wouldn't you mind?"

He lied, saying, "I was thinking of the Hall of Glory, sir."

"I bet so. I do." Mr. Chosen sounded happy. He announced, "I've always suspected that of you. You're like all of us. No differences at all."

"Maybe that's so, sir."

And maybe the sufferings and the joys he felt were nothing, more or less, than the grand yearnings of something stuhr-built.

Sometimes it felt good to think so.

It made the difference, sometimes.

XXXIII "You're improving. I know."

"I'm trying."

"I know how you're trying. I can tell." He said, "Just in these last hours, I've noticed improvements."

"You have?"

"Haven't you?"

"Well, maybe." She considered her feelings carefully. "I am trying harder to please. I know that."

"And it's not the pain you imagined, is it? The wires and I are good, kind masters. Aren't we?"

"Yes."

"Of course we are." He smiled, nodding. There was a faraway look to his eyes. "This brings me to a point. I want to warn you of something." He paused, then said, "I know of cases where new converts, fueled by their enthusiasms, have done terrible damage."

She listened.

"There's something I want you to promise—"

"The helmet—?"

"No." He laid a hand across her mouth, pressing. "I mean, yes. I told you what to do, and I meant that. I did. But I'm talking about something else now."

She spoke into his palm, saying, "I'm listening."

"If it comes to it, don't use a gun. Don't ever pick one up. Don't ever aim one. And never pull a trigger. Am I understood?"

She said, "Yes."

"Don't."

"I won't," she promised.

"Good."

She sat on the floor, telling herself to do exactly what she was told to do. She imagined guns, and the guns burned her hands when she touched them. She imagined the priest dead and her finding the helmet with the i-ply inside, and she pulled off the batteries and watched the stuhr fade and crumble to dust.

The priest began to stand. He said, "Come on."

They were in the front of the cabin, alone. Abitibi looked at the helmet propped up on the equipment, and she happened to see the priest as he glanced at it for an instant. She thought of him silencing her, covering her mouth, and a part of her wondered why. Why? They had been whispering. Everyone else inside was sitting up near the airlock, out of earshot.

"We're going up on deck again."

She lifted her own helmet.

"How do you feel?"

"Fine."

"The others say you ate last night. Finally."

"A little." And she had vomited once more. "Then they gave me some standard rations."

"You feel stronger."

"Much."

He said, "Good."

There were no windows in the boat's cabin. Abitibi had never seen a window on Leeshore. Yet ever since the sun had risen several hours ago, she realized, the cabin had been begging for the luxury. Every time she went up on deck, she was stunned by all the light; and whenever she came back down again, she discovered a dark and cramped place, gloomy and foreboding.

Hissing, the airlock pressurized.

Moaning softly, the upper hatch slid open and let sunlight pour across her face and her shoulders and pool around her booted feet.

She had to dip her eyes and wait for her faceplate to darken. She thought how Skyhook Island had felt much this way—the light nearly as bright, and brighter in the UV wavelengths—but when she was up on the narrow deck again, turning and watching, it was nothing at all like Skyhook Island. The lights there had reinforced the darkness on all sides. Here, almost without trying, she could see for kilometers on end.

The priest, standing close, said, "Lovely."

She looked at him.

"Don't you think?" He said, "Abitibi?" His armor was throwing sunlight everywhere. "I want to know. What do you think?"

"It's all . . . very different," she said, rigorously honest.

"You're free to have opinions with me. I want you to remember that, first and always."

She promised to try.

"You know," he said, "you're fortunate. Another priest might treat you differently."

He seemed so huge and wonderously strong.

"I'm very good with my people. I have a reputation among my peers." He said, "I know when the wires will help, and I know how to let people move inside the wires. To allow them to help me all they can." His face just showed inside his helmet. "Some priests, I want to tell you, are less . . . how should I tell this? . . . less competent than me."

"Are they?"

"You are fortunate. You should feel fortunate."

She tried.

"Come this way, Abby. To the front." They walked to the bow. Half of the conscripts were up on deck with them. They were watching the sails and rigging, and they were using sensors to look far behind. *Little Fist* was somewhere over the horizon, the priest had told her. It was coming, limping, and soon they would have to be ready.

"The haze is burning off."

She said, "Burning?" and looked around carefully.

"An expression," he explained. "We can see farther and farther, now that it's noon."

Their shadows were pooled around their booted feet.

"You're important to me," he assured. "Vital." He said, "I want to prove that to you."

She waited.

"So," he said. "Do you like being out in the sun? Hmm?" He laughed and touched the top of her helmet, the gesture powerful and affectionate. "Or would you rather be down in the cabin?"

"No."

"No, what?"

"I don't like the cabin. No."

"So why don't you ride here for a time." He motioned, taking in the sky and the sea. He said, "Enjoy," with a large voice. "All right?"

"Can I sit?"

"Whatever you wish."

She sat on a tall coil of glass rigging, shifting until she was comfortable.

"Later," he promised, "we'll talk."

She said nothing.

"About the future," he said. "It may be years and years before our rescue comes."

She tried to imagine such a length of time with this man.

"But for now, if you would . . . keep watching."

"For what?"

"Anything dangerous," he said. "You use your best judgement," and then he turned and left her alone.

She watched the haze burning off, and she watched the waves as if she had never seen waves before now. Every facet of the world seemed changed. There were no birds close to the sea, but sometimes, squinting, she could just make out high, high delicate shapes. Boeing birds, perhaps. A great flock of circling boeing birds.

"They're curious," she told herself. "It's all new to them too."

The water was remarkably clear. Peering over the bow, she saw nothing at first and thought there was nothing to see. But then a great pale fish appeared, rising zeppelin-style from the depths; and she recognized the species and guessed its size. "Huh." It was mature and enormous. She was staring at it through many meters of water, and it in turn gazed upwards at her.

She said, "Desert." Without shit and the dead falling, this was pure desert. A textbook example.

The sailors must hate it, she knew. Watching a big lone sailer drawing parallel to the boat, she thought how other fish could dive. But sailers hated the act, and they made lousy swimmers in three dimensions. She wondered how the sunlight bothered their eyes, and she decided to mention the problem to Jellico when they met again . . . and then she remembered their circumstances and felt a familiar ache. She had to push Jellico away in her mind. Away from the wires and down into her secret places.

The sailer was closer now.

It kicked with both of its tails, softly, and she heard the clear sharp *pop-pop* of the water and realized that the clean, dry air made sounds seem louder. Everything in the sunlight was closer, too. And so much sharper.

She leaned back onto her coiled rope seat. The sun turned her faceplate black and the sun's heat seeped into her helmet. She heard the lifesuit's cooling unit kick on. Thinking back, she couldn't recall a dozen times when the unit had been needed—Leeshore was so uniformly cool—and she felt a tiny breath of icy wind lift up over her jaw and face, making the sweat tingle. The wind ran through her hair and down her moistened neck, carrying away the passive heat.

Briefly, lightly, she began to doze.

Then suddenly her head snapped up and she said, "Watchful. I have to be," and she sat up and blinked and felt guilty of some crime.

Conscripts were behind her, working. She felt them there, and she heard them. There was a second sailer now too. It was kicking beside the first one. She guessed it must have been in the distance earlier, but in view, and she hadn't paid attention. Ahead of everything, straight on, was a huge cluster of islands packed flush with one another and with shallow channels laced between them. From here to the islands was nothing but glittering waves. No sailers. No lesser fish. No birds whatsoever. The islands themselves looked small and bland and virtually lifeless. Those fungal woods were fully mature, she knew, but under the sun they were the color and fine texture of shit. Dried, crumbling shit.

They were closing on the clustered islands.

Abitibi heard the conscripts working with the rigging, readying the boat to leave the open water. She glanced backwards over a shoulder, looking for the priest and not finding him. Half the crew was in sight. They were talking with clipped, code-like phrases and gestures. There was an intensity about them. A clear sense of purpose. She knew none of them by name, yet she understood them perfectly. Their armor and their helmets shone in the sun.

Looking forwards again, she blinked and breathed.

The wind rose, then danced sideways. She felt the sailboat shudder and groan. "I wonder," she said to herself, imagining the air heating up and moving faster with the heat, dancing more and more violently with each successive day.

There came a sound, odd and harsh. Abitibi turned. The second sailer was lunging at the first one, using its body to shove hard and then its mouth to grasp and bite. Abitibi was startled. Rarely, if ever, did they fight this way. Not sailers. She mumbled, "Maybe it's the light." She wondered if their eyes were failing. Maybe the one was confused, lashing out at some ominous, ill-formed shadow.

The aggressor bulled onwards. It shoved and snapped and kicked with its tails. The sailers were equal-sized. One had spirit. Abitibi stood, more curious than concerned, guessing what would happen next. The second sailer made a sharp, high-pitched wail and nearly bowled its victim over on its back. The first sailer fled. Kicking, it blindly ran headlong into *Four Winds.* Abitibi went to the railing. The conscripts had quit working and were holding onto the railing, watching, asking each other if the boat was at risk. Spray and gouts of foam came flying, then a mist of vivid orange blood. Abitibi said, "Goodness," and blinked, and all at once the aggressor went rigid; and she breathed and blinked again and saw a sudden little man standing out on the sailer's back.

She knew him.

The stuhr gun seemed a natural part of his hands.

She squatted and said, "Moon," and looked down the deck in time to see each of the conscripts lifted upwards and thrown back from the railing. She heard the sharp cracking of the gun, five distinct times, and the conscripts were bloody and twisting on the pebbled white glass of the deck.

She crept away from the edge and hid behind the rigging rope.

Soldiers came over the railing. Moon came over the railing. They went like crabs towards the cabin's hatch, keeping low. One soldier tried the hatch controls. There was a hiss as it rolled open. The other soldier deftly tossed a concussion grenade into the airlock, and all three stepped backwards and bent lower. The blast came after a moment. Abitibi felt the blast and then saw the flash and bright, white smoke, and she heard the inner door scream and burst. There was a rush of wind pulled into the cabin. A second grenade was lobbed, and there was a duller blast. The white smoke came down the deck, spinning and thinning and then gone. No one moved. No one moved. Then there was a sharp fast cracking sound, soft and then loud. For an instant, Abitibi didn't understand. Then the booms and sails were breaking loose and falling. There was a string of sudden holes in the deck. Conscripts were firing upwards, cutting away at the rigging. Carbon cloth and glass tumbled and crashed. Moon was out of sight. The soldiers were underneath a sail, both kicking and pulling at the black fabric. There was something frantic and hopeless about them fighting. While Abitibi watched, a conscript climbed to the top of the airlock, then aimed and shot. He shot until Moon scrambled out from under a boom. He spotted Moon too late, and Moon killed him.

Now the airlock showed nothing.

Moon crept forwards, cursing in Asian. He took a large grenade off his belt—not a simple concussion job—and threw it underhanded into the hole. He said, "Fuck it," without heat or life. The deck bowed upwards and cracked and spouted geysers of hot white steam. Pieces of the deck fell away, then nothing moved.

Ahead of Abitibi, butt up, was someone's stuhr gun.

She scrambled forwards and grasped the butt and laid flat, never once trying to think, aiming just as Jellico appeared on the railing on the stern. He and Moon were standing in a line. If she shot, she thought, she might kill two of the enemy neat and clean. And she was eager to shoot. But then she remembered something she had been told, and she suddenly felt glad for remembering.

Jellico called, "Abby?" and then saw her.

Moon saw her too. He saw her gun. Reflexively, he halfway aimed his stuhr gun before he caught himself. He lifted a hand as if to say, "Don't." He said, "Don't!" She saw his hard round face, the scars hidden by the distance and the tint of the glass. He told her, "Let it down!" and then something picked him up and threw him backwards. Bullets pierced his armor, front and back, and the stuhr turned to a plastic film. Moon was bloody. He resembled something wrapped in plastic, falling; and when he had been plainly dead for more than a minute, the priest slowly climbed up through a hole in the deck.

Jellico was hiding. Abitibi couldn't see him.

Standing, she dropped the gun and ran towards the priest, shouting. "I didn't shoot!" she called. "I remembered!"

The priest wheeled. His face gave an odd, almost frightened look.

She repeated herself. She thought he didn't believe her good words. "I never shot," she said. "Not once!"

The priest paid no attention to Abitibi.

She froze and turned and saw what he saw.

The deck was in shambles. Masts were tilting and booms were down, the rigging cut and frayed; and beyond, huge and looming, was the lee shore of a great dead reef.

Abitibi hadn't time even to tense herself.

The keel bit into the bottom, and *Four Winds* bucked and broke apart, people and equipment scattered pell-mell across the sunny tangled woods.

XXXIV

He was flying, enormous shards of glass around him in the bright clear air; and then there was a prolonged crash and numbed pain too, his body dropping through the canopy and down to the soft forest floor.

For an age, Jellico laid still.

The lids of his eyes stayed shut for their sheer weight. He listened to the waves beating against the shoreline—he had never heard such waves —and he heard the wind in the tops of the canopy. Then there was a small quiet sound that seemed wrong, and he put open his eyes and saw the towering form of the Alteretic priest. The priest seemed to be smiling. He said, "I want to kill you, you miserable bug," and he seemed to be snarling. His face hadn't changed its expression. "The trouble is," he said, "I need you. I need everyone I can get for myself."

"Where's Abby?"

"Safe," he said. "Unconscious, but safe."

Jellico pulled the stun gun from his holster. He aimed and fired and missed by a hair's breadth.

The priest swatted the gun away. He said, "Quit that," as if scolding a child, and he started to lift Jellico by his own breastplate. "Don't even think—!"

The knee caught him underneath his breastplate, in the diaphragm, driving out his wind and making him stagger.

Jellico rolled and rose and drew his knife.

The priest said, "Quit it," without breath, his face long and ill.

Jellico aimed for soft spots. He consciously tried to wipe his mind clean, moving without thinking, taking swipes at the gaps in the armor while the priest still staggered.

Even hurt, the man was quick. He never let Jellico near him.

"You son-of-a-bitch," he said. "You shit," he said, his voice swelling. "What do you think you can do? Hmm?"

Jellico charged.

One of the big hands had his wrist, twisting now, and the pain ran up to the base of his head. Clumsily, stupidly, he tried to kick again and was thrown for his effort. The knife was gone. He was sprawled out on the ground—

"Where you belong," snapped the priest. "In the filth."

Jellico was breathing. Thinking.

"Come on." The voice took a step away. "I'll take you to your sister. Get up."

He rolled and ran. The priest was on his heels, shouting and swatting at him. Ahead was a mass of fungi growing close together. Turning sideways, Jellico slipped between two trunks. The priest tried following and got pinned, cursing now, and Jellico charged up the slope and kept to where there wasn't room, staying low, using his arms to climb. Every limb turned rubbery. His lungs burned. Once he paused, gasping, and heard the priest crashing through underbrush below. He made himself run harder. He kept more in the open, moving fast. *Get distance,* he was thinking. *All you can.*

Last night, laying awake inside the sailer, a crazy stupid idea occurred to him.

Now it seemed like the only sensible bet.

He ran on. Higher, up near the crest of the island, he saw the big mature growth give way to a pasture of little squat blood-oaks. The wind was screaming; he had never felt such a wind. The plastic ground was bare and cracked and cratered, and he squinted and took the pasture in while he moved. What he wanted was up high, up near the summit, sitting pretty in the sunlight. Running harder, he began pulling at the straps and loosening the armor. His headphones began to sputter. The priest said, "Answer me!"

Jellico said nothing.

"I hear the breathing. Come on!"

He reached the spot and went down on a knee. First the breastplate, he thought. Then the backplate. Then the leggings and the rest. Working, he studied the ground and the angles involved, deciding how it could be done. The best way.

"You're breathing hard, boy."

He said nothing.

"What do you think? I'll let you go?" The priest laughed, trying to taunt. "You don't see, do you? If you're left, *Little Fist* knows I'm left too. If I take you and hide the evidence, then they might just believe that all of us are dead. Which is fine."

He set the armor down, wishing for time. He checked the angles and wedged the pieces in the ground so the wind wouldn't take them anywhere, and he got up again and felt his legs ache and go numb. He started to run again, stiffly. The priest asked:

"Are you rested?"

He left the blood-oaks, heading downhill. It seemed so strangely bright out in the sun, and now he was in shadows again, panting, the priest's signal stronger every moment. Jellico found a branching trunk and climbed. He went up through the canopy and saw how the old woods were bent and scorched at the margins of the pasture. Keeping low, he positioned himself beside a big bowl-tree. He watched the pale oaks dipping and rising on the pasture. The priest came jogging over the summit, bright and enormous, and he paused suddenly and panned a sensor in Jellico's direction. He said, "I'm coming close. I feel it." He said, "What if I turned around and broke your sister's arm? Hmm? Would that make you come out of hiding?"

Jellico kept still and quiet.

For an instant—a terrible long instant—the priest seemed to turn in the wrong direction. But then he found something and moved where Jellico wanted. The curled pieces of stuhr were below him, on his left. Jellico could see where the sunlight gathered and rose again, focused in a crude fashion, and he watched the dark brown form of a mature bomb-stool as a patch of its skin began to quietly burn.

Too late, the priest saw the array of simple mirrors.

"What's this?" he wondered, the voice distinctly softer. Almost a whisper now. "What are you planning?"

A thin dark spiral of smoke was rising from the bomb-stool.

"Jellico?"

He strode over to the bush, examining it with his eyes. Squinting, Jellico held his breath. He watched while the priest kicked away the armor. He heard him say, "I don't know what you've got going—"

The bomb-stool did nothing.

Jellico crouched lower.

The priest began walking away. He was shaking his head. He was moving like a man without concerns, saying, "I'll have you, and the four of us will make quite the team—"

The bomb-stool detonated.

Jellico rolled and dropped into the dark rich goo on top of the bowl-tree. The noise and heat and light swept over him. The woods tilted and fell, and he felt the cool goo sucking him deeper. He saw little of the blast. He rode the tree down. He never sweated from the heat, and the roaring was done when he stood and began walking, wiping himself a little bit clean.

XXXV

It was like old times, him working on his own. He felt comfortable. He had missed this business more than he had guessed. *Little Fist* was still a far faint glimmer over the horizon. Which was fine. He shouldered the pack and climbed into the gill, concentrating on what was left to do. If he hurried, he had all the time he needed.

Abitibi was laying in the gill, curled up but starting to move. She was moaning. She asked him, "Why am I tied?"

"Good afternoon, Abby. How do you feel?"

She said, "I hurt, Jel," with one voice. Then she asked, "Did *you* tie me up?" using another, harsher voice.

He confessed.

"Why?"

"I don't trust you just now."

She began to jerk, testing the knots.

"I'm sorry." He removed the pack and lashed it into place. He had picked what he wanted from the soldiers' gear, and Moon's. "Later," he promised. "I'll cut off those wires later. When we can make a camp."

"You're my brother."

He didn't know the voice.

"Do you think I'd kill you?"

"Would you?"

She said nothing. She jerked at the glass ropes, then stopped and asked, "Where's the priest?"

Jellico told.

She whimpered. He couldn't tell what she meant by the sound, watching and waiting, and she said, "Let me go. I've got to do something."

"What?"

"Let me go, Jel."

"Why?"

"Reasons," she said. "Jel."

"No," he said. "I don't know this person."

"Jel?"

"I'll be back. Relax. All right?"

She persisted with the knots. He turned and gripped the fleshy gills, lifting himself. The wind hit him with a hard gust, and he heard the surf beating against the shoreline. The sailer was inside one of the narrow kelp-choked channels, beached and sleeping. The wreck of the sailboat was at the channel's mouth, its bright hull easy to see. Crabs were already working. They didn't seem to mind the sunlight or the heat. They were eating the bodies and eating the stores. Fine, thought Jellico. All I want is the hardware.

His ears filled with a crackling noise. Then a voice.

"Anyone? Anyone? Can anyone hear me?"

He paused and thought about staying quiet. About what the priest had said, no one knowing for certain if they were dead or alive. But it seemed wrong somehow, playing silent. So he said, "Mantis?" once. Then again.

Static burst and sputtered.

Jellico jumped to the shoreline and deployed the aerial from his helmet, boosting his reception and signal strength. "Mantis?" he said a third time, and the voice answered.

"Friend!"

He walked towards the wreck, both of them talking. Jellico described the battle and Moon's death in crisp detail, and then he told about the priest. "No one to interrogate," he said. "You must be disappointed." The sailboat was on its side, pieces of the deck missing. He bent and climbed inside and began to sort through the mess.

Mantis asked about Abby.

He told him, adding, "It hasn't been too long, and she's tough. I think she'll be fine."

"In time. Sure."

He found a fluorocarbon sack, folded and dry, and he opened its neck and began to pick and choose. The stern of the cabin was flooded. The sunlight came through the cracks and holes. A mangled corpse was drifting in the seawater, in a narrow sunbeam. Jellico turned and moved in the opposite direction.

"What do you plan to do?" asked Mantis. "Will you wait on us?"

He said nothing.

"I bet you planned to escape all along, hmm?"

"I never hoped it'd be this easy." Everyone dead, he thought. No one to stop them from escaping.

"These winds are giving us fits out here," said Mantis. "This hole in the sky should last a week or more, and all the weather's changing. Your maps aren't going to be worth much soon."

He said nothing, grabbing an Islander-built tent off a tilted shelf. Camp tonight, he was thinking. Sure. And they won't know where to look.

"You can't have much of a life here."

Jellico rose and walked into the narrowing bow.

"But I'm not going to pressure you," Mantis promised. "I'm not."

"You can't."

"I suppose you're right."

"We won't listen."

"Exactly. You're quite right."

"Sure." He saw motion ahead—a scuttling crab—and heard the soft, unmistakable chippering of a wounded knife-owl.

"But you're wrong about not having someone to interrogate: We have you."

"Only by radio. At a distance."

"You've given this some thought."

He said nothing, tossing the helmet in on top of the tent.

"I'm impressed," Mantis said.

Jellico finished gathering up what he could save, the sack full. Then he climbed back out onto the sunny shoreline and walked with the wind at his back.

"Jellico," Mantis said, "I am fond of you."

"I like you too." It was true, and he realized that he would miss the man when he left.

"But Mr. Chosen wishes me to tell you . . . we've got strict limits. We can't make any promises about aid. You'll be going it alone."

"Nothing has changed then."

Mantis chuckled. "No, I suppose not." Jellico could imagine the bridge of the *Little Fist*, Mantis at the helm. Suddenly, he felt a twinge of regret at having to say good-bye. He leaped onto the sailer's back and looked westward, studying the high bright sky and the streams of bladder plants as they closed on the sun. Then he looked at the surf and saw a gigantic crab, milky white, walking up onto the land. The crab was blind. In one pincer was a bit of gold that caught the sunlight, casting a liquid gold beam. He thought of Moon. It must be the old engagement ring, he decided. The crab had gotten it caught on the top of its pincer.

"Jellico?" a voice asked.

Startled, Jellico looked down at the sack. He could see the helmet through the tough plastic. It was operating! He reached into the sack, pulled out the helmet and almost turned it off.

"Don't," said the voice.

That voice again. He blinked and waited.

"Don't worry about Mantis and his doubtful aid," the voice said. "I'm ready to help you—in ways that you can't even imagine. Just don't tell anyone about me. Not *anyone.*"

Jellico felt the weight that had been pressing on his chest begin to lift. To Mantis he said, "I'll talk to you later . . . soon."

"I'll be waiting," Mantis said.

Jellico pulled in the aerial and quit broadcasting, then looked inside the miraculous helmet and said, "This is crazy."

Silence.

"What are you?"

"Take a guess," said the chiseled-free hunk of god.

Jellico's legs collapsed. He fell on his butt on the sailer's back, stunned. Then he looked at the way the i-ply was wired to the helmet's speaker and faceplate and radio, thinking: *What have I got here . . . in my hands? Sweet goodness.*

The god said nothing.

It let Jellico chew on its presence.

Waiting.

Waiting.

Watching the big crab carrying the tiny gold ring and then a huge sky-blue miser bird as it swooped down. The bird came from nowhere and snatched the ring with its bill, twisting and jerking. And then it pumped its wings and lifted both the ring and the crab, rising up into the sky. Out of sight.

Clear up to the roof of the world.